THE GaMe

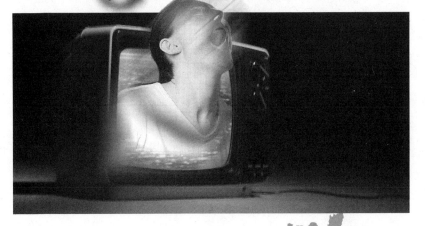

"Compel(s) us to keep reading ... Armstrong injects the trope with new vigor." *Booklist*

*L*ike Ben Elton's Dead Famous (2001), this offbeat mystery features a Big Brother–like reality TV show, a murder, and a cantankerous detective, Alban Bane, who must overcome his revulsion for everything and everyone connected with the show if he is to find out whodunit. There's also a touch of the hit TV series House here, too: like the small-screen physician, the cranky, pain-pill-popping Bane adds a delightfully sarcastic tone to the action. But, for all of that, the novel somehow manages to avoid feeling derivative. Armstrong's abundant enthusiasm for his material, combined with the semi-satirical plotline, compel us to keep reading, and his prose style keeps us chuckling. The sleuth who disdains the world in which he finds himself is an idea as old as Raymond Chandler, but Armstrong injects the trope with new vigor. This is a series to watch from a new publisher to watch. David Pitt/Booklist

STARRED ★ REVIEW

"Derek Armstrong writes with tremendous force and self-confidence." *ForeWord*

*G*ruesome, suspenseful, and rich with dark humor, Armstrong moves the reader through time and space with a keen sense of momentum and dash. His characters are diverse, bold, unforgettable, from the detective's adolescent daughters to the Renfield-like doctor on the set of Haunted Survivor. Armstrong's swashbuckling Scotsman is a welcome addition in the thriller tradition of Weisman and Connolly. Heather Shaw/ForeWord

"Dark tongue-in cheek ... thriller."
Library Journal

THE GaME

A NOVEL

By Derek Armstrong

KÜNATI

THE GAME

For information, contact Kunati Inc., Book Publishers in both USA and Canada.
In USA: 6901 Bryan Dairy Road, Suite 150, Largo, FL 33777 USA
In Canada: 2600 Skymark Avenue, Building 12, Suite 103, Mississauga, Canada L4W 5B2,
or e-mail to info@kunati.com.

FIRST EDITION

Designed by Kam Wai Yu
Persona Corp. | www.personaprinciple.com

ISBN 978-1-60164-001-7   LCCN 2006930183
EAN 9781601640017   FIC031000 FICTION/Thriller

Published by Kunati Inc. (USA) and Kunati Inc. (Canada). Provocative. Bold. Controversial.™

http://www.kunati.com

TM—Kunati and Kunati Trailer are trademarks
owned by Kunati Inc. Persona is a trademark owned by Persona Corp.
All other tradmarks are the property of their respective owners.

As always, for Kam.

In memory of my mother, Anna.

With Thanks: With my deepest gratitude to my editor James McKinnon and Kunati's great team. Also to Kam Wai Yu and the great people at Persona Corp. Thank you to novelists Pat Brown, Elizabeth Burton, Joylene Butler, Pattipeg Harjo, Jo Ann Hernandez, Dr. Audra Himes, Christopher Hoare, Lynn Hoffman, Jan Halloway, Alan Jackson, Paul Jacobsen, Michael Jensen, Karl Joreid, Michael Kayser, Roy Kimbrell, J R Lankford, Frances McFate, James McKinnon, Gloria Piper, Ali Potter, Dave Shields, Suzanne Synborski, Art Tirrell, and Don White for invaluable critiques, reality checks, advice, and encouragement. Special thanks to all the folks at deadlyprose.com, the best online critique group on the net.

Chapter 1

····································

January 13, 11:31 pm
San Quentin

The crazies were at the gate.

Rain and the late-night hour didn't keep away the death-row protesters. Alban Bane opened his tartan umbrella and jogged across the San Quentin visitor parking, splashing through dark puddles. The chanting rose to a crescendo as he approached: "Stop the killing! California murders! Stop the killing!"

Bane pushed through the sign-wielding crowd. Hundreds protested the execution, ten years overdue, of America's worst child killer.

"Excuse me, late for an execution, excuse me."

Cold rain pelted his face as he fended off signs, batting them aside with his umbrella.

They had a right to their opinion although he felt a bit of a simmer when he saw the image on the signs: a smiling picture of Tyler Hayden, killer of children, computer-retouched with an angelic halo. Bane was all for compassion, but a monster was a monster and he saw no need to canonize the beast.

He flashed his badge. "Hey, cop here, coming through!" But instead of clearing a path, they converged on him.

He tussled with a big pillowy man, at least three hundred and thirty pounds of him, who pummeled Bane's Red Sox cap with a sign. Bane blocked the blows easily with his umbrella but the man knocked off the precious cap, a battered treasure that had been on his head every waking hour since the Sox finally won in '04. He dove for the cap, yanking it from under the feet of a middle-aged woman in a yellow rain slicker.

He shoved his beloved cap backwards on his rain-soaked head and plucked the pillowy man's sign from his hands. "Union rules. I can't beat you back. And there's so *much* of you to beat." He threw the sign to the asphalt and pushed on through the crowd.

The immense inner complex was lit with news crew lights, throwing harsh shadows on black pools of water. The tangy smell of San Francisco bay and rain mingled with the sweat of the crowd.

He burst through the outer perimeter into a riot-equipped police line. They pushed him back roughly, and Bane fell into a news crew filming the chaos.

"It's Alban Bane!" The CNN anchor flipped his microphone around in a smooth motion. "Are you here to witness Hayden's last moments?"

Bane offered one of his PR smiles and winced as harsh video lights turned on him. "Someone gave me front row tickets."

Forty or so angry protesters rushed towards him. He jangled his handcuffs over his head. "I only have one set of handcuffs," he shouted. "One at a time, please!"

Someone grabbed Bane's bicep. He pulled back and turned away from the grip, but a familiar voice stopped him. "That smart mouth of yours'll get you in trouble, bro."

"It's served me well, old friend," he said as he yielded to the pull from his ex-partner, Armitage Saulnier. Together they pushed hard through the protesters and reporters until they made the main security gate and escaped inside.

Bane flipped off his baseball cap, shook his red hair, and smiled his goofy best at old buddy Armitage. "It's good to see you, Arm." He looked up at Arm's luminous green eyes, the man's most striking feature, against rich ebony skin. Fuzzy brown hair stood straight up as if ten thousand volts shot through him. Arm gave back a giant smile and pulled him into a bear hug.

Bane patted his wide back. "Ach, now, none of this! I'm a Scot. We dinnee hug."

They checked their weapons and showed their invitations from the governor to a guard. "You gentlemen are early." The corrections officer stared at Bane.

"Wouldn't want to miss anything," Bane said.

"Hey, you're *the* Bane." The guard handed back the badge, flipped open to reveal a picture of a smiling, boyish-faced Bane with shoulder-length red hair. *The* Bane meant that the guard—like most of the crowd in the parking lot—had seen the recent movie *Hayden*, which portrayed child-killer Tyler Hayden as some kind of dark hero. Ewen McGregor starred as Bane. Hollywood had not portrayed Bane as the relentless FBI agent who captured a monster, but as the *bane*, the ruin, of dark, Gothic champion Hayden. To thousands of Goths, teens and whack-jobs, Hayden was the cult-hero and Bane the "caustic Scot."

Bane and Arm followed a guard down long echoing halls, pungent with the smell of disinfectant, to the "Green Room." He hadn't expected it to be like this. The sterile austerity of the execution chamber with its mint green metal walls looked like something in a nineteen-fifties crime flick. A stark reminder of today's mission sat inside the glassed-in chamber: an inclined gurney covered in transparent disposable polyethylene to simplify post-mortem clean up.

"Pretty grim place," Arm said.

"I think the green is kind of cheerful, in a puke sort of way." Bane fished in his pocket, popped the lid off his Aspirin, and dry swallowed two tablets.

"Still hooked on ASA?"

"Ach, no. Just eight or ten a day. Keeps me bright and cheerful."

"Ten a day, three hundred and sixty-five days a year, for sixteen years—that's how long I've known you, my man."

"Your point?"

"Your stomach must be one big ulcer."

"No, but I piss every hour, all day long," Bane said.

Arm laughed, his tractor-like bray oddly soothing to Bane. "Guess you never get headaches."

"No, I give them."

"Well, now, don't you be telling me it takes an execution to get old buds together," Arm said, resting his hand on Bane's shoulder. "You missing the FBI?"

"Not a bit. Vermont suits me. I was tired of being worshiped by my fans."

Arm laughed. "You ain't about to change."

"Change is for wimps, old friend."

For a few minutes they slipped into the comfort of nostalgia, catching up on the last three years. Arm laughed as Bane complained about his teen daughters. Arm enthused about his own son, a budding twelve-year-old baseball star. They caught up on old friends. Neither mentioned their wives.

In minutes, the observation gallery would fill with pale-faced witnesses, anxious to see a man die. They would settle into rows of mold-injected plastic chairs, eyes fixed on the five slabs of shatterproof glass that separated them from the killer. For now, the silence was punctuated only by a ticking wall clock and a fly buzzing in a fluorescent light fixture.

The door slammed open; selected journalists and official witnesses filed in. The network correspondents looked naked without their camera crews in tow. Bane and Arm avoided eye contact with the journalists and slid to the back of the room.

Bane wasn't surprised to see Hugh King, although how the sleaze reporter got through the press lottery for one of the seventeen coveted media spots was a mystery as deep as *The Crime Times'* pockets.

King's shoulders stooped and he looked ten years older than his forty-five years. Seeing Bane he veered across the room, jostling correspondents aside as he crossed the gallery. "Bane! I wondered if you'd come!"

Bane folded his arms. "I came just for you."

Arm slammed between Bane and King in a quick block and towered over the reporter. "Well, I'll be! Hugh King!"

As Arm fended off King, the other reporters buzzed around Bane, drawn to him like mosquitoes to bare flesh. Through the years they had not forgotten ex-FBI task force leader Bane and his stubborn two-year pursuit of Hayden.

"Bane, is it true they found two more Hayden victims in Texas?"

"I'd guess you know more than I do."

"What do you say to reports that Hayden slipped out of Florida due to your negligence?"

"What do you expect me to say to that? 'Gee, you're right, I'm awfully sorry?' Any serious questions, folks?"

"Are you admitting negligence?"

"Are you daft?" Bane flipped the man's press pass up and stared at his credentials. "Dan, is it? Did you write these questions down, or do you just wing it?"

The other journalists laughed.

"Is it true another victim's family is suing you?" Hugh King shouted, still blocked by Arm.

"Any other questions?"

"Is that a 'no?'"

"That's—" He bit off another sarcastic reply. Journalists. He could play with them all night. "As long as there are reporters, there'll be stupid questions. As long as there are lawyers, there'll be suits."

"Did you see the movie?"

"No interest." Unfortunately, his daughters had used "borrowed ID" to see the R-rated movie, *Hayden*. They were celebrities in their school because of it.

"What do you think of Ewen McGregor playing you in the movie?"

"I was never that handsome."

The journalists laughed again. The questions kept coming. The correspondents stopped drilling him only when the victim families filed in to the room. After fourteen years, Bane still recognized them all. They wore their unmasked pain on tense faces and huddled together, whispering and crying.

Bane winced when he saw Leslie Chow, barely one hundred frail pounds, cut across the gallery, her glare and fists making it clear she still blamed Bane for her daughter's death.

"She sued your ass, didn't she?" Arm whispered.

"Three times," Bane said, as Leslie Chow stopped in front of him. He felt a pang of guilt. The juries had vindicated him, but that didn't make the deaths of the seven girls and six boys in California any easier. Teens the same age as Bane's daughters.

Leslie Chow's lip quivered, and in that moment Bane saw the face of Hayden victim eleven—the Chow's fifteen-year-old daughter Olivia. Tears washed Leslie's face, and she raised a hand to slap him. "Bastard."

Bane caught her hand, gently. He had no right to rob her of precious hate. He had lost his own wife to violence and knew the stages of grief: after the shock and the tears came hate, blaming, and emptiness. Leslie Chow couldn't strike out at Hayden, but she could fault Bane.

Mr. Chow wrapped his arm around his wife and guided her back to the orange plastic chairs. She sat on the edge of her chair, a photograph of her daughter clenched in her hands. A flow of tears dripped from her chin, splashing the picture of Olivia, frozen in time—a plain girl with straight short hair, unsmiling and too serious, but with her whole life ahead of her.

After the families settled into their chairs, the gallery stilled, as hushed as a funeral. The reporters hovered behind the seated families, some of them scratching notes. It seemed to Bane that all the families and journalists turned in his direction, some openly hostile, others sympathetic. The room grew hotter as the audience grew larger, and soon Bane was sweating.

A prison guard stepped into the gallery, held the door open, and said, "Detective Bane?"

Bane nodded.

"Urgent call, sir."

As Bane crossed the observation gallery, the visitors erupted in a loud chorus of voices. Bane heard snatches as he followed the guard.

"Why's *he* here?"

"Arrogant bastard."

"Asshole."

The voices faded as he entered the sentry station. The guard gestured to a chair in front of a telephone. "That phone, sir."

Bane scanned a row of closed circuit monitors. One revealed the execution chamber in stark monochrome. Another displayed the turmoil in the observation gallery.

He leaned forward and peered at the third—the death-watch cell. He rolled forward in his chair until his face was inches from the monitor and stared at Tyler Hayden. Hayden, the child killer, sat on a small cot, legs crossed, his back to the camera. Across from the killer sat an elegant man, straight-backed in a fold-up chair.

"You have volume on monitor three?"

The guard shook his head. "Not allowed, sir."

Bane winked. "How 'bout I offer you a two-four of your favorite brew? No? Help me out here. Trip to Vermont? Three nights with your favorite hooker?" When the man just shrugged, Bane snatched up the phone. He kept his eyes fixed on the monitor. "Bane."

His captain's voice was too loud. "They pumped the bastard yet?"

Bane held the phone away from his ear. "Not yet, Cap. Turn up your hearing aids, Cap. You're yelling again." Cap had lost his hearing in a shooting incident. Bane's eyes remained locked on Hayden in his cell.

Bane heard an exaggerated sigh. "Damned if I know why they do these things so *late*." And from the way Cap emphasized the word *late*, Bane understood him to mean, *It's three in the morning here, and I'm still working, so you damn well better pay attention.* "I need you back here on the next flight. A bad one. Near Bromley Mountain."

"I'll pass the ball on this one, Cap." He leaned close to the sentry's name tag. "Brad and I, here, are going out for hookers after this."

"Bane, I want you on this. No one works a crime scene like you do."

"The vic will be rancid by the time I get there."

"Be serious, Bane. Just once? There's a snow storm back here. No one's getting in for twenty hours or so."

"Meaning, I'm still wanted. Look, Cap, our team's worked plenty of homicides."

"Not this kind of sick crap. We're talking butchery." Cap's voice gained volume. "Bane, forget Hayden. Your job finished fourteen years ago."

"My job is never done."

"Always the joker."

"Keeps me sane, Cap."

"Drives the rest of us nuts."

"Not my problem."

"Our victim was tortured."

Bane squinted at the death-watch monitor. His hate had diminished over the years. He no longer needed to see Hayden sent to hell. If

Hayden's lawyer obtained another reprieve, and the child-killer rotted in prison, that would be just fine. Bane really wasn't sure why he was here. He'd left all this behind. His new life was good: two teen girls with boy troubles, a small bungalow near the lake, easygoing Vermont, and weekends in the country. Why bring back the shadows?

Still, it seemed important he witness Hayden's death, even if it brought back the nightmares. A journey begun must be finished.

"Bane, are you listening? The homicide was on the set of *Haunted Survivor*. You know how the governor fought to get that reality TV show up here."

"Never heard of it." His daughters would have to tie him to a chair and crazy glue his eyelids open to make him watch any kind of reality television show.

"You're a caveman. *Haunted Survivor* is the number one rated show. The gov's flipping over this."

On the death-watch monitor, the visitor stood and shook Hayden's hand. Who was he? By statute, Hayden could see anyone he wanted in his last twelve hours, but he had no friends. He had killed his own foster parents. He hated God, despised reporters. His lawyer, Laura Kincaid, was conspicuously absent. So, who was this man?

Cap shouted, "Are you there, Bane?"

"Ach, Cap. Fine. Too many reporters here, anyway." He glanced at the sweep clock over the door. *Seven minutes.* "Got to go. It's almost midnight."

Bane hung up, started to stand, but hesitated as Hayden turned and faced the closed-circuit camera. The killer smiled and nodded, as if he knew Bane was watching. He gave the camera a thumbs-up.

By the time Bane returned to the gallery, every seat was taken, and the journalists lined the walls. Bane slipped to the back of the gallery.

Beside Arm stood Noland Hix, Bane's former Miami FBI liaison. The man who let Hayden slip out of Florida. He towered over both Arm and Bane, a stooped scarecrow.

"Look who came," Arm said.

"Hix. You still alive?"

"And kicking." He held out his hand to shake.

"Too bad." Bane folded his arms.

"I was telling Arm we should go out for drinks after all this. Get caught up?"

"I'm as caught up as I need to be, Hix." He leaned closer, not wanting to cause the victim families any pain. "I'm surprised you had the guts to come."

"It's you they blame. Not me."

Bane forced himself to unclench his fists. "I'll give you credit. You're a screw-up, and you know it, but you don't give a damn."

"Saw the movie. They got you right. Cranky Scot."

"I heard they left you out. Probably a good thing for you." Bane leaned against the wall beside Arm.

The last to enter the gallery was the dapper man from Hayden's cell. He smiled as he scanned the crowd, then moved to the opposite wall. He was as straight as a poplar tree, and dressed in a black three-button Dolce and Gabbana suit, crisply pressed. His mature features were as taut and wrinkle-free as his clothes. The man noticed Bane's stare and nodded.

Bane knew this man from somewhere. He wasn't sure where or how, but he was curious enough to start across the room. The steel door to the execution chamber clanged open and Bane retreated to his corner.

Four minutes to midnight.

With a guard on each arm, Hayden, his hair cut short, stepped into the green death chamber dressed in new denim jeans and a blue work shirt. He smiled, revealing no sign of the jitters. He seemed to enjoy the attention and wore his sociopathy as openly as his trademark smirk.

Hayden had aged gracefully, his hair still blonde and his face marred by only subtle lines. Piercing blue eyes stared out of the movie-star face that had lured so many adolescents to their doom. He stepped closer to the glass and scanned the gallery, stylish and chic even in denim. New clothes were a San Quentin tradition, along with the last meal and the chance for final words—but it all seemed too good for him. He glanced at the gurney and then at his audience, although his expression revealed only disdain.

The warden stepped close to the glass and reached up to activate the microphone. After announcing the sentence to the witnesses, he said, "Tyler Hayden, do you have any final words?"

Everyone leaned forward. What does a psychopath say at the moment of his death? Hayden's smile widened, as if all his friends were gathered to see him off. "I am so happy to see all the people whose lives I touched." A rumble of anger cascaded through the room.

Journalists, stripped of their tape recorders and cameras, scribbled notes to capture Hayden's words for their version of history.

Now Hayden stepped closer to the glass. "A large audience. And the person we have to thank for this grand occasion is there." He lifted his elbow as if to point, but the cuffs snapped taut. His ice-cold eyes settled on Bane.

"Alban Bane, it was you, my friend, who drove me on and on, from state to state. These people have *you* to thank for that. We are like old friends."

Bane felt the heat of the killer's knife. Ignoring the journalists and the inevitable headline, he gave Hayden his middle finger.

Hayden laughed. "Who knows? If not for your pursuit, Olivia Chow might have graduated from college—instead of rotting in the ground."

Bane stared at the back of Leslie Chow's head. She bent over, her shoulders shaking. Even facing his own death, Hayden wanted to torture the families of the victims, to make them relive the nightmare.

Bane felt a rise of Scottish temper. He circled the chairs and rapped on the glass in front of the warden's face. The man jumped back. "Shut the microphone off!"

The guards inside the chamber stepped forward, and grabbed Hayden's bound arms. They tried to pull him back. "I have the right to speak!"

"The only right you have is to *die*," said Bane.

Olivia Chow's father shouted, "Burn in hell!"

Hayden's chilling laugh subdued the room. "I'll be there. Down in hell. With your children."

Leslie Chow screamed. Another parent leaned into her husband's arms, sobbing.

Bane stepped close to the glass, face to face with the killer, separated only by the transparency. He hadn't been this close to the beast since the night of the Hayden take-down—the night Hayden drove his long knife into Bane's abdomen.

Bane reached out his right arm and pounded on the glass. "Time to end this game. Pump this bastard silly." There, he'd given the journalists their story. Thank God they didn't allow cameras in the gallery.

One of the guards yanked Hayden back, dropping him to his knees as the warden snapped off the microphone. The gallery stilled, most of the witnesses now standing. Bane stepped to one side, allowing them to see Hayden's end. It was what they had come for. He knew they'd regret it. Death was never easy to watch, no matter what the circumstances. Arm joined him by the side of the glass, a silent comfort.

The guards dragged Hayden, feet trailing, to the inclined gurney. They lifted him and one guard released the cuffs. Hayden rubbed his wrists then lay down without struggle. As they strapped his arms, then legs, Hayden's head turned and he stared at Bane.

"Chill, bro," Arm whispered.

Hayden didn't flinch as they pierced a vein at each elbow with IVs. The saline solution flowed, and then the first of the two drugs, sodium thiopental. He remained alert, his eyes fixed on Bane through the glass.

Hayden smiled again. His mouth moved. With the microphone turned off, the witnesses heard no more of his demented words.

Bane pressed close to Arm. "You read lips, don't you?"

"For true." He leaned forward, concentrating. Hayden's lips continued to move, and Arm interpreted: "*The same words, over and over. Friend Bane*—he thinks you're his friend. Lord Almighty." He squinted at Hayden's moving lips. "*Friend Bane, I know who—I know who—killed?* I think so. *I know who killed your—oh—you bastard.*"

Bane saw Hayden's body relax, a quick spasm, then a draining away as the second drug, the pancuronium bromide, relaxed his muscles. Bane watched the EKG as Hayden's heart sputtered to a stop.

The EKG flat lined, though Hayden's eyes remained open as the prison doctor pressed forward with his stethoscope. Bane stared at Hayden's hateful eyes, hoping the beast was gone, knowing he would never be banished from Bane's nightmares.

The prison doctor nodded. Tyler Hayden was dead.

The only sound was the buzzing of the trapped fly.

"Tell me what he said," Bane whispered to Arm.

"Drugs. It was the drugs, bro."

"Tell me!"

Arm leaned closer. "He said—*God. . .*"

Bane shook his friend's massive bicep.

"I think it was—hell bro, I might have got it wrong! I think he said, *Friend Bane, I know who killed your wife. I take the secret to hell.*"

Chapter 2

....

January 14, 8:01 pm

Near Bromley Mountain, Vermont

The helicopter swept through a sky boiling with clouds. The Huey shook like an old roller coaster at Six Flags, undulating between barely visible mountains.

"We'll be there soon, sir," said the pilot.

"Don't call me sir or I'll call you son. Do you even have your driver's license, son?"

Alban Bane wished his destination was Burlington, his bungalow and his daughters, not a crime scene in the snowbound mountains of Vermont's heartland. He missed his girls, and he was exhausted.

Twenty hours after Hayden's revelation, a storm still raged inside him. Hurricane Hayden.

The helicopter rocked and he clenched the arms of the co-pilot's chair. The fatigue made him queasy. He looked away from the window, disturbed by spectral images. Sheets of snow transformed into ghostly faces, his tired mind projecting his nightmares: images of Hayden laughing and Susan Bane screaming, and the pale faces of decapitated heads seemed to fly towards the helicopter in phantom blurs.

"Air sick?" The pilot's voice was too loud in Bane's headphones.

Bane pressed the talk switch. "Don't want to mess up the upholstery. How long ago did Crime Scene Services get in?"

"Two hours ago. Damn storm's the worst I can remember." The pilot kept his eyes fixed forward. "You watch *Haunted Survivor?*"

"Ach, no. My remote's locked on the sports network." Bane knew he sounded a little curt, but his mind was fried.

"It's way cool."

Way cool. Bane wondered how the pilot, especially a man who seemed not much older than his daughters, could navigate in the remains of the blizzard and still prattle on about television. "What's it about?"

The pilot smiled. "They strand twelve people in this so-called haunted mansion, you know, Mason Place, for twenty-six weeks and film every moment with hidden cameras. It's like *Survivor* meets *Fear Factor.*"

Bane had no idea what the man meant.

The pilot laughed. "Some twisted minds behind that show. It's a real killer. I would have freaked if I was one of the contestants the night they released the rats in the bedrooms."

"Big laddie like you?"

"I mean, thousands of rats, man. I wouldn't stay in that house for half a year—not for a lousy million bucks."

The helicopter quivered and seemed to plummet, then pitch. "Hey, watch your driving."

"No worries, sir."

"Keep your eyes on the road, son."

"Funny, sir."

"Look, son, don't make me bust you for dangerous driving."

The pilot laughed, and the helicopter swayed even more violently. "I guess you think I'm too young. They all do."

"Doesn't matter what I think, lad. Let's just get there alive."

The pilot's voice droned on, and Bane wondered if there was an off-switch on the headphones. Instead, he slid the headphones from his ears. The scream of the compressors assailed him, but he preferred it to the chatty pilot.

Bane wasn't thinking of *Haunted Survivor* or the new case or how good it had been to see Arm after three years or how sorry he was the Chows had to hear the demented rant of their child's killer. Only one thought absorbed him.

How could Hayden know about Suze's murder?

Over a pitcher at the airport, Arm had spent ten minutes trying to convince Bane that Hayden knew nothing. Arm's theory: Hayden heard a little prison gossip, or saw the news coverage on Suze's homicide, all those years ago. "He just wants you to suffer, bro."

Bane wasn't so sure. The only man with answers had died hours ago.

Chugging back a second beer, Arm had promised to track down all of

Hayden's visitors and callers and e-mail the list to Bane.

Angry at his own stream of thought, Bane pushed the head gear back over his ears and pressed the talk switch. "Are we there yet?"

"Around the corner?"

"Funny."

Bane glanced out the windows. As they swept over the hill, the sheets of snow cleared and he saw a cleft between two mountains, a wilderness vista dominated by a frozen lake and surrounded by bent pine trees. The storm was clearing and a nearly full moon bathed the mountain valley in silvery light.

The old Mason Place mansion squatted like a dark stain on a snow-covered hilltop that rose like a single tit between the higher mountains. Who would build a mansion, a virtual castle, in this lonely valley, thirty-two miles from the nearest village? And who would think to shoot a live-broadcast reality television show in it?

Like every Vermonter, Bane knew the story of Mason Place. Mason was the Green Mountain State's bogeyman, a name parents used to scare children—"Be good, or Mordechai Mason will come after you." The industrial tycoon was more famous as a mass murderer than for a financial empire that rivaled his contemporaries—the J.P. Morgans and Rockefellers. Obviously Real TV wanted to exploit the legend and make a little money of their own.

Decades ago, Mordechai Mason, one of America's richest men, went mad, slaughtered his wife and eleven guests in a rampage lasting two days, becoming one of America's first recorded civilian mass murderers. According to Vermont legend, he pursued them relentlessly through the house, preying on them from secret passages. Authorities never found any hidden tunnels, but they did find Mason in his study, clenching a shotgun, his own face blown off. The featureless face of the apparent suicide led to an enduring legend: Mason had not killed himself, but had obliterated the face of one of his victims to ensure everyone would assume him dead.

Bane stared down at the state police cruisers, the pulsing glow of their reds sweeping the snow in blood scarlet. In the headlights of parked

SUVs, eight state troopers, trudged through deep snow as they walked a grid search pattern. Mason's pre-depression-era mansion loomed over them like a robber baron's castle.

As the chopper settled onto the snow, Bane patted the pilot on the shoulder. "Thanks for the ride. I only threw up once." The pilot laughed. Bane zipped his unlined leather bomber jacket. He had no winter gear, only his Sox cap and the tan bomber jacket his girls gave him last Father's Day. His girls laughed hysterically the first time he called it his "bahookie freezer," a bum freezer, because it was too short even to cover his butt. When he flew to California, he hadn't expected to need blizzard gear.

He slung on his worn leather shoulder pack. In it he carried pictures of wife and daughters, spare cuffs, two pre-loaded speed loaders for a thirty-eight caliber Smithie, fingerprint kit, satellite phone, evidence bags, disposable latex gloves, and an antique Leitz magnifying glass, a gift from Susan Bane, beloved dead wife. Hooked on the strap was his trademark tartan umbrella.

The pilot slid back the door and wind howled into the helicopter, lifting sheets of snow. Bane shivered. He didn't even have gloves.

Someone in a hooded coat waited for the prop wash to die, then ran for the chopper.

Bane's partner, Justine Kipfer, threw back her hood, her white smile marred by a missing upper incisor, lost in a martial arts tournament. "Hey, Bane," Kip shouted over the whine-down of the compressors. "How was death watch?"

"I asked the warden for a refund. Hayden didn't even wet his pants.. I mean, you'd think he'd at least piss himself when they pumped him full of that stuff."

"*Jesus*, Bane."

"Kip, this better be good. I was planning on two days of obscene sex on a California beach." His teeth chattered.

"Be *serious*."

"I'm always serious." Bane followed her across the snow, sinking to his knees in fresh drifts. He covered his face with a bare hand, his nose already raw from the biting wind.

He followed Kip to a back porch, a tiny room out of proportion to the massive house. She slammed the door shut behind them. "This is the television crew entrance. Believe it or not, we the people of Vermont own this monster. Real TV made a deal with the state to restore Mason Place for—"

Bane held up his bare hand, interrupting her. "I'm too tired to care about Real TV. It's all a plot to get people to forget how to read, anyway." He smiled. "But I would like to see our victim."

She shook her short-cropped black hair, still powdered with snow. Her dark skin hinted at her mother's Abenaki native heritage. Kip was Bane's best friend, after big old Armitage Saulnier. The Banes and the Kipfers always barbecued burgers together on Labor Day and even did the Christmas-present thing, although Kip's high-school-football-coach husband harbored some resentment toward Bane for the late nights. Her twelve-year-old son, Jeremy, a brilliant but disturbed child, was just old enough to have a crush on Bane's older daughter Mags.

Bane didn't unzip his jacket "So, what do we know?"

"Crime Scene Services is on scene but they haven't moved the body. We only got in here about two hours ago because of this storm." Kip spoke with quick authority. Proud of her down-to-business reputation and tough-girl persona, she was meaner in hand-to-hand than any man in the Vermont State Troopers. Her fierce devotion to martial arts chiseled her athletic body into a hard machine, and she toned down her ripe sexuality by wearing no makeup, cutting her hair military-style, and covering her body in loose pantsuits. She hid her Glock nine-millimeter cannon under a baggy wool jacket. The troopers joked she slept with it.

"Who's the victim?"

"Preliminary ID, doubtful. We found a set of keys belonging to one of the producers. Name's Lorentz. You've heard of Lorentz, right?"

"Not unless he's in one of my books."

"I know you hate TV, but you must catch the news, don't you?"

"I only watch HBBF."

"What's that?"

"Hockey, baseball, basketball football—*real* football. What you call soccer." He smiled. "I'm joking. He's a big television producer, right?"

"The Lorentzes are a big-time ex-husband-and-wife producer team. Went through a really nasty divorce."

They stepped into a ceramic tiled hallway, plain and salt stained, and lined with closet doors. On one wall was a long cork bulletin board, labeled *News and Bull*. He paused in front of the board, scanning the notes. Some of them were handwritten, some laser printed or photo-copied: *Ride to California wanted; Dell laptop for sale; Union meeting next Wednesday; Green Mountain Freedom meeting on 15th.*

Bane rapped the last message with his knuckle. "They employ locals."

"Part of the deal here. Lots of locals get jobs." She shook her head. "Can't even go to my corner grocer without seeing this propaganda."

"The *Green Mountain Freedom* movement's harmless. As busy as maggots, and about as smart, maybe, but harmless."

"Independence for Vermont? What's a little state like Vermont going to do all by itself? That's whacked."

"Scotland's a wee country, too," Bane said.

"We must put up with them, I'm afraid," said a new voice: low, soft, and feminine.

Bane turned. At the end of the hall, at an open door, stood a woman of lofty stature, elegant on heels, almost too straight and proper. Though her smile offered a dazzling display of perfect teeth, there was no warmth there. Her dress was daringly low-cut.

"Alban Bane, meet her highness, Abbey Chase," said Kip, her tone light, almost amused. "The producer of *Haunted Survivor*."

"I'm the one plotting to overthrow the evil book publishers."

"Ah, you're an eavesdropper," Bane said.

"I'm a television producer." Her smile didn't alter. She stepped forward with a grace that had to be practised. Her handshake was firm and dry. "Abbey Chase. Friends call me Abs. Employees call me Abbey." She smelled soapy and fresh, as if she had just showered. She settled into a provocative pose, revealing deep cleavage. She was blonde, blue-eyed beautiful, even in the glare of fluorescent light. "Do I know you? You seem familiar."

"I would have remembered meeting *you*, Ms. Chase." He forced a smile.

"I'm sure I know you from somewhere," Chase said, not moving aside, her head slightly tilted. She leaned forward, hands on her full hips. "I didn't make the connection. My, you *do* get around. You were on the news just last night, at Hayden's send-off. I saw you beating protestors with your umbrella. That was a laugh-riot."

"I like beating protestors—"

Her voice boomed over his. "FBI Special Agent Bane! Of course. I remember the whole story!" She snapped her fingers. "Cole is working on producing the Hayden story. It's his hot project right now."

"Been done, Ms. Chase."

"Yes, yes. That was pure spectacle and bull—pardon me, nonsense. No, this will be the real story. Exposing the truth. An exposé."

The idea of yet another Hayden movie buzzed around his tired mind for a moment. "Well, I'm sure it will be a big flop for you." Behind Abbey Chase, Kip waved at him.

"Tell me, Detective. Did you rehearse that line?"

"What line?"

"The line that's all over the news. '*The only right you have is to die.*' I couldn't have written better. '*Pump this bastard silly.*' Beautiful."

They reported *that*? "No, that's just me tired, Ms. Chase. Speaking of tired, I have a crime scene to attend." His hand dove into his pocket and snatched out two more Aspirin. He popped them into his mouth.

She seemed amused. "Well, I must get to the control room. Tonight, we release scorpions in our guests' bedrooms." The smile never left her face. A real corpse lay in her basement, but this vile woman stood here gleefully discussing scaring her guests to death with scorpions. "Oh, don't look so shocked. We remove their stingers."

"Ach, not my business, Ms. Chase. I guess television's not the art form it used to be."

The smile remained. "My, you *are* colorful."

"I know what fear does to people. After six months of this they'll need psychiatric help."

Abbey pressed her lips together, losing her practised expression for the first time. "Of course the premise is—daring. That's the whole point. Audiences don't watch *Leave it to Beaver* anymore."

Kip gestured behind Abbey Chase, looping her finger around her ear in circles—*nut case*. He almost laughed.

"By the way, I'll be interviewing all of the crew," Bane said. "Please make sure they don't go home after shift."

Abbey Chase's face remained aloof and beautiful. "They live here, Detective. We all do, for the duration. But Detective, please don't interfere with our production."

"That's what I do best. Interfere." He smiled. "And I'll be talking to your cast as well."

She clasped her hands in front of her form-fitting dress and her ice-blue eyes bored into him as if Bane was a wannabe actor auditioning for her show. "My dear Detective, that is quite impossible." She held up her hand. "I will cooperate in every other way." Her foot tapped. "Every other way. But, this is where you will require a warrant. And our lawyers will get an immediate injunction."

"I'm used to lawyers. And they love my insurance company."

"The 'cast' as you call them are secure in their environment, behind magnetically-locked impenetrable barriers. Hidden cameras peer into every room, around the clock. They have not left their haunted house environment for weeks. They don't even know what has happened here."

"Ach, come now."

"Haven't you ever watched our show? Or *Big Brother?*"

"I must be one of the few who hasn't."

One eyebrow shot up and her forehead furrowed. It was the first time she appeared less attractive. "Well, come to my office when you're finished. I'll show you why your request is ridiculous."

"It wasn't a request, Ms. Chase."

"We shall see, Detective. When you're done. Ask anyone where my office is."

She nodded once, imperious, and spun on her Italian heels. She moved with the grace of a gymnast.

Kip's laugh was low, almost whispery, but grew louder as the door slammed. "I think you've met your match, Bane."

"I hope you mean in wits," he said. "What an unappealing woman, putting aside her looks, of course."

"Ah, I knew there was a sexist in there." Kip continued to laugh. "She is something. She fills out a dress in ways I could only dream of."

Bane laughed along. It had been a good forty-eight hours since he felt the urge. Now, it fell out of him, a welcome release. "This should be interesting."

"At least."

"Stop enjoying this."

"Oh, hell, Bane, I haven't even begun to tease you. You should have seen your face."

They made their way to the door at the end of the employee entrance hall and went down a long flight of stone steps to a basement level. Like the hall, the stairwell was painted white and lit with fluorescents. At the bottom landing, Bane reached for a door labeled *Real TV: Authorized Personnel Only.* Kip shook her head. "No, not here."

She pointed down an even narrower stairway, lit only by bare dangling bulbs. Bane stared. *A sub-cellar?* The sub-cellar stairs, barely wide enough for one person, plunged into the limestone bedrock, dark and cool.

Bane pursed his lips. "A sub-basement. How nice."

"Don't be a wuss."

As he followed her, his head brushed a limestone ceiling, wet with condensation. He hesitated as the stairway narrowed even further and the air became stale and damp.

Kip led the way through a labyrinth of halls and doors. The stone walls and low ceiling pressed in on them, like the catacombs in Rome.

Bane and his wife had visited the catacombs on their honeymoon in Rome, though she had to drag him into the dark and ancient tunnels. He remembered her words, as if they were yesterday. "Look at my big FBI crybaby. What a baby." Even with Suze's prodding, they only followed the tour guide to the first tomb before claustrophobia, a fear Bane had never been able to conquer, had him racing for the exit, Suze clinging to his hand.

This sub-basement even smelled like the catacombs, musty and stale. He had to tuck and weave between the dangling bare bulbs. His hand brushed against something wet and *growing* between the cracks in the old stone. Bane wiped his hand on his pants.

"Watch your step, Bane." Kip pointed at a wooden cover on the floor, half rotten. "Silva nearly broke his leg there."

He stopped, and knelt by the trap door. "What's this?"

"They're wells. We found five of them." She kicked a stone through the break in the door. Bane heard a splash.

As they moved on, the corridor brightened, and the crime scene spotlights came into view. His breathing returned to normal.

He waved at Henry Cross, head of Crime Scene Services. Cross ducked under the yellow police tape with a tagged evidence bag. He wore a bright orange, one-piece forensic suit designed to minimize scene pollution, marked with glow-in-the-dark letters.

"My team's finishing here." He deposited his evidence in a chain-of-custody box. "You don't need a poly suit, but wear boots."

"You've collected exemplars of everything?" Bane didn't want to walk into the scene without a suit, carrying with him dust and lint.

"I know your standards, Bane. Dust, lint, hair, granules, foil lifts." He shook his head. "You always cost the state a fortune."

"You should see my bar tab." Bane slipped disposable crime-scene boots over his shoes, and latex gloves, then stepped into the tiny, low-ceilinged room. He held a hand over his mouth and nose, filtering the outhouse reek.

"So did you meet our Ms. Chase?"

"He met her highness," Kip said.

"Ah. Every man's wet dream, that woman," Cross said.

"Bane blushed as red as his tartan," Kip said.

But Bane wasn't listening. For once, his one-liners failed him. His eyes locked on the body.

Kip frowned. "We didn't move it."

Bane said nothing.

The naked body hung from a beam by the ankles.

Headless.

He closed his eyes and dizziness came over him, a combination of claustrophobia and memories. "A damn copycat."

This was no coincidence: a Hayden copycat, on the weekend of Hayden's execution, in the state where Bane worked homicide.

All business now, he reached into his leather shoulder bag and dug for a flashlight and his precious antique Leitz magnifying glass.

Cross tossed Bane a bottle of Vick's Vaporub. "The smell is because his sphincter let go."

"I'd never have guessed." Bane dabbed his nose with menthol, then studied the unrecognizable lump that might once have been Colin Lorentz, television producer. The upside-down victim's knees were at eye-level, thick knobs on hairy legs.

"Not a true copycat." Strangely relieved, he pointed at the fingers. "Hayden never did anything like this." Bane directed his narrow beam of light at the tied hands, trailing on the limestone floor under the headless neck stump. No fingertips on either hand. Hayden had never finger-capped. Knobbing of fingers and decapitation were typical of old-style mafia hits, designed to slow identification. Without fingertips or a head, there was only DNA match, body scars or birthmarks for identification. DNA analysis would take at least forty-eight hours, and was only useful if there was an exemplar from a known victim. He assumed Cross had already arranged for a hair follicle from the possible victim, Lorentz.

Bane leaned close, abolishing unwelcome memories by concentrating on the evidence.

Victim identification was very important to Bane's investigative method—forensic chronology. Without victim identification, he would never have suspected Hayden all those years ago. The victimology in that case, the history of one victim in particular, made Hayden a key suspect.

"Hayden raped his vics, didn't he?" Kip rotated the spotlight to light the jagged gash between the victim's legs. "Both boys and girls, right?"

"No semen, but anal penetration." Bane squinted, guessing the body's age at forty to fifty, based on skin elasticity and fat deposits. "But always adolescents. Never adults, like this." It occurred to Bane that the victim was about his own age.

He walked the grid, step by step, scanning with his glass and light.

"This was engineered for spectacle," Kip said, her voice low.

Cross nodded. "Why else would our perp pick the weekend of Hayden's execution?"

Kip's bushy eyebrows drew together into one line. "Major national headlines for sure, especially if they find out we have a Hayden-imitator in *your* jurisdiction."

Bane squatted on his heels and looked up at the body. Since leaving the Bureau task force, he had not seen one this bad. Vermont offered up mostly domestic and revenge-based homicides, and only a handful a year. "You're a bigger cynic than I am, Kip. So you're thinking Abbey Chase is a suspect?"

"A few ratings points can mean millions, right? The headlines will drive this show to better ratings." She shook her head. "You men always think with your balls when it comes to women."

"And you think Ms. Chase could actually hoist a body like this? Saw off a head?"

"She's the mistress of spectacle."

Bane found himself breathing too quickly, probably due to the claustrophobia. "Do we have a time of death?"

"Best guess, between six and ten Friday night, based on temperature and lividity."

Just before Hayden's execution. "Any sign of the head?"

"Haven't found it yet."

"Hayden always left the heads on the floor." *Dead eyes, staring up at their bodies.* Bane examined the finger-knobbed hands. "So how do we know this is Lorentz?"

Kip shrugged. "We *don't* know. A poll of missing persons on the set here indicates Lorentz is the only one unaccounted for—of this body type and age. At the time the roads were unplowed. Plus, we found a key to his office in that corner. The bitch—I mean, Ms. Chase—says Lorentz is the only one with the key, besides herself."

Bane stepped closer and examined the protruding vertebrae. "We're looking for another crime scene, right?"

Cross gave Bane a thumbs-up. "Only postmortem mutilation took place here."

"I have two teams on it," Kip said.

"Good," Bane said. "This scene brings to mind two things. One, I need some bi-carb. Hell of a thing to see on an empty stomach."

Kip smiled. She, of all people, knew his sense of humor was about dealing with sick crimes like this one. "And two?"

"Two, remind me never to watch reality television."

He circled the dangling victim, his flashlight scanning the gaping wound between his legs. Bane felt his scrotum tighten. Castration was one of the few things in a crime scene that could still bother him.

He frowned and knelt close to the hands, careful not to touch what was left of the body. "Wedding finger?" Unlike the other fingers, the perp cut the wedding finger down to the third joint. Bane peered at Cross. "Any sign of the finger or a ring?"

"Still searching."

"Who found the body?"

Cross folded his arms. "Stunt coordinator on this show. Name's Jackson Reid."

"Why was this stunt coordinator down here?"

Kip shrugged. "Haven't talked to him. The first trooper got through the storm by snowmobile from a nearby ski resort. Beat us by two hours, but he was alone and didn't hold the witness. Reid's disappeared."

Bane heard the annoyance in his own voice. "I'll want to talk to *that* trooper, and Jackson Reid when we find him."

"The trooper's crapping bricks in the kitchen upstairs. He's just a kid, first year on the force. He was on snowmobile patrol, spot-checking for drunks." She winked. "Before you get mad, it took a lot of initiative to come in by snowmobile. The poor kid's never done more than give out speeding tickets." She smiled. "I told him you'd have *him* castrated."

"At least. And Reid?"

"This place has a maze of sub-basement, hundreds of rooms, out-buildings too, miles of wilderness surrounding it—not to mention an uncooperative producer."

"You just want it to be her."

Kip nodded. "Yes, I do."

"Do you seriously suspect her?"

"Ex-wife is obvious if this turns out to be Lorentz. She dropped her married name, uses Abbey Chase."

"Any publicity is good publicity?"

"Why not? You saw her. All smiles and tits."

"That's a crime? I happen to like both."

"I have no doubt, Bane."

He moved his flashlight over the victim examining with his antique glass. The victim's body, what was left of it, was burly with dense knots of muscle and weathered skin. The victim's hands hung below the empty shoulders, palm to palm as if in prayer, tied with binder twine. The hands were callused. Big, hard-working hands, leather-tough and permanently tanned, criss-crossed with deflated veins.

"This is no Hollywood producer."

Bane leaned closer, examining the victim's feet. Crusty, hard heels. He scanned between the victim's toes with his glass, separating them with gloved fingers. "Tweezers?" Kip handed him a pair.

"You shot the feet?" When Cross nodded, Bane lifted his sample. He turned it under his old glass.

"What is it?"

"I'd say alfalfa. Hay. This man could be a farmer."

Kip peered over his shoulder. "Oh, come on."

Bane bagged the sample. "Callused heels. This man spent most of his days in big work boots. The alfalfa, well you find that on farms around here." Which meant that the crime scene might be a local farm. But why move the body here, to Mason Place? And how could the perpetrator manage that in a Vermont snow storm?

"Why, though?" Cross asked, sounding doubtful.

Bane scanned every inch of the victim's skin, working his way down to the dangling arms. Although not decaying, the epidermis was in early slough. He pulled back the skin with his gloved finger. "See this?"

Bane moved the magnifier so Kip could see.

"Looks like a . . . hole. Track marks? A junkie farmer?"

Bane felt the rise of his blood pressure. "Only one injection mark. Not a shooter. And recent, too." He examined the other arm. "And another one, here."

Lord Jesus, he thought. *This is too much.*

"What's up, Bane? I know that look."

He stood up, tossing the flashlight into his shoulder bag. Kip followed him from the crime scene.

"Two injections, one on the inside elbow vein of each arm."

"But what's it mean?" Kip asked.

"It means someone's playing a game. With me."

"What do you mean?"

"Hayden was executed around the same time as our victim here. Two injections, one in each arm. "The claustrophobia returned, and Bane felt the ceiling closing in on him.

This was no coincidence. This copycat perpetrator knew Bane would be on the crime scene, fresh from Hayden's execution. Whether the perp was an accomplice or a copycat, Bane knew he needed to talk to Hayden's lawyer, Laura Kincaid.

Chapter 3

....

January 14, 4:16 pm Pacific Time
Golden Gate Park, San Francisco

The Japanese Tea Garden was her favorite retreat, but today law-yer Laura Kincaid found no comfort. Dappled late afternoon sunshine broke through the rain clouds but did not improve Laura's mood. She sat in the teahouse, sipping her green tea and watching the tourists wind through the pagodas and koi ponds. They could enjoy the sun, happy in their blissful worlds. Laura envied them.

Almost finished, she thought. *Just get through this.*

Hayden gone. After today, she would no longer have to deal with his—associates.

Hayden had been evil, there was no doubt about that. When she first became his lawyer she had been enamored of his godlike stature, even his malevolent legend, but she had long ago come to terms with the fact that he was evil to the core and deserved to die. They had merely used each other. She accepted the high retainers and under-the-table cash bo-nuses while teasing him with promises of freedom. She justified it with easy grace. She was a struggling lawyer, over-extended financially and supporting a dependent mother with Alzheimer's. Hayden was incar-cerated, could do no harm to anyone; it was her duty to serve the needs of her client. And she had accomplished the impossible, keeping him on death row as appeal after appeal went before the courts.

She had not attended the observation gallery at Hayden's execution, watching instead with ice-cold satisfaction on video in the warden's of-fice. Given a choice, she would not have attended at all, but her presence was required, in case of a last-minute reprieve.

Thank God there had been none.

She watched him striding down the winding path past the arched bridge, his size fourteen cowboy boots crunching pea gravel as he angled towards the teahouse. Heads turned as he passed. A tourist lifted her camera to snap a picture of the towering cowboy in his dusty Stetson and his worn boots, against the delicate irises and floating lilies of the Japanese gardens. The tourist never took her picture. A single sharp glance from the cowboy and the tourist dropped her camera, grabbed the hands of both her children, and hurried away over the arched bridge.

Kincaid finished her tea, her breathing accelerated. She wished she could turn and run like the tourist and her children.

As he came closer, she reached into her bag and her hand tightened on the gun.

She relaxed. A little.

The resemblance was uncanny. The man was the very image of Hayden, tall, with rippling muscles and the same striking blue eyes. Dead, soulless eyes.

He vaulted over the rail, ignoring the glare of the waitress.

She had feared Hayden, but *this* man terrified her. She shivered. *Almost over now. Just chill. You have a gun.*

Austin Bartlett smiled at her, a stunning burst of white, but as cold and insincere as a movie star posing for fans. She nodded in reply. He wore clinging button-up jeans, heavily worn around the crotch. They revealed a manly bulge, nothing left to the imagination—and no place to conceal a gun. In spite of this, her hand remained in her purse, wrapped around the grip of a snub-nosed .38.

Laura Kincaid was no fool.

Never once, in all the years of meetings, had she felt comfortable in the presence of this giant of a man. His height was accentuated by the Stetson, which he never removed from his head, but she guessed he was six foot five without his hat and heeled boots. He was a man of few words, although clearly well educated. He was macho beautiful, and exuded a sexual magnetism that was undeniable, like a cowboy model for Stetson cologne or Marlboros.

She felt only revulsion for him, though she crafted a smile, the same one she had perfected in the presence of Tyler Hayden.

He sat down opposite her, and towered over her by at least a foot, even seated. His hard body could only be the result of perfect genes and daily workouts. His skin was naturally dark rather than tanned.

"Did you bring it?" She kept her voice controlled.

He gave a curt nod.

Kincaid offered him tea, but he said nothing.

"Give it to me, then."

Austin put his hand over her wrist. "Not here."

A tourist at the next table smiled at them.

Thinks we're lovers, thought Kincaid. She yanked back her hand, embarrassed.

Austin was right. This was not the place to exchange money. People were watching. She would have to count it.

"Where, then?"

"Over there." The man jerked his head to one side, indicating the north garden, behind the teahouse, past the Zen garden and the bamboo grove.

As they walked, she was startled when Austin brushed her shoulder with light fingers. A sensuous touch for such a big man.

"Don't."

"I thought you liked men." A husky laugh. "I know you liked Tyler."

"Keep your mind on business." What was this all about? She had never given Austin any indication that she was interested, beyond the occasional lingering glance. She felt a moment of uncertainty.

Prior to January thirteenth, at midnight, they had needed her. Her usefulness as Tyler Hayden's advocate was finished.

"This way." The man led the way up a path covered in pine needles. She hesitated. She didn't want to go out of sight of the tourists, but she wanted the money. She had worked for it.

Chill, she thought. *I have a gun.*

Austin stopped in a tiny clearing and turned to face her, looking down, actually smiling. "You're beautiful."

"Whatever. The money."

The giant man cocked his head, listening. "Father wanted you to know you did excellent work."

"I did all I could." Kincaid grew impatient. They had paid her well, over the years, to defend Tyler Hayden, but they had also asked her to go above and beyond normal duties. At first, just small things. Carrying verbal messages that seemed to mean nothing. Then phoning people. Hayden was always interested in Alban Bane, and she saw no harm since her client was safely in prison, on death row, so she told herself. Cryptic messages, every other week, to Austin Bartlett.

She had been stunned the day she read the small story in the *Chronicle* on the murder of Bane's wife—West Coast news *only* because of Bane's profile as the man who caught Hayden. When she confronted Hayden about it, he had smiled, closed his eyes, shivered, and reached out and covered her hand with his. She could have sworn he had an orgasm in the silence that followed. She had almost called Alban Bane, but knew that such a call would lead to an investigation she could not survive. That was years ago, but the memory still gave her sleepless nights.

As his execution became imminent, his only other regular visitor was his psychiatrist.

She was stunned when the doctor asked her to give up the appeals. "He just wants to die now," the doctor told her. "Just respect his wishes."

Her golden goose would die.

The last few months crawled by. More messages. Cryptic letters. Then, the execution and the thrill of knowing that Hayden was gone.

She could not totally justify her actions, she knew that, and several times she had come close to mailing the anonymous letter to Alban Bane. It sat in a safety deposit box, her insurance policy, postage already affixed, and tomorrow she would send Bane the information that would shake his world.

Austin smiled. "You're so beautiful. No wonder Tyler wanted you."

"He said that?"

Austin was a handsome caricature of his half-brother. Although Tyler's face was more delicate and beautiful, Austin was a more manly interpretation of the genes that made Hayden so pleasing to the eye. He was taller, broader, stronger, the veins standing out on knotty muscles under brown unblemished skin. The eyes were the same. In any other circumstance she would have found Austin irresistibly attractive; now, she felt only revulsion.

Laura Kincaid trembled.

"It's all right, Laura. I want you."

"No."

"I could make you scream with delight."

"No." *Hell, no.* She found she couldn't breathe.

Nearby a child laughed, and Kincaid relaxed. What could he do, here, in this public place?

The man handed her a canvas shoulder bag. "It's in there." He watched, as Kincaid pulled back the flap of the bag and started thumbing through the stacks of hundreds. "You want to count it?" He sounded amused.

Kincaid nodded. She had worked hard for this. Not exactly breaking the law—not in any serious way—but what she had done was ethically wrong and could lead to her expulsion from the Bar. This would help compensate her for the sleepless nights.

"I have something else for you," Austin said.

His hand closed over hers, and he yanked her closer, with strength that was impossible to resist. He pressed her fingers to his swollen crotch. "This is for you, too."

She snatched her hand away and reached into her bag. "I'm armed."

Tyler's half-brother smiled. "I want you."

"I don't want to ever see you again," she snapped. Her hand came out of her purse, with the snub-nosed .38.

He cupped and lifted his crotch. "My gun's bigger."

She stepped back, the gun leveled at his chest. "I'm serious. I'm leaving now." *And I'm mailing that damned letter to Bane. To hell with you. To hell with your father.*

He stepped closer. "The safety is on."

She took another step back and felt a branch stab her back. Startled, she wavered, and in that moment he lunged forward.

She dove to the ground, tumbling sideways on the soft bed of pine needles and the gun came up again.

"It's all right to be afraid," he said. "I like that." He laughed.

God, he's so fast. She hardly saw him move as he swung in and plucked the revolver from her hand.

Chapter 4

January 14, 10:44 pm
Mason Place, Vermont

The house seemed endless, a rambling maze of spacious halls and stairways. By the time the production assistant led Detective Bane to the lobby outside the producer's office, it was nearly eleven—twenty-three exhausting hours after Hayden's execution.

The executive assistant smiled at Bane. "Five minutes, Detective. She'll be right with you."

"Thank you."

"Coffee?"

"Please. Just black."

She nodded. "Right back."

Bane used those moments to call San Francisco. He rummaged in his worn bag for his phone, and punched the speed dial number for the home of Laura Kincaid. Again, he got her answering machine. He tried her office, cell phone and pager. He looked at his watch. On the west coast it would be 7:54. This time, he didn't leave a message.

Bane pretended to study the many framed wall photos of Abbey Chase with various presidents and movie stars as he moved in small steps in the direction of her office. He worked his way to the arched oak doors. They were open a crack, and he peered inside.

Colin Lorentz's ex-wife sat behind a Chippendale desk. He watched her for a moment as she typed on her computer, her forehead furrowed with concentration over a face that required no makeup.

He pushed open the door and stepped in. "Hello again, Ms. Chase."

She stiffened, then snapped the laptop screen closed and whisked a file folder off the desk into a drawer. Bane heard the click of a lock.

"Detective?" Her calm voice contrasted with the haste he had just witnessed. She gestured for him to sit.

"You're a little jumpy, Ms Chase?"

"Who wouldn't be, in the circumstances."

Bane sat facing her and glanced around the study, taking in the high bookcases laden with antique leather-bound books, gleaming mahogany desk, teak wainscoting and crystal chandeliers. "A pretentious office."

She blinked several times, batting her long lashes. "You love to throw people off guard, don't you? This is Mordechai Mason's private study. I had it restored." Behind her, big bay windows, draped in floral yellow, revealed a frozen lake, nestled at the bottom of a snow-capped mountain. The moon hung over the mountain, among silver clouds and glittering stars, a perfect postcard Vermont nightscape.

"Isn't that a little morbid, making your bunker in the den of a mass murderer?" He flipped open his note pad and unclipped a felt tip pen.

"Good for the image, you see?" She laughed, but it was a nervous sound. "Oh, Detective, I don't believe in ghosts." She reached for an unopened pack of Marlboro Lights. Her hand shook as she picked up a silver lighter, rolled it in her fingers, then put it down beside a splendid Tiffany-style butterfly lamp and pushed away the cigarettes. "Quitting. Damn hard under the circumstances."

"Do I make you nervous?"

"You? No." She had changed since they last met, only hours ago, now in an Armani suit. The Chanel bag on her desk seemed staged and out of place for a late winter's evening, high in the mountains of Vermont, and it seemed that she had showered and changed in preparation for this interview. But if so, why had she appeared surprised by his entrance?

"So—you're nervous because?"

"Because? Because someone was brutally killed on my premises. Are you always such a jerk?"

"I'm allowed to be a jerk. I have a badge."

She smiled. "Do you always wear your hat?"

"Does it bother you?"

"Wondered if you're hiding a bald spot."

He yanked off his cap. "Still have all my hair."

"So—so, who is it?"

"We have five missing people, all from your crew. Including Mr.

Lorentz. Time of death and the blizzard limits us to a high probability that it's one of those five—unless you had people on the property you didn't report."

"Security's tight, Detective."

"Not tight enough." He fished in his pocket for the Aspirin bottle, nearly empty now, and dry-swallowed two.

"Do I give you a headache?"

"More or less. So, what about Colin, your ex?"

She swiveled the chair away from her desk and crossed her legs. "He's away on business."

"When did you last see him?"

"Three days ago." Her ice-blue eyes settled on him. "Colin's a busy man. He flew out before the storm, on our private helicopter. To New York—he's dealing with our financial partners." There was the slightest quiver of uncertainty in her voice.

Bane thought of the old-style mob finger-knobbing. "And would these financial partners happen to be sharks?"

"What?"

"Mafia. The Mob. Mario the mechanic. You know."

"Really, Detective. What do you expect me to say to that?"

"I expect you to lie."

"Then why ask?"

"Because I have to." Bane didn't believe in interviewing suspects. It rarely helped solve crimes. But here, little Hollywood in the mountains of Vermont, he needed orientation. To get a feel for things.

She fingered a ring, looking away for the first time. "I'm not involved in the financing."

"You know we found your ex-husband's key at the crime scene."

"Yes. I identified it." Her eyes rolled closed and she took a long, ragged breath. She shook her head. "Look. I'd know if he was dead." She held up her hand. "Not wishful thinking. Cole's alive."

If so, Colin Lorentz would now be a suspect. "You parted on good terms?"

"Acrimonious at the time. But we were together too long not to stay friends." Her hand swept back her wavy hair in a nervous gesture. She leaned forward, clasping her hands on the desk.

"So, my question about the Mafioso? Or are they triads? Biker gangs? You tell me. Not wholesome people, right?"

"You're a funny man, Detective."

"So this Mafioso loan shark thing smells about right, then?"

"I don't know. I have my own suspicions. Nothing obvious." She smiled. "I can't decide if I like you or not."

"I hope not. It's bothersome when suspects like me."

"Am I a suspect?"

"You're a suspect—until you're not."

"What's that supposed to mean?"

"It means, Ms. Chase, that everyone who had opportunity—and even some who apparently did not—is suspect. Until they're not. So, could you tell me, Ms. Chase, where you were Friday evening?"

Her glare would have made most people wince, and it was clear that she was a woman used to being in charge. "You think *I* am capable of murder?"

"Everyone's capable of murder."

"Like *that*?"

He stared at her. She was canny, this Chase. She was an expert in diversion. "You are capable. Like that."

Her shoulders stiffened. "*Really*, Detective." She opened her notebook computer, although Bane now realized it was one of those tablet PCs that converts to a laptop. She tapped the screen with a digital pen. "I had dinner here, in my office. Then I went to our post production suite."

"You need a computer to tell you where you were on Friday?"

"I'm a very busy woman, Detective Bane. I have no alibi. I had a pesto linguini right here at my desk. By myself."

Bane let the awkward silence hang for a moment, hoping to shake her. He watched her closely, judging her body language. "Did Mr. Lorentz have any distinct birthmarks, anything that might be unique? Devil's pitchfork tattoo? Scars from your honeymoon? Anything at all."

"I've decided. I don't like you."

"Good. We've got that settled. Birthmarks?"

"Not really." Her voice dropped to a near whisper. "So the body is—as bad as—as bad as they say."

"Who are they?"

"Jackson Reid spilled the grisly details to the crew. The rumors have spread."

"We have been unable to locate Mr. Reid."

The pale trembling lips hardened into a firm line. "Probably skulking in the north wing." She shook her head. "The unfinished wing. An awful man. I don't know why my husband hired him."

"Why do you need a stunt coordinator for a reality television show?"

"Some of what we do is dangerous for the guests. Thursday, we're releasing snakes in the guest quarters."

Bane frowned. This woman was horrible. "What about Reid?"

"Truth is, our financial partners insisted. He's more of a watchdog than a stunt coordinator."

"So, we're back to my Mafia theory."

She snapped forward in her chair. "You'd know better than I. He was an awful man, that's all I know."

He shrugged. "Can you show me this north wing?"

"Of course I can." She picked at her sleeve, straightening the cuff.

He nodded and his eyes settled on her computer, a shiny metal-cased ultra-slim tablet. "I assume Mr. Lorentz has one of those?"

"A tablet? Yes, we're on a wireless network. Keeps us all connected, with the latest production journals and scripting." Again, she wagged her finger at him. "Very clever, Detective. Of course, if it will help your investigation, why don't you take Cole's tablet? His whole life is on that hard drive. He'll be so pissed off when he finds out I gave it to you." She rubbed her hands together and smiled.

"You want him pissed off."

"He knows who's boss. His password is *Abbeysucks*. No spaces."

"I see."

"It was a between-friends joke. My password is *Colinblows*." She smiled, again. "I'll have to change it now that you know."

"I understand." He wrote down the passwords. "Did Colin have any enemies here?"

"Who knows? Television's brutal. It burns people up, you know. Reality television is a growth industry, and Real TV is on the cutting edge. Unique concepts are hard to come by. We stepped on a few people on our way here."

"Anyone in particular?"

"Not really. Everyone."

"Would you be willing to provide a sample of your hair?"

"I beg your pardon?"

"Your hair, Ms. Chase."

She frowned. "I don't see why."

"Now, don't play daft. DNA, Ms. Chase."

She pursed her lips. After a moment of hesitation, she brushed her Armani jacket and pulled off two hairs. "Call me Ms. Cooperative."

Bane didn't touch the hairs and let her slip them into a sterile bag. "Now, about the cast interviews."

She launched from her chair and half jogged across the room. On the far wall, she pressed an oak panel between the bookcases. Bane followed her and watched as a hidden door slid back revealing a dozen small monitors.

"These are live scenes in the contestant wing."

He leaned closer to the bank of screens, fascinated. "The cast?"

"Yes. We don't call them that, since they're real people, not actors. But they're on camera twenty-four hours a day."

"You're telling me this to forestall a warrant." Bane squinted at a monitor. "Their space is locked?"

"Oh, yes, since October of last year. They're my prisoners. They can't get out unless we let them out."

He studied the tiny images for a moment. In one room, apparently a library, three of the guests sat in plush wingback chairs, chatting. In another room, two played billiards. Another pair tossed darts. The images changed.

"I have it set to change the camera views every fifteen seconds."

He saw three contestants in their beds, and another sitting alone, writing in a notebook. "This stuff is—"

"Big budget?"

"I was going to say sick shit."

She pressed the panel again, hiding the monitors. "Come, Detective. Let me give you the quick tour. You'll see that everything's secure. How would that be?"

He forced a smile. "That would be a good start."

"Come along then, Detective." She swept through her massive double doors into the long hall, casting her assistant a sharp look on the way by. "This is part of the original house, you see?" Her voice was animated, full of pride. "We restored everything. The pewter candelabra sconces, the mahogany panels, even some of the original art."

Abbey Chase marched at a brisk pace down the long hall. "Mordechai Mason killed all his heirs, of course. The state owns the house. We have a ten-year lease. We're assuming America's fascination with reality television and crime will continue. I have a lot of projects simmering, you see?" She stopped in front of two magnificent carved doors, deep cut with delicate floral patterns. She opened a door and revealed a glass conservatory, filled with tropical plants. "Cole's private oasis," she said, in a hushed voice. "Cole loves plants, you see?"

"Apparently." Dieffenbachia, bamboo and rows of exotic orchids crowded the massive greenhouse. It reminded Bane of the winter garden in the Vanderbilt mansion museum, though the massive Empire-style desk in the room's centre destroyed the illusion of a winter sanctuary.

"Tell me, Ms. Chase, wouldn't it have been less expensive to build all this—your haunted mansion—on a set?"

"On a sound stage? Of course. But it could never be as magnificent as this. I'm sure you'll understand why we thought it important for the guests to know the history of this place, with its mass murderer legend. Adds to their fear—and publicity value."

"So Mason Place is all about publicity? What about a new murder? Is that good publicity?"

She leaned on Lorentz's ornate desk. "I suppose some could spin it that way. I hadn't thought that far ahead."

"I'm willing to bet you've already phoned your publicist, Ms. Chase."

She swept a tiny metal computer out of its swivel cradle on Colin's leather-topped desk and handed it to him. "Cole's tablet. Remember, *Abbeysucks.*"

"How could I forget?" He slipped the pad-sized tablet and the AC adapter into his leather shoulder bag.

"When Colin shows up, tell him I gave it to you with my blessing. He'll flip." Her smile lingered.

She circled Colin's desk, walked to the glass wall and gestured with her hand. "Glorious, isn't it?" He joined her and looked out on the back of the sprawling stone house. "There are over forty gables. One hundred and sixty-eight rooms. All built with Vermont's famous granite, limestone and marble."

"Too much house, too big a crime scene."

"You see, on that side, those forty rooms, we converted for our contestants." He noticed the rooms were firmly shuttered, with no view to the outside. "They have the cobwebbed library, the creaking grand dining room, the scarlet master bedroom. Your voice echoes, even if you whisper. A masterpiece of the macabre. We even added some moving walls to create dead-end halls and rooms that seem to vanish."

Gargoyles leered down from the peeked slate roof, their faces demonic in the harsh spotlights. "It seems pretty outrageous to me. Playing with human fears."

"We have a famous psychiatrist to safeguard the mental health of our guests." Her voice hardened.

"Famous, maybe, but reputable?" What psychiatrist would be party to this insanity? "What's his name?"

"Doctor Jonathon Wingate."

Bane chewed his lip. He had read several of Wingate's books and attended two of his lectures at Quantico. He sat in the back row and fell asleep. The doctor spoke with a thick British accent, but with the charm and intelligence of the elite few blessed with brilliance. He was one of the foremost experts on sociopathy, and his book was standard reading for behaviorists at the FBI. "That's a bit of a triumph. How did you get him?"

She smirked. "Was that an insult, Detective?"

"A tiny jibe."

She held up her hand. "Right. Reality TV is junk television, and Doctor Wingate has the ear of presidents, world leaders, and the psychiatric community."

"Obviously you paid him handsomely."

She waved her hand dismissively. "Not a penny. I think he's using this scenario to write his next book. After all, reality television is a major part of the American psyche now. And, as you said, we play with people's minds." She walked briskly toward the hall. "Come with me."

Bane followed her through the opulently restored executive wing, trying not to let his eyes linger on her nearly perfect body. "Our crew lives in the east wing of the house. Our editing suites fill the main basement." She stopped and opened a door. "This is what I wanted to show you."

They stepped into a dark, short hallway, then through another door into a darkened room. "One of our camera rooms." Bane followed her. The entire opposite wall was glass. He looked at a stunning interior view of the main foyer of the house. The hall was larger than Bane's entire house, and swept up to a frescoed dome.

She pointed at the row of cameras. "One-way glass. These are just a few of the seventy-eight cameras." She caressed one of the cameras with her long fingernails. "You see? The contestants are always on camera. And they can't get out of their world."

"I promise I'll scare them. Isn't that what you want?"

She sighed. "A team of psychologists and psychiatrists pre-planned all of their experiences. Introducing your interviews is a variable that would alter the outcome."

"Psychiatry is about as predictable as roulette. And this all sounds pretty sick. Screwing with people's minds. You could trigger a psychotic episode, or worse." Like the crime scene below them in the basement.

She stabbed her finger at one of the cameras, her voice rising again. "But none of them committed this crime! Every moment of their lives is on camera. You can have the tapes if you'd like. We've taped every single moment of their lives."

"Tell me, Ms. Chase. Are you a voyeur?"

She laughed. "A little bit."

"Kinky. Tell you what. I have the crew to interview, so we'll leave the contestants—*for now*. But let's be clear on this, Ms. Chase. I will inter-view the guests when *I'm* ready."

"That's all I ask."

He followed her back to the hall and down some stairs to the base-ment studios, emerging in a long modern hall. Unlike the restored grand halls of the main floor, the basements were plain and modern, painted white with office-like drop ceilings, too bright under fluorescents.

Bane followed her into a large room. "Our Brain Room," she said. "Where we brainstorm our ideas, and meet over the shows."

A massive V-shaped table dominated the room, centered in front of a large screen plasma monitor and a bank of smaller screens, busy with live scenes of the contestants.

Bane scanned the room. His eyes locked on a portrait in a platinum frame on the far wall of the halogen-lit room.

He rounded the table at a brisk pace, staring up.

A man and a woman.

Abbey Chase leaned close beside him. "Stephen and Leslie Chow. They own fifty-two percent of Real TV. My partners, I suppose you might say." She leaned closer. "You are a little red, Detective?"

He stepped back, staring at the portrait.

Leslie Chow had crossed the San Quentin observation gallery to slap him. Later, as Hayden drained away, IVs taped to each elbow, Leslie Chow had glared across the gallery one more time. At Bane, not at the man who had killed her daughter.

The same weekend, Bane had a copycat homicide victim with twin hypo punctures, on the set of a reality television show—owned by Leslie and Stephen Chow.

Detective Alban Bane did not believe in coincidences.

The pain of his old Hayden scar blazed hot.

Chapter 5

Stephen Chow watched his wife bow toward the altar three times. The ritual never failed to move him, although unlike his wife Leslie, he never shed tears.

He had grown up in the tiny village of Chungzan, in southern China, a place where men did not cry, and face was all that mattered. He was born Chow Chan Zi and changed his name to Stephen when he went to Hong Kong. He made a small fortune there as a movie mogul, pumping out dozens of martial arts films. Then he bundled up his childless wife, a portfolio of B movies, their eight-figure bank account, and moved to Hollywood. America had brought success and fertility. He built a Hollywood studio that enjoyed some middling success. He never had the son he craved, but Leslie finally had a child, a sweet girl named Olivia.

He stared at Olivia's picture, his only child's image framed in solid gold and wrapped in coils of sweet lavender incense—their precious daughter, smiling and forever young.

Chow bowed in turn and placed a plate of Olivia's favorite California grapes on the altar.

"I love you. . ." his voice cracked as he spoke to the picture. "My sweet Livia." He cleared his throat. It was so difficult not to cry. He sniffed and pretended to blow his nose. He put his arm around his wife, so frail and sad, and guided her to the marble balcony. They stood in the heat of the late afternoon sun and listened to the surf crash on the cliffs surrounding their peninsula estate.

Their home. *Livia*, the grandest estate in Rancho Palos Verdes and named for their sweet Olivia.

It should have been her home. She never saw the splendid mosaics and frescoed domes of the palatial mansion, never enjoyed a walk along the oceanfront cliffs or strolled through the lavender garden. Only her spirit lived here, in the room with the nicest view facing the ocean. A shrine stood where her bed should have been. Her memory resided behind gates that could have protected her.

Olivia's brutal murder had driven Stephen Chow into a frenzy of activity that ultimately produced his wealth. The ancestors took their precious daughter and gave back compensation. A long series of reality television shows were staggering successes.

But it felt like nothing to Stephen Chow. It meant nothing without Olivia.

To see Hayden die painlessly was more than he could bear. Chow had fought to move the trial to Florida, whose governor was a friend, where eight girls and one boy had been raped and killed by Hayden. In Florida, the government was less liberal, and the courts were harsher. With tearful sentencing testimony from Leslie and other parents, Chow was sure Hayden would have earned an electrocution. Chow needed to see Hayden twitch, wanted to watch the killer's eyes bulge, wanted to remember every moment of Hayden's pain as he urinated in his pants and his teeth clenched the leather strap and he bucked in the restraints, muscles knotting in spasms of pain. He wanted to smell the burning flesh and imagined thin tendrils of smoke as Hayden fried. Instead, the monster had escaped to a peaceful sleep.

In Chow's tortured mind, Bane had killed Olivia. Bane's task force let the monster out of Florida, sent him on a horrifying spree across the Midwest then to California where he found sweet Olivia. And Bane, the rigid and proper FBI agent, waited for search warrants and evidence before moving.

Chow played with a tangle of Leslie's shining hair, fighting the rush of tears that threatened to spill even after all these years. Leslie had breached with Olivia, given her all to birth their only daughter. Leslie could have no more children. Her grief over Olivia's murder had been so intense that she tried to kill herself. Chow had come home from another day in the studio, shortly after Hayden's second appeal, to find his wife on their bed with an empty bottle of sleeping pills in her cold hand and a note begging his forgiveness—asking him to marry a fertile woman.

They had not spoken for the next month after her ordeal at the hospital and, strangely, had grown closer. And sadder. And still Chow could not let himself cry. He channeled the despair into hate.

Now, only two things drove Chow's life.

His primary mission was to expunge the world of anything Hayden touched. An army of private investigators searched for the parents of the monster Hayden. He would make Hayden's ghost suffer. In the depths of hell, Hayden's tortured spirit would scream in torment as Chow purged the world of the monster's memory.

And he would ruin Bane.

Bane with his two children and his cottage on the hill. In a black room of Chow's tormented mind, he knew he had lost his grip on sanity. But it no longer mattered. Without fulfillment, without happiness, there was only darkness and revenge. And contrary to Shakespeare, Chow believed revenge was a dish best served hot. Searing hot. Chow looked down from the balcony at the marble statue in Olivia's likeness, forever sixteen, a memorial in the formal gardens she had never enjoyed in life.

Only the guards and the prowling Dobermans spoiled the view. He watched, frowning, as two of the guards smoked a cigarette. The slung rifles were a constant reminder of their prison fortress.

Chow's cell phone rang.

His wife looked up at him, her eyes bloodshot.

He frowned, opened his phone, listened then said, "It does not matter. Any cost. Just do it."

He folded the phone, kissed his wife's forehead, and left her in their sanctuary. She must not be touched by the dark threads of madness that wrapped Chow's life. To her, there was only the memory of Olivia, the gardens, chairing fund-raising drives, her social parties—a numbing and blissfully unaware life.

Chow compartmentalized his psychosis, aware of it, afraid of it, unable to resist it. The only way to keep Leslie safe from the insanity was to separate the dark forces of Chow's existence from the banal storybook life reported in the tabloids.

At six o'clock, he met FBI Special Agent Hix in the garden by a marble dolphin fountain. Stephen Chow didn't shake Hix's hand. Chow turned his back and strolled down a pea gravel path that wound through tea roses in full bloom. Two silent bodyguards followed them.

"I understand Bane was assigned the case," Chow said, trying to keep the distaste out of his voice. Chow despised Hix and would have preferred not to meet the agent at *Livia*. The estate was his sanctuary from a world of barbarians like Hix.

"Yes. Of course." Hix snorted.

"Is your FBI Director Harris aware of the homicide?"

"Not yet. It hardly warrants the director's attention." Hix spat a massive gob of saliva onto Chow's gardens.

"Don't do that, *guailo*."

"Guailo?"

Guailo—*white barbarian*. If that description fit anyone, it was Hix. "Never mind." He glanced up at a mockingbird on the branch of a peach tree. So beautiful. What a shame to bring this *guailo* into his sanctuary. He smelled a pink rose, inhaled the perfume deep, to purge the stench of his guest.

"I have done everything you asked," Hix said.

"I should hope so. All these months of planning." Chow didn't mention the money, the "sweet grease" as he called it in the mother tongue.

Chow felt the rise of anger but he controlled his voice and studied the face of beloved Olivia on one of the garden statues. "So, you are going to Vermont?"

"I won't be called in to Vermont unless this is designated a Federal crime."

"It will be," Chow said. He plucked a red rose. "I have already called the state governor. And Senator Stephens of Vermont."

"It's a local homicide."

"My studio is not a local business. The victim might not be a local resident."

"How do you know that?"

Chow crushed the rose in his hand and threw the petals at Hix's feet. "Let me be clear what's expected of you."

Hix nodded, once.

"I want Bane ruined. Shame him. Destroy his credibility. Hurt him."

Hix smiled, an ugly expression on his angular face. "You don't even have to pay me for that."

Chapter 6

January 16, 8:16 pm
Burlington, Vermont

Bane stood on his creaking porch, home at last, the snow knee-deep, and fumbled for his keys. The sound of his daughters' laughter broke through the tempest of his emotions and he felt a warmth he hadn't felt in days. He took a deep, shuddering breath.

Home. Their warmly lit Victorian cottage sat on the hill overlooking Shelburne Bay. He had married Suze here, in her rose garden, under an arbor laden with blood-red roses. They raised two girls in the century-old cottage. He hoped to die here, wheezing his last breath amongst their country antiques and Native American paintings, with a photograph of his Suze clenched in arthritic hands. More likely, some maniac would blow a hole in his chest, and the daughters of Alban and Susan Bane would sell their precious things at auction.

The laughter died as he pushed back the door and snow blew into their living room.

"Hey, Pops," Jay shouted. His fourteen-year-old daughter sprang to her feet and kissed his cheek. "You look gone."

"Hi Baby." Bane pecked her back. "Aunt Di left?"

"Just." Jay smiled, revealing a tangle of braces.

The winter chill left Bane as he studied his daughters. They didn't quite turn out as planned—two candy-sweet darlings, named Jennifer and Margaret. Jennifer grew up to be Jenny, then rebelled at the cutesy name, and insisted everyone call her *only* by her initial. Just Jay. A real tomboy, with a passion for horses and baseball.

Margaret grew from his pretty doll, so like her mother, to become Mags, the punker, his sixteen-year-old hellion. Bane grounded her for a week the day she shaved off her beautiful blonde hair.

A piercing scream, distorted by television speakers, drew his eyes to the TV image of a woman covered in blood, wrapped in a stained towel.

Both Jay and Mags frowned, and Jay quickly changed the channel. Jay ushered Bane to his favorite denim-covered La-Z-Boy chair, the hockey night chair, and sat on the arm, massaging his shoulder. "We saw you and Uncle Arm on the news, running through those reporters."

"That was fun." Bane leaned over, pried the remote from Jay's hands and hit the last-channel button.

Their show came back on. The wild-eyed woman on the screen scrambled crablike up a winding stair, a bloody towel barely covering her breasts. She tripped on a Persian rug and fell. Mags stifled a laugh.

"This is funny?" Bane let his voice rise.

"It's chewy!" *Chewy*. That was Jay's favorite slanguage. In middle-aged speak, Bane knew it meant "*cool*." She saw his look and added, "We don't have to watch it."

"It's reality television." Mags tilted back her face, the way her mother used to, and smiled. Infuriating. Impossible to ignore. "That's Kelly. She just took a shower, and all this blood came out of the nozzle." A short burst of laughter escaped her.

Bane folded his arms. "Mags, I just. . ." His voice caught, and he let the words go unspoken. What was he going to say? *I just saw a man die? I just saw a monster die—the psycho who killed sixteen kids your age—and maybe, just maybe, he knew something about mom. . .* Bane ground his teeth. No way would he take out his frustrations on his girls.

Mags rolled her eyes. "It's just ketchup and stuff, *Landlord*."

"I read in a book once that daughters actually call their fathers, *dad*. Or *pops*. Or *daddy*. Even *father*." When she stuck her studded tongue out at him, he added, "I'm not in the mood for *Magsitude*." He walked to the television and turned it off, then stood in front of the screen, staring them down. Mags scowled, stood up, and marched to her room.

"What's up with her? She seems worse than ever."

Jay sighed. "She was looking through the albums again. Of mom."

Bane slid on to the couch and stroked Jay's hair. "I'm sorry, Jay." He retrieved the remote control and turned on the television. Diversion time. "So what's this about?" Though he needed to catch up on sleep, he wanted to spend some time with his girls.

"Pops, it's the hippest show." Jay's bright smile swept away the dark memories. "All my friends watch it."

Bane studied the screen. The show went to station break and an animated logo rolled across the screen, letter by letter—*Haunted Survivor*—suddenly impaled with a knife. Blood spewed out of the letters, and the words melted away like ghosts, revealing the logo for the Real TV network. A scream pierced the moaning music.

"This is *Haunted Survivor?*" *Oh hell.* He had not yet sat down to watch the show.

"These 'real' people are stranded in a creepy haunted house. The only way out is if the audience votes them off."

"I would think they'd want to be voted off then."

"Then they wouldn't win the million bucks," Jay said. "All these gross things happen. On one show they filled the rooms with hundreds of big hairy spiders. And the show with the centipedes was really putrid. The hidden cameras film as the 'survivors' freak! It's sooooo ace!"

Bane drummed his fingers on his thigh. The cop in him knew there was more. "And?"

"And there's lots of eye-candy." Jay collapsed in giggles. "Kenji's my fav! He's a hottie. Mags likes Junior, but he's gay."

"He is not," Mags shouted from her room.

He muted the volume. *How do I tell them?* He put his hand on Jay's shoulder, squeezing. *Just say it.* "My new homicide is on the set of this show."

Jay's head snapped around, eyes widening. "That's so lame."

"I'm not joking. I was just there."

Mags' door opened and she stood there, tapping her foot. "*Get out!*"

They both glanced at the television. She looked relieved as the camera moved in close on a handsome Asian with rock star hair that dangled like a sheep dog in front of his eyes. In the corner of the screen, a blue graphic indicated *Live*. She pointed at the screen and nearly shouted, "It's not Kenji!"

Bane sighed. It was all Hollywood and glitz to them. "None of the contestants. They're all accounted for." He saw the relief on both of their faces. His voice hardened. "But someone died." He wanted to say, *Don't you understand? I have to go back there tomorrow, there's a killer on the loose.*

"Your bag's ringing." Mags ran to the door and grabbed the leather bag, tossing it onto his lap.

Bane left them to watch their favorite show as he fished through the bag for his satellite phone. He slipped into his study, sat at his antique button-down leather chair, and answered, "You've got Bane."

"This is Stephen Chow." The man's angry tone cut through the fog of weariness. "Detective Bane. I really didn't expect *ever* to hear from you. Your message said official business. I trust this is important."

"Just wanted to hear your cheerful voice, Mr. Chow."

"To the point, Detective." His curt voice conveyed disgust, as if he was talking to a worm wriggling under his heel.

Bane hardened his voice. "I'm hurt. After all I've done for you."

Chow said something in Cantonese.

"Temper, temper. I assume you know about the homicide."

"Of course. It's my set, hmm? Well, obviously I don't need an alibi. I was with you that night, Detective. So what is it you need, hmm?"

"Doesn't entirely remove you from suspicion, Mr. Chow. You have lots of money."

"Why would I sabotage my own show, hmm?"

"Ratings? One point means a lot, right?"

"Right. So, I killed a stranger to gain two points?"

"That's the idea."

"You have no right to speak to me this way!"

"Yes, I do. Freedom of speech, remember?"

More Cantonese grumbling.

Before Chow could hang up the phone, Bane said, "Now might not be the best time to mention you're my prime suspect."

After a moment of silence, Chow said, "I suggest you contact the law firm of Dillard, Dillard and Derie."

"Don't like lawyers much, myself." The connection terminated.

Bane sat at his desk, spinning the phone with his fingers. That didn't go well. The Chows, far off in Hollywood and protected in their impenetrable towers of power, required finesse his tired mind did not possess. Bane couldn't believe he seriously considered the Chows as suspects.

He needed to tumble into bed. He spent a few more moments with his daughters in front of the television, watching the last moments of *Haunted Survivor*. He wouldn't be seeing much of Mags and Jay in the coming week, so he endured trash television for a while. Exhausted, Bane gave them a stern, "In bed by eleven," and left the room. He glanced back and saw Mags reach forward to caress the cover of Mom's photo album. He sighed.

A shower and some sleep would clear his head. The hot water helped revive him. As he soaped, his fingers ran over the scar on his abdomen, over the ten inches of ugly white flesh where hair would never grow. He lathered it until it throbbed.

The scar burned now, as it had during Hayden's execution.

Friend Bane, I know who killed your wife. I take the secret to hell.

He leaned into the shower nozzle; the hot water massaged his face.

A Hayden accomplice? Or an admirer copycat? Mr. and Mrs. Chow seeking revenge against the FBI agent who let Hayden escape Florida? A ploy to raise ratings? His instincts told him none of these.

A copycat killer in his home state. The place where his wife died.

Bane couldn't prevent the sudden, vivid image of his wife, lying in the black-stained freshly fallen snow, her naked body in a fetal position behind their tool shed. The heat of her blood had sculpted shapes in the drifts, the work of a mad artist. Blood in the snow. Size eleven shoes. His prime suspect had an alibi, all other leads went nowhere, until her case lost all traction, like a bald tire on ice.

Bane spun the hot water tap, letting too-hot water shake him from the unwanted vision.

He was not too exhausted to pick up the small silver frame beside the bed and kiss the picture of Suze, his wife. "Good night, babe." Tomorrow would come soon enough for the nightmares. Tonight was for dreams of Suze.

Bane slept for five hours, exhaustion taking him deep, until he awoke in a sweat from a vivid nightmare. He shivered, staring at the alarm clock. Three in the morning. More dreams of Hayden, but this time the monster was chasing his wife with the butcher knife.

Bane picked up her picture, nuzzling it close.

Awake. he sat up and thought about the case until heavy threads of fatigue finally took him back into dreams, and this time he stayed there until the alarm sounded.

Bane made his girls hot cinnamon oatmeal for breakfast and chased them out of bed, ignoring their complaints. They chatted about school, their Aunt Di, and Jay's horse-riding lessons. Mags wouldn't open up about the football-player boyfriend Bane had heard of. He drank black coffee, and made sure they finished their orange juice.

Jay put down her glass. "Forgot!" She ran to the fridge, its outside crowded with bills and reminders, and snatched an envelope from under a magnet. "This came."

Bane took the envelope. There was no postage, only a laser-printed label with his name and rank, no address. "How did this come, hon?"

She looked at the letter, then back at her father. "It was there when I got home. In the mailbox."

He put it down. A cop can't be too careful when he gets a personally delivered envelope in his mailbox, especially a cop with a high-profile history. If he lined up all the pissed-off perpetrators Bane had arrested in his career, they'd reach two city blocks right down to Shelburne Bay.

He fetched a pair of latex gloves. Jay's face scrunched up, and Bane thought she was going to laugh.

"When did you pick up the mail, Jay?"

"After school, yesterday." Jay frowned. "Around four."

They both watched as Bane handled the envelope by the edges. "You girls go get changed for school."

"Worried about anthrax?" Mags leaned closer.

"Now, young lady!" His voice rose to a level that took them beyond debate.

Mags pouted, stuck out her gold-studded tongue and went to her room. Jay looked worried, hovered for a moment, but finally left him when he hustled her out the door.

The letter was probably nothing, but he'd had plenty of death threats in his career. Although he was not paranoid enough to run to the lab with it, Bane didn't want his girls around. Slowly, he slit the short end and peered inside. A single page, fine linen.

Bane slid the page onto the ceramic-tiled tabletop. No evidence of powder. With a light touch, he pressed open the page.

The letter was laser printed on fine linen stock, in a plain typeface, signed only with the typeset old English-style moniker "G."

On it, a single line:

Welcome to The Game.

THE GAME ■ 61

Chapter 7

....

January 17, 11:26 pm

South Hampton, Long Island

Colin Lorentz always loved the sunroom, even in winter, even at night.

He stood by the glass, watching the gusts of Atlantic wind lift sheets of fresh snow, sending ice crystals impotently against the glass.

He enjoyed the heat of the cheery, snapping fire. He enjoyed the sweet mingled odors of the pine on the fire and the fragrance of the cognac. He drank deeply, enjoying the smooth warmth.

"The ratings are the highest ever." He smiled at his friend, Emerson.

"Yes. Very gratifying."

They toasted. "You know, you needn't worry."

Emerson's face lit. His smile was wide and reassuring. "Is that so?"

"No. We can use Bane to our advantage." Colin laughed, gently. "You know he's the one who. . . arrested Hayden?"

"Is that so?"

Emerson put down his glass.

"Yes. He's smart. Even Hayden said so when I visited him. But this is all bound to improve our ratings."

"Surely it will."

Colin held out his snifter for a refill, thinking suddenly of Abbey and *Haunted Survivor* and how he had missed the big scene with the snakes. *Funny how things work. From bankruptcy to unprecedented success with a simple idea.*

The homicide on the set had changed the dynamic of the already successful show, thanks to Colin's anonymous tips to key journalists. Frantic to add information to the leaked fragments, the reporters converged on the remote site. A frenzy had begun with the reporters circling like sharks. And *Haunted Survivor* could only go from number three in the ratings to top spot. A Hayden copycat was sure to spur new interest in

Colin's movie project as well. Lorentz's future seemed assured. Nothing could stop them now.

"Are you going to tell me why I'm here? Abbey will be worried sick, going off without a word." His friend didn't answer, and, for the first time, he felt uneasy. "Have I done something wrong?"

"No. No." Emerson smiled.

"Are you sure? Is this about Jackson Reid again?"

"Not at all. I have taken care of that."

"You have?"

"What about Mancuso? I've tried to pay him back."

"Mancuso's no problem."

No problem? Mancuso's initial seed loan of six million—the money Colin had needed to rescue his bankrupt company and build *Haunted Survivor*—had climbed, after interest, to nearly thirty million in just months. This was serious money, although with the success of *Haunted Survivor*, more of an inconvenience. He had already repaid principal and half of the interest with his friend's help, and he no longer had to worry that Reid, Mancuso's enforcer, might break his leg. But to call Mancuso no problem seemed foolish. The Sicilians were unlikely to hurt the goose who laid their golden egg, but they were still dangerous.

He swirled the gold liquid in his snifter and inhaled. If his friend wasn't worried, why should he be? He owed Emerson everything.

Colin was content. After twenty-two years of pilots that flopped, shows that spun into obscurity, a career notable only for its pursuit of the hit amongst the trash—finally he had produced a runaway smash. A hit that ensured his future. His only regret was that Abbey Chase was no longer his partner in life, only in business. But the millions to be made more than compensated for his personal emptiness, and Abs was still a friend, perhaps some day more. She must not, of course, ever find out about Mancuso. Or Emerson. Or Colin's other partners. He did what he had to do. And if it hurt a few people, then that was life.

His partner turned and refilled his snifter. "Do not stress over this. You have been perfect."

"Thank you."

His friend stepped closer. "In fact, I think you should go away."

Colin nodded. "I plan to. I'm working on the Hayden movie."

"So I hear."

"You don't approve."

His friend shrugged. "It is not for me to approve or not. It seems to me, however, that no one will be interested in this old serial spree."

Colin drank deeply of the cognac, enjoying the burning sensation. "Oh, yes, but with the execution, and the new developments. . ." He stumbled, tripping on the Indian silk rug. "Oh, must be getting tipsy."

"Yes." Emerson laughed again. "What new developments?"

Colin set down his glass on the sidetable by the fire, almost dropping it. He reached forward to stop it from falling and instead knocked it to the floor. It shattered, spilling cognac on his friend's priceless rug.

Emerson patted his shoulder, squeezing softly. "Do not worry. The cleaner will be in tomorrow. What new developments?"

"Oh, a private detective I hired is on the trail of Hayden's biological father. And we think we've found an accomplice."

"Well, your vaunted Detective Bane never found such a person."

"That's what's exciting— " His voice trailed off in confusion. "I must have drunk too much." He stumbled.

His friend reached out, gripped his elbow and helped him to a wing-back chair "There, there."

"I feel—" Dizziness took him, and he realized that something was wrong. Was he having a heart attack? A stress fit? Dull pain throbbed at his temples, and his vision blurred. He couldn't have had that much to drink.

"Just sleep, Colin. Sleep." His friend's smooth, wonderful voice took him into a blurry haze, a dull cloud, and for a moment, through it, he thought he saw the smile fade on his friend's face—replaced by something dark and hungry.

Chapter 8

January 18, 10:01 am
Mason Place, Vermont

Bane wasn't up for another bouncing helicopter ride. His four-wheel drive Dodge Ram had no difficulty clawing through the snow and the three-hour drive back to Mason Place helped him think. The roads had been passable until he headed south from Rutland, skirting the Green Mountains.

Welcome to The Game.

It did feel like a game, and clearly someone was playing it that way. The note delivered to Bane's house made it clear the game was personal and directed in some perverse way at him.

He redialed Laura Kincaid's office and home, over and over, hoping to get her in, certain that she had the answers he needed.

Streamers of snow still fell. The pickup truck's sweeping wipers pounded a throbbing beat that pulsed with Bane's headache.

Friend Bane, I know who killed your wife. I take the secret to hell.

What kind of twisted game was he in?

His phone rang. Kip didn't bother with greetings. "Where are you?"

"Dashing through the snow." He squinted into the noon haze, easing back on the accelerator as the truck slid too fast into a corner. Even with four-wheel drive, the big Dodge slithered across the pavement, shuddering as wheels lost their grip.

"Hands-free phone, I hope?"

He skidded around an icy blind corner and accelerated out of a spin. "Ach!" Bane slowly accelerated up the next steep grade. "You find Reid?"

"No. It's damn peculiar. We've searched every room. And the entire valley, and all the outbuildings. Three times. No idea where he is."

"Did you pull the architects' plans from the county?"

"You think there are hidden rooms and passages?"

"The internet never lies. I checked online this morning and found a dozen references to them, so it must be true." He waited until she stopped laughing. "Mason was supposed to have hunted his victims from—well, let's just say Mason was a mad man. I believe the stories. There have to be hidden passages. It explains how our perp moved the body without being recorded by the Real TV's security cameras."

Bane kept both hands on the steering wheel. "Weapon?"

"Forensics indicates a knife, rather than a saw. A very sharp knife."

"Needs a skilled hand, or an expert in anatomy." Bane braked as the road disappeared to the left. "The knife—could it be a scalpel?"

Some of Kip's words faded out due to sat-phone crackle as he coasted down a steep mountain grade. "I checked. . . the Doctor. . . name's Skillman. . . missing some scalpels. . . plus he. . . in the Gulf War."

That was interesting: the Real TV clinic doctor had a war background. Bane asked Kip to do a deeper check on Doctor Skillman. "There's another development." He told Kip about the note delivered to his house and that he had already sent the note on to the lab for tests.

"Sounds pretty personal."

"I had Cap put a trooper on my daughters."

"I bet he thought you were paranoid."

"Ach, no, but the girls did." When the trooper showed up to escort them to school, Mags and Jay freaked on him.

"We're starting the searches over." She paused. "What's up with you, Bane?"

"Nothing."

"No wisecracks?"

"Too tired. I'll have to grab my joke book." Bane hit his brakes. "Gotta go. The driving's bad."

Thirty minutes later, Bane wound up the long mountainside driveway to Mason Place. The crowd of journalists swarming at the gates, in the leavings of Vermont's worst blizzard, out to cover a local homicide, was not completely unexpected—not with the Hollywood connection, the Chows, Abbey Chase, Colin Lorentz, the glitz and the glamour. News vans jammed the entrance, kept clear only by closed iron gates and two parked state police SUVs. He inched through the journalists, as unyielding as rugby players in a scrimmage. Microphones batted the side of his truck as he blared the horn, and braver reporters threw themselves in front of the grill. One reporter shouted, "Detective Bane. Any comment on the Hayden copycat?"

Damn. They already knew. From local to national news overnight.

He nearly ran down a journalist who slipped through the troopers at the gate. As the wheels locked and the startled man fell back into the snow, Bane managed to put the brakes to his own anger at the same time. He'd stop all this. He'd find this copycat and find him a permanent home in the Vermont penal system. To do less would be to admit that Hayden had become a specter even more powerful than he had been in life.

Bane jammed his Sox cap on his head, snatched up his bag, buttoned up his tartan vest, and ran for the house. He flashed his badge at a sleepy-looking Real TV security guard.

"Mornin'," the man said with a nod.

Bane knew from that one word that he was a native Vermonter. "Mornin' back. Didn't see you yesterday."

The guard slipped his uniform cap off a shiny, balding head. "No, sir. Ira Evans, sir, that's my name. Lord liftin', I missed all the excitement, didn't I?"

"You did that. Off yesterday?"

Ira's big black eyes stared back at Bane. "Home catchin' up on the chores and a good thing too, so says I." Ira was a big man with big hands, a big face and a big frown, every inch Bane's vision of a Vermonter.

"Where you from, Ira?" He was the most expressionless Vermonter Bane had ever met, as placid as Shelburne Pond on a windless day. No nervous habits, no batting eyes, rubbing of the nose or phony smiles for Ira Evans. His only noticeable habit seemed evident from tobacco stained fingertips.

"Winooski, sir." His voice was flat and toneless.

"You been with Real TV long, Ira?"

"No, sir. Meaning, sir, them flatlanders contracted me privately. My company—that's Kirby Security, sir—we've been under contract with the State for ten years at this very house. Real TV assumed our contract, sir."

Bane stepped closer, his mouth inches from Ira's face, and dropped his voice to a gentle whisper. "You know this house, then?"

Ira backed away a pace. "Lord, yes, sir. I know this house just fine, sir. Terrible place. After a break-in by some teenage hoodlums—that was around Hallowe'en five years ago, sir—my company stationed me here for a whole week, and I even had to sleep here. Hairiest time of my life."

Bane studied his unruffled features but somehow couldn't visualize this craggy man frightened. Bane *could* imagine Ira walking up to a bear and saying, '*Boo!*' and the bear running right up a tree. "Is that so? And what happened?"

"Nothin'. Saw lots of wildlife. Wished I had my huntin' rifle, that's for sure. I'd have had venison for the whole winter."

"Well, how about that?" Bane offered his most neighborly smile and ignored the comment about hunting out of season. "Tell you what, Ira. Do you suppose your boss would mind if I asked you to be my guide? I sure need someone to show me around this big place."

Ira shrugged, sliding his hat back on a shiny head. "Sir, that would be up to her." He jerked his thumb over his shoulder. "Ms. Chase that is, sir. She be the boss lady."

"*She's* something." Bane allowed his voice to sound exasperated. "Hollywood." Bane invited Ira closer with a finger gesture. The man hesitated, looking uncomfortable, but finally took a baby step closer. "Do you know much about the secret passageways in this house?"

He nodded. "I doubts anyone knows this place better'n me, sir. But I ain't found more than a dozen of them Mason passages, sir."

"And you're thinking there's more."

"I am thinking that, sir."

Bane studied the man, letting the silence draw out. Ira stared back with placid eyes. "Can you show me?"

"You ask that Ms. Chase, sir. She says so, I'll oblige ya."

"I know you will, Ira."

"Not a problem, sir."

"Ira, where were you on Friday?"

His eyebrows shot up, but his face remained calm. "Right here, sir. I came on shift right at 7:26 am. Lunch break at 11:30."

"So precise?"

"I was a beat cop."

Bane nodded. "Burlington PD?"

"Yessir. Anyhows, off shift around four."

Ira turned his back and went back to studying the security cameras. Around Four. Suddenly, not so precise: 7:26 am on shift, 11:30 am on lunch, *around four* off shift. Bane would have to check into this ex-cop security guard. "Ira? Are those cameras taped or just live surveillance?"

"Taped, sir."

"I'll need those tapes."

"Sure 'nough, sir." He turned away again. "If the boss lady says okay, sir."

Bane stared at his back for a short moment. Ira seemed atypically aloof for a local, but he wouldn't judge him until a background check. He had noticed the green ribbon on his lapel, indicating sympathy for or membership in the Green Mountain Freedom movement. The G-Men, as they were affectionately known, were an interesting group of Vermonters that made regular local headlines and worried the Feds because of their quest for self-government. The G-Men struck resonance with many because of their platform to ship all flatlanders out of the state. But Bane had no particular issue with the independence movement. Two of his friends were in the Green Mountain Freedom Party, the political arm of the movement.

Bane found Kip in refuel mode in the massive crew kitchen, deep in the finished primary basement of the house, sitting at one of the tables over a cup of java.

The kitchen was impressive and would have been the envy of a fine hotel. The granite counter tops and stainless steel cabinets glittered and the gas burners blazed. Two men and three women in white smocks tended simmering pots. Though it was early, Bane's stomach rumbled at the delicious odors of garlic and sweated onion and bubbling chicken broths, pungent with fresh basil.

A white-uniformed Asian man stood behind a counter, hands on hips, broad, muscular, and barely five-foot-two. "You work here?" Bane asked.

"Mistah, this is my kitchen," he said in phony pidgin. "I'm bossie here." The fierceness vanished, replaced by an instant smile.

Bane knew acting and knew the man was jerking him around. "I'm sorry. You must be Chef Edward Kim."

"That's me, Mistah."

It was impossible to guess the age of Edward Kim's round, happy face. His eyes darted everywhere at once, and his tiny body seemed wound for action. "Who are you, Mistah? One of the police mans?"

"Yes, I am, Mr. Kim. I'm Detective Bane."

"You want coffee, Mistah Detekive?"

"I could use a boost."

Kim ran—he didn't walk—to the sink area. Bane followed to the long main counter that divided the kitchen from the eating area, and watched Kim grind coffee beans by hand: the aroma of heaven. "Don't go to any trouble."

"Nothing's too good for you, Mistah Detekive."

"Is that so?"

Kim didn't answer. He popped a can of Carnation sweetened milk, poured it into a gigantic mug, and microwaved the milk as the coffee grounds boiled in a pot.

"This flies in the face of my coffee knowledge. Your coffee drip machine broken?"

"This is only way to make coffee. Always boil beans, never drip, drip, drip." He laughed as if he had made a big joke and flew through his kitchen, a blur. He poured the coffee over the heated milk, then put the steaming cup on the counter in front of Bane. "Try it, Mistah Detekive. Try it."

Bane sipped his coffee. His head jolted back as if someone had thrown a switch and electricity flowed through his sagging muscles. "Holy java," he said. "This is something else."

"You like?" Kim paused, just for a moment—more of a hover, really—and smiled his charming best. "Vietnamese coffee is the bestest."

"I like. Great coffee. I can tell I'll be spending some quality time in your kitchen."

"Eddie's secret."

"Speaking of secrets, can we talk, Mr. Kim? Can you slow down for a moment?"

The man paused, wiping his hands on his apron. "Sure, Mistah, but ten minutes to lunch times. Can we work and talk?"

As Bane followed Kim, he greedily drank his coffee. Kim's frenetic pace made Bane dizzy, although after the high-test coffee, he was jumping, too. He pursued the chef through the kitchen with questions, firing them in between chops of Kim's massive cleaver.

"You notice anything strange? In this house?"

"Everything's strange here, Mistah." He chopped vegetables with a *thwack, thwack, thwack.* His skill with the massive knife was surgeon-precise.

"Anything in particular? Any strange people?"

"All strange people, Mistah. This is television. All strange people."

Bane smiled. "So what's your background?"

"Sometimes, I does a cooking show. You see it, hmmm?" He didn't wait for an answer. "But I'm off-season now, understand?"

Again, Kim didn't wait for a response as he flew to one of the massive refrigerators. He pulled it open. Bane didn't follow him in. Eight full sides of beef and several pigs hung from meat hooks inside.

Chef Kim effortlessly brought out a side of pork and began slicing it thinly with his cleaver.

His skill with his knife was impressive. With his wired-up power, he had more than enough strength to chop off the victim's head in one crisp blow.

"Do you know Mr. Lorentz well?"

For the first time Kim's wound up, muscular body froze. The big smile faded, like a house going dark in a thunder storm. With the meat cleaver still in his hand, half raised, he said, "I knows Mistah Lorentzee. Not like he."

The cleaver swung down, missing Bane's splayed fingers by a wide margin, but so forceful Bane felt the wind of the chop. He pulled back his hands and took a deep breath. "Why is that, Mr. Kim?"

"I not talk about he." Kim's wide hands caressed the side of pork. "Busy now. Come back later."

It was time for a harder hit. "Now, Chef Kim. Now, or—" He jangled handcuffs.

The knife came down with a reverberating thud, penetrating the wooden cutting surface. "Mistah Lorentzee promised me a new show. He lie. Big stupid liar." He leaned across the cutting table. "He always lie, lie, lie. Okay? Am I suspect?"

"Where were you last Friday, between five and eight—"

Kim interrupted. "Always here, Mistah. Ask anyone!"

Eddie Kim deserved more scrutiny. Bane didn't buy the cheesy pidgin English and the stereotyped Asian cooking show persona. And Eddie Kim had skill with knives and plenty of power.

"I guess the crew talk to you a lot. Over lunch?"

"Oh, the crew talk. They always talk to Eddie, you know? Always talk, talk, talk."

"What about?"

He reached for a knife. "Bad people. Bad, bad people." He shook his head. "No good people here."

"Why bad?"

"Laugh at contestants. Make fun of them!"

Bane chugged back two more of the super high test coffees as Eddie chased his crew around the big kitchen, a cleaver in his hand. "Lazy bones. Always lazy bones. Faster. Faster."

Bane watched for a while, then sat at a table and fished in his battered leather bag. He yanked out Colin Lorentz's Tablet PC.

It was awkward navigating with a pen—*I'm too old-fashioned*—but he managed to boot up with the *Abbeysucks* password and read some of Colin's emails starting over three years ago, when the show was just an idea in Abbey Chase's head. Lorentz's mail made for an intense two-hour read. He was particularly interested in the frequent mentions of the Lorentz's financial woes:

To: Colin Lorentz
From: Abbey Chase
RE: What do you think? Maybe Real TV?

Cole, I've got a winner. Real TV will buy this one for sure. They're always looking for new reality television concepts. We scare the shit out of twelve gorgeous real people, totally isolated from the real world in a scary house, and play mind games with them: missing people, moving rooms, snakes and spiders, doors that go nowhere, sound effects—and of course every room has hidden cameras. Here's the best part: the LAST 'survivor' has to live ALONE in the house for the last week, and we throw every-thing sinister at him and if he survives the last week he wins a million dollars...

Bane leaned back in the chair. This woman, Abbey Chase, was beyond nasty. Pushing the envelope of reality television, playing mind games, all in pursuit of the almighty ratings god. It carried a stink of greed. He read the reply in Colin's *Sent* folder:

REPLY E-mail
Abs, are you on drugs? No, really. Where do you think Lorentz Chase Productions finds a million dollars for the prize, never mind the millions to produce this monster? A lottery? LCP is bankrupt as it is.
Hell, Abs, I actually think the idea might work, if we were big enough. Maybe we could pitch it to Chow over at Real TV without developing it.
Cole.

Nearly bankrupt? That was interesting.

His satellite phone rang. "Bane."

Cap's too-loud voice boomed back. "The DNA confirms your suspicion. Not Lorentz. And no match to known perps in the DNA database, including CODIS." If there was nothing in the *Combined DNA Index System*, then the victim had no recent record.

Bane leaned back in his chair and watched Eddie Kim fly around his kitchen. "What's up, Cap?" He knew Captain D. Jefferies didn't call with DNA results. Cap didn't do that. He only called to give Bane hell. To yell and vent. Or to deliver bad news.

"Just had a call from San Francisco PD."

"That so?"

"Hayden's lawyer. Laura Kincaid."

Bane said nothing. But he knew. She was dead. Another move in this bizarre game.

"Found her dead. Put her own gun in her mouth."

"Right. And I can fold laundry. Shit." The one person who might know something about Hayden's involvement with Suze's murder—and some of the other coincidences—was dead.

"Who's in charge?"

"Sergeant Susan Lee." He gave Bane her number, then fell silent a moment. There was something else on his mind.

"Heard you called Stephen Chow."

"So?" Bane exaggerated a yawn, making sure his captain heard it.

"He's a personal friend of our governor."

"Ah. Another reason not to like the man." Bane hardened his voice. "I'm not done with Stephen Chow. Just so you know."

Cap hesitated, then said, in a quieter voice, "All I'm saying is, be more discreet."

"You know me better than that, Cap."

Bane immediately dialed Detective Susan Lee. A childlike voice answered, and he almost said, *Is mommy home?* "Detective Lee?"

"This is Lee," said a lilting voice.

"I am Lieutenant Detective Alban Bane of—"

"I was just going to call you, Detective. We've had a suspicious death here that may be connected to you."

"Laura Kincaid, yes. Call me Alban. Or Al."

"Susan. Laura Kincaid had a letter addressed to *you* in her purse."

Christ. Bane placed both elbows on the table. "What did it say?"

"It's short. A suicide note. Just—*I apologize to those I have hurt. I cannot live with the guilt.*"

When she didn't continue, Bane said, "That doesn't mention me."

"No. It's *addressed* to you."

"Oh." *Hell.* One more death to think about.

"Could you send the note?"

"Sorry, Alban. It's in our lab. I'll fax a copy and the report." She sighed. "Don't expect much. Laser-printed and unsigned." Bane thought of his own unsigned, laser-printed note, *Welcome to the Game.*

"Just so you know, this is a homicide."

"Almost certainly. She left behind a dependent mother who has advanced Alzheimer's. I doubt she'd kill herself. Her practice was flourishing—thanks to Hayden."

In the spirit of cooperation, Bane told her about his unsigned, hand-delivered note. They filled each other in on their respective cases, and he let her know his suspicion that it might have something to do with Hayden. He asked her to describe what she knew of Laura Kincaid's last moments.

"Witnesses heard a gunshot. I'm just putting together a time line, but we have fairly consistent witness reports. Just before the shot, tourists saw a man with Laura Kincaid in the Japanese Tea Garden. This man was very striking, blond, about six foot six, dressed like a cowboy."

"A cowboy in San Francisco? Is there a gay club nearby?"

"We actually thought of that. But no. Doesn't mean he wasn't on the cruise in the park."

"That's helpful, Susan. Keep me informed."

"You too."

He put the phone down. Kincaid didn't commit suicide, and clearly the big cowboy was the perp. Hired hit? Most hit men didn't draw attention to themselves by wearing cowboy hats in San Francisco. Lee seemed competent. Bane would leave the Kincaid investigation to her.

If Laura Kincaid was murdered, and if this was a related case, then he might be dealing with more than one perp.

Bane punched speed dial seven on his phone.

Armitage Saulnier's New Orleans drawl made him smile. "You've got Arm."

"Arm, it's Bane."

"You sound like crap."

"Thanks."

"You're in the news again!"

He chuckled to relieve his stress. "See? Vermont can be exciting."

Arm's laugh was short, and then it was down to business. "So what's up, bro?"

"A favor."

"You ask, it's done."

"Can you run something for me through the VICAP database? We might have a mob connection." Bane described the copycat scene, the finger capping, and his concerns about Jackson Reid being a possible mob enforcer. "Run cowboy hit men, too, six foot six, blond. That's all I have."

"That's some case you caught." Arm's voice boomed with confidence, but Bane detected the note of worry.

Bane glanced around the kitchen, making sure no one was close enough to hear, then spilled it all. He told Arm about the *Game* note, Stephen Chow, the lawyer Laura Kincaid, Detective Susan Lee, his suspicions about Lorentz and Jackson Reid, Kip's theories—everything. When Bane finished, Arm didn't reply for a long time, so long he thought the line had dropped. "Arm, you still got that bud in Revenue?"

"Sure do. I'll ask him to run down Lorentz's financial transactions. Might be able to find out who the moneybags is."

"I always said you were the smartest partner I ever had."

"Smart mouth, anyway. And here I thought you liked me for my looks."

"Don't go for green eyes, Arm."

"Unless attached to nicer legs."

"Damn straight. Can you pull Lorentz and Chase Productions, Real TV and Stephen Chow without raising too many red flags? I need to know where all the money came from. Who their silent partners are."

"You be careful, now. This stinks like a pile of crawdad leavings."

"What about Hayden's phone logs?"

"Can't find a sympathetic judge to give the court order."

"Why not?" What judge wouldn't see the merit?

"Some big shot's running interference."

That didn't sound good. Who had that kind of influence? The Chows, certainly. Vermont's own governor, a man who seemed bent on protecting Real TV. But it was difficult to believe either of these would be willing accomplices of a killer.

"How about the Hayden visitor logs?"

"Besides his lawyer and his psychiatrist, only one other visitor: your producer, Colin Lorentz."

"And you were planning to tell me when?"

"Like to surprise you."

"How many visits?"

"Five."

"Christ."

"Amen to that, brother."

"Give me dates and times." Bane wrote it all down. One visit last Friday, just around the time his ex-wife claimed he flew away on business in New York, and just before the execution.

Arm gave him the details, then fell silent. As if reading Bane's mind, Arm added, "Our task force couldn't have missed Hayden accomplices."

Bane stretched his neck, winding out the sudden tension kinks. "I know. But it seems we screwed up. See what you can find out. Maybe a relative on his adopted parents' side? Or his real parents? The court wouldn't release their identity, remember?"

"Never understood that order."

"Records are in Boston, right? That's where he came from."

"I'm all over it." Arm clicked off.

Bane knew Arm's high-level VICAP clearance would get him into nearly any database; he was one of the ASACs, Assistant Supervisory Agents in Charge, for a high-level department in CID, the Criminal Investigative Division.

After he ended the call, Bane punched up the cell phone number for Colin Lorentz and left another urgent message.

Obviously Lorentz and Reid were the keys to unraveling the case.

Bane went back into the greedy world of the Lorentzes on the Tablet PC. Abbey Chase hadn't lied about their relationship, and he skimmed through all the back and forth emails, some laden with sexual tension or laced with affection. He compressed two years of television development into an hour of reading.

But there was one thing she *had* lied about and he almost missed it, buried in an e-mail from William Kent, their director:

Our scout knows of this mansion in Vermont, owned by a famous mass murderer. We gotta use it, whatever it costs! Winter up there will add to the isolation of the guests. I drove up there. Wow. Forget building on a sound stage. A one-hundred-and-sixty room mansion built by an eccentric billionaire who made his money manufacturing bombs in WW1. He went mad, killed his wife, her entire family, some friends, then himself. Great background story.
There are secret passages that spider through the old mansion—you couldn't ask for better than that! They reach into every room of that house, a mysterious web of hidden doors and halls. . .

Secret passages. He wasn't surprised Abbey Chase had hidden the truth from him. This meant the contestants had access to the entire house. If any of them knew about these passages, he would have to add them to the long list of suspects.

Even more important, it gave his teams a place to look for the all-important missing witness, Jackson Reid, the man who discovered the victim, then disappeared, and who might have links to the mob.

Abbey Chase's lie also gave him a solid reason to treat her as hostile, no matter who she was connected to.

She could squawk all she wanted. It was time to interview the crew and contestants of *Haunted Survivor*.

Chapter 9

....

January 19, 5:37 pm

Real TV Control Room, Mason Place

Abbey Chase jabbed her finger at the monitors, her face red. "You see *that*, Detective?" she said, her voice almost a shout. "Every single room in the house is *right there*, in front of your eyes! Jesus save me from idiots." The heat of her anger activated her delicate floral perfume, an odd contrast to her sudden savagery.

The activity in the control room churned around them. She glared at him as if he were an annoying insect. "Take a hint, Detective. We're live in the Pacific Time Zone. Oh, hell—" She whirled and leaned over the wide bank of editing controls, one breast nearly bouncing out of her low-cut gown. "Camera fifty-five, damn it!"

Her editor slid a lever labeled fifty-five, his fingers fumbling.

"We only have one chance at this!" She put her hand on the editor's shoulder, standing between Bane and the bank of monitors. "I *live* for this, Detective. I can't see you now."

Bane folded his arms on his chest. "Producers don't direct—I looked it up in my *Idiots' Guide to TV*. Either here and now, or we fly you in to Burlington for questioning."

She put her hands on her hips, eyes fierce, lips pressed together. He didn't move. "Get out of my control room."

"I would, but I'm enjoying this."

She spun again, leaning close to a monitor. "Okay, here we go!"

Bane stepped closer. "I will now have to interview your cast—your contestants. Don't bother arguing. I don't bargain with liars."

"Well, aren't you the snitty Detective." She held up her hand. "Now! Camera nine."

A new image transformed the large central screen of the control room.

"Look at that," snapped one editor.

William Kent, the pro-wrestler-look-alike director pushed Bane aside. "Zoom in! Damn it, you're too slow." His voice boomed and made Jason jump. "No! Camera twenty-one. Kenji's bedroom. Look, they're on his bed!" Kent was overweight in the extreme although the layers of fat did not conceal muscle. His face convulsed with an energy that made his bushy mustache twitch.

Bane stared at the large screen that dominated the crowded control room. Fully distracted from his mission now, he leaned around Kent's massive shoulders and peered at the monitor. The bottom right of the screen was overlaid with bold type: LIVE.

The camera zoomed back from a close up of snakes.

Dozens of snakes slithered out of a tiny opening in a bed's headboard. As the view widened, Bane saw a sleeping face. The snakes dropped on to the pillow by the man's head.

"I'm hoping those are rattlesnakes. I'm itching to charge one of you."

The crew shushed Bane with one voice. As he watched, he realized the snake handlers had to be using the hidden passages to release the snakes.

"Look at that! That's a super shot! Closer. Closer. There." Kent's arms flailed around as he gave directions.

A snake slid across the bed spread. The Asian man—Bane recognized him as the heartthrob of his daughter Jay—rolled over, his naked chest revealed as he tossed back the blanket. His hand landed on a snake. It hissed at him.

Bane scowled. "This just gets better and better. Cruelty to animals. Assault with a deadly snake. I'll think of something."

"Shut up!" Kent whirled. He leaned in close to Bane, his breath reeking of coffee.

Abbey Chase knifed a look at Bane before moving in closer on the big screen. "You're trespassing here, Detective. And I assure you this is perfectly legal."

"He's waking up," a technician said, his voice hushed.

Bane watched as Kenji's eyes opened. For a moment he didn't move. His fingers convulsed. He turned his head, slowly. No reaction. He froze, staring at the snake, inches from his face.

"Kenji's too cool," Kent yelled. "Go to camera fifteen. Junior's going to flip. Keep an eye on Margaret. She hasn't woken yet. No, wait! Let's see this."

Kenji sat up, a snake in his hand, ignoring the others that swarmed across his bare legs.

Hell, Bane thought, *I would have thrown it across the room.* But this Kenji just leaned closer, wrapping his hand around its head. Gently, he put it down on the bed, and it slithered away to join a dozen others.

"Damn his Zen crap. Shit." Abbey Chase pointed at a small monitor. "Go with Margaret. She's waking up!"

Just before the camera changed, Kenji pushed back the blanket and slid out of bed. He was naked.

"Yummy shot, though," Ms. Chase said.

"What are those scars?" Bane leaned closer to the monitor, peering at Kenji's hairless chest. White, ugly scars, half a dozen or so, lifted in sharp relief on his brown skin.

Abbey didn't turn. "He never told us. Adds character."

Knife scars, or something bigger than a knife—Bane was sure of it. He had his own knife scar for reference.

The central screen, labeled 'Live Camera' changed to a woman wearing only a Minnie Mouse T-shirt.

A snake slid across her T-shirt. She batted it as if it was a mosquito.

"I can't believe this." Bane couldn't help himself.

Ms. Chase grabbed his arm, pulling him aside. "You're in the way, Detective." Bane moved to one side, following her.

"Turn down the gain. Her scream will feed back." Kent's big round face lit with a smile.

Margaret screamed, a piercing howl. She scrambled out of bed.

"Christ, if those were poisonous snakes, she'd be dead by now." Jason the editor laughed.

"She could still catch a nasty bite. Those milk snakes have sharp little fangs." Kent's laugh boomed, filling the small control room. "Quick, go to camera twenty-nine. Junior's freaking!"

Abbey Chase leaned close to Bane and whispered, "Stop scowling, Detective. We have to give our viewers excitement. Our snake handler assures us this is perfectly safe. The contestants have had their needles."

Bane continued calculating the various things he could charge the Real TV crew with: intimidation, assault, cruelty to animals, being sick bastards? The feeling of revulsion was so intense he wanted to do *something*.

The entire control room erupted in laughter. Bane leaned around the wide-shouldered director in time to see a young man, naked from the waist up, brushing snakes off his chest. He screamed as sharply as Margaret, then ran from the room.

"Follow him." Kent stabbed his finger at the monitor. "Camera twenty-six—no seventeen—shit! Jason, you're losing him." The views were from behind as the young man in his briefs ran down a hall carpeted in writhing snakes, coiling and uncoiling around his bare legs. "Junior's totally freaked."

"This psychological trauma could be felonious," Bane grumbled.

"Shut up, damn you!" Kent didn't turn as he yelled, but his voice filled the room. The director was imposing even with his back turned.

"This is what the show's about, Detective," Abbey Chase snarled at him. "They signed releases. Stop interfering. This is an important scene. We've been teasing viewers with it for weeks, and we sold out our ad time at double premium."

"You're doing it live?"

"West Coast only. Central and Eastern time zones get a later live show, plus a prime time special tomorrow. We promised our viewers."

Bane shook his head, eyes fixed with helpless fascination on the big monitor.

"Okay, Junior's running to big brother Kenji! That's what I thought. Get camera thirteen ready as he runs in—okay, now!"

Junior burst into Kenji's room and ran into his arms.

"Oh, the gay community will love this! We have to—cut to camera thirty-eight. Our Miss Hong Kong is waking up."

A close up of a stunning Chinese woman filled the monitor.

"Zoom back. Easy. Easy. Perfect!" A snake slithered across her bare neck as she bolted awake, eyes wide, mouth open to scream.

"You're all sick bastards." Bane couldn't believe people wanted to watch this show. Worse, he was sure his daughters were watching right now, Aunt Di's protestations notwithstanding.

"Back to thirteen!"

Now Kenji held Junior by his elbow, his voice loud on the control room speakers: "It's all right. They're just milk snakes. No poison."

"I hate snakes!" Junior shouted, and he scrambled up onto a chair, his face drawn back in a look of terror.

"Camera seventeen," Kent yelled. "There goes Ahmed!" The camera view changed to a handsome, dark-skinned man. He was nose to nose with a snake as his eyes opened. He jolted back, but didn't scream, or fall off the bed, like some of the others. Slowly, he slid out of the bed. "No fun! Go to six! Kelly's flipping."

The screen dissolved to a long shot of a bedroom. A woman stood on the bed, climbing the headboard. She was naked, her breasts bounced.

"Did you filter that?" Kent glanced to the right. The large central monitor revealed the same scene, but with blur filters hiding nipples. "Perfect, cut back to Kenji's room. Thirteen!" On the control panel main monitor, Kenji was full-frontal naked on the smaller monitor. Abbey Chase leaned closer, not hiding her interest. Kenji had a snake in each hand, but he looked calm. Bane glanced back to the plasma monitor and noted they had cube filtered his genitals. Kenji's face was inscrutable. He gently put the snakes down on the floor to join the others, then walked, barefoot, to his closet and pulled out a pair of shoes and pants. He calmly walked back through the snakes and handed the clothes to Junior, turning the shoes upside down and rapping the heels. "No snakes," he said.

"Kenji's not afraid of anything," Abbey Chase moved away from the panel, sliding between Bane and the director. She whispered, close to Bane's ear. "I love watching him traipse around naked, but I regret casting him. We've never had so much as a yelp out of him."

Kenji remained calm as he dressed himself, surrounded by snakes. His face revealed no emotion. With his scars and calm demeanor, he must be used to danger. Bane's cursory background check on the contestants had come up with zero history on Kenji Tenichi. Kenji was already on Bane's top-two list for contestants to interview. The blade scars, so similar to the one on Bane's torso, made him think of the forensics report indicating the perpetrator decapitated his victim with a knife. Bane decided he would run a deeper check on Kenji Tenichi. He had nothing prior to Kenji's immigration to America from Japan.

Bane watched the monitor as Kenji led Junior into the hall. Other contestants immediately gravitated towards him. "They're just milk snakes," Kenji said. Bane saw the calming effect the man had on the other contestants.

"Party pooper," editor Jason said.

"Asshole!" Kent pounded his big fist into the control panel. He looked back at Abbey Chase. "You should never have cast this jerk. Christ! I was counting on twenty minutes of screaming! He did the same damn thing with the rats." He jumped forward, sliding one of Jason's toggle switches. "Damn it, Jason! We're live. Go back to Kelly, on fifteen!"

Kelly, still half naked, with only a sheet clutched around her body, ran down the hall, screaming. Bane had seen something similar on his own television with Jay and Mags: Kelly, covered in fake blood, screaming and running up the hall. Now she jumped into Kenji's arms. He carried her, squirming, down the sweeping stairs to the domed lobby, which was free of snakes.

The only other calm presence was the dark-skinned Ahmed, still in his bedroom, picking the snakes off his bed as if they were litter.

Bane made a mental note about Kenji and Ahmed: they were both calm in the face of danger, and strong enough to be perpetrators. The scars on Kenji's body required explanation. He would interview these two first.

Bane whispered in Abbey Chase's ear. "I want to interview this Kenji first. Then Ahmed."

"Not now, Detective!"

"Now," he said, calmly.

She whirled, her eyes full of fury. "You're interfering with us here,

Detective. If you want access to my guests, get a damned warrant."

"And you, Ms. Chase, are—" he almost said 'a first class bitch' but instead paused, then finished, "interfering with my investigation. I do not need a warrant on a crime scene to interview suspects." Bane leaned closer and allowed his voice to lift a notch. "Now, Ms. Chase!" He didn't tell her he wanted to do this while the guests were still in fight-or-flight mode, drunk with their own adrenalin from their run-in with the snakes. "Please don't make me charge you with obstructing justice. I'd love to get you in my sweaty little interrogation room in Burlington."

Kent glanced back at Bane, sneered, then laughed. "You two, both of you, get the hell out of my control room. Now!" He whirled back around. "Damn it Jason! You missed—oh, let me. . ." He leaned over Jason and slid camera dissolve levers.

Abbey Chase led Bane from the control room and they stood in the hall, ignoring the bustle around them.

"Christ, Detective, you don't pull your punches, do you?"

"And you are a liar. Which means, you're now a suspect." He let that sink in. "And I'm making a list of things to charge you with."

She smoothed her designer dress, her breathing gradually returning to normal. "If you interview my contestants because they *might* have had access to the basements through some obscure secret passages—well, it could change the show dynamic. You really want to risk the litigation? Millions, Detective!"

Bane shook his head. "Litigation and I are old friends. I could arrest you and ship you off to Burlington right now. You up for a few nights in the lockup? They like hot numbers in designer dresses in the overnight cells." *God help me, I will do it*, he thought. *Just give me a reason.*

"On a trumped up obstruction charge? Don't be ridiculous. I'd never see the inside of a cell. It's you who should be worried. *Millions* in liability." Her sneer made her ugly.

"Lass, I was afeared of my wee ma. My dear wife could scare the crap out of me if she had cause. My partner Kip can beat the stuffing out of me. But, you, lass, I just feel sorry for you." He kept his voice low, to disguise his revulsion.

"That's you're way of saying I don't intimidate you?"

"Aye."

"I *will* be calling Governor Ritchie."

"Say hello for me."

"You'll be lucky if you have a job!" She turned to re-enter the control room.

"You'll let me know, won't you? I have a lot of things to pack in my office."

She stared back at him, door held open. He could see the turmoil in the control room.

"I will interview the guests. *Now*, Ms. Chase."

Her shoulders stiffened. "Go to hell!"

He snatched his two-way radio off his belt. "Kip, bring two troopers up here! We have a guest for overnight lockup."

Kip's voice crackled back. "I'll be sure her highness is comfortable."

Abbey Chase turned her head. Her glare would have turned back a room full of her own snakes. "Fine! I'll arrange access. Now, excuse me!"

She slammed the door.

Bane stared at the door, his hands curling into fists. Why were the beauties always so difficult? Suspect or obstacle? He wasn't sure yet.

Behind him, Bane heard a soft laugh. "I take it we're on for interviewing the guests."

He turned to face his partner Kip and two troopers. "I was always a good poker player."

"I saw that snake scene on the big screen in the—what do they call it—the Brain Room? Not very funny." She nodded at the control room door. "I assume you were watching."

"Squirming, more like," Bane said. "They're all freaks."

"You don't like her, huh?"

He shook his head. "Nope. She doesn't like me either."

"No one likes you much."

He clapped his hand to his chest. "You hurt me."

"See, it's your sarcasm."

"I'm only that way with suspects."

"And your friends."

"See, I have friends."

"Yeah, but they don't like you."

"Aren't you a fortune cookie philosopher?" He cocked his thumb over his shoulder. "She's like a twisted Ms. Hyde, our producer babe. Ready for some Hollywood?"

"For sure. Can't wait to see these hunks up close and personal like."

Bane imitated one of her special slow-mo winks. "You're married."

She laughed. "My husband and I have an agreement. Look, don't touch."

"Don't let glamour cloud your judgment, Kipster."

"Hey!" She punched Bane's arm, a little too hard. "Never happen."

They took Trooper Samuel Roth with them for control. Real TV had a guard on the magnetically-locked, shatterproof glass door that directly accessed the contestant wing. The door was visually jarring with modern metal and glass and keypad combination pads set into an old oak frame. Bane noticed the holstered gun and baton on the guard's belt.

After a lot of badge-flashing and a call to Abbey Chase, she met them at the door to the guest quarters, accompanied by another of her security guards.

"You *are* persistent." The anger was gone and she smiled, looking as if she had just washed and freshened. Ms. Hyde had vanished, for the moment.

"You're stalling again," Bane said.

Her face flushed, but her smile did not fade. "Of course I am, Detective. The live-shoot is finished, but we're still capturing some of the after-reactions for the follow-up show next week. Anyway, you didn't want to walk through wriggling snakes, did you? My crews had to clear the halls and rooms."

Kip's eyebrows shot up. "You're something, Ms. Chase."

Abbey Chase frowned at Kip and Bane realized there was genuine animosity between them. "Anyway, we're good to go now."

"No filming, Ms. Chase," Bane said. "I mean it. If one second of my interviews hits your little screens, you'll see the inside of a jail cell for just a day less than two years. Besides, I look fat on camera."

"I doubt that, Detective."

"Was that a compliment?"

"An observation. Cameras are off. Nothing of your interviews will air." There was enough hesitation in her voice to make him doubt her.

"I mean it. Anything airs, I'll charge you."

She waved her hand. "Oh, I believe *you*." She punched a key combination, which Bane memorized, then the magnetic lock slid open. And they entered the haunted halls of Abbey Chase's perverted imagination.

Chapter 10

January 19, 11:39 pm
Set of Haunted Survivor

They followed her up a long hall and through another door. Kip and Bane slowed as they entered the immense domed foyer, held aloft by polished granite pillars. Bane paused to study the fresco work in the dome, a disturbing but eloquent scene revealing drunken satyrs and nymphs.

"Ms. Chase, have your guards always been armed?"

She sighed, leading the way across the inlaid marbled floor. "They're licensed. And it's just a precaution. With a homicide, why take chances?" She stopped in front of arched double doors and held up her hands. "They're all in here, calming each other down." She cupped her hands in front of her, rubbing them. "Cold in this wing." She shivered. "You want a group session or one-on-ones?"

"A little of both. I want to see the group's reaction. Then Kenji and Ahmed."

Ms. Chase's hand hovered over the doorknob. "Why those two?"

"They seem the most mysterious. I read your files on them. Kenji's background is mostly fictional according to my checks. Ahmed Matwali Atwah is Egyptian—"

"That's racial profiling!" Abbey Chase snapped.

"You didn't let me finish. He's on a watch list with the anti-terrorism task force." Bane watched her face turn shades of red and purple. "I'm not sure what your friend Governor Ritchie will think of you casting an illegal immigrant who's on the terrorism watch list."

Her face drained of color. "You can be a real pain, Detective." She sounded hurt, rather than angry.

"So I'm told. So, how did they end up on your precious show?"

She turned, her smile a contrast to the hardness in her eyes. "Kenji's a hunk, pure and simple, and the more mysterious the better. And Ahmed is very political. We're doing television, Detective. The more strife, the merrier. Ahmed never stops fighting with Carlo—the animosity is real, based largely on religious differences. Carlo, the guilt-ridden sinful Catholic, and Ahmed the angry Muslim."

Bane shook his head and glanced at Kip, silently communicating, *The more strife, the better.*

Abbey Chase turned the knob and threw back the doors.

The roar of angry voices quieted down when the police stepped into the library. A big fire burned in the man-high hearth and clusters of contestants sat in different areas of the immense room under the hunter trophies—lions' heads, a massive tusked elephant head and a rhino head. Long streamers of cobwebs clung to leather-bound books, sweeping up in tangles to a forged-iron chandelier.

"What now?" A frightened woman said. She was plain but pretty, and Bane knew from his research that her name was Margaret, from Nebraska. "More games?"

Some of the earlier panic had subsided. They still seemed jumpy, and the staccato blinking of their eyes was evidence they were still in "fight or flight" mode. Ahmed didn't stand up, but remained by the fire, legs crossed. Considering they had not had an outside visitor since the show began—other than the snakes, rats, and spiders—their reaction seemed artificial, as if they had expected Bane's visit.

A shrill voice yelled from across the room. "You people are perverts." A stunning black woman, dressed in a clinging terrycloth robe, marched forward and towered over Abbey Chase, nearly two inches taller than the producer. "You can't do these things. You just can't!"

Ms. Chase took a deep breath. "Mya, this contest has high stakes. You knew that. We're not even half way. There's worse to come, I assure you."

"Bitch," snapped Mya, and she strode across the room, elegant in spite of her fury.

Ms. Chase clapped her hands, silencing the contestants. "People, we have a problem." After snakes and rats and blood spouting out of showers, Bane was sure they felt that "a problem" worthy of the producer breaking her own rules must be truly terrible. "This is Detective Alban

Bane and Detective Justine Kipfer with the Vermont State Police."

Jay's heart throb Kenji said, "A fictional detective?" He gave them a perfect Hollywood smile. "This is not a convincing play, Ms. Chase."

"Sorry. You might find this hard to believe. But they *are* real."

Bane opened his badge as the guests crowded around.

Again, Kenji was their spokesperson. "Come now. That is a prop."

"Yeah, bought it for five dollars online," Bane said. "Look, people, this is going to be a long day. And you're all suspects." He ignored their protests, studying them one by one.

He tagged them with first impressions: Kelly, the busty babe; Junior, the gay poster boy; Margaret, the country girl; Josephine Po, the Miss Hong Kong; Ahmed Atwah, the strikingly handsome Muslim; Kenji, the Japanese movie star look-alike; Mya, the stunning, statuesque black woman; Ray, the grey-in-the-temples stock broker type; Carlo, the simmering Ricky Martin clone; Loretta, the California blond; Mario, the Italian stud wannabe; and Nelson, the young white dentist from Philadelphia. Abbey Chase had cast all the racial stereotypes.

"Who do you think you are?" Ray, the stock broker shouted.

"I think I'm the guy who decides if I fly you to Burlington. It's not as comfortable as all this." He waved his arm. "And, I think you'd lose your chance for a million greenbacks."

The contestants fell quiet, the crackle of the fire suddenly loud.

"Here's how it's going to work—"

Country girl Margaret interrupted him. "You're Bane!" She pointed at him. "You know, *Bane*! From the movie *Hayden*."

"No, dear," Chase said. "That was an actor. This is the real pain. I mean the real Bane."

"Then, something really has happened?" Kenji spoke perfect English, tinged with the very slightest of accents, more curious than surprised.

Junior stepped forward. "What happened?"

"There has been a homicide." Bane looked at each in turn, seeing their doubt, then fear, as they realized he might not be an actor. Mya and Carlo looked furious while Junior and Margaret looked terrified. Kenji and Ahmed revealed nothing in their faces while the rest seemed on edge, afraid and doubtful at the same time.

Bane cleared his throat, angry at his line of thought. "We'd like to interview each of you. We're here to help and to protect you. We have an entire troop division on site. This is one of my troopers, Trooper First Class Roth." Margaret's wide eyes fixed on Trooper Roth's holstered gun, and it seemed to calm her.

"Who was the victim?" Kenji cocked his head to one side. "None of us, it seems. We are all here. Is it one of the crew?"

Bane chewed his lip. Kenji was sharp. He zoomed right in on the one thing Bane needed, the missing element that could move the investigation forward—a victim identification. Bane still felt sure the victim was a farmer. But why kill a farmer? What could be his connection with contestants on a reality television show. Even if they could exit the house through the tunnels, how could they be suspects if the victim was from a distant farm? It made no sense. His only course was to eliminate each contestant from the suspect pool.

"We do not have an identification, Mr. Tenichi. But the crime scene is here. In the house."

A rumble of voices threaded through the group.

"How can there not be an identification?" Kenji stepped closer, his face a calm mask.

Bane stepped closer to Kenji, impressed and worried by his stature in the group. "Let's talk privately, Mr. Tenichi."

"So the show is on hold?" Kenji turned to Abbey Chase.

"Of course not. Our format doesn't allow for this contingency. We go on."

"We can't stay here!" Mya shouted.

"That is up to you." Ms. Chase's voice was as icy as her eyes. "But any who leave, go with nothing—not even your weekly stipend."

"Screw you!" Mya turned away.

"You are being a little unfair, in the circumstances," said a pale-faced Ray Polson, the stock broker contestant from New York.

"Unfair?" Abbey Chase smiled, but it was not a warm expression. "Perhaps. Those are the rules. Stay or leave, it's up to you."

Carlo, the Ricky Martin look-alike, put his arm around Kelly, who looked like she belonged on the set of *Baywatch*, and she slid against him, the sexual heat obvious. "You can't be serious—"

Abbey Chase's voice rose over his. "We're not going to talk about this. The show goes on, and whoever is left at the end gets the million. Any who leave lose their two-thousand-a-week allowance." The contestants fell silent. "Now, please cooperate with Detective Bane. He's here to help us all." Her blue-eyed glare in Bane's direction made a liar of her words.

"We're going to talk to each of you separately. Mr. Tenichi, would you come with me?" He nodded. "And Detective Kipfer will start with Ahmed."

"Cops are all bigots," Junior said, his mask of fear dropping.

Bane smiled at him. "And you're next."

"You can use the billiards room next door. And the games room." Ms. Chase led the way.

Kenji and Ahmed followed them. As they left the library, Bane looked back at the contestants and said loudly, "Trooper Roth will ensure your protection. I advise you not to discuss the crime until we talk to you in-dividually." The group dove into a huddle, whispering like conspirators.

Bane noticed Ahmed's dark, calm eyes appraising Kip as she led him into the game room. He felt sorry for Ahmed. Kip could be brutal in an interrogation, and she was merciless with alpha males.

Abbey Chase followed Kenji and Bane into the billiards room.

The detective turned to face her. "Alone, if you don't mind."

Her head jerked back. "Very well. I'll stay with the contestants. Calm them down."

"Tell them nothing."

"Of course. Really, Detective!"

Kenji picked up a billiards cue and broke a rack of balls on a full sized table. The table was antique, like everything else, finely carved, with old-style netted pockets and centered in the vaulted teak room under a wrought iron chandelier.

"You seem very calm, Mr. Tenichi," Bane said.

"Fear is an illusion." Kenji bent over the table and took his next shot.

Bane stepped closer, studying the man's statuesque facial features, visible between the long bangs. He couldn't quite figure out how Kenji could play through all that dangling hair, but the man made a perfect bank shot. He brushed back his hair, and Bane caught his first good look at the alert, unblinking eyes—brilliant, too-intense eyes that disturbed at some level.

"Why don't we sit down?" Bane gestured to the wingback leather chairs.

"I prefer to stand." He knocked balls around with his hands.

"May I ask, Mr. Tenichi, why you seem so unconcerned? After all, this could be someone you know."

He began racking the balls. "It is not a matter of lack of concern. I accept what has happened. Regret will not help, will it? May I ask, Detective, why you chose to interview me first?"

Bane took a deep breath. A perceptive, cool young man. "Just random, I suppose."

"I doubt that very much."

"Maybe I'm a racist, like your friend says."

He contemplated Bane for a moment through the sheepdog bangs, then smiled, flashing white teeth. "I doubt that, too." He put down the cue and they sat in two chairs by the embers of a dying fire in a soaring marble hearth. "I will cooperate of course, Detective Bane."

"Of course." Bane slid to the edge of his seat, close to this too-cool suspect. "Now tell me, first, how did you end up on this show?"

He spread his hands in an expansive gesture. "I am the token Asian. Junior is the token gay. Ahmed is the Muslim, Carlo the Puerto Rican jock, Mya our sexy black person." He laughed, a rich rumble that poured from his throat like the purr of a jungle cat. "This is politically correct Hollywood. It is a long story."

"But why did you audition?"

"A diversion, I suppose."

Bane sighed. Not the answer he was looking for. "Before *Haunted Survivor*, Mr. Tenichi, what did you do?"

His voice remained flat. "I have tried virtually every profession."

Bane frowned at Kenji's evasiveness. "Actually, Mr. Tenichi, I ran background checks on everyone here. Crew and guests. I find it most peculiar that you have no background. No history at all."

He watched for the slightest suggestion of nervousness. Kenji's eyes, barely visible as glittering black highlights under the bangs, did not blink, his lips remained in a steady line, his hands were rock-solid calm. "Does that make me a suspect?"

Bane nodded. "Everyone is a suspect. Your lack of background moves you to my A list."

"That is very forthright of you, Detective." He smiled again.

"Even the National Police Agency of Japan—you are from Japan, originally, correct?" Kenji nodded. "No record. No birth record. Not even so much as a speeding ticket."

Normally, when Bane was in confrontational mode, his suspects would lean away, become agitated. Kenji Tenichi actually slid forward, perching on the end of the chair until their knees almost touched, his face closer. "I value my privacy. I was born in a small fishing village." His voice was low and husky, so much so that Bane could barely hear him.

Bane smelled Kenji's breath, fresh like a sea breeze. "There would be birth records. Look, Mr. Tenichi. I don't buy your stereotyped Buddhist Monk routine. It's pissing me off."

Kenji tossed his hair. "I am who I am. I do not ask you to buy anything. I grew up northeast of Kyoto on the island of Honshu not so far from the city of Fukui. I am a follower of Soto Zen Buddhism, founded by Baneen. How much of my biography do you wish me to reveal on national television?" He nodded at the gilt antique mirror, where Bane knew there was a camera hidden.

"Ms. Chase assured me that this will not air."

This time Kenji's laugh was soft. "Do you believe her?"

"You do not?"

Again, the easy shrug. "This is television. Do not be naïve, Detective."

"Naïve isn't one of my weaknesses."

"No. But rudeness is."

"Way to make friends, Kenji." Bane smiled. "I need enough background to check you out. Your biography with Real TV indicated you lived at a temple at Ehi-ji. They have no record of a Kenji Tenichi."

"Eiheiji," Kenji corrected. "My uncle is a teacher-monk there. And my temple name was Miyazawa, after a famous poet of my country. A well-known evangelist. We did not use our birth names."

Bane wrote the name on his flip pad. "You understand I will check this name."

"Of course."

"I noticed something in tonight's pandemonium."

"Snakes?"

"Besides snakes—and how calm you seemed to be."

Kenji shrugged. "Snakes, spiders, rats are all very common things for me, Detective. In my village they are everywhere. What did you notice?"

Instinctively, Bane scratched at the knife scar on his abdomen. "Scars. Many scars on your body. Knife or sword. Blades, certainly."

Kenji smiled perhaps a little too quickly, the first sign of nervousness. "Martial arts."

Bane's pencil tapped the pad in a short rhythm. "With real blades?"

"In the temple we use kendo only in early training. Later, we use real swords."

Bane tried to stare him down, letting his silence, exaggerated scowl and unblinking eyes offer intimidation. But Kenji's smile never faded. "I'm not sure I believe that."

"I do not lie."

Bane was getting tired of this monk persona. "Lies make us human."

Kenji tossed his bangs back. "What made you so cynical?"

"This and that. Spare me the Kwai Chang Caine Kung Fuey crap."

"I guess I am not human. I do not lie."

"Right. So, Kenji, are you aware of the old tunnels and passages in this house?"

"Certainly. I found those weeks ago." Kenji stood up, gliding out of his chair with a grace that seemed surreal and moved to a panel beside the fireplace. He pressed an oak cornice, and a narrow door slid open. Bane would not have found the panel himself, and an entire troop of officers had not been able to find the entrances. "You must understand, Detective, we have been here for many weeks. Exploring and talking are the two diversions we have. We do not even have television, although they gave us this games room and a library of old books."

Bane examined the entrance to the hidden passage. Perfectly crafted to fit the wood paneling, the door would be invisible to the eye, and rapping on the panel would be useless. The designer had engineered the door to sit perfectly in the molded surround.

Bane peered into the dark, narrow corridor. "Where do these go?"

"Everywhere. From attic to sub-basement. Perhaps even further. I found bat guano which suggests connected caves. I did not explore that far since my. . ."

"Yes?"

"My activities are monitored. I am not supposed to leave the wing."

"See, now that's where I stop believing you."

Bane stepped past Kenji into the passage trying not to let his latent claustrophobia crowd his curiosity aside. The door was barely wide enough for him. Inside, the corridor was unlit and hardly wide enough for a grown person to walk without moving sideways and bending his head. Bane's hair brushed something, and he instinctively ducked then looked up. A camera sat on a clamped arm, pointing out through the inside of the looking glass. Bane looked back into the room through the one-way glass. Abbey Chase had set up her cameras throughout these tunnels. Again, she had lied.

Bane glanced to his right, down the dark tunnel, fishing in his bag for a flashlight. The pencil beam pierced the dark, low corridor, which narrowed and sloped, bending around and disappearing. It was smaller, narrower, and lower than the sub-basement corridors, and Bane knew he could never go in there. Just thinking about it made him queasy.

"Excuse me, Detective Bane?"

Bane stepped back into the Billiards Room. "Yes?"

"I believe your partner requires you," Kenji said.

Bane walked around the billiards table. Kip stood at the door with that *I-have-to-tell-you-something* look on her face. She gestured for him to follow her and stepped out into the dimly lit hall. "What's up, Kipper?"

"There's been another homicide."

Chapter 11

....

January 18, 8:11 pm

Beacon Hill, Boston

Hugh King, of *The Crime Times*, shivered, the sweat of his earlier sprint chilling him.

He paused, listening, but heard only the splash of distant cars in salt slush, and the screech of two fighting alley cats, out of place in upscale Beacon Hill.

No more footsteps. Just the thud of his own heart, loud in his inner ear. The visceral rush gave him adrenal energy.

He straightened his rumpled sheepskin and walked on, striding towards the honking horns of distant Grove Street.

He was half way through the alley when he heard the boots again, clattering on the cobblestones, a distinct, fast-paced *clop-tap, clop-tap*.

For a moment, panic immobilized him. He squinted into the dark ahead. Grove Street was too far, nearly a mile. Overhead he saw lights, and heard televisions, a woman shouting, laughter. But the fire escape ladders were pulled up. Hugh was in the world of the homeless and the drug dealers, a shadowy night world that coexisted uneasily between the upscale brownstones, like a dark dimension in an old episode of *The Twilight Zone*.

The big man with the cowboy hat and worn old boots had followed him all day, and though Hugh had covered crime all his life—including dangerous run-ins with some of the worst serial killers and sadists imaginable—this silent man with the lifeless eyes, made Hugh wish he carried a gun. The cowboy never ran, never seemed to hurry, yet he was always there, no matter how many cabs Hugh took to try to shake him and regardless of how fast he ran. Always there. *Clop-tap. Clop-tap.* The black shadow was relentless.

"I see you," the cowboy said, his voice flat, gravelly, unhurried.

The words echoed back from the alley's cobblestones and the backs of high brick north-end Boston row houses.

Again, Hugh ran, his breath coming in ragged gasps, his polyester shirt stuck to the long hairs of his chest.

The tall man in black followed, visible in the gloom only because of his white smile.

Hugh regretted leaving the Common. His attempt to lose the man had only made things worse. He had left Arlington, certain he had finally thrown the man. Now he was alone in the dark, except for the cats who stalked rats and the giant who stalked him.

He forgot the earlier thrill of discovery.

The pressure in Hugh's chest intensified, and his breath came in heaves as his lungs burned. He glanced behind him, his eyes adjusted to the gloom. When he was sure the man was not in sight, he slipped behind a garbage dumpster and thought about jumping inside, amongst the leftovers of the affluent. The stench stopped him.

He crouched in the shadows, listening, waiting for the dark man to pass. A cat hissed at him. He covered his mouth with a gloved hand to mask the white jets of breath, visible in the reflected light of the second-floor windows.

His hand slipped to the precious envelope in his zipped pocket.

A plump rat squeaked at him, inches from his foot, glittering eyes glaring, yet more friendly than those of his dark stalker.

Hugh King took deep breaths, calming himself.

He hadn't slept much since Hayden's execution. He felt it now. The crash off the adrenal highs. He hadn't dreamed that Hayden's execution would yield anything but a great front-page story.

He had seen that big FBI agent whispering to Bane, growing agitated as Hayden died on the gurney. King had studied Hayden's relaxed face and his moving lips. Reading lips was one of King's more useful skills as a journalist.

Friend Bane, I know who killed your wife. I take the secret to hell.

And King made the obvious leap of logic: if Hayden knew about Bane's wife, perhaps was even responsible for it—revenge?—then he must have had an accomplice. A person who cared enough to kill for him. Maybe a lover or family. Someone close, someone who cared.

Now with bribe money and a flash of insight, he had taken the first steps to proving it. And with the knowledge might come destruction. The shadow in the alley.

Who was this guy? Rival reporter? Cop? FBI? No, none of these. The eyes told Hugh all he needed to know.

A killer.

Please, God. Just let this pass. Let me write this one story.

He clenched his keys, one thrust between each knuckle, his only weapon. He knew they'd be little use against the towering cowboy with the dead eyes.

He listened. Nothing. Was the shadow man gone? King waited, his own breathing too loud. Ten minutes passed: still nothing.

Far off, he saw a Jeep Cherokee pass the alley exit and he ran, more carefully this time, conscious of the icy film on the cobblestones and his buttocks, sore from his earlier fall. He ran fast, bent in a painful stoop, hands chugging alongside his chunky frame like pistons.

He heard the booted feet on the stones and a shout, "I see you!"

Too soon! He had left his hiding place too soon.

His left hand fumbled for his cell phone, flipping open the tiny Motorola and punching nine-one-one as he jogged, his breath wheezing.

King's foot caught a lifted brick, and as he lurched forward, the phone clattered from his hand and spun across the alley to land at the bottom of a fire escape.

A face emerged from the shadow, where his phone had landed. Hugh King screamed, tumbling to his knees.

The face shouted back at him. "Whatchya want? Whatchya want?" Spittle flew from the mouth, and dried vomit clung to the chin. A homeless man.

Hugh scrambled to his feet, looked around wildly for his phone, then over his shoulder. He saw the shadow, striding with dark purpose, its face invisible in the gloom.

Hugh ran on, leaving his cell phone to the homeless man.

He heard the booted footsteps behind him, closer now.

Tears ran down his cheek. *Not now*, he thought. *The damn story of the decade, and I'm going to die.*

Anger drove him on. And shame. This was no ordinary mugger. King had stumbled on a conspiracy, always the journalist's dream, but like a greedy fool he had told no one of his suspicions. No one knew he was in Boston. Not even his editor.

A goddam conspiracy! Why didn't I tell anyone where I was going?

He had the first traces of evidence, including the photocopied records of Hayden's visitors, smuggled to him by an over-priced San Quentin guard. The list had driven King to Boston, to the Hall of Records, to the discovery that might some day earn him a Pulitzer.

Even King was shocked by the network of Hayden accomplices, with connections right to the Senate. Not even Bane could know that. He would have breaking news. And material for his next book.

If he survived.

His breath came in wrenching gasps.

Who is it? he thought wildly. Who was this tireless cowboy? As King had left the gold-domed state house, with his photocopied treasure from the Hall of Records, he had seen the man's face for the first time.

The cowboy had not even bothered to look away, staring at Hugh with the cold assassin's eyes.

The road was closer now, enticingly close, occasional cars splashing by. King knew he should not look back, not when he was so close. But he couldn't resist—just as when he was twelve years old, throwing stones at yellow-jacket nests to see what would happen, then running as fast as he could for the safety of the screened porch, looking over his shoulder as the angry swarm came closer and closer. . .

He looked.

The man was almost close enough to touch King's shoulder with his long fingers. With a sharp cry, the shout of the twelve-year-old chased by wasps, King ducked and ran, sliding on the stones, running not to make a deadline, but for his life.

Chapter 12

Bane and Kip followed an agitated trooper Peterson, the same man who had discovered the first body. Chilled by the biting wind, they walked a straight path to a dilapidated barn that leaned into rotting posts. Bane wore only his butt-freezer bomber jacket and Sox cap.

"You didn't think to grab a parka?" Kip asked.

"With any luck I catch a cold and get to call in sick. Get some time at home."

Kip laughed.

"You discovered the body, son?" Bane asked Peterson.

"Yes sir. My third go-through on this search grid, sir!"

"Relax, Peterson. I'm not going to fire you—yet."

The trooper's dancing black eyes indicated he wasn't about to relax. "I didn't enter the scene, sir. I saw the body, and stayed—I stayed out, sir! And I controlled the scene."

Bane nodded. "Keep it up, you'll get brownie points."

Kip leaned close to Bane and whispered, "I think he's grateful you didn't give him a formal. They're all scared of you, you know."

"Yeah, you told me no one likes me. I remember." Bane halted a few paces from the barn, close enough to see through the open doors. Mounds of green plastic garbage bags filled the barn.

"That's close enough. We wait for Crime Scene Services."

Cross and his forensics team arrived by chopper forty-five minutes later. By then, the journalists, shivering in their vans outside the gates, had spotted all the activity, and as Cross's helicopter landed they swarmed the guards, trying to break the perimeter. Camera teams perched on stone gateposts shot with zoom lenses over the heads of the state troopers. Soon the news crew helicopters would hover overhead, circling like turkey vultures.

A trooper at the gate knocked one cameraman from a gatepost. The journalist stood up, waved his arms around and shouted.

Henry Cross waved Bane and Kip closer. Bane and Kip followed the trail of the forensic team to avoid contamination. As he came closer, Bane said, "Not a Hayden copycat this time, right?"

Henry Cross nodded. "No. And blood splatter indicates this *is* the scene of the crime."

Bane and Kip remained outside the inner perimeter to ensure they didn't corrupt the exemplars. Bane chewed his lip, impatient to enter the inner crime scene. "I wonder if this is our missing Mr. Reid?"

"What makes you think so?" Kip shielded her eyes from the spotlights and studied what was left of the victim.

Bane didn't answer. Short of birthmarks and scars, there was nothing much to identify here, except the victim seemed lean, hard, well-muscled, his skin dark, almost olive.

"Jackson Reid was Mediterranean demographic."

"With a name like that?"

"Pseudonym." Bane remembered the man's picture in the Real TV file—the image of a stern, hard-bodied, sun-kissed Mediterranean type. Short, muscled, with the hard look of a handsome Sicilian. It had occurred to Bane that Reid was a real tough guy.

Bane had no evidence that this might be Reid beyond physical characteristics, but he felt intuitively that this lump was the missing stunt coordinator.

"Could be Italian, perhaps Spanish," Cross said.

"Birth marks or scars? Unique features?"

"Moon-shaped birthmark on his buttock."

"Sure it's not an ass hickey?"

"Funny, Bane. It's a birthmark."

Bane gestured at trooper Peterson. "See if anyone else from the crew is missing." Peterson glanced at the crime scene, his face pale, then turned and dashed back towards the house on Bane's mission.

Kip watched the trooper run. "You didn't tell him this might be the man he let out of custody."

"What's the point?"

Kip smiled. "See, you have your soft side."

"Don't tell anyone. Could ruin my rep." He cleared his throat. "I want to send the K-9s out into the woods."

Kip's eyes focused on something as she glanced out the barn window. "Damn them!" She ran outside and swung down the path to the parking lot a hundred feet away, outside the wider ring of crime scene tape. She had sharp eyes and fast feet, but the Real TV cameraman disappeared into the house long before she caught up to him. Bane doubted he got much, even with a zoom lens, other than the crime scene activity. He probably hadn't been able to focus on the victim from that distance.

Kip returned, grim and furious, but breathing evenly. "He got away, damn him. Don't know what he taped."

Bane shook his head. "I guess we'll see it on the news."

Cross approached them, holding out two crime scene orange poly suits. Bane slipped into his sterile jumper easily but Kip struggled to pull it over her bulky parka.

"You look like a big orange marshmallow," Bane said as he pulled on the disposable boots.

"Okay, you can go in." Cross said.

Bane nodded. "You've shot all this?"

"Yeah, you're clear."

"Printed footprints?"

Cross gave a thumbs up. "That was easy in the freeze. I also dusted for fingerprints."

Bane stepped closer to the body.

He pointed. "Kip, see this?"

"Uh-huh. Wedding finger again cut at the third joint."

"Were any of the crew missing after the first homicide married?"

Kip held up three fingers.

Bane bent low to the ground, careful not to disturb the victim. Cross swung the crime scene spot to light the area. "Cross, any idea on time of death?"

"Body temperature roughly indicates time of death within the last six hours or so—and yes, I'm taking into account this cold."

"Trooper Gabaldon?" Bane shouted out to a trooper second class who manned the perimeter. "You and your team search every one of these garbage bags." He motioned to the mountain of green plastic to the rear of the barn.

"Sir, that will take days."

"At least."

"Isn't that a job for Crime Scene Services?"

"Nice try. Get started, or get job-hunting, son."

Kip laughed. "And you wonder why no one likes you."

Like the first victim, the body was naked. Bane pulled out his six-inch Leitz magnifying glass and spot flashlight, and examined the bluish feet. "Bring a camera with macro."

Cross waved at a crime scene cameraman. "What do you see, Bane?"

Bane leaned even closer. "Looks like—not sure until we get it out of there. Something clinging to the ankle hairs here. Shoot it first."

After the camera man was finished, Bane leaned close, tweezers in his gloved hand. Gently, he pulled out the sliver and studied it under his glass. "It's a flake of paint, I think, white or light color." Bane glanced around the barn after he bagged the sliver. "This barn's unpainted."

Kip leaned close, peering at the sample, holding her breath to prevent the vapor from frosting the bag. "What are you thinking?"

"He was killed here. The blood splatter makes that clear. But maybe he was *held* somewhere else?"

"A prisoner?"

"I don't know. Reid's been missing for days. So, how did the perpetrator get the victim here, to the garbage barn?" Bane glanced at a small rolling bin with handles. "They bring in the garbage in these bins. Gabaldon! Search all these bins, and dust even the inside for fingerprints. Luminol for blood splatter." He ignored the Trooper's exaggerated salute. "Cross, I want exemplars of all the paints used in the house."

Cross nodded. "Shouldn't be hard to match. The lab can even age the paint."

Bane checked the inside elbows. No needle tracks this time.

He followed his own trail back to the perimeter to minimize displacement of forensic evidence. "So, tell you what. I'm done here. See what else you can find, Cross."

Bane moved closer to Kip. "We could use more detectives up here. We need to find those tunnels, starting with the one Mr. Tenichi showed me. He can show you some of them, I'm sure."

She tried to smile. "More detectives? In your dreams." She wiped the mentholatum off her upper lip. Vermont didn't have many detectives in the Bureau of Criminal Investigation, and many of them were attached to the Drug Task Force. "I could assemble some troopers."

"No troopers. Tell you what. I like Peterson. Let's make him a detective."

Kip said nothing. She knew he was kidding.

"Deputize the kid. He'll worship you."

"It's you he follows around like a puppy."

"I need detectives, not pups. But we do need doggies. Try to get another K-9 team. The dogs should be able to sniff out the passage entrances. We can sledgehammer them if need be."

They entered the house and Kip stripped off her parka. Bane enjoyed the sudden warmth. As they walked the long employee hall, Bane scanned the corkboard again. Unlike the last ones he'd read, these messages were darker in tone: *"Quitting this hell hole and need ride to LA"*; *"Meeting of union to organize safety committee to monitor police activities"*; *"Vermont is for Vermonters meeting moved to Friday"*; and numerous creepy messages like *"Get out while you can"* and *"We're all going to die."*

"Cheerful bunch," Kip said, as they passed through the door into the west wing, where the executives and crew lodged.

Bane asked, "Did you ask Ms. Chase about a cot in the crew's bunk room? For later."

"You really want to sleep here? Our pilot's willing to fly us back to Burlington."

"I don't believe in ghosts," Bane said.

"What about your daughters?"

Bane sighed. He wanted to go home. More than anything. "The perp's escalating. Besides, the commute's a killer."

Kip shook her head. "Well, Ms. Chase did us one better. Bunks for any troopers who need them. And she gave us rooms. On the inner courtyard."

"Wow. Isn't she sweet?"

They passed through the Real TV security post, a metal detector with a solitary guard. Bane waved. "Hey, Ira."

Ira stiffened, his lined face calm but his eyes darting with a nervous energy Bane hadn't seen at their first meeting. "Sir." He nodded at Kip. "Ma'am."

Bane pointed at the holstered gun, a big Colt. "That's new. You have a permit for that?"

He nodded. "Lord liftin', we all do. Boss's orders. She wants us armed, don't you know?"

"How does someone get past this post, Ira?"

"What do you mean, sir?"

Bane lowered his voice. "Fairly simple question, Ira."

Ira scowled. "Lots of ways, I suppose, sir. The east wing, where the guests are, that's locked down tight, as secure as Rikers. But, the west wing, we're just here for basic security." His voice dropped. "Some of the crew actually smuggle out tapes. You know? They're worth a lot on the black market. Especially them bedroom scenes with Carlo and Kelly."

Bane nodded. "We're talking bodies, Ira." Bane had done a complete background check on him. Ira had twenty-six years with the security company after an injury took him off the Burlington PD force. He had been a beat cop with an ordinary record, then had wrecked his personal car, off-duty on New Year's Eve, and killed his wife. His own injury had been minor, resulting in a permanent limp, but he was discharged from the force. His buds on the force had not charged Ira, even though Bane saw a notation in the file that he had been drinking before the accident and blew point eight.

Ira's face was unearthly serene again, and his voice emotionless. "Well, three ways I can think. I mean, they have them garbage bins on wheels that they roll up from the kitchens. Lots of garbage comes up, and we only spot check that. Really stinks, some of it." He frowned, quickly. "Of course, from now on, I'm openin' every bag."

"Stop worrying about your own ass, Ira. How else?"

"Them secret passages we talked about. But I showed your men all them passages—alls I knows about, anyhow. And there's the windows, 'course."

"Were you on duty last night?"

"All night, sir. Since eleven."

Bane leaned closer. "Tell me, is Ms. Chase worried?"

"You could say that, sir. She ordered up eight more guards, and these 'uns are *flatlanders*." He emphasized the word with sizzling energy. *Flatlanders*. Non-Vermonters. People from outside the Green Mountain State. "Them flatlanders'll be here tomorrow." He sighed. "I don't know where we'll put 'em."

"I'll need the security tapes, Ira."

"Your man picked them up."

Bane nodded at him. Kip and Bane made their way up the hall into the west wing.

She put her hand on his arm. "He bothers me, Bane."

Bane paused, glancing back at the security post. Ira had his back to them, his hand on his gun. "Ira's just an old Vermonter."

"Racist."

"Separatist groups often are."

"When we first met he said, 'What're you, some kinda injun?' I mean who says injun? And he seemed so cold."

Bane studied Ira's hunched back. The guard turned and glanced at Bane and Kip, as they whispered, and Bane gave him a wave and a smile. The guard frowned and turned away. "Yeah. Well, he's not smart enough to be an organized felon. And one thing I'm sure of—this crime is highly organized."

"He's plenty smart," Kip said. "He pretends to be stupid. You saw the green ribbon?"

Bane nodded. "Independence movement." The green ribbon was worn in solidarity with the Green Mountain Republic of Vermont movement, the more radical of the separatists. The more conservative groups wore a gray ribbon.

"I don't like *those* people. Nearly all of the security guards wear those damn things."

"Now who's prejudiced?" Bane frowned.

"Ever been to their website? They have links to all kinds of splinter movements. Armed militias, everything. They support the Green Mountain Freedom Party, but they're more radical."

"Thought you didn't trust the internet." Bane pressed his lips together. "I like some of what they have to say. We're becoming a state of Walmarts and paved highways." But would the Green Mountain Freedom fighters kill to send a message to flatlanders? Maybe not, but a madman in their midst might.

"Kip, I think I'm going to join the Green Mountain movement."

Chapter 13

....

January 21, 3:49 pm

The Red Room, Mason Place

Doctor Jonathon Wingate's too-kind eyes—warm brown marbles that spoke lies—locked on Bane and the detective saw a momentary flicker of recognition. Of course, Bane remembered Wingate.

The psychiatrist smiled and rounded his plain but massive mahogany desk. He crossed the room on long shanks and extended his hand. Feathery, elegant fingers wrapped around Bane's hand in a quick pump. His tailored suit, worth a month of Bane's salary, hung tightly on a lean and muscular frame.

"Good afternoon, Inspector," he said, his words polished with a rich British accent. "You have been busy."

"It's just lowly Detective." He swept his Sox cap off his head.

"Ah, you Americans and your obsession with baseball." He smiled. "But you're Scots originally, aren't you?"

"I'm American," Bane said, feeling his own heat. For some reason, though proud of his heritage, he felt fiercely 'American' in the presence of this well-heeled Brit.

Wingate carried himself rigidly, a crisply athletic and imposing man with big shining eyes that seemed interested in everything. "Please sit."

"Not a social call, Doctor." Bane remained standing as the doctor swiveled his tall-backed chair. "I've read some of your books."

"Oh, which ones?" He turned, silhouetted slightly by the stark cloudless sky of the floor-to-ceiling bow window behind him. His polished shoe tapped.

"*Profiling Group Psychosis*. Pretty boring stuff." In truth, Bane had memorized every line of Behavioral's standard text, but it was important to annoy Wingate. Bane's interview style relied on emotional friction.

But Wingate's expression didn't change. "Yes, well, that was years ago, Inspector."

"Learned a few things since then?"

"I am on to you, Inspector." Wingate winked. "I use much the same technique in my sessions. Sadly, it will not work with me."

Bane hardened his voice. "Why were you at Hayden's execution?"

The only sign of surprise was a single lifted eyebrow. "Really, Detective. He is—rather, he was—a patient."

"I got that. I just don't get why."

"Why are you surprised? I am, after all, the recognized expert in fear-induced psychosis and sociopathology. High-profile case, you understand?"

Bane took a deep, calming breath. As Hayden's psychiatrist, Wingate might know his secrets.

Friend Bane, I know who killed your wife. I take the secret to hell.

Did he know? "You were using him, he was using you?"

Wingate spread his hands in a dramatic flourish. "Something like that, Inspector." He leaned forward across his desk. "I saw you there at San Quentin. Gloomy place. If not for the timing and those reporters, I would have had a talk with you." He clasped his elongated fingers into a tent on his desk. "As a psychiatrist I find it queer that you would attend. Contrary to what those poor parents believed, revenge is not a form of healing, hmmm? They call it closure. Falderal, I say."

"Falderal?"

"I can be sesquipedalian at times. There I go again. I have a love of long words, you see?" He leaned back in his chair. "My patient, Mr. Hayden, went to great lengths to impeach you with his last words." A frown played across his tall, angular face. "Blamed you in front of all the victims' families. Totally uncalled for."

"I'd have done the same."

"That's quite the admission."

"Ach, not the family torture thing. The blaming."

Wingate shifted in his chair, the leather creaking under his weight. "I do not believe I could ever do that again. See a man die like that." He shook his head. "I think I shall never forget."

"I rather enjoyed it." How did Bane really feel about it? He thought of Hayden, smiling as he died, his life draining away as his lips moved, repeating the horrendous confession over and over. Bane should have felt some satisfaction at his death, but it was harder to watch than he had imagined. The terrible revelation that Hayden might have known something of Susan Bane's murder had hijacked Bane's emotions, transferring hate and revenge-lust to horror and helpless anger.

"Do you always say the opposite of what you mean?"

"Nearly always."

Wingate sighed. "Tyler Hayden was my patient. I tried to give him some comfort in his last moments. At his request I attended. You should understand, fourteen years on death row, as appeal after appeal goes by without success." His lip twitched.

"I'm all teared up."

"Yes, I can see you are."

"You being Tyler Hayden's psychiatrist is a bit like asking Einstein to make a paper airplane."

"Why, thank you, I think. Oh, I see. You question my motives. You, of all people, should recall that Hayden was high-profile." He leaned closer. "An admission, Inspector?"

"Yes?"

"I volunteered. You see, I felt Hayden could be material for my next book."

"That's rather cold of you, Doctor. Is that what motivates you here? Helping build psychosis-inducing booby traps for Ms. Chase?"

"Perhaps. She would do this with or without me. I like to think I am mitigating the damage."

"How altruistic of you."

"My work here can, potentially, help many."

"That sounds vaguely sociopathic."

Wingate leaned back in his chair. "Well, that is quite the assertion. How do you come to such a radical conclusion?"

"Sociopaths believe their work is justified. They feel no social attachment to the people around them. They rationalize their behavior."

"So, by that definition, you are a sociopath."

"Aye. Except for one thing."

"Please educate me, Inspector."

"I don't pretend some higher cause. There's nothing noble in what I do."

"It is just a paycheck?"

"No, not much of a paycheck. I feel good about what I do. But I don't care if anyone else knows."

Wingate took a long breath. "You are quite a lot more interesting than I assumed. Inspector, what I am doing here is not so different from what you are doing right this minute. Provoking to study reaction."

"I see you're on to me. But there's a difference in scale, eh Doctor?"

"Somewhat." His smile was warmer this time. "I shall, of course, help you in any way I can. Without divulging patient confidences, of course."

Bane had used Doctor Wingate's theories, books and observations throughout his career, and in some ways Wingate was a silent mentor. It disappointed Bane that a man like Wingate, a man he respected, could be involved with Hayden and Chase. "Doctor, with Hayden dead, he's no longer protected by privilege."

Wingate placed his hands on his lap. "Well, yes, I believe that is so. But what could he possibly have to do with our current situation?"

Bane stared out at the frozen lake, snow glittering as the afternoon sun broke through the clouds. How did he ask this question without sounding self-serving? "In your sessions, did he ever mention my wife?"

Wingate blinked, his tall forehead furrowing. "Well, no. That is a tad out of left field—is that the American saying? What does your wife have to do with Hayden?"

Bane looked down at his hands, embarrassed at veering into personal territory. "You're telling the truth?"

"The truth is rather subjective, is it not?"

"No."

"Well, then, yes, I am telling the truth. Why would I lie?"

"Everyone lies, Doctor. We lie to make ourselves feel better. We lie to ourselves because of conceit. We lie to others to prove our superiority. We lie to change outcomes."

Wingate chuckled, dry and short. "Ah. Nearly verbatim from *The Truth About Truth*. I'm flattered. So, what is this about your wife?"

"My wife was murdered."

"Oh. I *am* so sorry, Inspector." He rolled his chair closer, leaning over his desk, big panda-bear eyes pulling Bane in with apparent warmth.

"It was twelve years ago."

"After Hayden's incarceration? Then I do not see how Hayden could have known anything about your wife."

"I don't, either."

Wingate shook his head. "A terrible thing, Detective. It seems to me, without consulting further, that you have not let your wife go." His voice was warm, the professional confidant. "If you ever want to talk about it—even just as a friendly associate—feel free to drop by. During this interminable twenty-six week show, I am a virtual prisoner here."

Emotion cascaded through Bane: gratitude, anger, confusion, and a melancholy that overcame his earlier sense of disappointment. Bane had been so sure Wingate would know something.

"Did Hayden have visitors? Friends or family? Accomplices you know of?"

Wingate snapped out of his chair and walked to a nearby bookcase. He pulled out a book, crossed a plush gold and scarlet Chinese dragon rug and handed it to Bane. "All I know of Hayden, that I feel comfortable disclosing in any case, is here."

Bane glanced at the title. Hayden's Hollywood star face smiled back at him from the cover, a strange contrast to the book designer's blood red background. A single drop of blood rolled off the title—*Madness Unveiled: Studying the Mind of the Vampire Killer*. In elegant type on the bottom, by Jonathon Wingate, Ph.D, M.D. "Yes, I've read it."

Wingate sat on the edge of his desk, his hand pressed over the book cover. "Is that so? Then you know he had no relatives, and Hayden claimed to have no friends. Indeed, his lack of social interaction certainly contributed to his particular form of sociopathy."

"Yes." Bane's eyes fixed on the cover of the book. One of Hayden's blue eyes stared at him from between Wingate's splayed fingers.

"You seem obsessed, Inspector." Wingate leaned forward and laid a hand on Bane's shoulder, startling him. "Ah, you are very tense."

Bane stiffened. Wingate had hijacked his interrogation. Talk of Hayden, and his wife, had accelerated his heart, raised a bead of sweat under his collar and churned Eddie King's lunchtime noodles into a gaseous nausea. "Let's talk about the contestants and crew. Do you have any particular concerns?"

"Certainly you know that patient-doctor privilege prevents—"

"They're *all* your patients?"

"Do not sound so incredulous. Of course they are. Every one of them. It is part of my contract here." He smoothed a wrinkle in his suit jacket. "You know, everyone is so frightened. I am here as a consultant on the show, but it has become nearly a fulltime job, just to prevent the crew from quitting en masse. Both crew and contestants."

"I can imagine. How do you avert it?"

He spread his arms in a big shrug. "I am not entirely successful. Three of the crew quit just today."

Bane allowed his voice to lift in volume. "And you, Doctor? You seem rather fearless."

"Really, Inspector. We are both professionals. I deal with fear every day—professionally, of course. And you? It must be your daily fare, what?" He slid off the desk. "Is that all?"

"No. Let's talk about Chase and Lorentz."

"I have no intention of talking about my employers."

"Well, that's a shame, because I intend to stay here, right in this very spot, until you do."

Wingate sighed. "You think it is professional for me to discuss them?"

"Do you think I care about professionalism? I only care about finding the sick son of a bitch who slaughtered our John Does."

"You are an interesting man, Inspector. Very interesting, indeed. But, I do require my office. I have a session in five minutes."

"That gives you five minutes to spill."

"Spill? How colorful, Inspector. How can I be rid of you, then?"

"You could try to physically lift me and carry me out of your office. Or, you could tell me something helpful."

"I will try. But I won't compromise patient confidentiality."

"So, did you tell either of them how dangerous this reality television concept would be? How it could trigger fear-induced psychosis."

He snorted. "That is overly simplistic. But of course I gave realistic projections. I believe Abbey's exact words were 'I'd screw with the Virgin Mary's head if it would get better ratings.' Colin was less crude, but he made it clear that the contestants' mental health was not a concern. The show's stars signed releases and so forth."

Bane stared into Wingate's eyes, putting on his fiercest interrogator's glare to hide his disgust. "So, you're saying they hired you as a consultant and then didn't listen."

"You have spoken to Abbey Chase."

"But you, Doctor Wingate, are sufficiently godlike in stature to carry some weight. With your mythical persona, and Chase's awe of the rich and powerful, I doubt they would proceed without your endorsement."

"Should I be flattered or enraged, Inspector?"

"Either. Both. I don't care. But don't sit there and lie to me."

"My, you are quite something, Inspector."

"You didn't actually advise them to tone down their show, did you Doctor Wingate?"

"Shamefully, I admit my guilt. Am I a suspect?"

"Everyone is a suspect. Just as everyone is your patient."

"Ah. Touché, Detective." He turned and smiled. "However, you might remember, I was in San Quentin—with you."

"I had not forgotten that convenience, Doctor. It continues to disturb me greatly."

"Inspector, you are a difficult man to please."

"So I'm told." He tapped his watch. "I am not leaving your office, Doctor, until I get something useful."

Wingate laughed. "Fine. Inspector, there are two contestants who are not my patients. Or, rather, they have not come to me."

Bane waited, pretending to admire the view. He saw a deer, hovering at the edge of the pine forest, scenting the mountain wind.

"Kenji seeks his own counsel. And Ahmed has not responded to the mandatory assessment ordered by Ms. Chase."

Bane wasn't surprised. "Can you at least tell me if *you* consider any of the contestants dangerous?"

Wingate folded his arms. "I would not be able to tell you," he said. But then he nodded, once, ever so slightly.

"Off the record, yes."

Chapter 14

....

January 21, 9:45 pm

Hell's Pit, Vermont

Colin woke to the sound of water. Drip, splash, drip.

He tried to open his eyes, but they felt glued shut.

Must have fallen asleep, he thought. A gentle rocking motion lulled him back to sleep, back to nightmares. He fought to stay conscious.

Hung over. Must be hung over.

He shivered, cold. His arms wouldn't move, then his legs seized with cramps.

The pulsing pain and paralysis warned him something terrible had happened. His mind worked, piercing the achy fog, trying to remember. He remembered only drinking cognac, warm cognac, golden cognac, by a warm fire, with his friend. . . .

Open your damn eyes.

His stomach churned, queasy but empty. Needles of pain focused his efforts. Why couldn't he move?

A twinge shot through his thigh, he felt light-headed.

For a dizzy moment, he saw only a smudge of muted color, intensifying his urge to heave, and then his eyes focused on a bucket. A bucket? The room seemed to spin, revolving around him in a sickening blur.

Not a room. He was somewhere else. Not a room.

Colin remembered fragments now: drinking cognac by the fire, Long Island, his friend, laughing, feeling the warm kiss of cheery flames. He shivered now. His head throbbed. What else? What had happened?

Colin's breath churned around him in an icy mist.

A rivulet of blood rolled over his chin, across his cheek, down his forehead, a long stream of scarlet.

No. Oh God, no.

Colin tried to move, as he struggled to comprehend.

Upside down.

He was upside down, dangling.

He hung from the ceiling—no, not a ceiling, a roof—not a roof, a—rock? He was trussed up like a lamb for slaughter.

Colin's eyes darted up to the stalactite, taking in his bound ankles, his naked body.

A spasm rippled through Colin, and settled to his fingertips. His hands felt sticky.

And then he knew. His friend had drugged him. Not a friend...

He thrashed, trying to pull his hands and legs apart and ended in a fit of coughs.

His partners had no more use for him. Or they were teaching him a lesson. A few broken bones. Speed up payment. One more chance. Clammy fear clung to his naked skin like an icy bedsheet.

He fought to remain conscious. Tried to think. What had happened? *Calm down.* What happened? Had his partner conspired with Mancuso to cut him out, to pocket all the profits. He had to... he had to... Abbey would be in danger. Abbey would be...

He tried to shout out, knowing he could talk to them. He could... He could... His mind wouldn't focus. What could he do? Talk to them? Talk to whom?

A rush of pain channeled through him, and he shivered.

Cold. So cold.

His vision blurred.

I'm upside down. Hung upside down. What did that remind him of? His dizzy mind tried to remember, to comprehend.

Hayden had hung his victims.

No.

His own hands trailed below, bound with rough bailing twine.

Lord Jesus.

Colin had no fingertips. Just reddish brown nubs.

The pain blossomed, a dull tide of agony. Delirious, he thought, *How can I... How can I... How can... Oh... Fuck you...* He understood now and the wave of comprehension brought a new surge of pain.

He laughed. Stinging tears mixed with warm blood as he hummed the maniac tune. The theme music to *Haunted Survivor*. He would star in his own show. He would be the next victim of the. . .

A sudden jumble of fragmented memories swept through him: Abbey Chase, the twenty-one-year-old scriptwriter with the dazzling boobs and the even more dazzling ideas; their first kiss; their first pilot television episode, a flop; walking down the aisle, surrounded by all their friends; the doctor saying sadly, "You can never have children" and then Abbey's tears; signing the divorce decree; laughing over clam chowder on the beach; making love in the sand, drunk, laughing; the smiling face of his first mistress; lawyers, always the lawyers. . .

And then the pain again. The delirium faded and he was in the cave once more. Yes, that's where he was. Some kind of a cave.

Colin fought the nausea as he stared at his truncated fingers, and a frenzy took him. He bucked in the ropes.

Queasiness swept over him, and warmth spread out from his thighs, a stream of heat washing his chest.

Gone and wet myself.

The cave spun. He saw the stalactites and stalagmites, reaching out to each other, glittering in torch light, so beautiful. Then, the pail below him. His blood dripped from finger nubs—drip, drip, into the bucket, already a quarter-full.

Clarity came with a thick sluggishness that emulated the blood dripping from his congealing wounds.

His attacker was gone. Thank God in heaven. If only Colin could loosen the ropes before he bled out.

"Help!" he shouted. His voice echoed back at him.

He must survive. He had so much to live for now. Abbey. And *Haunted Survivor*. And his movie.

"I have money! I'm rich!" He shouted, and his voice slurred like that of an alcoholic who found the bottle empty.

He felt a moment of hope. Money solved all problems. He would buy his safety. He would promise not to tell. *I won't tell, I won't tell, I won't tell. . .*

"I have millions! Anything you want!"

Someone laughed. A shadow lanced across the rocky floor.

Sudden dread paralyzed him.

But then the anger came. Just when his career was finally taking off. Just when he had his precious hit. Not just a hit, but the biggest hit in television history. He was Colin Lorentz. Surely, they'd want a ransom.

"I have—I have friends. Ask for any—thing. A ransom. . ." His words slurred and cracked. He bucked in the ropes again, fighting to loosen the bonds at his wrists. New pain arced up his arms, wakened by his renewed struggles.

He felt the rope loosen. Felt new hope. New pain.

"I can pay you."

More laughter.

The wind moaned through the cracks in the rock, a haunting sound, and he felt new fear.

Colin tried to reach out with tied hands, with numb fingers, to stop the spinning.

He choked back a shriek as ten brown nubs tumbled across the rock, rolling like dice on a craps table. He stared at them.

His fingertips.

Now the scream came, and it echoed back from high rock.

"Money! I have money! I have friends!"

More laughter.

He stared at his finger nubs, the nails stained with his own blood.

"The FBI director is a friend!"

Laughter.

"Millions of dollars!"

The scrape of a booted foot on rock.

He tried to swivel in his bonds. Tried to see. He saw the tips of boots. Tried to look up. To see.

His friend had drugged him. Wanted all of the production for himself. Not his friend.

But the boots. His partner never wore boots. Who was this? Who? Cowboy boots. Worn, stained cowboy boots. A hired thug? A hired hit? He felt hope. A hired strongman could be bought.

The boots tapped.

Colin tried to see. He focused his eyes, looked up, but could only see the jeans, worn jeans, stained brown from butcher's work.

"I am famous! I can help you!"

A gloved hand from out of the shadows held his arm and stopped the spinning.

Colin screamed as the knife swept down.

Chapter 15

· ·

January 21, 10:52pm
Mason Place

On their way back from the third series of interviews with crew and cast, they passed the whist room, which now served as the executive lounge.

Bane heard a familiar voice. He froze at the double doors and stared in at the two people chatting in Queen Anne chairs by a roaring fire. "Oh hell. Hugh King of *The Crime Times*," Bane said. King saw Bane at that moment. He waved at the detective. Abbey Chase turned in the chair, pausing in her interview with the *King of bad press*.

"What is it? Bane?" Kip leaned around Bane and peered into the mahogany paneled room.

Bane stepped between two marble columns.

"Bloodhound Bane! Agent Bane, there you are!" King laughed like a pre-teen girl and propelled from his chair as if his legs had Go-Go-Gadget springs. "Can you believe this? Another one?"

Bane ground his teeth, willing himself to stay calm. "Ms. Chase, didn't we agree, no journalists?"

Hugh King's smile faded. "For shame. That's gratitude! I made you a superstar."

"In your book, your blather made me a fool." King was the first so-called journalist to call Hayden a serial, and he named him the *Vampire Killer*. He had interfered with the FBI investigation at every turn, once even polluting a scene. Two years after Bane arrested Hayden, King had splashed news of Susan Bane's homicide across the nation, with headlines Bane would never forget—*Wife of Hayden Nemesis Raped and Killed* and *Hayden Cop Hasn't a Clue on Own Wife's Homicide*—picked up by wire services around the world.

Bane folded his arms rather than reaching out and choking the man who had made his life a living hell. "Kip, call a trooper to escort this—

person—from the premises."

"I'm a guest," chided King.

"This is a crime scene."

Abbey Chase lifted out of her chair, elegant and perfectly coiffed. "I invited him. Colin's using him as a consultant on *The Vampire Killer*, our new movie on Hayden." She hesitated In a quieter voice, she said, "*The Crime Times* is also a wholly owned subsidiary of Real TV—"

Bane lunged between them, glaring down at Hugh King, his voice lifting sharply as he cut her off. "I'll say this once, wee man. You can leave on your own power or I can have you escorted. Either way, you are not to return."

Hugh King stepped back, his face paling.

"Detective Bane!" Abbey Chase snapped. "This is my property. I'll have whatever guests I choose!"

Bane leaned closer to King. "This entire property is a crime scene. And *he*—any reporter—is not welcome."

Bane hadn't noticed Kip leave the room, but now she returned with a trooper. "Mr. King was just leaving," she said, her face a calm mask. "Make sure he joins his friends *outside* the gate."

"Bane, you can't get rid of me this easily!" yelled King as the trooper pulled him from the room. "One way or the other, you're front page tomorrow!"

Bane focused his emotions. "Bye-bye." He waved.

"What about the Hayden accomplice?" King yelled from the door. "Let me go, damn you!"

Bane held up his hand. "Wait."

The trooper dropped King's arm. King straightened his sleeve and gave Bane a look of poison. "You realize, besides yourself, I am the biggest expert on Hayden. You didn't think I missed that rather obvious conclusion, did you?" He stepped closer, his stooped shoulders drawing straighter as his confidence grew.

"Biggest asshole is more like it. So you're the one spreading these rumors in the press pool."

"It's not rumor, and you know it, dog!"

"A dog that bites." *Hell*, Bane thought, fighting to control his Scottish temper. His voice had risen to a snarl, very doglike.

"I know it. I know it! But I have information! And I nearly died to get it."

Bane's self-control took over. He buried his personal emotions deep. "You're full of shit." Bane stepped closer. "Full of lies, half-lies, guesses, exaggerations."

"Deductions, dog. And in this case, you'd better listen!" His voice was shrill. "*Bloodhound Bane returns to bungle another case!*" He laughed and dropped his hand; spittle flew from his mouth. "Tomorrow's headline!"

Bane grabbed him by his shirt, pulling it out of his pants as he lifted the reporter. He leaned in until he was nose to nose with King. "What's your damned information?"

"Bane," Kip whispered in his ear.

Bane released King and the reporter dropped, then stumbled back.

King's breath came in rapid heaves, but he stood defiant. Abbey Chase looked back and forth between them, perhaps a potential witness for future litigation.

As King calmed, his smile returned. He knew something important. Bane could tell by his weasel expression. "Spill it, or you'll spend a night in lockup."

"On what charge?"

Bane smiled. "Assaulting an officer."

King laughed, but Kip said, quickly, "I *did* see an assault."

Hugh King glanced at Abbey Chase for support but her face revealed nothing. "Dog, you never change."

"Or lockup as a material witness," Bane said, more seriously.

"Fine. Okay. All right, already!" He tucked his shirt into his pants. "I'll cooperate. But you give me an exclusive." When Bane didn't answer, he shouted, "I mean it, dog! You give me an exclusive, or the headlines you read about yourself will make you squirm!"

Bane took a step forward and King took a step back. In a calmer voice, Bane said, "They will anyway, I have no doubt!" As he reached forward, the reporter jumped back, but Bane calmly smoothed the collar of his shirt. "Fine. If you give us valuable information, I might give you a small exclusive. I wear tartan socks. How's that? Exclusive enough?"

"Be serious." King's too-eager black eyes blinked several times.

"Fine. You get the story first."

"You wouldn't lie to me, would you?"

"I might."

"Okay! Jeez!" He tried to smile, his lip trembling. "I found something your buddy Armitage will never track down. In all your investigating Hayden, you missed it."

"I missed a lot. My highschool prom, seventh anniversary. Sleep."

"Doubt all you want." He fished in his pocket and pulled out a folded paper. "Read it. This runs in tomorrow's paper. And don't say I never cooperated."

Bane unfolded the paper. It was a galley of the following day's *The Crime Times*. The headline read: *Vampire Killer May Have Had Accomplices.*

Kip leaned close. "That was one of our theories."

Bane nodded. "Everyone, I want some time alone with Mr. King."

"I want witnesses!" King looked at Abbey Chase, who shook her head. The troopers also left the whist room.

"I'll stay," Kip said.

"No one's staying. Just the *King of Bad Press* and me." Bane leaned close to Kip and whispered, "Don't worry. I promise to assault him only with my bad sense of humor."

She scowled at him and made fists, but she said, "Fine."

When Abbey Chase didn't leave the whist room, Bane said, "Police business, Ms. Chase."

With a final glance at Hugh King, she left the room.

"I told you all I plan to." King sounded frightened, but he sat in one of the armchairs and sneered.

"Forget that we love each other like brothers," Bane said, keeping his voice calm. "Lives are at stake here, King."

"Lives are always at stake. Crossing the road, I risk my life. More important is integrity of the press."

Bane breathed steadily. He paced the room as he read the story on the press proof. He was conscious of King tapping his foot, but he didn't look up until he'd read every line, devouring the story like a hungry wolf. Wow. What a story. "You mention accomplices in your article."

King sat down and crossed his legs. "Yes."

"Who?"

"Going to charge me with obstruction again?" King laughed. "It's an old song."

"I might. Or I might bore you with the history of clan McBane. The tale could last days." Even as Bane struggled with an urge to bash King around the room for a while—without witnesses—it occurred to him that if King could find this information, his people could, too. Surely he could find the information without bribe money and dirty tricks?

King's maddening smile never faded. "There's a bigger picture here."

Bane took a deep breath, forced himself to control the anger he felt whenever King was in the room. "Tell me about this assassin. The one you mention in your article."

King cocked his head to one side. "You don't believe me."

"I think you're so full of lies they fall out your butt hole. But I'm listening."

King sagged back in his chair, his tapping foot, darting eyes and pale face revealing his stress. "Fine. Hell, Bane, this guy is a big, big dude. Christ, I tell you, I was scared. And you know I deal with this all the time." His eyes darted. "I'm not joking. Six foot six, I think. Hard to tell. In a Stetson and cowboy boots, you know? Those goddam boots, clopping after me, relentless. In his hat and boots he was seven feet in all! I'm not exaggerating."

Bane's eyebrows lifted. Detective Lee had described a big cowboy in Golden Gate Park, last seen with Hayden's dead lawyer Kincaid. "So, he chased you through the OK Corral. Is that it?"

King was too sharp not to notice his surprise. "What? You know about the cowboy?" Now he was interrogating Bane.

"Don't be clever. Describe Billie the Kid for me."

"There's something about him. The eyes. They're evil. Only ever saw eyes like his once before." He plucked at the lint on his slacks. "You know."

Bane shook his head.

"Hayden!"

"Are you telling me Buffalo Bill's another Hayden? Just because he chased you up an alley in Boston? Come on, King, tell me what's going on in that pea brain of yours."

His lower lip trembled, the only sign of emotion. "Maybe. I don't know. But I know one thing. Hayden was given up by his parents for adoption. His father was a connected, wealthy Bostonian." He spun in the chair, leaning forward.

Bane chewed his lip. He had pursued background checks on Hayden's real father, but had been blocked at every request. "Go on, Sundance."

King folded his arms. "I'm not saying more."

"But you said you thought this—let's call him Jesse James—is a killer like Hayden."

King blinked rapidly; he was sweating. "Maybe! I don't know. If he is, he's scarier, let me tell you."

Bane shook his head. "Only Satan himself is scarier."

"You weren't there!"

Bane snorted. "Come on. A Jesse James in Boston. A giant? Did he have six shooters blazing? You think I'm buying your exaggerations? He was five foot ten and wore a Fedora, right?"

"Screw you, Bane."

"And your mother."

"It was a frigging cowboy! No six shooter, but he didn't need one."

"Okay, okay. A cowboy. Clint Eastwood type."

"Colder, bigger, scarier."

"If he was so bad, how'd you get out alive?"

"Was that a jibe?"

"King, you're not even a match for Annie Oakley."

"Go to hell."

King and Bane stared at each other, faces inches apart. "So? Convince me," Bane said. "If I'm to believe you, tell me how you got away from the

Okay Corral. You get winded running through a reporter scrum."

King gave Bane the finger, but he said, "Fine. Fine. I ran right into a squad car! They passed the alley, saw me running—they thought I was a thief. Cuffed me and took me to the station!"

Bane laughed, at first in a light rumble, then he couldn't resist a deep belly laugh at King's expense. Bane could see it. King, trembling, out of breath, his face slick with sweat, saved by a pair of uniforms out looking for the burglars who plagued upscale Beacon Hill. "I would love to have seen that." He caught his breath. "I bet you didn't argue much."

King's pale face mottled pink.

"I know you. You called your mommy—I mean, your editor. He bailed you, just like he did in Florida."

King didn't answer and didn't have to.

"Fine. So what? This could have been a mugger with bad taste in clothes. Look at me. I'm a cop with bad taste." He tugged on the lapel of his tartan vest. "A coincidence. Doesn't make this man an assassin, King." He rolled his eyes.

King folded his arms. "Uh-uh. I've been doing this too long. I know what's what, dog."

"That's why you work for a supermarket tabloid."

After ten more minutes of King's "I'm not saying," Bane knocked on the door and shouted, "Dump King in the snowdrift outside the gate."

With King gone, Bane sat alone in the room, enjoying the heat of the fire. He couldn't get the idea out of his head. For years he had tried to discover the identities of Hayden's parents. No Boston judge would issue a warrant releasing the sealed records of Tyler Hayden's adoption. King, on the other hand, had probably bribed someone. Hayden's birth parents were wealthy, connected Bostonians. Wasn't everyone in Boston wealthy and connected?

Bane called Vic, an old detective friend on the Boston PD, and asked for some help with a friendly local judge. Vic promised to try, but doubted Bane had anywhere near enough grounds to justify release of sealed adoption records.

Bane twirled his phone on the whist table, staring at the fire. They still didn't even have victim ID, and he was sure that victim ID would lead to the perpetrator.

He punched *last number dialed*. His first follow-up call was to Japan. The police in Honshu, the island contestant Kenji Tenichi claimed to be from, had no record on him, or on his "temple" name, Miyazawa.

"Anything else, sir?" the perfectly polite logistics officer asked in clipped English.

"No—wait, yes. Do you have any unsolved homicides on Honshu?" Bane gave her some dates, asked her to focus on knife-related crimes. The vicious scars on Kenji Tenichi's chest still nagged at Bane. They promised to send him a list.

Bane made his way to Lorentz's study in the conservatory. He searched Lorentz's desk one more time but found nothing of interest.

He called his daughters, talked to the trooper guarding them, finally collapsed on Lorentz's leather couch, and waited for return calls to his various inquiries. He had hardly slept in forty hours.

Dozing, he returned to alert status at the click of the door.

He sat up and waved Abbey Chase in.

She smiled. "I'm sorry, Detective. I didn't want to disturb you. I think you need sleep. Please." She gestured at the couch.

"Please stay." Bane did need sleep but Abbey Chase had the pulse of the show.

She sat beside him. "I apologize."

"For what, Ms. Chase?"

"Can you call me Abbey?"

Bane stared deep into her marvelous ice-blue eyes, sorely tempted. He both despised everything she represented—greed, Hollywood, big city—and loved her energy, charm and, frankly, looks. He remembered their shouting match in the control room, as she gleefully directed the snake scene, and her apparent coldness and ruthlessness. But that was her professional persona. What was she really like?

He made a small concession. "Abbey in private then. Call me Alban."

"In private." She yawned. "This has taken a toll on me, too."

"Imagine that stress times one thousand. That's what your contestants live with."

She stiffened, but no snappy come-back. "That's business, Alban."

"Business doesn't make you less responsible, all of your insurance notwithstanding, Ms. . . Abbey."

"I just wanted to apologize for my blowup. It was uncalled for."

Bane smiled. "Which one?"

"Funny. Very funny."

They both smiled, for a moment just two ordinary people.

"Heard from Mr. Lorentz?"

She shook her head. "I left another message." She took a deep breath. "He doesn't answer to me."

"Something on your mind?"

"Yes." But then she didn't speak, her face thoughtful and unsmiling. The blue eyes swept up and captured him in their gaze. "I have a little confession."

"Yes?"

"I didn't intend for this, you understand?" He nodded. "But I did recruit both crew and cast with strife in mind."

"I know."

She blinked, several times. "Well, what you don't know is that—and I feel awful about this—secretly, I'm delighted by all of this. Our ratings are soaring."

"I know that, too."

"Oh. Well, I thought it only fair—this has nothing to do with me, you understand? I had a call from Governor Ritchie."

"How is the old buzzard?"

"He is most concerned," she said.

"Aren't we all."

"I believe he's calling in the FBI."

"A nuisance, to be sure." When the silence continued too long, he said, "Abbey, we'll stop this maniac."

"Yes. I believe you will." She placed her hand on his. He jumped.

"What's the matter, Alban? Surprised I'm warm to the touch?"

Bane pulled his hand, but she clung to it. "Ms. Chase."

"I'm frightened like all the rest." She put her other hand on top of the first. "I'm just glad you're here."

He yanked his hand away. Had he given her some body-language clue he found her attractive? "I'm not available, Ms. Chase."

The old Chase returned, eyebrows hooking together. "Don't flatter yourself." She slammed the door on her way out.

Bane felt a bizarre rise of emotions. His professional persona fought his personal attraction for Abbey Chase. He could almost feel her hand. Good old-fashioned guilt reared up to confuse the issue. He thought of Suze, buried but always his.

Still, it was hard to take Abbey out of his thoughts, to concentrate on either sleep or the case.

The ringing of the satellite phone woke him. "Detec-a-tive Bane, sir?" asked a rich-voiced man, with a thick accent.

"Yes, this is Bane." He stifled a yawn and looked at his watch. Only two hours of sleep. He slid off the couch and walked to the bay window with its magnificent view of the snow-covered mountains, touched in the gold of sunrise.

"Superintendent Kizawa. J. P. A." He spoke slowly, precisely.

As his Japanese counterpart relayed his news, Bane paced the winter garden. Superintendent Kizawa told of a string of grizzly serial killings, all perpetrated with a knife, around the time Kenji Tenichi was on the island. As he told Bane the details, the detective noticed similarities to the new crimes.

"May I ask, Superintendent, do you have an undercover on American soil?"

"A what? I cover American soil?"

Bane smiled. "Just wondering if you have an agent or officer working over here." He told Kizawa of Kenji, gave him names and descriptions.

"No. No, Detec-a-tive. No. This is he you asked back-a-ground on? He is not one of mine."

It was tenuous, vapors really, with no real evidence the crimes were linked to Tenichi—just the convenience of coincidence, some nasty scars, and his knowledge of the tunnels in Mason Place. But Kenji Tenichi was a prime suspect.

Bane thanked the inspector, and stood for a moment in the window, watching day spread over the eastern ridge. Vermont always took his breath away, and as the late winter sunrise spread golden fingers across the glittering snow, he found new strength.

They spent another day questioning Real TV crew and the senior people.

The most disturbing interview involved Doctor Skillman, on-site Real TV doctor. Bane hoped he'd never need emergency medical care from the Real TV doctor.

The albino, freckle-faced man had a frizzy blond Afro, very seventies, with eyes that darted in every direction. As they talked, Doctor Skillman became more agitated, pacing in circles in his tiny clinic, fumbling with a tray of scalpels, at one point even thrusting one in Bane's direction.

"Calm down, Doc. Nice 'fro by the way."

"Fro?"

Bane swept his own hair. "I just asked where you were between five and—"

Skillman's voice burst over Bane's like a bomb exploding. "I told you I was drinking with Doctor Wingate!" The doctor twirled the scalpel, and it caught the fluorescent light on its sharp edge.

Bane unbuttoned his wool jacket and pulled it back enough to reveal his .38 revolver. "And what if I told you Wingate was in Washington?"

Skillman's freckles seemed to darken as his skin paled. "Must have been a different day, then!"

"So Friday?"

Skillman played with a hypo needle now. His pupils were dilated.

"Self-prescribing, Doctor?"

Skillman's reaction was unexpected. He giggled. "I was here. Here, in my clinic. That's right!" He started humming.

The man was stoned out of his mind. "You didn't, by any chance, study medicine by correspondence course?"

Skillman snapped back his arm and threw the hypo. It speared the door with so much force it stuck.

Bane stared at the vibrating hypo. "Maybe you got your license at the Looney Tunes Asylum?"

Skillman giggled some more. "Looney Tunes. I like that. Looney Tunes."

Bane folded his arms. "Tell me, Doctor Skillman. Do you like games?" *Welcome to The Game.*

Skillman giggled. "I like games fine. Can't help myself." He turned away for a moment, then swung back around so abruptly that Bane reached instinctively for the grip of his gun. But the nutty doctor broke into a song, a familiar tune: *"I can't help myself, help myself, can't help it. . . And the funny part is I feel no guilt and no shame. I guess where there's no action there's no blame. . ."*

Bane had to conclude he was mad, or playing at being mad. Just one more name to add to the long list of suspects who required deep background checks.

Abbey Chase continued hot, then cold, offering food, support, rooms for Bane's men, her Real TV Brain Room as temporary headquarters—then, in the next instant refusing interviews and threatening litigation if they bothered the contestants.

Bane's team quickly moved into the Real TV Brain Room, filling the white boards with notes and observations from each crime scene. It felt good to have a base of operations, a sanctuary with a door that could be locked, although the framed picture of Stephen and Leslie Chow loomed over their activities, a constant reminder of the link between Vermont of today and the ghost of Hayden.

The remoteness of the crime scene and the seriousness of the threat required shifts of Bane's men to stay at Mason Place. Until Bane got closer to an answer, he'd stay too.

He called his daughters, laughed with them at their day's antics, missed them so much it hurt—but lives were at stake.

He would stay at Mason Place.

Chapter 16

January 22, 1:22 pm Pacific Time
LA, California

Ken Li opened the door to the limousine, his nine millimeter auto-matic visible as he swung around.

Stephen Chow offered no smile as he stepped into the stretch limo. Li didn't care. He was paid well to protect Chow, to focus on the people around his employer, to kill with prejudice if it meant keeping Chow alive, and to tune out everything he heard. Which was a good thing, for Stephen Chow was an asshole.

Twice in the last month he had steered his boss clear of dangerous situations. The first was a violent protest that quickly spun out of control at the gates of San Quentin after Hayden's execution. The other—well, Li preferred not to think too much about the cowboy named Austin, a man who enjoyed his work too much.

Li slammed Chow's door and slid into the Lincoln's shotgun seat. "Let's move."

The chauffeur pulled away from the curb and cut off a courier on a bicycle. The courier shouted and gave the driver the finger. The chauf-feur shouted back at the courier.

Li's black eyes darted from mirror to mirror to road in an allegro-tempo dance. They took it all in with radar-like sweeps—the steady stream of Porsches and Merecedes, a river of pedestrian tourists on the sidewalk, the bit actor from a hot TV show signing autographs on the south sidewalk, the dog walker with a clutch of dogs not bothering to scoop poop, the little girl who dropped her ice cream.

He had a vested interest in Chow. Not just the money. Chow had promised Li a future role in his movies and shows. Already his boss had cast Li in a martial arts movie, to be shot in eight months. It helped that Li had the dark, sleazy look and hard body of a stereotypical martial arts villain. If Li could make it as a star in Chow's movies, he would be able to move his family to America. His wife and three good strong boys waited in Hong Kong. Nothing was more important than family.

Li scowled. Another horn-blaring traffic jam.

"Don't take Santa Monica Boulevard," Li ordered.

Patterson, the chauffeur, didn't reply or look at him.

Patterson was a humorless beast, too big behind the wheel. Though the ape was a hell of a driver, always finding a way around traffic jams and cool in a crisis, Li mistrusted the *guailo*—white barbarian. His open prejudice served him well in a city where no one could be trusted, but made it impossible to develop friendships in America.

"Stop staring," said Patterson. "You some kinda fag?"

Li smiled. He cupped his crotch. "In your dreams." He enjoyed their daily verbal sparring.

"Asshole," Patterson snapped.

"Seefut," Li said—*asshole*. "Dieu neh." *Fuck you.*

If Chow heard the exchange he gave no indication. The privacy glass was up and he was talking on the phone. In fact he was shouting so loud that the words penetrated the driver's cabin: "No, shut up and listen. Reid's dead, you know? I don't care! Your man is dead." He looked at Li through the glass and rapped the partition with the phone. "Mind your own business," he said in Cantonese, frowning.

Li turned forward but continued to listen. Chow was in full rant: "Don't threaten me, Mancuso. You're nothing to me! Fuck you, too." Li tried not to think about what that outburst might cost in extra hours. On their last trip to New York, when Chow met with Mancuso in Chow's Four Seasons penthouse, Mancuso and Chow had smiled and shaken hands, while Li was left to face down three of Mancuso's enforcers. Li's hand had never left the grip of his pistol.

The limo fought through the traffic and sped south, the ocean flashing by on the right. Chow continued to conference by phone, sometimes yelling at studio executives, other times at partners. Most of it Li tuned out.

He continued to stare at the driver. All these white barbarians looked the same, with their big ugly noses and round eyes. Patterson was black haired, furry and big—and how could you trust someone who looked so hairy, like an animal? But it was more than the driver that nagged at Li. On some days Li could smell danger, and this was one of those times.

Chow was screaming again, this time talking to that reporter from *The Crime Times*. "Look, King. I paid you a lot of money. A lot. I want the name. No, now. By phone. Don't give me any shit, King. I want to know the father's name."

Chow listened, not speaking for a long moment. As his eyes scanned past the center mirror, Li noticed his boss paled. His hands shook.

He was silent after he terminated the call. His boss poured himself a tall Napoleon brandy from the limo bar.

Chow drank, in silence, for the rest of the return trip to *Livia*, the walled peninsula compound he called home, named for his daughter Olivia, butchered by Hayden. *Livia*, surrounded on three sides by cliffs and crashing surf and on all sides by walls and surveillance cameras, was more a fortress and shrine than a real home.

The first sign that anything was wrong was at the guardhouse. There was no sentry.

"Stop the car," Li said.

"Probably taking a whiz," Patterson said, frowning.

He knocked on the glass divider. Stephen Chow put down the empty snifter, scowled at him, then slid down the partition.

"No guard, sir," he said in Cantonese. "Cheung should be here."

Chow glanced at the car locks.

"Sir, we should call the police." Li leaned over the divider.

"No fucking police."

"I know how you feel, sir. But I don't like this."

They argued back and forth in Cantonese, and finally Li said, "Let me go first, then. Stay here. Lock the car."

Chow nodded. "Leslie's in there." His voice carried a sense of urgency Li had never heard before. He glanced at the empty guard house, then up at the tall closed gates.

"I'll find Leslie, sir. You lock the car. Patterson, look after him."

Li slipped out of the car, slung low in a catlike crouch. He was afraid of very little, but he knew that Chow's enemies went beyond dangerous and the knowledge gave him a nervous energy that crackled under his skin. As he slid along the stone wall, he rationalized to himself, *Only a fool is without fear.* Mancuso's thugs he could probably handle. But the cowboy? The cowboy went beyond scary.

Li scrambled up and over the stone wall like a monkey, levering with his strong forearms. He dropped to the other side, paused and listened. No dogs. Where were the Dobermans? He whistled softly. Nothing.

He drew his Browning and crept along the sea wall, listening to the surf below. Over that cliff was a hundred foot drop to sharp teeth of rock and a surf that rose wild and foamy.

He paused behind a statue of Olivia, a marble sculpture that made Chow's daughter appear as elegant and peaceful as Guan Yin, the goddess of mercy. He peered at the house. It seemed peaceful enough. Too peaceful?

Still no dogs assailed him as he sprinted through *Livia's* formal gardens and vaulted over trimmed hedges. The crashing of the surf was a distant sound now, but there was nothing else to hear. No dogs. No birds. No guards.

By the pool he found two of the Dobermans. One had his throat ripped out and ugly spurts of blood had washed the mosaic-tiled deck in scarlet. The other dog had been eviscerated.

The dogs always attacked together. He was either dealing with more than one trespasser, or with someone of vast strength. Someone like Austin Bartlett, the cowboy. But right now the only thing that mattered was Leslie. She was the only half-decent person in the compound, a woman who treated Li with genuine respect.

The library's garden doors were open.

With the stealth of a predator, Li slid into Chow's study, gun in hand, pausing as his eyes adjusted.

Crouching behind Chow's desk, he heard muffled voices.

Then he heard her scream.

No longer cautious, he ran through the open doors into the foyer, spinning in a full circle as he surveyed with his gun lowered. A rhythmic sound thudded in his ears and it took him a moment to realize it was the racing of his own heart. He crouched, waiting for it to slow.

Another scream.

Leslie's voice. Someone had invaded the Chow's house, killed the dogs, probably the guards—and Leslie was his prisoner.

Li felt the first pricks of heat, then the rise of sweat on his forehead. He was surprised to find his hands shaking. *Guan Yin have mercy.* He had never—*never*—been afraid before. *Merciful goddess, keep me safe.*

He sprang up the sweeping staircase and dove around the marble pillar at the top.

As he rounded the corner, he heard the laugh.

"Come in, Li," the man said.

Li took a deep breath, then stepped into the wide hall. At the far end, hanging from the chandelier, he saw the mistress of the house. Leslie Chow. Hung by her ankles.

Li absorbed the details in seconds. The fingers on one hand were missing. Blood dripped into a basin. The look of fear on her face. Her recognition. The hope in her eyes as she saw him.

But no attacker.

He heard the sound behind him. Instinct drove Li around, muscles tensed. Too late. A hand came down on his wrist and he was thrown against the wall with bone-shattering force. His gun spun across the granite floor.

Pain shot through his shoulder and he fell to the floor. His right wrist was broken, his gun hand useless. His right shoulder throbbed, probably dislocated, but he used the pain to drive himself to his feet.

This man was strong, towering over Li and nearly double his weight. Those cold, dead eyes and all those white teeth.

Li swiveled and lunged in, relying on his speed and martial abilities. He managed a full roundhouse kick, then dipped low and brought himself up in a low, anchored stance. But his kick had not connected. Something brushed against him as he whirled into a new stance.

The man smiled. He held a long double-edged blade, dripping with blood.

Li crouched lower, but a spasm shot through him and he winced, losing his stance. His hand went down to his abdomen. It felt wet and sticky.

What is that smell?

He looked down, knowing he shouldn't take his eyes from the assassin, but unable to resist.

The wound was long and deep. He saw his own muscle sliced open, and something round and pale, protruding. He realized it was his own intestine.

Chapter 17

∙∙

January 23, 3:17 pm
Mason Place

The day was windless, a rare treat in January. From a stark blue sky the sun shone on the glittering fresh snow. Bane heard the helicopter before he saw it, the thrum becoming a roar as the sleek black chopper landed beside the clunky Vermont National Air Guard Hueys, like a bird of prey swooping in amongst fat chickens.

Bane ran under the blades. As the door slid back, and the big guy emerged, Bane found new energy and shook off the last of his fatigue.

Bane and Arm topped each other's fists like school kids.

"Hey, bro!" Arm's voice roared, loud even over the whine down of the compressors.

"Welcome to the asylum."

They met Kip at the crew's entrance. Arm ducked under the door frame to enter. He peeled off his coat and Bane noticed Kip's eyes darting up and down, appraising the newcomer.

"This lusty married woman who's sizing you up, Arm, is my partner Kip. Kip, this is Arm, my old partner. He's married, too."

Kip's tiny hand disappeared into Arm's callused palm. "Spoilsport," Arm said.

Kip blushed. "You're such an ass, Bane."

Bane pried apart their hands. "Hey now, I explained all this. You, married. You, too. Married."

"Got the message, bro." Arm flashed a smile, then he was all business. "Where can we talk? Privately."

"No team?"

I'm here semi-informally. You have to ask the Bureau's CID into your jurisdiction—if that's your wish, they'll be here in hours."

Bane shook his head. The FBI tended to assume control in task force situations. "You're all the help we need, old friend."

"He's never that nice to me," Kip said with a smile.

"For true, but give him time," Arm said. "He gets crustier the longer he hangs around with someone."

Kip led the way down to the finished basements of the house, through the winding halls to the Real TV Brain Room. Arm rumbled on about Mason Place. "Wow, ain't this something. Just look at that. How about that, now."

Arm paused at the entrance to Abbey Chase's Brain Room, Bane's new command centre. "This all looks familiar. You've moved right on in."

His practised eyes swept the room. Forensics files covered the big boomerang-shaped table, and Cross had scrawled his observations on one wall of Abbey Chase's floor-to-ceiling whiteboards. Bane's barely legible scrawl dominated the other whiteboards.

Bane studied Arm. "We call this the nut house."

Arm walked around the table and stared at the bank of closed circuit monitors, his eyes settling on the big plasma screen. Arm studied the contestants. "I wonder if them cameras are on when they shower."

"Perv," Bane said.

They spent an hour bringing Arm up to date and Bane told them both about his background check on Kenji Tenichi and the interviews with Skillman and other cast.

"So what turned up in the VICAP database?" Bane asked. "Let me guess. Zilch."

"Just about right. But on Lorentz, the IRS has a bulging file. Charged with tax evasion twice, settled both times with massive fines. Nearly bankrupt just last year." Bane scratched notes on the whiteboard. "Each time Lorentz flew to California, supposedly on business trips to meet the Chows and Real TV executives, he also dropped in on his buddy Hayden, in San Quentin." His fingers drummed on the table.

He pointed at the Chows' portrait on the wall. "This bothers the mudbugs out of me. They own the majority share of this production here. And I'm not comfortable with coincidences."

Bane told Arm about his conversation with Stephen Chow, the subtle threat of litigation, the referral to their law firm.

"Chow's not all there, that's sure. You don't blame the man who caught your daughter's killer. They ain't right in the head."

"You don't need to be 'normal' if you have a billion bucks in assets."

"Anyways, listen to what I got on that Doctor Skillman you asked about. He's a war vet. Then practised in Miami. At the same time Hayden was preying on his victims."

"Fourteen years ago. I think I'll hug you."

"Scot's dinee hug, remember?" Arm grinned. "But there's more; he had a patient you'll be interested in—I pulled the records from the insurance company."

He frowned so hard his eyes folded into slits. "One of his patients was Sammy Franks."

Sammy Franks! Bane had a quick image of Hayden's third victim, dangling from his ankles, just twelve years old, bled into a bathtub. Poor Sammy Franks. His parents had not been at Hayden's execution, but Bane never forgot little Sammy.

"That one, you might have called me on."

"Sorry, bro, they radioed me the news in the chopper."

Doctor Skillman's patient became Hayden's victim. Now Skillman was here. Was Skillman the Hayden accomplice? It couldn't be another fluke. Bane told Arm about his interview with Skillman.

"For true? Well, there you go. He needs more checking. But I'll leave the detecting to you young detectives. I'm more about breaking down doors and target practicing on perps."

Bane tapped on the board. "How about her highness Ms. Chase? Anything?"

Arm slid off the table. "Well, once married to Lorentz, but you know that. She comes from money, good New York money. Daddy's a banker." He stopped in front of Bane. "You interested in her, bro?"

"She's a suspect. Not a major suspect. Greedy, will do anything for ratings, but kill? I doubt she's involved in anything like that."

"Not what I mean, and you know it. She's a hot number, that's a sure thing.""

Bane shook his head. "I always say, murder's no excuse not to have fun. But what about mob links?"

"Ha! That's the thing. We found six million going into Colin Lorentz's account."

"Where from?"

"From a numbered account. No trace possible."

"Loan sharks."

"Big time. Anti-corruption squad's all over this one. Your buddy M is the thinking, bro."

"You're not serious?"

"That's the word on the street."

Mancuso! The worst of the families—and involved with Lorentz. He specialized in loaning to distressed corporations, then foreclosing. That was how he built his so-called legitimate enterprises. "Mancuso. This just gets better every day."

Arm's eyebrows shot up. "That sure surprises me, bro. Seeing as he's in your neck of the woods. Literally."

"And he never invited me to dinner?"

"This can't be another coincidence," Kip said. "Another link to your past, Bane."

"I don't believe in coincidences," Bane said.

"His summer place is a horse farm in Vermont," Arm said. "He breeds thoroughbreds. Has a virtual compound here."

Bane dry-swallowed another aspirin. "Thoroughbreds. Nice."

Kip jumped in. "We found alfalfa on our first victim. In Vermont, alfalfa is ubiquitous on horse farms."

"You don't say?" Arm smiled as if he already knew that.

"I think we'll need to visit Big M," Bane said.

Arm nodded. "First we have to get ourselves invited to his compound. Alfalfa won't be grounds for a warrant."

"Like you said. Mancuso and I are—close."

"In what way?" Kip asked.

He shook his head. He never thought about it himself. Not anymore.

One of Arm's eyebrows shot up. "You once told me partners should share everything."

"I was talking about my wife. Your wife. That kind of partner."

"Hell you were." Arm sat on the table. "Tell you what, Kip, I'll tell you if Bane won't."

Kip's head tilted to one side, her eyes alive with interest. "Secrets? I love secrets."

"Me, too," Bane said. "I never told anyone Arm's a sex change."

Arm smiled. "Those hormones made me grow big, sure enough." He rapped the table. "You going to tell the young missus, or am I?"

"Blood oaths aren't worth much these days."

"We never swore no blood oath."

"We're brothers, right?"

Arm laughed. "Now, we're brothers. Ha!"

"That's right. Sacred trust, and all that."

"Good. Let's share with sister. She may need to know if you end up shot dead one day. Which you probably will. Everyone hates you, you know."

"Nice thought." Bane smiled. "Fine, I'll tell her."

Kip smiled. "Is this about your deep-cover organized crime days?"

Bane paced the room, circling the big table. "Good guess. What's not in my Bureau file was that I was Mancuso's enforcer, once. As an under-cover."

She laughed. "A Scots Mafioso. I love it."

"See, Arm, she's laughing at me."

"Women love to laugh at men," Kip said.

"Let's just say, I was close to Mancuso. I was deep, deep cover, so deep that I—"

"You got a little dirty?"

"Good guess again, Kip. A lot dirty. Bloody, too. Don't look so shocked. I didn't kill anyone. I broke some bones."

Kip shrugged. "You do that, now."

"Long story short, I—" Bane stopped pacing and stood in front of the big plasma screen watching Kenji Tenichi play billiards. He never missed a shot.

"What? You what?"

"Oh, tell her, bro," Arm nudged him.

Bane didn't turn.

"Then I will. Susan Mancuso was Bane's wife. Mancuso's his father-in-law."

Chapter 18

· ·

January 24, 9:03 am
State Capitol, Montpelier

No one in the crowded office spoke, waiting for Vermont's Governor Ritchie to finish his anti-Bane harangue.

Bane tuned him out, wandering around the Spartan office, studying framed prints of the Governor with various dignitaries. He noticed his own colonel and captain were carefully expressionless. Arm stood at the back of the room by the bookcase, smiling. Six of the Governor's aides were in the room, nearly invisible and totally silent.

"I don't see why you called in the FBI," the governor said.

Bane turned. "Oh. Sorry. Didn't realize your rant was complete."

Cap gave Bane a sharp *don't-do-it* look.

"And I don't see what this has to do with you, Governor," Bane said, ignoring his captain.

Governor Ritchie stared at Bane with appraising, cool eyes. "Why is that, Lieutenant Bane? I'm the governor. Your boss."

"Bosses and I don't get along. I have a long history of snubbing them. And, technically, my bosses are sitting over there." He pointed at the Colonel and Captain. Cap winced. "I didn't even vote for you."

"Bane, like it or not, I can have you fired."

"Really?" He yawned. "Since you aren't on the state police force, I must assume that you mean you'll pressure my Colonel into firing me? Correct?" The Governor nodded. "Now, I thought extortion was against the law. Arm, am I right?"

Arm smiled. "For true."

Ritchie launched himself from his chair, his chubby cheeks mottling red, then leaned across his glass and steel desk. "I'm not stupid, Bane!" His fist came down on his glass.

"That's a matter of opinion, sir."

"*Christ*, Bane," Cap said.

"I have called FBI Director Harris." A cold smile played across Ritchie's features.

"Not my boss either." Bane sat on the edge of the governor's desk.

"Have a little respect, Bane," said Colonel Clancy, his voice low and even.

Bane stood up. "I respect the office." He brushed off the corner of the desk. "See. Not a mark."

"Well, that's something." Governor Ritchie shook his head. "I talked to Director Harris about your friend here. ASAC Saulnier." He stared at Arm. "And he requests your return. And, as for you, Detective, your chief and I have discussed where this investigation should go, haven't we, Colonel Clancy?"

Bane studied Colonel Clancy. The commander of the Vermont State Police was a gray-topped man, never quite a mentor but always a supporter. The colonel nodded, but Bane saw the brief roll of his eyes, an expression that told the detective, *Just lay off, Bane. Let him boil over for a while, then we'll get back to business.* "Yes, we discussed it, Governor," Clancy said.

Governor Ritchie picked up a silver gavel from his desk and caressed it. He had once been a judge. "I heard you put out an interagency notice on Colin Lorentz."

"Yes." Bane said.

"On what grounds?"

"Material witness. He's missing. He has links to Mancuso's family and to Hayden."

"What's Mancuso got to do with this?" Ritchie snapped.

"Let's see. Mancuso financed Real TV. That's your pals' company."

"The Chows."

"Right. Our second victim has now been positively identified as Elvio Manetti, a.k.a. Jackson Reid. A Mancuso enforcer."

"So the mob's involved."

"Wow, you're sharp." Bane shook his head.

"And the Chows." Ritchie put the gavel down. "My poor, dear friends, the Chows."

"Yes. Your good friends. That tells me something. They own Real TV and have refused to cooperate. And they're tied in with Mancuso. I would have issued a notice on them but—well, you know—with the wife dead and all, I thought I'd give him a day."

"Bane, you're a heartless bastard."

Bane folded his arms, doing his best to control his temper. "You play in a pool with piranhas, you might get eaten."

"You see what I mean?" Ritchie shouted past Bane, staring at Colonel Clancy. "He's just a stone cold bastard."

Bane smiled. "As a matter of fact, I am considering issuing a notice on you, governor. Just for questioning, of course. I'd like to know how connected you really are to all of this."

The governor's red face grew even hotter, cherry bright. "You shut your mouth, young man! You will respect the office of governor." Bane felt the wind of his breath from across the desk.

No one in the office spoke. Colonel Clancy and Captain D. Jefferies seemed most interested in their shoes.

"That's better." Ritchie pushed back his chair and walked around the desk, knocking his "in" box from the edge as he passed.

Bane reached out and caught the box. "Governor, although I'm known as a joker, I'm not joking."

Governor Ritchie froze in mid-stride. "You've gone too far! Too far, damn you! Colonel, I want this man removed from the case. Put on paid leave."

Bane stepped closer to the Governor. "You're embarrassing yourself, Governor. Colonel Clancy has no grounds. You have no right. And I'm late for dinner. My girls haven't seen me for days!"

Cap coughed. Arm smiled. Colonel Clancy continued staring at his shoe.

"He speaks like this to Senator Stephens and General Franklin," Clancy sounded apologetic.

"Then why on earth do you keep him?" Ritchie said.

"He's the best we have," Clancy said, mildly.

Bane stared at his boss, embarrassed by the admission. Clancy had never praised him, let alone in public. "Does that mean I should ask for a raise?"

"Don't push, Bane," Clancy said. From his clenched teeth, Bane assumed he was pissed.

After a long moment of silence, Ritchie circled his desk and sat in his high-backed chair. "There appears to be a link to the Green Mountain Freedom movement?"

"That's a little like saying there appears to be corruption in politics, sir." Bane clasped his hands behind his back and waited for the storm.

The governor sprang out of his chair, his face red with fury. "Bane, who invited you to this meeting?"

"I believe you did. Sir." Bane shrugged. "I can leave."

Clancy stood up. "No, no, Lieutenant, stay. We're talking the Green Mountain Freedom movement." His calm eyes fixed on the governor.

"The Bureau database indicates they're a peaceful movement, sir," Arm said.

"They're building a militia in the mountains," Clancy said.

Ritchie became more emotional. "They organize protests on every bill-passing. That Seth Allen is not some bumpkin, and don't you think he is. Claims he's a descendent of our great Ethan Allen, if you can believe that! If he's behind this, it'll be organized." He stood up and paced. "I just knew they were behind this! They fought me on the Real TV license of Mason Place. Didn't want flatlanders in Vermont. They're behind this, and that's all there is to it."

"There we go," Bane said, mildly. "The case is solved. I can go home."

"This whole thing—it's bad for the state. Bad for tourism. Bad for our relationship with Real TV. They brought millions to Vermont. And jobs too!"

His tone suggested that this was all somehow Bane's fault. *Maybe he's right*, Bane thought. *Maybe this is all about some sick revenge on me*. But the scale made it improbable. There was more to this than revenge.

"Millions upon millions! And Abbey Chase is threatening to pull out now!"

Bane sucked air through his teeth. Stop him before he rants again.

Ritchie's diatribes tended to last ten minutes or more. Bane tried to be serious. "This is a difficult situation. We have a potential psychopath or a revenge copycat. This investigation will not be resolved in one week."

"Damn you, Bane, that's not what I want to hear." His hard black eyes settled on Bane, unblinking and hostile. "Well, since you've called in the Feds, Bane, I've gone over your head," he said in a softer voice. He punched a button on his phone. "Brenda, send in the Special Agent in Charge." He stood up, his large stomach brushing the edge of his desk.

Bane glanced at Arm. He looked unusually tense.

Ritchie gestured at the door. "May I present Special Agent in Charge Noland Hix."

Bane sat back in his chair, pressing hard into the upholstery, concentrating on control. Willing himself to remain calm.

Hix.

He dry swallowed two pain killers.

Hix smiled. "Governor Ritchie, sir. Gentlemen." He strode into the room on long legs, crossing quickly to the glass desk. He shook Ritchie's hand, then the Colonel's. Arm, his face a careful mask, nodded once. "*Assistant* Special Agent in Charge Saulnier. I didn't expect to see you again so soon?"

Bane had been sucker punched. He stared at Hix's outstretched hand as if it contained poison ivy.

"Calling the Feds is my prerogative," Ritchie said, his voice rising in volume. "The Director sent SAC Hix here as the FBI's acknowledged highest-ranking active expert on Hayden and sociopathic spree killers."

Bane didn't rise to the bait and locked eyes on Hix's angular features, struggling to control his anger. The scar on Bane's abdomen flamed, burning hot now, nearly as hot as the detective's blushing face.

"The Director felt that an expert was required, and promoted Hix to Special Agent in Charge for this operation," Ritchie said. "He was quite furious that ASAC Saulnier was here without assignment. The director was more than a little surprised you were here." Now the governor's voice lifted, the anger gone, but a note of triumph in his voice. "He has asked you to return with your explanation."

Arm was as steady as a rock, his breathing even. "I see, sir."

"And SAC Hix is in charge, federally."

Bane kept his voice low and even. "This is a state investigation. It is *my* case, and Arm is my choice as a Bureau liaison."

Ritchie leaned across his desk, hands flat. "*You* brought in the Feds. Which, by the way, seems provocative given a link to an independence movement that despises the Feds."

Bane ignored Ritchie and faced his Colonel. "This is a state homicide investigation."

Colonel Clancy stood up, and put his hand on Bane's shoulder. A show of support. "Of course it is, Lieutenant Bane. You are still in charge." He squeezed, hard enough that Bane felt his warning.

Hix circled the desk and stood beside the governor. "You have guests and crew from fourteen states in that house. You have a violent offender, possibly a copycat serial perp. Federal involvement is appropriate, in the circumstances."

Colonel Clancy cleared his throat. "I don't see how."

"These two homicides seem to copycat Hayden. Doctor Tillman at Quantico has already established an early profile." Hix tossed a bulging FBI file on the desk.

Bane didn't reply. Two days before, Bane had requested that his friend, Doctor Peter Tillman, construct a profile and—it seemed—Hix had intercepted it.

Governor Ritchie smiled. "Ah. See. That's what I'm talking about. Fast track action, gentlemen."

Hix patted the file with his spidery-fingered hand. "It's preliminary, but I'm sure Detective Bane would agree that the copycat element is worrisome."

Bane cleared his throat. " Only one of the homicides was a copycat."

"Exactly!" snapped Hix.

Governor Ritchie rapped his desk, as if for order. "Well, well. There we go. I trust you gentlemen to resolve this." He looked at each of them in turn. "I have to answer to my constituents—through the damn press. I have never—not in my whole career—seen so damn many of them.

Did you see that zoo in my parking lot?"

Bane nodded with the others. Nearly a hundred journalists, dozens of news vans, all on the scent of a Hayden copycat.

Ritchie stabbed his finger at Bane. "I want these Green Mountain Freedom assholes stopped dead."

"Actually, I don't believe this is a political crime at all," Bane said.

"It's the theory we're pursuing," Hix said, staring at him, smiling.

"I'm sure it is, Hix. That doesn't surprise me at all. And I wouldn't put murder past someone in politics."

Arm laughed.

The governor scowled.

"Even if you accept that a separatist group believes murder on some crazy reality television show will raise awareness, what would they gain?"

"Public sympathy when the Feds come in?" Arm proposed.

"Exactly. Which, if true, means you've played the hand they dealt you governor." He stared at Hix.

Ritchie said nothing.

"Fortunately, you're wrong. The GMF may be involved. Somehow, I think they are. But this goes beyond them. It's idiotic to focus on only one theory at this point."

"Are you calling me an idiot?" Ritchie slammed his desk so hard, the glass top cracked.

"You said it, not me," Bane said, mildly.

Colonel Clancy stepped close to Bane and said, softly, "I think you should apologize."

Bane popped yet another aspirin. "I forgive you for being an id—" Clancy's hand clamped down on Bane's shoulder. "I apologize for not voting for you." He shrugged off Clancy's hand. "Best I can do, boss."

They left the governor's office, leaving Hix behind and not speaking until they stood in the busy atrium overlooking the foyer.

Colonel Clancy spared Bane a tired smile. "That went well, Sergeant."

"Don't you mean, lieutenant?"

"I haven't decided yet." He smiled, quickly. "Let me know how it goes with Big M."

"Yes, boss."

Arm and Bane remained at the top of the stairs. "You're doing all you can, bro."

Bane shrugged. "I know. But *Hix*." They walked the pillared hallway. "Christ, he'll blow this." Bane's voice echoed on the granite walls.

"With Hix here, you'll need me, if only for damage control."

"Amen to that." Bane paused by the marble water fountain. "You know, if this whole thing is targeted at me, some sick revenge thing, then I'm responsible for two—"

"Bullshit!" Arm roared it so loud, civil servants froze in mid-stride and looked in their direction. Arm frowned, his forehead scrunching into deep furrows. "Just you cool your jets, bro. No sense in taking blame for someone else's acts. That's just plain dumb-ass dumb."

Bane rolled his neck to work out the sharp tension pain. "Sorry. I've just got a Hix-ache." He popped another pill.

"Don't you let him get to you. You know how to handle him."

"He's smarter than he looks. That's the problem."

Arm leaned close. "You're not telling all, bro. I know you."

Bane didn't know how to tell his best friend what he tried never to think about? Suze, crumpled in the snow, tossed like garbage in the drift. Only days after. . .

"Spill, bro."

Bane closed his eyes. "Hix—" He didn't know how to say it. He rarely thought about it. "I . . . I once suspected Hix in my wife's murder."

Arm said nothing.

"I told Burlington PD about my suspicions. We ran it down. He had an alibi. So it was settled. He had dinner with Senator Stephens that night."

Arm leaned back, his almond-green eyes piercing and angry. "But that doesn't make sense, bro. He's Bureau. Why'd you suspect him—besides that he's an asshole?"

"Long story. Damn, Arm, I don't like to talk about this."

"It's been twelve years, bro. Let me have it."

Bane hid a frown. "Let's just say I was away a lot."

"Okay."

"I was testifying at all the trials for Hayden. And—Hix made a pass at Suze."

Arm's voice echoed off the studio set walls. "I'll ring his scrawny neck." He slipped into a whisper. "Suze didn't—she wouldn't. He's a creep."

Bane closed his eyes. No way he was going to cry. "No. No. Suze told me about it. That's how I know. He visited her, while I was away, pretended to console her. Then made a not-too-subtle pass. She slapped him."

Arm laughed. "Good for her. I can see that! That's what she'd do."

Bane smiled in spite of himself. Arm had actually been worried Suze might have slept with twiggy Agent Hix. "And I confronted the worm. I slugged him, but—you don't need all the details. There was a reprimand on my record over it. Broke his nose."

"So you suspected Hix because she rejected him?"

Bane nodded.

"But he had an alibi. So let it rest."

Bane nodded again.

"You're never going to forgive him?"

Bane shook his head.

Suze had been killed two weeks later. Bane saw her only twice in those precious two weeks between their fight and her homicide. His last real memory of Suze was the fight over Hix. They made up, made love, but he still smarted from it when Super Bowl Sunday arrived, black Sunday, the cursed day when Suze met her end.

Arm rested his hand on Bane's shoulder. "I'm staying here. If I have to take a holiday or leave of absence, fine. I'm staying on. Count on it, brother." When Bane said nothing, he added, "Now, let's go have it on with your father-in-law."

Chapter 19

······································

January 24, 1:03 pm
Green River, Vermont

The Bureau helicopter swept south past Mason Place, into the snow-covered hills of horse country. They flew over the valleys where some of the rich and famous of New York had their most private Vermont estates—flatlanders, as the Green Mountain Boys called them. The pilot hovered over the Mancuso farm while Bane and Arm looked down.

"That's a chunk of real estate," Bane's voice crackled in the headsets. "Got to be a thousand acres."

Miles of white fences separated vast stretches of pasture dotted with horses. The estate followed the winding Green River, a perfect painter's landscape of the Green Mountain State, now blanketed in soothing monotone white.

They landed at Mancuso's private airstrip where a craggy-faced man in late middle life met them at the tarmac. "Gentlemen. I am Angelo Manetti."

Bane shook his hand. "Manetti?"

"Yes. Elvio was my brother."

"I see." *Was.* The second victim at Mason Place, Jackson Reid was an alias for Elvio Manetti, the crime family enforcer, although it had not been disclosed to the press.

Bane could read nothing on his elder brother's face. "I am sorry."

"Thank you." Angelo's voice was flat and emotionless. He studied Arm. "You must be Agent Saulnier."

Arm nodded.

"You're a big guy." He said it so coolly that Bane could almost hear the subtext, *Size doesn't matter in my world, gentlemen, remember that.*

"Please leave your side arms here, at your helicopter." He spoke very good English in a deep voice, although a slight hesitation and deliberate slowness of his speech implied it was not his first language.

"FBI rules," Arm said, brusquely. "Can't do that, sir."

"This is private property. You have no warrant. You are here solely at our invitation and I am responsible for Mr. Mancuso's safety." He looked up at Arm, and though he was nearly twelve inches shorter, his fierceness made it clear he was not intimidated.

Arm folded his arms across his expansive chest. "Ain't happening."

Bane took a deep breath. He knew how stubborn Arm could be. "My Daddy-in-law wouldn't hurt me, right Manetti?"

Both Arm and Manetti laughed, then Arm surprised even Bane by pulling his piece and throwing it on the seat of the chopper. "Fine. Don't need a gun, anyway." Bane placed his .38 snub beside Arm's big cannon.

"I have to pat you down," Angelo said, glaring up at Arm.

Arm smiled. "Just don't get too intimate."

"Why? Closet gay?" Manetti smiled.

"Would explain a lot of things," Arm said. "Like why I feel like putting you face down, butt up, on the snow."

"Hey, I do the jokes," Bane said. "Arm, really, I want you to stay here."

"No, bro."

"Yes. Daddy-in-law won't like meeting you."

"I'll keep the chopper warmed up. Be careful."

Bane smiled. "Daddy won't hurt me, Arm."

Bane and Manetti walked down a plowed roadway, between two long paddocks. Both pastures were crowded with thoroughbreds despite deep snow, most munching on alfalfa and timothy hay in round metal mangers. One horse watched the visitors with a wary eye, following them along the fence.

"Heaven's Gate, one of our promising yearlings," Angelo said.

The bay colt snorted at them, blasting white steam out of his flared nostrils. Angelo pulled a carrot from his pocket. Heaven's Gate danced up to the fence. He backed for a moment, looking at Bane with wide eyes and flattened ears. Then he snatched the carrot from Angelo's hand. He pulled off his glove and caressed the muzzle. "Good boy."

"I thought you mafia types cut off horses heads," Bane said, staring hard at Angelo "Put them in people's beds."

Angelo stared at him like he was mad. "You got a death wish?"

Bane moved closer. "Can we talk? About your brother?"

"I'd rather not." Angelo cupped his arm around the horses long neck and pressed his face close. In that gesture, Bane saw Angelo's sadness.

"It's important. If we are to find your brother's killer."

"I take care of my own, Detective Bane."

"Hey, I'm family."

"Screw you, Bane." Angelo tussled the yearling's mane then continued walking towards the barn.

The walk to the main yard was a long one. Trainers worked with horses out in the cold winter air, taking advantage of the break in the weather. Both the outdoor and indoor tracks were busy with green fillies and colts. As they walked down the roadway, they passed half a dozen magnificent horses in various states of warm-up or cool-down.

He led them to the fence of a plowed outdoor track. "Here we are, gentlemen."

Mancuso walked a mare around a cool-down track. Standing next to the seventeen-hand horse, Mancuso was shorter than Bane remembered, somewhat stooped with age. He was unmistakably the unsmiling man who refused to attend Bane's wedding, but now topped with a steel-grey mop of hair, his black eyes framed by bushy white eyebrows.

"Alban Bane. I hoped never to see you again." Mancuso, a man who could have Bane erased with a single word, walked to the fence and stared at him. His face went beyond neutral. "Except, perhaps, at your funeral."

"I'm hoping it will be me at your funeral, Mancuso."

Mancuso smiled. "Have you found my daughter's killer yet, Alban?"

Bane concentrated on staying cool though he wanted to slam this man's face into the oak fence boards. "No. You?"

"No. So, what do we have to talk about?"

"I don't know. Your granddaughters, maybe?"

Mancuso's smile widened. "How is Jen-Jen?"

"She prefers Jay. She's fine. Asks about you a lot."

"Oh? What do you tell her?"

"That you're too busy breaking legs and killing people to see her."

A single grey eyebrow lifted. "*I don't kill people.*"

"Forgot. Your minions."

"Yeah. People like Al Smith."

"I always liked the name." Bane smiled. His alias from the Bureau days. "Original, yes? Smith."

"You never used to be this sarcastic."

"Oh, fifteen years of serial killers, mobsters and losing a wife can do that to you."

"How about spending the rest of your life in a wheelchair?"

"It'd be okay if it was one of those nifty motorized jobs. I'd install an ipod and be happy."

"You have changed. Death wish."

Bane shrugged.

"And Maggie?"

"She's dating boys."

"You watch those boys, Bane."

"I try. I guess I'll be chasing them off in my electric wheelchair."

Mancuso laughed. "I like you better this way, Alban."

Bane followed him through a long barn. Bane had only ever seen barns like this in Kentucky. Plush arm chairs lined the planked walkway, and there were salons and observation galleries between the big stalls. It was more a house than a barn. Well-dressed men and women sat in sofas studying shining horses and sipping martinis. On the south end they passed an indoor arena with a full-sized track and a glass-enclosed gallery worthy of a racetrack.

"We need to talk to you about Elvio Manetti." Bane paused at a stack of hay. He leaned back against the bales with his hand behind him and pulled free a clump of alfalfa hay.

Mancuso said, "If you want hay, you can have as much as you want."

Bane thrust the hay into his pocket. "Then you won't be minding if I borrow this." He pulled a loop of twine off a hook and coiled it into his pocket.

"Your first victim was tied with twine." Mancuso was expressionless.

"You are well informed," Bane said.

"Always." Mancuso's riding boots tapped. "Well, about Elvio, shouldn't you be talking to his brother Angelo?"

"He seemed indifferent to my request," Bane said.

"As am I, Alban," Mancuso said.

"I doubt you are indifferent."

"I hope I haven't wasted your time."

"Mancuso, forget our differences. We may have a copycat serial killer on the loose in Vermont."

"Dreadful. Just terrible." His voice was flat.

"There will be new victims," Bane said.

"How sad." He continued walking.

"A killer like this destroyed our lives, Mancuso."

"A killer like this? You don't know anything about my daughter's killer. You don't know if it was one of my rivals—"

"You know how hard it is to talk to the families."

"—one of your enemies—"

"I have enemies? Oh dear."

"—a random maniac—"

"Not random."

"—or someone who just hated you."

"That's my theory. But there are so many."

"I'm still thinking about wheelchairs, Alban."

"I know you are."

"Do you know why I haven't?"

"Because you think I'll find who killed our precious Susan."

"Right."

"Damn hard to do from a wheelchair."

"Right."

"What makes you think I can after twelve years?"

"Because you're stubborn, Alban. And I know you loved her. If I thought otherwise, you'd be worm food."

"Wow. I never heard anyone speak in clichés. Neato."

"I'm reconsidering my decision."

Bane opened his tartan vest. "No Kevlar. Fire away."

"Suicidal?"

"You think it takes me twelve years to get around to suicide?"

"I think you love your daughters. I love my granddaughters. I think you might still find out who killed my daughter. Those are the only reasons I don't add you to my manure pile. And why you don't off yourself."

"There you go, then. Do you know, Daddy-in-law, that Tyler Hayden had a deathbed confession?"

"It wasn't in the news."

Bane took a long breath. Verbally fencing with Mancuso was worse than he imagined. "Which news? Your network or the public one."

"Either."

Bane told Mancuso about Hayden's deathbed confession.

Mancuso stared at Bane for a long time. His face mottled red. His breathing accelerated. For a moment, Bane was sure Angelo Manetti would be called to chop of their fingers, one by one.

"So, it *was* your fault."

Bane nodded. "Not family wars. Not rivals of yours. My enemies."

"I should—" Mancuso let out a long breath. "I won't. I knew it, really. I knew it all this time."

"I did, too."

"But you've eliminated all the people who might hate you?"

"And some who loved me."

"People love you?"

"Now who's sarcastic?"

"A lot of people must hate you."

"Yes. Including you."

"I'll pretend you didn't say that."

"I eliminated you the first year."

"So where does this leave us?"

"With too many coincidences. A Daddy-in-law mafioso who sends an enforcer to the set of a reality show owned by a man who wants me dead. The enforcer's dead. A serial killer who knows something about all this, but is 'worm food' himself, now, and who is linked—more coincidence, I don't think so—to this same show, and to you, somehow. An apparent revenge against Bane? Maybe. I could say the same of my wife—your daughter. Another coincidence. Hmm. A pattern, here."

"You're something, Bane. You weren't this fearless when I knew you."

"Back then, I had something to live for."

"So now what?"

"Now, I start over. Assume it's all linked in one big mess."

"Then, go. Do it."

"Thanks for your blessing. It's not what I came for, though."

"Manetti?"

"Manetti."

"Fine. I'll tell you. Off the record."

"Of course. Always with you, Daddy-in-law."

"Truth is—"

"Ah, the truth. A whimsical concept."

Mancuso shook his head. "Truth is, I've been watching the Chows for years. I suspect them."

"In Susan's murder?"

"And you didn't?"

"A little. I don't think they're that mad."

"I do."

"So, you partner with them."

"Every chance I get. On condition my men are part of any deal."

"Well, mystery solved, then."

"Be serious."

"No, really. It helps. Who else have you planted?"

"You know I can't tell you."

"I hoped."

They walked again. They stepped out into the sun in a wide paddock filled with fillies and colts. The young horses crowded around Mancuso searching for treats and for the first time Bane saw him smile. "God's country up here," Mancuso said.

"You believe in God?"

Mancuso crossed himself.

"Funny. And here I thought you believed *you* were God."

"My enemies think I'm the devil. No. Just an old man with lots of enemies, money and houses."

"I was surprised to discover you lived in my state."

"Wasn't aware it was *your* state." Mancuso smiled. "Green River's my favorite house."

Bane pressed his lips together. "I can see why. Beautiful here. But Suze never mentioned it. You bought this after we married?"

"Shortly after. It was to be hers one day. Now, it will be my grand-daughters. My dying wish."

"You're dying?"

"We're all dying, Bane. But I'm further along the road than some."

"How wise and full of shit. Old Scottish saying, 'We're all dying and we're all lying.'"

"That's a Sicilian saying."

"Right now, you're lying. You leave my daughters out of your world. They have no use for all this."

"It's in my will. What they do with it is up to them. Sell it, give the money to charity."

"Nice." Bane worked on controlling his temper.

Mancuso stopped suddenly. He turned. His face revealed nothing. "Bane, the only time I ever want to see you again, is if you have news that you have my daughter's killer."

"And then?"

"And then, I want you to bring him to me. For justice."

"And if I don't?"

"A meaningless question, Bane. In that case, I find you."

They glared at each other, Bane acutely aware of his empty holster. The weapon lay on the helicopter seat. He knew Mancuso had erased more than one law enforcement agent in his bloody career.

"I want you to leave. Before it is too late for you to leave."

"Back to wheelchairs again?"

"We understand each other." Mancuso's forehead creased.

"I'm so touched."

"Shut up, Bane. I blame you for Susan's death. I do. But I want her killer. It's the only reason I can stand here, right now, wanting to have you—well, let's leave it at that. Bring me her killer. Bring me Manetti's killer. We'll call it even, then. Goodbye, Alban."

Bane started to follow, but Angelo appeared out of nowhere and blocked the path, his gun a visible bulge under his jacket.

"One more question?"

Mancuso kept walking.

Bane stepped closer to Angelo and put on his fiercest scowl. "I'll ask you, then."

Angelo turned and walked back through the long barn. "Ask."

"Finger capping is an old Sicilian method, isn't it?"

Angelo's pace didn't break. "In the movies."

Bane jogged to catch up. "Your brother was finger capped."

Angelo stopped again by the chopper as the rotors wound up. When he turned his eyes were fierce. Bane had surprised him with that news. All pretence of politeness was gone. "You should leave, now."

"I want to find your brother's killer."

Angelo pointed at the helicopter. The compressors already howled as the rotors reached a high spin.

"Is your family involved in a war?"

"You have quite the imagination, Detective."

"Just tell me what you know," Bane yelled.

"There are always wars."

"That's a yes?"

Angelo shrugged. "I don't need your help with my family." He folded his arms. "You should think of your own."

Bane said, "Is that a threat?"

Angelo turned and marched back down the hill.

Chapter 20

....

January 24, 5:03 pm

Burlington, Vermont

Arm swept Bane's daughters into his arms as if they were rag dolls and kissed them both. "There's my favorite girls!" Mags hung all over his biceps, a little too clingy and in awe.

Bane began to relax, enjoying the girls' laughter. The smell of lasagna wafted through the house.

They were about to serve dinner when the phone rang.

As Mags and Jay laughed at one of Arm's jokes, Bane took the call at the kitchen table. Caller ID indicated Kip's cell phone. "What's up, Kipster?" Bane glanced at his watch. Seven o'clock. She should be home by now.

Kip sounded tired. "Couple new developments," she said. "I caught Eddie Kim rifling through Reid's—I mean Manetti's—room."

He sat up in the chair. "Cool. His phony accent drop?"

"Not yet." She was silent for a moment, as Arm and his daughters roared with laughter. "You having a party without me?"

"Just dinner. Sorry."

"Lucky bastard."

"So, you take a can opener to our chef, yet?"

"Uh-uh. I've just cuffed him."

"Force feed him American food for two hours. He'll break." In the background, Bane heard Kim, "*Just looking. Only looking is all. No use to keeping me.*"

"Long night," Kip said, sighing. "How was the governor?"

"Shouted a lot."

"Mancuso?"

"Awesome. Threatened to stretch my testicles. Thinks he's the Godfather or God, not sure which."

"He is, isn't he?"

"Well—yes. You must be tired. Why not put chef in lockup for eight hours? Get home."

She laughed. "I might do that. We're still in Manetti's room—"

Bane heard Eddie Kim's anxious voice in the background: *"No arrest me. No, no, no. Have work to do!"*

"Be quiet, Mr. Kim," Kip snapped.

Bane smiled. "Want me back? I can hop a chopper."

"No. I'll fly him in to you."

"Kim say anything at all?"

"He's admitted stealing stuff to sell on the black market. Looking for mementos of the victims to sell on Ebay. He confessed he smuggled out the tapes of the cast. Made a bundle selling tapes of *Haunted Survivor* contestants bonking each other." Kip laughed.

"Aha. He produces porn reality TV." Bane said. "Good work, Kipster."

Bane thought about returning to Mason Place, but he was hours away, so he enjoyed a cozy, cheerful dinner by the wood-burning kitchen stove. Mags' lasagna filled him with warmth. His daughters radiated a happy glow he hadn't seen for months. He didn't mention Grandpa Mancuso.

Arm had a way of making everyone relax and remember what was important in life. Laughter, food, good times, friends. After dinner they moved to the living room, where Arm had the girls opening up about boyfriends Bane didn't know they had.

Mags jumped to her feet, laughing at one of Arm's jokes. "The news! You'll be on!" She snatched the remote. "We've been watching you guys every night. Dad, you're all they talk about at school."

Bane felt a flush of warmth. *Dad.* Mags never called him that. *Landlord* most of the time, *Father* if she was mad, but never *Dad*—not since she was eleven.

Mags clicked on the news, a national channel.

The murders at *Haunted Survivor* were the top story. "Another development in the *Haunted Survivor Killer* case," said the newscaster.

The broadcast cut to Bane's interview with Kenji in the billiards room of Mason Place.

Bane sighed. "I guess I shouldn't be surprised."

On the bottom right corner of the screen was the network logo and flashing words: *Breaking News, courtesy of Real TV.* "We go now to Zoë Okiko, host of the Real TV hit show, *Haunted Survivor.*"

"Everyone's a liar," Bane said. Abbey Chase lied about the cameras, and though he wasn't surprised, he felt profoundly disappointed. She cared only about ratings and television and sponsors. The last vapors of his Abbey Chase illusion evaporated.

Jay lunged forward on the floor only three feet from the big screen. "Oh, Pops, you got juicy close to Kenji! Is he as gorgeous in real life?"

Bane sighed. "Oh ya. So gorgeous I'm thinking about swinging gay."

Jay and Mags laughed.

He heard his own voice on the television speakers: "Maybe I'm a racist, like you're friend says." They cut Kenji's reply.

Great. More Bane bashing to come.

"You said that?" Before Bane could answer, the broadcast replayed it in a comical loop: "I'm a racist. . . I'm a racist. . ."

"Give it a break, Abbey," Bane said.

The news cut to a long, shaky zoom shot of the garbage barn, scene of the second crime. A sultry overdubbed voice narrated, "Sadly, there's been a second homicide on the set of Real TV's hit show, *Haunted Survivor.*" Vaguely. through the fogged window, Bane saw the lumpy silhouette of the second victim, a shape amongst the refuse. Not enough to give television audiences nightmares, but sufficient to make it clear they were seeing a body.

"That settles it. Chase spends a week in lockup," Bane said. "You girls—out!" Mags and Jen didn't move.

The camera swiveled. Kip ran towards the cameraman, shouting, "Get the hell out of here—" The rest was bleeped and the scene became a muddle of jarring images as Kip chased the cameraman to the house.

The scene cut to Real TV's Zoë Okiko, the diminutive but sensuous Native American host of *Haunted Survivor.* Her raven hair cascaded over delicate shoulders, glittering in carefully placed studio lights.

"I am reporting live from the set of *Haunted Survivor* in a special feature report. This breaking news is courtesy of Real TV." Projected behind her were quick cuts of dramatic footage: a helicopter-shot image that revealed troopers with flashlights, dozens of SUVs and a long zoom shot of Bane at the barn entrance.

"Detective Alban Bane, best known for his dramatic capture of the notorious *Vampire Killer*, Tyler Hayden, fourteen years ago, has been too busy to respond to requests for interviews. Our killer, however, has been less reluctant. This is important breaking news."

The superimposed Breaking News logo flashed red. "This network has received an anonymous note hinting at future *carnage*." She exaggerated the word, and a long shot—a repeat of the shaky camera shot of the second crime scene—emphasized her grim meaning. A shot of victim number one followed, pixilated to hide gore, but graphic nevertheless.

"Christ," Arm said. "My Lord Almighty."

Arm and Bane rose in one motion; Bane snatched the remote from Mag's hands, turning up the volume.

Zoë licked her full lips. When she continued her voice was low and sultry. "I quote from the letter." The camera cut to an image of a letter, written on three-folded fine linen stationery, unsigned, printed from a laser printer. "*My Dearest Detective Bane*," she read.

"He's writing to you!" Arm said.

"At least I have one fan." His finger hovered over the off button on the remote.

Zoë read on. "*You have played The Game admirably so far. I have watched with great interest. Clearly, you are a worthy player. . .*"

"You were right, bro. You're the target!"

Bane glanced back at his daughters, cowering on the couch. "I hate it when I'm right. I hate it when I'm wrong, too. Can't win."

Zoë continued: "*Your play is perhaps too much 'according to Hoyle.' Your moves are slow, Detective. One of the disadvantages of living by rules, I suppose.*"

Bane closed his eyes, listening, trying to hear the perpetrator's voice, instead of TV star Zoë Okiko. Stilted. Formal. The language almost too constructed.

"Since I will be stepping up the pace, I implore you to ignore your rules and procedures."

Bane opened his eyes. Zoë looked directly at the camera as it dollied in for a tight shot.

"Are you listening, Detective Bane?" Zoë read from the letter again. *"I will give you every opportunity to make countermoves, but you must be somewhat more adroit. Ignore the rules, to win the Game. If you can. Kind regards, The Gamester."*

The Game. *Welcome to The Game.* Now he had named himself: *The Gamester. Oh Lord Almighty, a psychopathic overachiever out for revenge or sport.* Bane knew psychopaths were often driven by super egos. According to popular myth, Jack the Ripper had churned out a stream of taunting letters to investigators, most of them phony. One of the letters, felt genuine by authorities, ended with *"Catch me when you can."* The Ripper letters started a nasty trend, with serial killers emulating "Jack" by sending cheeky dares to reporters and police.

This *Gamester* fit the profile of an organized serial psychopath, not a bit afraid that the note might provide valuable evidence. Arrogant. The killer challenging Bane to find him. It didn't seem natural—as if it was all a Hollywood production with actors playing at being psychopaths.

"Maybe this whole thing is some elaborate, sick, reality show."

"You mean, killings and all?" Arm stared at Bane.

"Why not? Who says Hollywood executives can't be psychopaths?"

Zoë's commentary interrupted them. "We at Real TV can only hope Detective Bane is up to this challenge. Surely we must wonder at this point."

Her picture dissolved to a video shot of Alban Bane taken fourteen years ago. An idealistic FBI agent, short hair, no baseball cap, trim and muscular. In the clip, Bane shouted at someone, looking for all the world like a drill sergeant in the face of a recruit. The camera pulled back to reveal that he was yelling at sensationalist reporter Hugh King, leaning into his face, hands holding his shirt, ready to knock out his teeth.

"Join us for a special broadcast, tomorrow at eight PM Eastern Time, profiling the deaths at Mason Place on the set of *Haunted Survivor.* We will have extensive coverage of the controversial Alban Bane, including the unsolved case of his murdered wife. Please join us."

The broadcast went back to the news desk, and on to other stories.

Bane turned off the television. He stepped back to his daughters, hugged them both, one arm around each, heard them sniff, pushed their heads into his shoulders.

"It's a prank. Just TV hype—a Real TV publicity grab." Except Bane knew, from the language of the note, that it wasn't fiction, that this new note was similar to the first note. And he knew his daughters would be watching Real TV, tomorrow night, as the show revealed crime scene photos of their mother, lying in the snow. Unless he stopped it.

Mags and Jay cried, even hugged Arm for a while, and then they all sat on the couch until nearly midnight. They didn't speak, though there was much to say.

Later, after Mags and Jay finally went to their beds, Bane sat beside Arm and said in low voice, "Real TV has to be stopped." He was already thinking of ways to make Abbey Chase's life miserable.

"Freedom of the damn press," Arm whispered. "America. Gotta love it." He went to the bar, and poured two stiff Johnny Walkers on ice. They clinked glasses.

Bane put down his glass, without drinking. "I think this Gamester's right about one thing."

"What?"

"Maybe we have to stop following the rules." He looked at Arm. "Show of hands. Who's for dropping all the rules?"

Arm and Bane held up their hands.

"We bad."

Chapter 21

· ·

January 24, 6:46 pm

Jackson Reid's Room, Mason Place

Nah Yoon pulled at the cold metal cuffs on his thick wrists and watched the dark-haired beauty snap her phone closed. Beautiful, this detective with her too-big gun and her yum-yum breasts.

Not now, Lady Policeman, he thought. *Not now.*

He tugged again at the handcuffs. "I no speakee," he said. Pretending ignorance had always been Yoon's power tool, the Eddie Kim persona that allowed him to survive in America. He had come here on a snake head's promises of a country paved in gold, the land of the free and greedy where the police were not terrorists but protectors. For over ten years, his Kim persona had kept him safe from the authorities, together with a perfectly forged green card and passport.

"Sit down, Mr. Kim," she said, and she gestured at the bed. She closed the door and Yoon felt trapped. His heart rate climbed, his eyes darting around and looking for escape.

"I no speakee." He remained standing and waited for her to make a mistake, to lower her guard long enough for him to run. He couldn't let her have his fingerprints, because then she would know, they would all know. This beautiful, tall policewoman with the yum-yum breasts would know all his dirty secrets, and he would be in leg cuffs and sent back to North Korea before the next sunset to face a firing squad, or worse.

"Why are you here, Mr. Kim? In Jackson Reid's room?"

"I not say." He rattled the cuffs. "Too tight. Too tight."

Sweet Buddha, I despise playing the fool, he thought. But he had nothing else. This woman police was no fool, and she was strong, and armed. He had felt her steel-hard muscles as she spun him in an arm lock and snapped on the cuffs. Her quick Tae Kwon Do moves when she arrested him had made it clear that he could not better her in a fair fight.

"Mr. Kim. Just tell me why you are here."

"I lookee for somethings. See?"

She sighed, and in that small gesture he heard her exhaustion, and his hope. He saw it in her eyes. This house wore on her, just as it did on him. Haunted. He felt the ghosts in this very room. The ghosts were everywhere here. "You said that already, Mr. Kim. Not very helpful."

You surprised me, Lady Policemans, he thought. *I couldn't think of better.* He realized she wasn't really a white woman. Her dark skin was richer and more beautiful, like a stunning upper caste lady from Delhi, and though she wore men's clothes, she was all woman. Yoon felt oddly aroused, handcuffed by this raven-haired, dark-skinned goddess. Lie? Tell a partial truth? Yoon wasn't sure what would be best, but he was certain this policewoman wouldn't believe anything he said now.

He gauged the distance to the door, but she was blocking the way, her hand hovering near the grip of her gun. He could never get past her. He used peripheral vision and memory, trying to recall anything that might be used as a weapon, but there was only a pile of books, the bed and the old lamp. Not even a window to break in this basement room. He was trapped, and it was hopeless.

"All right. I will tell the truth."

She folded her arms over her wonderful bosoms. *Sweet Buddha, just let me feel those,* he thought, and he almost laughed.

"Your English has improved."

"Yes. I am sorry," he said and smiled. His smile was his best feature, and it made him cute—so his wife had told him all those years ago.

Then, he had second thoughts. No, not the whole truth. She wouldn't believe him, and he couldn't prove anything. Jackson Reid might be a blackmailer—part of the Mancuso family, the group who took over Yoon's debt to the snake head—but if this policewoman found out it meant instant deportation. If he could lay on the charm and tell half the truth, he might be able to claim asylum, although any claim for refugee status would be destroyed if the police knew about his unwilling ties to the Mancuso family.

It was too complicated to explain, and no one would believe his grim story about snake heads, about how they had promised him a new life in America, made him endure months in the hold of a rusting ship with only white rice and water as he and other refugees grew sicker and sicker. Snake heads took his life savings plus most of his income in America in exchange for silence—a poor trade just to escape the horrors of home. She wouldn't understand the years of extorting him, breaking his arm with a hammer, and how he had fled in desperation to the Italian families for protection, only to become their virtual bonded slave. Yoon was used to people abusing him. He must have earned evil karma in a previous life because he had never enjoyed good fortune in this one. He had learned that the police were the last ones he should bring his troubles to.

Partial truth, then. "I am an illegal. It is... if I... I go to my own country, I will be executed."

"For what?"

"I..." She wasn't stupid. She wasn't going to accept a lie. Not now.

"Yes?" Her face became hard, less beautiful.

He felt his own heat, the flush of anger. Unable to stop himself, he shouted, "I... killed the man who... he raped and killed my wife. Okay? He..."

Her eyes widened. Fear? She was concerned for him, touched by his story? A police lady?

Then she was going for her gun. *She's going to shoot me. She's no different than any policeman.*

He heard the sound, the whoosh of old sliders, felt the cold draft. One of the passage doors had opened, one of the secret ways, and someone was behind him. He quivered, hesitated a moment, before diving sideways towards the bed.

Something struck him hard, and his breath whooshed. Sharp pain shot through his spine, paralyzing him. A burst of heat radiated out from his neck.

She yelled, "Don't move!" but he fell and heard no more.

Chapter 22

· ·

January 25, 9:53 am
Carriage House, Mason Place

No more rules. No more by the book.

So far, it wasn't working. Ten minutes of Bane intimidation on the sound stage—the very set where Zoë broadcast her lies the previous night—had resulted in no new information from the pro-wrestler look-alike Real TV Director.

William Kent lunged at Bane again, his soccer ball face inches away. "What are you implying? Damn it, I'm a busy man! I've got a show to run."

Bane recoiled. "If you're going to get cozy, at least wash your teeth."

"Step back please, Mr. Kent," Arm said.

William Kent was imposing in every way. Bane suspected the pro-wrestler persona was deliberate, just as pidgin was Eddie Kim's defense. Abbey Chase used her sexuality, her dominatrix persona. Hollywood. They must have thought him a fool.

"This is *my* goddam operation," Kent shouted again. His breath was hot and sour, the bitter wind of a coffee addict.

"And it's *my* crime scene."

"Meaning?"

"Meaning, we can shut *you* down," Arm said, towering over even the immense director.

"Which I've more or less decided to do," Bane added.

"Your governor would never allow it." Kent wavered for the first time, his voice dropping a full octave.

"Well, try to run a show with you, Abbey Chase, Zoë and half of your contestants in my jail," Bane said, his anger rising with the mention of the governor.

"You're bluffing."

"If I am, I'm damn good at it." Bane smiled. He jangled his handcuffs.

"Not sure if these will fit your fat wrists, but I'm game to try."

The director turned and crossed the set. It was constructed in the old carriage house of the mansion, a high-raftered building that was larger than Bane's entire house. The garage was now a set, a sound-insulated studio dedicated to the rising star Zoë Okiko, hostess of Real TV's number one show, *Haunted Survivor.*

Bane folded his arms, waiting.

Kent returned, eyes fierce, a forced smile on his face. "I don't see how this can help you." He handed Bane the note Zoë read on the air the previous night.

"Let's start again."

"Detective Bane, if you don't mind I am getting the set ready for Zoë's next segment."

"I'm in no hurry." Arm moved in behind Kent. "Here's what you will do. You will cease broadcast of details of this case, or I'll shut you down. Simple as that."

"You can't give me orders!" He stepped forward, his hands in fists.

Arm pressed close behind him, as solid as a stone wall.

"I can. I will." Bane wagged his finger at him, as if he were a naughty child. "Abbey Chase already broke one promise. I may charge her. You will not be as stupid, will you, Mr. Kent?"

He swiveled sideways, his head turning back and forth so that he could keep both Arm and Bane in view. "I— Fine! But I can't control what the news broadcasts."

Bane lifted his shoulders in a slow shrug. "I promise you something. As sure as you eat super-sized french fries, I will throw you in jail for obstruction if the news picks up any more Real TV film. And, if Zoë broadcasts her report about my *wife*—or runs crime scene photos of my wife's body—I'll make sure you resist arrest."

"I wouldn't resist arrest."

"I say you would. And just to show you how sincere I am, read this." Bane handed Kent the arrest report he had pre-written dated tomorrow's date.

Kent snatched the triplicate form. His eyes darted back and forth.

"William Kent, when informed of his arrest, attempted to flee. Detective Alban Bane, badge 878389, pursued. In the ensuing struggle, Kent's right wrist was broken—" He dropped his right arm.

"See, I can do Real TV, too."

"You wouldn't."

Bane laughed. "Arm, would I?"

"Oh, yes."

Kent's voice sank to a husky whisper. "Now, you look here. You have no right."

Arm moved in so fast Bane hardly saw the movement. He bent Kent's arm down and back, turned him, and snapped on a pair of handcuffs before the flustered man knew what was happening. "How's that feel, Mr. Director? Bet they pinch a bit?"

"What are you doing?" He tried to lift his arms and dropped them with a grunt, his wrists cuffed behind him.

"Just trying them on," Arm said. "Go ahead. Run."

"No."

"Do it."

Bane smiled at Arm's little melodrama. "There are several things you can be charged with already, Mr. Kent. Obstruction. Interference with an investigation. Assault of an officer—"

"I never assaulted no one!"

"You could. I say you will. All carry substantial mandatory jail time."

William Kent tugged at the cuffs. "Okay. All right! I won't. We won't even mention your damn wife."

"Add slander to the charges," Bane said.

"Just take them off!" He struggled in the cuffs, bruising his wrists.

Bane nodded at Arm, who released the man. Kent rubbed his arms and scowled at both of them.

"We understand each other?" Bane pulled his own cuffs off his belt and twirled them on an index finger.

"Perfectly." He was still heaving, his face flushed. "Damn butt-hole Vermonters," he grumbled as he stomped out of the studio, not looking back. "Never should have come to this hole."

After he slammed the door Bane said, "I think you'd make a great Mancuso enforcer."

"I'm enjoying this. Let's do more."

Bane glanced at his watch. Where was Kip? He tried phoning her again. No answer.

Kip needed rest, and he wouldn't bother her. He could find out about Eddie Kim later. Besides, two K-9 units arrived that morning and were already searching the house.

He scanned the set and stepped onto the seamless background, where Zoë hosted the show, then stood in front of an aerial photograph of Mason Place.

"What's up?" Arm stood beside him.

Bane pointed at the north wing. "This wing is not renovated, so far."

"Yeah, so?"

"Well—we searched it. Many times."

"Yup."

Bane stared at the lofty ceilings, soaring over the second floor. "There's got to be attics up there."

"You searched the attics, didn't you?"

"Sure, but I don't remember any access or stairs to an attic in the *north* wing." He felt a moment of hope. An unsearched area of the house. Bane snatched his two-way. "K-9 three, come back, this is Bane."

After a moment of static, they heard, "Trooper Fordor, sir."

"Take the dogs and search the north wing again. You're looking for access to the attic."

"Understood."

Bane clipped the radio onto his belt. "Probably nothing." His satellite phone vibrated and he snatched it out of his pocket. "Bane."

"Hello, Alban. It's Susan Lee."

The San Francisco detective sounded out of breath. Car horns blared in the background. "Hi Susan. How's your case?"

"I followed your suggestion."

Bane squatted on his heels, digging in his bag for a note pad. "You attended Hayden's wake?"

"You wouldn't believe this, Bane. Okay, long story short. I'm there now. There's hundreds of freaks here."

"You've got backup?"

"Of course."

"Be careful, Susan."

"I will. Look, I'll make this fast. I knew you'd want to hear this right away." He waited as he heard shouts, then her voice, "Get out of the way!" Then, more voices.

"Sounds like a crowd."

"Damn Goths. Hayden had himself a fan club." She sounded out of breath. "Okay, I've only got a minute. I just heard the bulletin before I came down here. Chow's wife, Leslie, she was killed. Same M.O. as you've got going up there, is what I think."

"I heard."

"Three guards and two dogs killed too."

"Unfortunately Stephen Chow escaped?"

She laughed. "I see someone. Got to go!"

"Susan, are you there?" He glanced at the signal light and realized the connection was dropped. He stood up and glanced at Arm. "A detective investigating Laura Kincaid's homicide. She's following a lead."

Bane didn't call her back. If she was on a suspect the last thing she needed was for her cell phone to ring. But he rang in to SFPD. They would tell him nothing.

Bane had never met Detective Susan Lee, but her sharp mind and enthusiasm made her likeable.

"Why do you look like your favorite goldfish just died?"

Arm's eyes looked mournful. "Didn't get a chance to tell you, bro. Director Harris called. Got to head back."

"I understand."

"As detective in charge, you *could* ask for me to be assigned as a consultant," Arm said, his voice soft and tinged only with the slightest southern warmth.

"I already did. My office will call your office."

"Make you a bet?"

"The Governor's going to call?"

"Not that he'll call. Fifty bucks he calls in an hour."

"I say half an hour."

"Bet."

Bane sighed. "You know, I thought I'd left all this behind. All this sick shit."

"No such thing, bro. It follows you."

"I know." Bane thought of Suze, murdered in their own backyard. Even in his beautiful Vermont, violence could be found. Brutal, senseless violence.

The sun was at noon as they left the carriage house and headed back to the main mansion. Bane shaded his eyes against the sparkling glare reflecting on fresh snow.

Arm paused. "I sure know why you like it so much here, bro."

"I like this place as much as Mexico in a heat wave."

"I mean Vermont."

He stopped, his boot half lifted from crusty snow. "What's that? Wolves? You have wolves up here?"

"Sure we have wolves." Bane listened and heard only the wind whistling through pines. Then he heard it too. Baying. "No, those aren't wolves. That's our canine unit. They've found something!"

They ran for the house entrance, burst past the sentry station and ran up the hall, following the sound of the dogs. Bane registered, in passing, that the guard was a new man, armed with a gun and wearing the ribbon of the Green Mountain Boys on his uniform. He made a mental note to follow up on the security company and the Green Mountain Boys as they ran through the west wing, and veered into the unused north wing.

They barreled past startled crew and more Real TV security guards with green ribbons. They got lost a couple of times in the maze of hallways and came to a few dead ends.

Then he heard the German Shepherds again, louder now, wildly howling.

At a ruined wall, recently demolished with sledge hammers where

Bane's men had broken down the drywall to access the sealed up wing, they saw flashlights ahead.

They stepped into an old kitchen at the end of a long hall. The dogs chomped and snarled; one snapped at Bane as he slid to a stop.

Two Real TV camera crews were filming the chaos.

"Take those cameras away."

"We're wireless and broadcasting," snapped back one cameraman.

"Get them out of here."

The cameraman didn't move.

"Smash the camera," Bane ordered.

A trooper did just that. The other camera filmed the event.

"Oh, great. We're on the news again." Bane walked past the smashed camera, pausing only to stomp on an unbroken lens.

Young trooper Fordor, head of the canine unit, pointed up, jerking his thumb to the high ceiling. "They're trained to howl like this only when they smell blood."

"Bane, I'll boost you." Arm cupped his hands for Bane. Bane rapped on the ceiling. A third and fourth camera crew arrived and filmed Bane pounding on the ceiling.

"Hollow," Bane said. "Get sledge hammers and ladders. Use them on those cameras first. Then smash a hole up here."

The camera crews backed off, moved outside the broken wall, but continued filming from a distance.

Bane's men climbed aluminum ladders and hammered through the roof, leaving a gaping hole. He looked up into the darkness, his neck prickling as if some voodoo master had pricked a doll of his image. "Attic. With no entrance."

They all pointed their lights up and the darkness swallowed their flashlights.

"Has to be an entrance, bro. We just haven't found it."

Bane drew his .38. "I'll go."

"I'm right behind you," Arm whispered, his Glock drawn.

"You think the rafters will hold you, big guy?"

He shook his head. "I'm coming."

Bane climbed the ladder and slowed near the top. He stepped up one more rung, but kept his head tucked. Then, with a sudden uncoiling of his back and neck, Bane levered off the ladder into the attic, swinging flashlight and revolver up in a quick three-sixty. He felt Arm's hand steady his leg.

Bane did a slower scan. Nothing. Darkness.

The attic was vast. He did another full circle, squatting at the ragged mouth of their makeshift opening as Arm joined him. They squatted, back-to-back, guns lowered.

Below them, the dogs continued to howl.

The floor was old, nailed to the cross-beams decades ago. It was painted white. The paint was flaking.

This is it, he thought. *Our second victim was held here, a prisoner awaiting execution.*

Bane's shirt clung to his back, wet with chilling sweat.

"Be careful, Arm." Bane didn't explain and didn't have to.

A jumble of old wooden crates and boxes lay in a heap near a wall. As Bane crabbed across the floor towards them, his hand slid in something thick and sticky. He swung the light up.

A lump rose in his throat. Couldn't swallow.

A headless corpse, hanging by the ankles from the rafters.

Under the empty shoulders was a tub of blood. The body had been drained in the trademark style of Tyler Hayden, the Vampire Killer.

"Hell," Bane said, trying to fight a tumble of images. Sixteen Hayden victims flashed through his mind.

"That's for sure, for sure. Hell, Hayden-style," Arm said. His light rotated through the rafters, then froze. A second body.

Two headless corpses. *Two.*

"The copycat technique is better researched this time," Bane said, keeping his voice even, unemotional, as he fought the torrent of memories. "Bastard's copying Hayden." The words came hard.

Bane stood up, his face almost directly level with the shoulders of one of the victims. He panned the light across the naked bodies. A man. A woman. No head, no fingertips, wedding fingers cut off.

A serial perp. He had left the FBI to get away from this horror, and here it was, staring him right in the face once again.

Bane knelt under the first victim, a female. A single drop of blood fell into a bucket.

"Arm. The female vic is recent."

In one motion they scanned the attic with flashlights.

Chapter 23

····································

January 25, 1:12 pm
Chinatown, San Francisco

Detective Susan Lee climbed the steep hill, winding between busy pedestrians and vegetable stands, her diminutive body blending with the busy near-noon crowd. She was invisible here, at home and familiar with the sights, smells and sounds of Chinatown. Car horns blared, mingling with the rumble of haggling pedestrians. The sumptuous aroma of dim sum and spicy noodles blended with the rotting stench of rain-soaked garbage.

The suspect had not noticed her, and continued to stride up the hill, walking in the rain gutter to avoid the flow of bartering merchants, gawking tourists and local residents.

At a noodle shop, her stomach rumbled as she thought of shrimp balls and rice noodles. Or just hot tea.

The hard rain beat down, washing the busy streets, a sheet of fast flowing water skimming the sidewalk without deterring the shoppers. Hundreds of bobbing umbrellas made navigation treacherous. Lee, with her turned up collar and slicked black hair, and the tall blond suspect, marched on without them.

She snatched the two-way from her belt. "Frankie, where are you?"

Static answered her.

"Frankie, what's your twenty?"

"Stuck in traffic." She heard the blare of horns. "I've dispatched a uniform unit."

"Negative on the uniform," Lee snapped. "You'll spook him." She had worked too hard to lose him now.

She had followed him since Hayden's much publicized funeral which she'd attended in hopes of seeing associates of Laura Kincaid—Hayden's lawyer. The crowd at the funeral home had surprised her, though she expected the reporters and the television crews. What shocked her was the fans—Goths, vampire cultists, punkers—and hundreds of women, tears spilling down their faces as they stood in line to view the body of Tyler Hayden. Lee watched them bend over the coffin to touch his cheek.

There was no one over twenty-five in the long lineup, except the television correspondents and the journalists, and her own men, peppered too obviously through the crowd.

The man she was following had arrived late. He wore tight jeans that revealed hard muscles. His shirt was open, revealing a wide hairless chest. Brilliant blue eyes stared out of a face that was just too handsome—and, for some reason, vaguely familiar.

Lee skirted the back of the line and slid up the alley, entering the funeral home from the back, through the preparation studios reeking of embalming fluid, and into the chapel where Hayden lay.

The blond man bent over the open coffin. He stroked Hayden's cheek, smiled, then bent and kissed the monster.

That was when she saw it. The visitor could have been Hayden's brother. Younger, blonder, even more muscular, but the resemblance was unmistakable. He was no fan. He was a blood relative.

Her heart beat too fast, and sweat broke on her face. She pulled back into the preparation room and radioed for backup. When she slid back into the gallery, the man was gone. She ran to the street, pushing through the snarling Goths and vamp cultists. She was barely five foot-two, but she stepped on toes and kneed groins until she emerged on the street.

He turned a corner and ran up the street just as the rain began to fall.

Now she was alone, without backup.

Damn. She couldn't take him down without backup. The man was a giant. He had a look on his too-handsome face that told her he wouldn't hesitate to kill, even a cop. Yet she was disappointed too. She had hoped to find the "cowboy" mentioned by witnesses at Golden Gate Park.

He was a hard man to follow, in spite of his height. He strode fast, and Lee had to jog to keep up. Twice he had lost her, but then—almost too conveniently—she found him again.

"I need backup, now," she snapped into her radio. "Dispatch, no lights or sirens, and no uniforms."

"Stand by," answered a harried dispatcher.

"Now, damn it!"

"What's your twenty?"

Susan Lee gave her position and cursed her partner Frankie Parkinson. The fool had lost them.

Detective Lee loosened her .38, hand resting near the grip.

She wouldn't lose the blond Hayden clone, but she wasn't about to take him down alone, either. *Just follow, Susan*, she thought. *Don't get near this one.*

The tall man, now drenched with rain, his shirt clinging to a rippling body-builder physique, rounded a corner. He hesitated, glanced back down the hill, and for a moment she felt certain he saw her. The blue eyes, even at that distance, focused on her. She dropped her head, as if scanning for puddles, and turned to inspect bok choi on a vegetable stand. The merchant immediately moved forward, but she rolled her eyes right and squinted into the hard, slanting rain.

The man had gone.

She ran now, certain he had spotted her. Sweat stung her eyes. She radioed again for backup, but they reported they were just entering the lion gates at the bottom of the hill.

No choice. She snatched the .38 from the holster, pressing against the cold stone of the corner building. Restaurant patrons stared out the window. She leaned around the corner, just enough to scan, her gun held up and back in case of ambush.

Nothing.

The alley was empty.

She rounded the corner, and ran, lithe and athletic, breath coming in economical chugs, but she didn't reholster her gun, all her instincts on full alert. As hard splats of rain struck her cheek, she blinked away rainwater and sweat.

She stopped, crouching slightly, catching her breath.

As she lifted her radio to report, a voice startled her.

"Are you looking for me?"

Too late, she turned.

Chapter 24

January 25, 1:37 pm
North Wing, Mason Place

The attics connected in a gloomy web of interconnecting crawlways, joining the soaring gables with their massive trusses. Bane left two from Fordor's team as sentries to guard the immediate crime scene until Cross's forensics teams arrived, while the rest of the search team fanned out through the dark, frozen world of cobwebs, mouse droppings and squealing rats. For Bane the excitement was akin to sex. He always felt that way when he felt close to a suspect.

"Getting aroused, bro?" Arm whispered. He knew Bane better than anyone.

Closing in on a perpetrator after a long chase made Bane's heart race. In his hospital room, after the Hayden take-down, Arm asked him why he looked so happy when he could have died. Bane had said something like, "Arm, taking down Hayden is like sex. Hayden almost killed me. Sex almost kills me. I get all trembly. My heart pounds. My temperature rises. My blood pressure goes through my skullcap. I'm leaking body fluids—I know, gross—my muscles tense, adrenalin pumps. I'm a mess, but a good mess. If I die tomorrow, I'm happy. I caught Hayden."

He felt a tremble of that messy excitement now, and Arm knew it. This was the hidden lair of their perp, or perps.

Bane and Arm swung through the north wing loft, and again Bane was amazed at the magnitude of Mordechai Mason's colossal house. His back ached from constant bending in the connecting crawl spaces. He rested on the attic floor boards beside Arm, both feeling the strain, their breath heavy from exertion, their heat sending clouds of vapor into the frigid air. But he felt good. He was close.

Foreplay.

Bane had bumped his head enough times that he learned to stumble along in a permanent stoop, keeping his flashlight tilted up to spot the rafters and the spider webs. Arm trained his light low on the loose old floorboards and rusty nails.

Excited voices came to them from adjoining attics. Bane and Arm turned instantly towards the sound. It sounded like Fordor's voice, "Don't move, mister." Then Sergeant Silva's voice, "Stop!"

They scrambled through a low annex attic. They had cornered a suspect.

Bane heard, "Freeze! I mean it! Your last warning, mister." The shouts that followed told Bane that the suspect had not listened. He scrambled as fast as he could, his .38 in hand, Arm right behind him with his drawn nine-millimeter.

Bane splashed light down the long crawl way. Eyes. A dark face. The man burst into the annex, knocking Bane backwards.

Bane spun on his heel, gun grip coming down on the suspect's back.

A satisfying thunk. Not quite sex, but it felt good.

The man fell hard. Arm was on him, bringing his elbow down. The suspect grunted, stayed down. Arm snapped the cuffs in an expert move, and rolled him over.

Ahmed! His eyes were wide, and his lip curled back in a snarl.

Sergeant Silva barreled through the corridor, a big semi-automatic in hand, and Bane caught the momentary look of disappointment on his face as he saw Arm standing over the cuffed suspect like a triumphant hunter.

"Damn," Silva said, holstering his cannon.

Bane smiled. Silva was an aroused hunter too, and didn't like losing the prey to someone else. "Sarge, why don't you take Ahmed down to our makeshift headquarters," Bane said. "Read him his rights."

"You have the right to remain silent. . ." Silva Mirandized Ahmed as he dragged him away.

Bane nodded at Fordor, peering in through the low corridor. "Continue the search, Fordor. We still have missing persons."

Fordor puckered his lips and scowled, but nodded.

"You're bleeding there, bro," Arm said, with a flashing white smile that mocked and charmed at the same time.

"A scratch." Bane lifted his hand. He hadn't felt it. The rising climax of the take-down pumped too much adrenalin to feel pain.

He stared. A long gash crossed his hand, probably from one of the protruding nails, already ugly with long ropes of blood.

"Needs stitches," Arm said.

Bane frowned. "You want that madman Skillman to stitch me? I'd rather bleed out."

"I can do it," Arm offered. "Just find me a needle and thread."

"With your big, clumsy hands?"

Arm laughed. "Don't be a baby. You're worse than my son."

They climbed down the ladder and back to the west wing, then wound their way down to the clinic. Arm teased Bane about this being his golden chance to interview Skillman, to catch him off guard.

"Yeah, he'll torture me if I bring this up now."

Arm smiled. "Then I'm waiting right here, outside the clinic door."

Skillman looked up as Bane entered. His eyes darted past the detective, taking in big Arm standing at the door, then back at Bane. He seemed wired for power, as if he was energized by either too much caffeine or drugs from his own locked dispensary. He swept back his straight-up blond Afro and seemed wary, as if he expected a trap.

Bane showed his gash.

"*Sweet,*" Skillman said.

The nutty doctor slammed the door on Arm and pushed Bane to a gurney. He examined the wound, yanking back Bane's sleeve with hard fingers that spoke more of battlefields than bedside manners. "Better do tetanus." He held up a syringe. "A precaution."

Now was not the time to ask him tough questions. The doctor jabbed too enthusiastically and as Bane jumped he saw the flicker of a smile on the sadistic doctor's face.

"We'll have to stitch that cut. Stitch, stitch, sew, sew." He laughed.

"A Band-Aid is good enough."

"I don't think so." To prove it, Skillman tugged on the loose skin. Bane almost yelped out loud.

The skin had pulled back, revealing a jagged tear in the muscle tissue.

It looked worse than it felt, until Skillman probed with unkind fingers. Bane winced as the suture needle jabbed through his skin.

Skillman smiled as he held up the needle in forceps, pink with Bane's blood.

"You seem a little rough for a surgeon." Bane grunted as the doctor plunged it in again and a spasm of pain shot up his arm. "Is that battle-field technique?"

Skillman giggled like a girl.

He dabbed Bane's arm with hydrogen peroxide and bandaged the wound—one little cut that suddenly felt like a Hayden slash.

"Thank you." Bane pretended to leave, then turned back and said, "Say, Doc."

Skillman turned, his eyes revealing annoyance, but a half-smile on his face. "Yes, Detective?"

"I noticed you once lived in Miami. From your background file."

Skillman tossed the dressing in a sterile dispenser bin. "Yes, yes. For sure. For sure. So?"

Bane winced. "About fourteen years ago, wasn't it?"

"About right. Why?"

Oh nothing, Bane thought. *Just that Tyler Hayden killed one of your patients around then.* "You must have had a lot of patients."

"Detective, are you playing games with me?"

"You like games?"

"You asked me that last time."

"And you like them fine."

"Like them fine, just fine."

"About your patients?"

"I see. You have access to my patient records."

Bane nodded. "I bribed an insurance company."

Skillman sighed, pushing back the tray of surgical instruments.

"One of your patients was Sammy Franks?"

Skillman's eyes rolled in an expression that Bane, the dad, knew meant, *Oh come on*, but he also noticed a slight quiver of the man's lip. "This game's no fun."

Bane waved his bandaged hand. "Tell me about it."

His eyes darted around as if looking for an escape. "Well, of course. I suppose I know what you are talking about. . ."

"Your patient Sammy Franks was a victim of Tyler Hayden."

His head bounced up and down with that strange Skillman energy. "Just awful." His lips pressed together into an ugly scowl. "What a strange coincidence that I would meet you all these years later."

"Strange coincidence? If I piled up all the Hayden coincidences here at Abbey Chase's hall of horrors in one place, I'd have one mighty mountain of bullshit."

Skillman looked puzzled.

"Sorry, I'm tired. I'll think of a better analogy later."

Skillman bounced from the ball of one foot to the other and back. "I don't understand."

"Just explain to me, Doc, how it is you happened to be the doctor of one of Hayden's victims, then fourteen years later, you happen to be the doctor at a remote site with Hayden copycat killings?"

Skillman stared at him. "What am I supposed to say?"

"Supposed to say? Just lie to me. Everyone else does."

Skillman giggled. "You want me to lie?"

"Why not?"

"I don't have to."

"Why?"

"Patient privilege."

"Sammy's dead. Hayden's dead. By any chance was Hayden your patient? That I can find out."

"No."

"Did you know him?"

Skillman hesitated just long enough to tell Bane the truth. *Yes.* But, of course, he said, "No."

"So, you were lovers? Friends? You got off on watching him torture kids? What was it?"

"I think you should leave my clinic."

"We can discuss this in *my* clinic if you want. Cozy place with bad coffee, bars, hard chairs, and you shit in a crapper in the corner of your holding cell while twenty or so locked up felons watch."

Skillman giggled.

"Turn you on, Doc?"

Skillman turned away, his face flushed.

"Why'd you apply here? At Abbey Chase's madhouse."

"Change of scenery."

"You like all this, don't you? I saw how you got aroused when you sewed me up. You into kink? You watch on the monitors, don't you, live as Carlo screws Kelly. Right? You like the screaming?"

Skillman turned. He grinned.

"You gonna arrest me? Arrest me, arrest me, throw me in jail!" He laughed.

Bane stared. Mad as Hayden. "Not yet. But I'm watching you."

Bane left the tiny clinic. Arm struggled not to laugh as he saw his face. "Aw, you poor boy."

Bane patted his inflamed wound. "I felt better before I went into that hall of horrors." He told Arm about Skillman. "Needs deeper checking, Arm."

"I'm on it."

They found Cross on the crime scene, so Bane decided to interrogate Ahmed, to confront him before he lawyered-up and while he was still crashing from his adrenal highs.

Before they entered their converted headquarters in Real TV's Brain Room, Bane dug for his phone and dialed Kip again. No answer. "That's strange, Arm. I'm not getting Kip. It's going to her voice mail on the first ring."

Before he could put away his phone, it rang.

He answered, "Bane."

"This is Captain Lawrence Oxford. I'm Detective Lee's supervisor."

"Yes, sir," Bane said, instantly alert.

"There's been an incident." The captain's voice was deep, he sounded stressed and angry. "Detective Lee was shot. With her own gun."

Bane closed his eyes, his lips pressing together into a thin, hard line.

"I'm sorry, sir," he said. He leaned against the wall.

Detective Susan Lee's captain continued, but Bane only half listened. "She was my best detective. Backup arrived too late to help her."

"Do you know—" Bane's voice caught with unexpected emotion. He had never met Detective Lee—Susan—but he felt somehow close to her. "Captain Oxford, she pursued without backup?"

"She was always—" Oxford cleared his throat. "She didn't wait for backup."

"I'm sorry, Captain. I didn't mean—" *Oh screw this*, he thought. *Screw this, and screw Hayden and to hell with diplomacy and games.* "Do you have a suspect?"

"No identity, and no one in custody. We're screening the witnesses on the street. They just remember a tall white man. Blond, blue eyes. Big."

"Was he wearing a cowboy hat?"

Oxford sighed. "No. That's the first thing we canvassed witnesses on—considering, the Laura Kincaid homicide."

"I see, sir." He took a long breath, trying to visualize what Susan Lee must have looked like. She had a childlike voice that somehow made her seem small in stature, but a fierce enthusiasm.

Bane looked at the phone trace on his screen, to ensure the call originated from SFPD. He noted Captain Oxford's encrypted ID. Then, he did the only thing he could do, sharing everything he knew with Susan's captain. The captain listened without interruption as Bane explained his thoughts on Laura Kincaid, the cowboy, the suspicion that the cases in the east and west were linked, and even that he had suggested Lee attend Hayden's funeral. And he shared the status of his own case.

Again the captain cleared his throat. "I was going to ask you to fly in. But clearly that's not possible."

"Not right now. Though I would like to."

"Bane, I know of you. I know about your work on Hayden. That was good work."

Bane said nothing.

"It seems we have a conspiracy here. Multiple perps."

"There's no doubt about that now, sir."

"Will you share everything you learn?"

"Without hesitation, sir." Bane took a breath, held it. "Did Susan have family?"

"A mother who lived with her. And a son."

"She was a mother?"

"Husband left her."

God. "For what it's worth, will you convey my condolences?"

"Detective, this isn't your fault."

Anything Bane could say would seem shallow.

"Every detective in my department has this as a priority. They all liked Susan."

Bane nodded. "Will you let me know when the—when the funeral is scheduled."

"Yes, I will. Good luck out there."

Bane closed his phone. The least he could do was to fly back for her funeral.

The headache came stabbing back. He popped more aspirin.

Susan Lee. He had sent her to her death.

Arm stared at Bane in silence. Bane knew he understood most of what happened, even just hearing one side of the conversation.

Ahmed glared at Bane as they entered the Real TV Brain Room, his handsome face dark and canny. He had the start of a shiner. Next to him was a blond man, also dark-skinned, but blue-eyed in the classical California beach boy way.

The blond man stood up, elegant in a pressed suit. He didn't offer his hand. "Robert Davidson, Real TV council. I was here consulting with Ms. Chase on—let's just say on your intrusive investigation here." Bane knew what the lawyer meant. Abbey was planning a possible injunction to prevent further access to the guests. "Ms. Chase asked me to act as Ahmed's lawyer." He spoke crisply, but the hesitation in his words suggested he was either considering his words, or covering up an old stutter or accent.

"Fine. Sit. And shut up." He spoke to Arm as if Davidson and Ahmed weren't in the room, "Lawyers. Sometimes I think there are more of them than street bums."

Bane sat on the table, close to Ahmed. "You are from Egypt, sir?"

Ahmed said nothing, revealed nothing, his eyes unblinking, his hand held in a prayer-like gesture in front of him on his lap.

The lawyer whispered in Ahmed's ear.

Ahmed nodded.

"Legal immigrant?"

Nothing. Not so much as a flinch, twitch or blink.

Again the lawyer whispered. Again Ahmed nodded.

Bane glanced at Arm, saw his eyebrows lift. *We don't have time for this.*

"Are you aware, sir, that you are on a terrorism task force watch list?" Bane stepped closer to the suspect, focusing on the black expressionless eyes. Nothing. No humor, uncertainty, fear, tension. Nothing. Not bad for a man in handcuffs, just captured for fleeing a crime scene where two bodies still hung from the rafters bleeding into buckets.

Mr. California Lawyer leaned close to Ahmed. They whispered. Bane watched the lawyer's face, hoping for insight. "My client was unaware of this list."

"Does your client know why he might be on a terrorism watch list?"

This time, finally, Ahmed answered for himself. "American racism." His voice was low, filled with hate, very clear and accent free.

"Is that so?" Bane let his voice harden. "Now tell me, Mr. Atwah, what were you doing in that attic?"

Ahmed leaned towards his lawyer.

"Can't think for yourself, Ahmed? You do look a little retarded."

"That's provocative," the lawyer said.

"I hope so."

"And insensitive."

"To whom? Retarded people?"

The lawyer nodded.

Bane scanned the room. "Well, I don't see a lot of retarded people. Except a suspect and his retarded lawyer."

Ahmed's glare would have made most men recoil, eyes that said, *I'd kill you as soon as look at you*, but Bane just smiled at him.

Mr. California Lawyer said calmly, "This interview is over, gentlemen, if you cannot behave."

"Who do you answer to, sir?" Bane stood up, hands in pockets, and smiled at the lawyer. "Mr. Stephen Chow, by any chance?"

The lawyer's tanned features paled. "I'm here to protect the interests of Real TV and all of our contestants. You will limit your questions to my client, please."

"Why?"

"Because I'm not the suspect."

"Everyone's a suspect. You, especially, Mr. Surfer Dude."

"You're rude," the lawyer snapped back.

"Practice."

"Do you have any questions for my client?" The lawyer shouted now, his face scarlet. Ahmed stared at him as if he were a fool.

"A question remains unanswered."

The lawyer nodded at his client.

Ahmed looked away. "It is very boring being the only man of God in this terrible place. I used the passages, at times, to get away from the godless—"

Arm stepped up and shouted in Ahmed's ear, "The secret passages?"

The lawyer frowned. "What is this, gentlemen? Good cop, bad cop?"

Bane smiled at him. "You watch too much television, Mr. Davidson. We're both bad. And Arm's FBI."

Ahmed rocked in the chair and ignored his lawyer. "I was bored. I have no friends among the contestants." His head wagged from side to side in a strange waving motion. "More American racism. Since nine-eleven, any faithful Muslim—"

Bane interrupted, "Oh, spare us. You're not here because you're a faithful Muslim. You're here because you were found in a crime scene with two bodies. It's not just your lawyer who's retarded."

"Bane!" The lawyer bounced to his feet. "I'll have you in front of a disciplinary committee."

"They don't bother with me, anymore."

"Why?"

"Because I call them all kinds of nasty names."

"Then why are you still a cop?"

"Because I'm good." He smiled, and leaned closer to Ahmed. "If you're so faithful, aren't you a hypocrite just for being a contestant?"

Ahmed no longer looked at his lawyer for answers. By engaging him, this was what Bane hoped for. The man's anger would take control, sweeping aside the California lawyer. "This show is a forum. I hope that my religious views are taken seriously by viewers."

Bane laughed. "I've watched the tapes of the shows. They've cut every single religious debate. They cut everything except angry close-ups of you yelling at the others. At Carlo the Catholic. And then scenes of Carlo and the others laughing at you when you leave the room."

Ahmed bowed his head but Bane saw his shoulders stiffen.

"And I think your whole explanation is bogus. You're the type who thrives on conflict. You don't run to the secret passages to escape it."

Ahmed stared at Bane.

Bane pushed harder. "So you're the show's token Muslim. Tokenism designed by Ms. Chase to introduce tension among the contestants."

Bane paced, hands in pockets. "And you just happened to be out for a stroll—to get away from the infidel?"

Ahmed nodded, curt.

Arm leaned close. "You expect us to believe that?" He shouted it, an inch from Ahmed's ear.

Ahmed didn't flinch. "Believe what you will. You Americans always do." He sneered. "Americans think they are the whole world."

Bane stopped pacing. "You are saying you found the bodies, correct?" Ahmed nodded. "So, how do you feel about the bodies you found in the attic? They were white Americans, weren't they? How did you feel about *that?*"

Ahmed blinked, rapidly. Thinking. He was thinking it through. Bane was hinting that he might have believed Ahmed didn't kill them, just asking how he felt about finding them. In a deliberate voice he said, "Sad. Most sad. Then frightened. Very frightened. I heard your men and ran."

His eyes told Bane he was telling the truth. "I believe you."

The anger faded slowly from his handsome face. "You believe me?"

"Yes. You didn't kill them. I know that."

Ahmed seemed startled. "Why?"

Bane pointed at his hands. "The scene was fresh. You had no time to clean. Even with gloves, there'd be splatter."

Arm snorted. "That's not conclusive."

Bane continued to stare at Ahmed's humorless face. "I just want you to help us. I do not suspect you. You don't need surfer boy here to protect you. He can't protect himself."

Ahmed froze then said, "How can I help?"

"Tell us all you know. When you came to the attic, what happened?"

He swayed, closed his eyes as if remembering something, opened them. "I—I went a new direction in the passages I had never gone. It was dark, and cold."

"All the contestants know about the passages?"

Ahmed nodded.

"Go on."

"I was mad. I had fought with Carlo. He is this—sex pervert—it does not matter—we fought, I was angry."

"What did you fight about, Mr. Atwah? Jesus and Mohammed?"

Ahmed gave a quick shake of his head, his eyes darting back and forth. "I. . . he wanted to. . ." Again, he closed his eyes. "We were talking about the—the killings. I thought he was accusing me!" As his voice rose, a slight accent surfaced. "When I confronted him, he told me—he told me he knew who did it."

"Go on."

"He said, it wasn't me. He knew who it was. Not one of us. Not one of the contestants." His voice quickened, and his words ran together. "Not us. But he wouldn't tell me."

"But you know something, don't you?" Bane controlled his tone, trying to keep the excitement out of his voice.

Ahmed half rose out of his chair, then sank back. "I don't know. He—The only time he spoke to an outsider was. . ."

"Yes, go on."

"To the doctor. He went to see the doctor."

Bane took a deep breath. Ahmed, always the calm contestant in all the tapes he had seen—never flinching in the face of snakes and spiders and rats and bloody showers—seemed terrified now. Bane saw it in his eyes. Ahmed spoke the truth, as he knew it.

The doctor. Doctor Skillman, with his wild Afro and his glittering scalpels. Bane would have to talk to Carlo, and then again to Skillman—this time in a proper interrogation format. And he would need to have a straight-up look into Doctor Wingate, too. A breakthrough was close.

"How did you get up to the attic?"

Ahmed slid back in the chair, reclining, half closing his eyes. "I. . . I went further in the passages than ever before, and I worried that I might—it does not matter. I couldn't go back. I needed to be alone. But then. . ."

"Yes?"

His hands were in fists, nails digging into his own palms. "There were screams. Screeching. Terrible. Terrible." The emotion cascaded across his face, breaking like a dam bursting. "There was laughter. Like demon laughter. Horrible." He shook his head, and slumped back in his chair with a thud.

Bane folded his arms. "But we heard no screams." Bane unlocked Ahmed's handcuffs.

"Thank you." Ahmed rubbed his wrists. "Well, they were muffled. As if. . . as if. . ."

"As if they were gagged?"

His forehead creased. "Yes. Yes. That must have been so. They were terrible. They seemed loud to me. Nearby but muffled. Yes."

"Go on. You heard laughter. A man or a woman?"

"A man demon!"

"And the screams. A man or a woman?"

He didn't answer at once. "A woman. It was a woman!"

"What did you do, Mr. Atwah?"

He closed his eyes. His face was pale, and his lip trembled. He relived his own hell. "I have seen death. Oh yes, I have seen death." He shook his head. "This was evil. This man is Satan himself. The shrieking continued. I couldn't move. So much pain. A woman, screaming, crying, screaming, sobbing, pleading—terrible. Terrible."

He covered his face with his hands, and Bane waited until the man's breathing became normal. "Did you run?"

Ahmed pulled away his hands, and Bane saw no tears. "I ran. I ran. But I ran in a circle. There was something dark and terrible. Chasing me. I heard its breathing—"

"Go on."

"It wasn't human. I heard its laugh. I heard it grunting. I heard it breathing. I ran. I thought I would die. I thought—"

"Then what?"

"Then, then—well, it stopped. I heard your dogs. And the demon disappeared."

"Mr. Atwah. We will have more questions. But this is all for now."

The lawyer, pale now, stood up. "You are not holding him? Charging him?"

Bane shook his head. "I will require more of your time, Mr. Atwah. Sergeant Silva here will take you to the doctor—" Bane saw the fear in Ahmed's face, and added, "Our doctor in Burlington. Would that be all right?" No one asked why Bane wanted a doctor's exam. It would be important, in future, if Ahmed was to testify. It was also an excuse. A way to get Ahmed out of Mason Place where he could be protected, without the Real TV lawyer.

Ahmed nodded, a rapid bouncing of his head. Clearly Ahmed couldn't wait to get out of Mason Place.

"You understand it means you will be out of your—contest. The show."

Ahmed spat on Abbey Chase's brushed steel table. "I have had enough of this."

Bane nodded at Silva, who escorted Ahmed from the room. After the lawyer had left, Bane leaned on the table, head bowed, thinking, puzzling it out. "Ahmed—wrong place, wrong time, but a witness. And he had heard the voice of our perpetrator. We will need that."

Bane turned to face Arm. "It wasn't him."

Arm frowned, looking doubtful.

"They'll luminol his clothing to be sure he has no blood on him."

Arm said nothing.

"But he was lying."

Arm snorted. "Of course." He crossed his gnarly arms.

The detective smiled. "He lied about the screams of the victims. And about being chased."

"Okay, Einstein, spill."

"Under stress, witnesses almost always use pronouns and personalization to express what is real. The truth. Like when he said, 'I ran. But I ran in circles.' That was true. But he lied when he said, 'There was something terrible.' No personal pronoun. He made that up."

"Oh come on, Bane. That's a stretch."

"No, it's SCAN. Don't you use SCAN? You're FBI."

"I took the course. Nothing but psycho-babble. Waste of six hundred presidents."

"You're wrong. Under stress, it plays out that way. Like when he talked about Carlo. He said, 'He practically accused me.' That was the truth. But when he mentioned the screams—the screams you and I didn't hear—he said, 'There were screams.' Not, 'I heard screams.' I don't know why, but he's hiding something."

"But you don't think he's our perp?"

"No. He's scared. Piss-your-pants scared. But not our perp. I'll have Kip interview Ahmed in Burlington." Bane dialed Kip's sat phone. No answer again. This just wasn't like her. Though her husband Pete would shout, Bane called their house phone.

Her husband answered. "Yes?"

"Pete, it's Bane."

"Christ, Bane, when are you sending Justine home?"

Bane clenched the side of the table. "What do you mean?" The phone trembled in his other hand, against his ear.

"Bane, she's a mother. She needs to see her son once in awhile. She's not even answering the damn phone."

"She didn't come home?"

Silence. A queasy feeling churned through his stomach. Finally, "Bane, what are you saying? Are you telling me—?" A dish dropped, shattering on the floor.

"Pete? You there? Pete?"

"What have you done, Bane?" Bane held the phone away from his ear. "You damn cops. What have you done?" Pleading, anger, fear—it was all in his voice.

Oh Christ Almighty. Bane closed his eyes, squeezing the phone. "Pete, I'm sure it's nothing." *The hell it's nothing. The hell it is.*

"Bane, you find Justine, and find her now!"

The bodies in the attic. A man. A woman. Naked. Featureless. *Dear God.*

"Bane, where's my wife?"

Bane couldn't speak. He felt a shiver, cold and icy. Heard Pete's pleading voice again. Bane closed his eyes. *No more,* he thought.

Chapter 25

....

January 25, 5:33 pm

The Caves, Vermont

Justine Kipfer continued to work the ropes.

Her wrists were bruised and raw, but the pain focused her efforts. That and thoughts of Jeremy and Pete. She couldn't leave them. She couldn't bear the thought that they might know how she suffered.

When she awoke, hours ago, blinded by the pain, Eddie Kim was beside her. They were trussed up, ankles and wrists, but she was able to kick him with her bare feet and shake him with her tied hands. He remained unconscious, and she was worried for him. She worked on in silence, not daring to yell out or shout for help.

She could smell bat guano, a harsh ammonia stench.

When she had first opened her eyes she had stared up at the brown bats, some of them stirring and angry. It took her a moment to realize she was in a cave, lit by the flickering flame of lanterns. Her many years of spelunking had taught her that the bats hibernated in the winter, and if they were awoken by careless spelunkers, they would likely die, unable to sustain themselves until the insects of spring. They're going to die, these bats. She was going to die. Eddie Kim was going to die.

Soon, she forgot the bats, as her rational mind wrapped comforting hands around her hysteria. She sat up, dizzy, bruised, but alive.

Magnificent stalagmites swept up to meet elegant stalactites, forming delicate pillars of calcium carbonate. As her eyes adjusted, she saw a vein of good Vermont granite on the opposite cavern wall.

The cold was worse than the pain of her bruises and the cuts in her wrist. She was naked, as was Eddie Kim, and soon the chill would make the pain irrelevant. Although the caves were not too cold, they were damp and the rock felt cool.

The unspeakable had happened. Captured by the very predators she hunted. She had been stripped of her clothes. She closed her eyes, controlling her breathing. The fear of rape was worse than any death.

She opened her eyes, relieved. No. She had not been raped. Attacked. Stripped of her personality with her clothes. Dignity torn away. Shamed forever. But she had not been raped.

Yet.

She didn't remember how she had been taken from Mason Place. Only that there had been two men. Two men she didn't know. None of the contestants, none of the crew, none of the suspects. Strangers.

She had not expected the sudden entrance. The panel had sprung open behind Kim, and two men burst into the tiny room from the dark passage. One clubbed Eddie Kim and the other knocked the gun from her hand in a quick, skilled kick. Then, the shock of pain as he struck her chin.

She had rolled to her feet, ignoring the pain, and took him down with a flailing roundhouse kick. She heard the satisfying rush of air out of his lungs as he crashed into the bookcase. But the other man was on her, and something hard came down on her head.

Her memories from that moment were sporadic. A feeling of motion. Of being rolled. The stench of garbage. Ropes binding her hands and legs, and the cloth in her mouth. The kitchen garbage bins? Struggling against her ropes.

He had injected her, too, silencing her muffled cries.

How did she get to a cave? Did Mason's tunnels connect to some cave system in the nearby mountains? She would have to discover that later.

She shivered, cold. Her flesh on the cold rock no longer felt the bruises or the pain. There had been pain, but that had faded to a lack of feeling. The chill in the caves kept her alert but shivering, and she forced herself to squirm and thrash like a landed trout, to keep warm, to prevent succumbing to total delirium. She kept her fingers and toes moving to force the flow of blood.

Kip forced herself not to think of Pete or Jeremy. At first, keeping their faces in her thoughts had made her fight harder, but soon it drained her will. Seeing their sad faces and teary eyes paralyzed her, then made her thrash on the stone floor in wasted bursts of madness.

"Eddie," she whispered. She kicked him again.

He grunted. This time he stirred.

She waited for him to stop struggling, trying vainly to shut him up, worried they might return. But he yelled and lashed and squirmed with an energy that reassured her. He was far from dead.

As he calmed, he began to ramble, and Kip knew it was his hysteria. "What you do? What you do to me? Let me go! Let me go! I American! I have rights!"

He thought the police had captured him, were torturing him, and in a moment of lucidity she understood that in his birth country the police did that sort of thing. "Eddie Kim. Listen to me!" She kicked him again. "Listen to me, now!"

He stopped squirming. "I have rights!"

"This is not an arrest, Eddie Kim," she whispered, trying to make him understand. "Eddie, I'm tied up too!"

She heard his sharp intake of breath. He rolled over, his eyes wide with fear as he looked at her. She turned away, trying to hide her breasts, embarrassed to see his penis flop over in her direction. "What happening? What you do?"

"Eddie, stop looking at me!" She felt stupid saying it. Her nakedness was the last of their worries, but he was staring, eyes locked on the rise of her breasts. "They could come back any moment." He still stared, damn it. "Eddie, listen. Turn around. Use your fingers to untie me. Do you understand? Eddie!"

With a last quick look at her nipples, he turned. "I understand. Yes, I understand." .

To give him credit, he was calmer than she had been when she awoke. She understood immediately that he had endured hardship and pain in his native country. As he rolled over, she saw scars on his muscular back, probably laid into his flesh with a whip, crisscrossing his brown flesh in ugly white welts. The scars were years old.

She rolled over and pressed closer. His fingers grabbed her cheeks. "Hey! Let me do it. Eddie. I'll do it!"

She worked on his ropes with her fingers. She had no idea why they took the handcuffs off Eddie, but right now all that mattered was getting him untied. She couldn't see, but she felt the knot, a bulging knob of rope that Eddie had pulled too tight in his struggles. She worked the ropes, ignored the pain in her fingers, and focused on making each movement economical. The knot was hard, but she managed to keep a two-finger lock on the bailing twine.

Finally, she worked it loose. She felt the first loop un-kink, and then it was easier. She pulled loop after loop, until finally, Eddie's hands sprung free.

"Now me, Eddie. Hurry. They'll be back soon." Though he didn't appear to be cowardly, she worried he might leave her, desperate that she not arrest him. When he didn't work on her ropes, she said, "Eddie, I'm not going to arrest you. This proves you are innocent. Do you understand?"

She rolled over to face him.

Eddie stood over her.

And beside him, smiling, was their kidnapper.

Chapter 26

January 25, 6:58 pm

Mason Place

Doctor Jonathon Wingate kept his back turned to Bane, watching the troopers with flashlights walking search patterns across the court-yard outside his bay windows.

"What do they expect to find?" the psychiatrist asked mildly.

"Anything," Bane said, his voice level. "Whatever. We're searching every room. Every inch of the valley. More than half of Vermont's state troopers are here. And volunteers from Burlington PD."

"Why just the valley?"

"We're in Mason's passages. We're searching every neighboring farm."

"The proverbial needle in the grass?"

"Haystack."

Wingate turned. His handsome face was drawn, tired. "And what do you expect me to offer? Empty words of hope?"

"For that I go to church."

"You a man of faith, Bane?"

"I believe in God. He doesn't always believe in me."

"That is an admission."

"I don't pray for solutions, Doctor. But I pray. Okay?"

"I am not disapproving, Detective. Just surprised."

"Why?"

"You are a man of many layers, are you not?"

"Whatever that means. There's a difference between stupid faith and enlightened belief, Doctor. I don't believe that if I pray, Kip will appear magically right here in this room. But that doesn't' mean I'm a non-be-liever."

"You believe, but no faith?"

"Exactly."

"You are an odd man, Bane."

"So, I do not pray that you'll help me, Doctor, but I beg you. What do you know that can help me find my partner? You know something."

"I do not know what to say."

"Two more victims. Two people kidnapped. One, my best friend. Which takes priority? Stopping the madness, or your confidentiality rules?"

"You know my awkward position, Detective. I really would like to help. Justine Kipfer is a lovely, lovely woman." He sighed.

"So, your way of saying your rules are more important than my friend? Doctor, statistically some 12,000 patients die each year because of medical doctors following rules from health companies only willing to pay for certain tests; 9,000 homicides go unsolved due to investigative rules; 133,000 criminals take a walk because of court rules that allow clearly guilty people to get off on technicalities. Most of this can be directly linked to assholes who follow rules."

"Oh, dear. You researched all this just to impeach me?"

"No. I use this speech a lot. Especially on my captain. And lawyers."

"You do not believe in rules?"

"No."

"But are you not a rule-enforcer?"

"No. I don't give out speeding tickets. I stop killers." He popped four aspirin.

"I can prescribe something stronger, Detective."

"I like aspirin, the wonder drug."

"It can increase risk for Reye's Syndrome, ulcers, fatty livers, hemorrhaging in the brain or intestines. It is a blood thinner, Detective."

"I'm touched. You care."

"A doctor who cares is unusual?"

"My doctor's a cantankerous old fart."

"I am a people person."

"You're changing the subject again." His hand dove into his bag. He pulled out a small photo album and flipped to pictures of a laughing Justine Kipfer at Bane's last Labor Day barbecue. He thrust the picture in Wingate's face. "Rules are less important than lives, Doctor."

Wingate flinched. "I am very uncomfortable with this, Alban."

"First names?"

"If you expect me to take you into the intimate world of confidences it is better as friends than professionals, no?"

"I suppose."

"Jonathon."

"Jonathon—I promise you, nothing you disclose will ever be revealed in trial."

"By your own admission, everyone lies. Yourself included. Cynical perhaps, but insightful. I am to believe your promise?"

"A promise and a lie are two different things. Friends will lie to each other, but not break a promise, right Jon?"

"Jonathon."

"Okay, not close friends."

Wingate smiled. "It is a sign of denial, that in the circumstances you can still joke."

"And no matter what the circumstances you are still polite."

"I am over-compensating for this uncomfortable situation."

"Politeness is a symptom of lying."

"Sarcasm is a symptom of insecurity."

"Lies are one thing. Lies are natural. Humans have the instincts of the hunter, bred into us over thousands of years. Subterfuge, cheating, traps, all natural hunting tools—these are the precursors of lies. Every successful hunter, every career, every happy marriage—is built on lies."

"Your point?"

"Stop lying to me—friend."

"Have I lied?"

"Lie number one, the day I met you here, you lied about your purpose at San Quentin."

"I did?"

"Lie number two. You've broken patient confidences before."

"I have?"

"In building this show. You can't build these scenarios without knowing what your patients are most afraid of."

"They signed permissions to disclose for the purposes of Real TV."

"Lie number three—"

Wingate held up his hand. "Please. Please spare me the embarrassment." He shook his head. "I still happen to believe these rules have meaning."

"Jonathon. Don't go all law school on me. Lives—not rules."

Wingate smiled. "Fine. No rules. I will help you, as I can."

Bane breathed out, relieved. "Do you believe any of the cast or crew are involved in this?"

"In 'this' what? What is 'this' exactly?"

"We're wasting time."

"No, we are not, Detective. If you do not know what 'this' is, how can you expect to solve your case?" He smiled. "Yes, I listen to the news."

"This seems to be about revenge."

"On you?"

"On me."

"Does it not seem a little too elaborate for a simple game of revenge? Is not that a vain assumption, Alban?"

"Yes."

"What is the simplest explanation of this complex situation?"

"An organized sociopathic killer with a mission."

"That is simple?" Wingate smiled. "Well, then, we should make quite the team. I am the leading expert of sociopathological disorders. You have—how do you say it?—captured? Caught? You have arrested several sociopaths."

"Your point?"

"My point is, it is not that simple. I believe you have indicated you have multiple perpetrators?"

"A conspiracy of sociopaths?"

"Sociopaths do not socialize." His eyebrows lifted. "I must remember that line."

Bane sighed. "I've always found if you want answers, don't ask a psychiatrist."

"I am approaching this as a diagnostician."

"I see. Elimination."

"Exactly. Eliminate everything false. What is left is our answer."

"If a conspiracy, and if revenge-motivated, then I would assume Hayden had friends or family as psychopathic as he was."

"That is possible. Psychotic behavior can be genetically influenced, in some cases, and sociopathology can be learned, even in a familial unit. But I am fairly certain none of the cast or crew are related to your Hayden."

"*My* Hayden." Bane hated the sound of that.

"But, if this is a game, Alban, then could not this apparent revenge motive be subterfuge?"

Bane was grateful for Wingate's calm analysis. With Kip's loss it was difficult for him to think this through on his own without emotions tangling with logic.

"So, what about a simpler conspiracy?" Wingate's eyes half closed.

"What do you mean?"

"Take away the 'of sociopaths.' After all, statistically sociopaths are rare. We all tend to care about our fellow human beings to some degree, no matter how selfish we might be."

"A cult?" Bane massaged his sore neck.

"With a sociopath leader, charismatic, capable of inducing sociopathic behavior in followers?"

"We don't have any little men with funny mustaches running around. Abbey Chase?"

"She's dictatorial, not charismatic."

"The Green Mountain Freedom movement?"

"Yes."

"Are you saying you hear about GMF in your sessions?" It made sense. He just had a hard time visualizing Vermont youth in Nazi armbands. Separation for Vermont? Was that worth killing for? It seemed ludicrous, at least to a sarcastic, mostly sane detective.

Wingate nodded.

"Who?"

"You tell me. You are the big detective."

"Ira?" The stern, prejudiced security guard with his green ribbon pin.

Wingate nodded again.

"I have a watch notice out for him. He didn't show up for work today."

"See, dear friend, you do not need any help from me at all."

"Has any patient mentioned the passages? Mason's tunnels?"

"Certainly. They are a source of anxiety. Ray cannot sleep because of them. Kenji cannot resist exploring them. Carlo has—how do you American's so colorfully put it—quickies? Quickies with Kelly in the dark passages."

"Tell me something useful."

Wingate shrugged. "I do not know what useful means to you. Those passages have doors to every room—"

"Including Jackson Reid's room."

Wingate nodded.

"I have Arm searching his room."

"Door releases are almost always in the underlip of the moulding."

"You know a lot."

"I absorb a lot. The caves, Alban. The caves is what you are looking for."

Bane stared at Wingate. Caves. No one had found caves, but Bane long suspected there must be. Vermont's mountains were famous for limestone caves.

Bane snatched his radio from his belt and started for the door. "We're looking for caves."

"Go to the sub-basements, Alban," Wingate shouted after him.

Bane pressed the talk switch. "Silva's team to the sub-basement." He turned back at the door. "Thank you, Jonathon."

"Gratitude is hard for you, is it not?"

Ten minutes later, Bane met Arm in Jackson Reid's small room.

"Found nothing, bro."

Bane squatted on his heels. White dust. "You see this?"

Arm nodded. "Limestone. The sub-basement's full of it."

"I remember."

Bane pounded on the wall behind the single bed. It seemed solid, no hollow sound. He ran his fingers along the molding.

"I tried all that. Let's go to the sub-basement."

Bane felt a bump. "My wife always said I was a sensitive touch." He heard a faint click. The inner panel slid back on old cables and gears.

A tiny opening, barely wide enough for a man to squeeze through.

"How about that," Arm said.

The glow from Reid's room spilled into the pitch dark tunnel. It was barely wide enough for one person, and so low that Bane would have to bend his head to move in there. Could Arm even lever through that?

I can't go in there. Bane sampled the air. Damp. Musty. *But Justine's in there. Kip.*

Bane fished out his flashlight, swung the beam along the cornice moulding, and found the switch. He clicked it on. Nothing. Arm swung his flashlight up, revealing the dangling light fixture.

"Someone broke the bulbs, bro."

"We're hot on somebody's trail, that's for sure."

"This is a break. We just follow this, maybe we'll find—" What was he going to say? Justine. A body? He shivered.

"I've never seen you like this, bro."

"That's cause I try not to get close to victims."

"Your jokes. Sarcasm. All that. It's your shield. Except it doesn't work for Kip."

"It's easy when you don't give a crap about the victims. Oh, not that I don't give a care, I do, but they're not people I know personally."

"That's why you hardly ever do interviews with victim families?"

"Aye. I let other people hold their hands and cry. If I start having tea with the families I'll be a wreck."

"Like now?"

"Like now."

"Well get over it, bro. Because that's your partner in there."

"Aye. I checked the Detective's manual. There's nothing in there about dealing with a partner snatched by psychos."

Bane fished in his leather bag and pulled out four glow-sticks. After his first experience in the sub-basement, he had loaded up with a pack of six-inch chemical glows and two flashlights. He shoved three glow-sticks into his shirt pocket and one in his pants and handed Arm a handful. They activated the chemicals.

His head brushed the ceiling as they entered the tunnels. Bane froze. He couldn't do it.

You have to, Bane.

He focused on a memory of Kip's face. He could almost hear her voice. "Bane, you're a wuss."

Bane glanced over his shoulder and saw that his big friend was forced to crouch. He glowed blue in the cold, eerie light.

Where are you Kip? We're coming to find you.

The circle of light penetrated only a few yards and his flashlight beam disappeared into inky blankness. *Get on with this, Bane. No more victims! Find Kip now!*

They pushed forward with tentative shuffling steps into the sloping tunnel. Sweat broke immediately. He shivered. He knew it was childish, a fear born of decades-old trauma, but the claustrophobia would not be abolished with a thought.

He pulled the dangling light strings. The bulbs were all broken, the shards of glass crunching under his boots. As they crept forward in the darkness, Bane felt Arm's breath hot on his neck, oddly reassuring. They swept the corridor with flashlights, the beams punching through the darkness outside the ring of glow-sticks. Bane came to a corner. He pressed his back to the near wall and slid around it, exploring with the flashlight first. Dust motes swirled in the flashlight beam. He swung the beam up, looking for lights. Another shattered bulb.

He looked back, past Arm. They could no longer see the entrance. It felt as if they were suspended in space.

He reached for his two-way and called in backup. After Silva acknowledged, he shuffled forward.

"Bro." Arm put his hand on Bane's shoulder. Arm knew all about his claustrophobia. "I can go on alone."

A surge of anger strengthened Bane. Kip needed him. Arm wouldn't go on to face a serial perp alone. Bane focused, pushing aside the phobias of childhood.

The air was musty, still, slightly acrid.

Even with Arm at his back, the smothering claustrophobia pressed Bane. He flattened himself against the cold wall until the feeling passed.

Kip needed him. His partner. His friend. Her son needs her. *Please Justine, hang on. Be all right.*

Something brushed against him and swung to one side. His heart raced. Cobweb. Where the hell were they? He stood for a moment, disoriented.

The close, suffocating feeling returned as the passageway narrowed again and the ceiling closed in. Bane forced his breathing to return to normal and walked on. Behind him Arm grunted, and in the light of the glow-stick he saw that his friend was sideways in the tunnel, barely able to push on through.

Bane lost his footing. Arm grabbed his shirt, pulling him back. Stairs!

"Going down."

The steps were small, only half steps, so narrow that only their heels found footing. There was no rail and they found themselves leaning hard into the lath and plaster walls as they descended. Bane leaned too hard and his hand went through the rotting plaster. He pulled it back, wet and slimy. He shone his light into the hole.

Eyes stared back at him.

"Christ!" Beady rat's eyes. The rat chattered at him.

Arm laughed. "We'll tell stories about this some day, bro,"

They inched down the stairs. At the bottom the floor was limestone. Bane knelt and picked up dust between his sweaty fingers. It felt the same as the dust in Reid's room. He scanned with his light for blood or footprints.

"I think we're in the sub-basement, bud," he said, trying to sound calm.

The tunnel ended at a wall. Bane felt his heart racing. A dead end! But he fought the phobia. His rational mind took control There was a door here. There had to be.

On this side of the tunnel the catches weren't hidden. He pushed the lever and the door slid back.

Bane stepped out. After the confining passageway, the limestone sub-basement felt expansive. He paused to catch his breath. The panic passed.

For ten minutes they searched the maze of basement corridors. All the bulbs were smashed, as in the tunnels. It was time to bring in rein-forcements.

They heard it at the same time.

Groaning hinges, ahead in the darkness. Their flashlights swung, stabbing into the dark. The limestone walls, shattered glass and cobwebs resolved in the light, an eerie blur of monotone shapes. But they saw no one.

A door closed. He glanced back. Arm nodded. He had heard it too.

Bane pressed his back against the clammy stone wall. He paused, letting his heart slow.

They were not alone.

Now there was only the sound of rats squealing. They shuffled along, inching forward. A blind corner slowed them even more. Bane carefully scanned with the light, listened, then peered around the wet stone edge. He squinted into the gloom. Barely visible, an old wooden door. Arm slid along one wall as Bane pushed it open. The hinges squeaked.

Bane stopped again, and slid the safety on his revolver. This time he was sure. They were not alone.

"I got your back, bro," Arm whispered.

Even with Arm pressing, close sweat beaded Bane's forehead. He searched the hall with the beam of light. He released his breath.

A door slammed. Someone ran.

Bane ducked under a low doorway and jogged through the hall, Arm close behind, his head brushing the low ceiling. Bane's foot squashed in something wet. With only sound to guide him, he went in the direction of the slamming door. They paused, listening. Another door opened.

He ran faster, careless of the dark.

The hall bent to the left, disappearing into the gloom. Bane slid along the inside wall and slowed his pace. Footfalls echoed. Distant, regular, but clearly footfalls.

Bane took all the glow-sticks out of his pockets and threw them down the corridor. They tumbled and clattered; one shattered exploding in a snap of sparks and acrid smoke. Three of the others landed twenty feet away.

A hulking shape appeared, a dark shadow dimly washed in blue. The man stepped back.

"Halt! I order you to halt!"

The man was just out of range of the flashlight.

Arm pressed against Bane. Another sound now, perhaps a third person's fast breathing. A cough. Right there, in front of them. Another cough. Closer. But nothing visible in the ring of the glow-sticks or the flashlight beams.

Bane stepped forward. The shape of a large man hulked. He took another step.

His foot slipped, skittered sideways.

The floor sagged under him, then with a sharp crack broke through. "Arm!" His hand scraped smooth stone, and a finger nail tore away as he tried to hold on.

Bane dropped into the darkness.

Chapter 27

· ·

January 25, 10:31 pm

The Kipfer Bungalow, Burlington

Pete stroked Jeremy's hair. Jeremy looked up at him, his breathing shallow, his eyes red from crying.

The last day had aged both Pete and twelve-year-old Jeremy. The stress hardened Jeremy's face, so much like Justine's, into a semblance of what he'd look like as a man. The roundness was gone, the childlike pout had drawn into an adult frown. The change shook Pete profoundly.

Together they watched the twenty-four-hour Real TV network. In between various reality television shows where contestants ate animal parts, spied on loved ones, and posed as multimillionaires, the network broke away to numerous live segments updating the investigation at Mason Place. They broadcast, over and over again, digitally enhanced images of the body in the shed, the police chasing away the cameraman, and clips of Bane and Justine interviewing guests.

Real TV delighted in the carnage, endlessly showing images of the second victim, tossed with the garbage, and cuts to crime-scene photos of Hayden's crimes, with analysts explaining how the *Haunted Survivor* killer was clearly a copycat.

Pete covered Jeremy's eyes, but his son pushed the hand away.

Where are you, Jus? He watched the terrible parade of pictures. How could they broadcast this garbage? Was it even legal?

The doorbell rang.

Pete muted the television.

Someone had come to tell him something.

An odd-looking gray-haired man stood on their porch, hunched with fatigue, it seemed, yet his face alive with amphetamine energy. A flood of lights stunned him blind. Through splayed fingers held in front of his eyes, he made out two videographers on his lawn.

"Go inside, Jeremy."

He pushed his son inside. Jeremy retreated to the couch.

"You're not welcome here," Pete snapped.

"Pete Kipfer? I am Hugh King of *The Crime Times*. Could I have a moment?"

Pete moved to slam the door.

"It's about your wife!"

He held the door open just enough to glare at the gaunt reporter.

"Dad! You're on TV," Jeremy yelled.

Hugh King nodded. "We're live, sir."

Pete closed the door.

"I have news of your wife, sir!" the reporter shouted.

Pete opened the door a crack. "Turn off the cameras. Then I'll talk."

"I can't do that, sir. This is news."

"Get the hell off my property!"

"I can't do that either, sir."

"I'll call the police."

"I think they're all busy."

Pete sucked air through clenched teeth, and held his breath. He didn't open the door wider, but he didn't close it either. He glanced back over his shoulder, and saw himself on the television, his head turned away to reveal only his bald spot. Was that him? In the washed-out video lights, he appeared so slumped over and tired.

"What do you want?" He turned to face the reporter on his verandah. "Is this about—?" He wasn't going to tell them anything. They might be here fishing.

"Sir, just a comment. A reaction."

The reporter was predarory, hungry looking, with his flinty stare and scowl. A sadist, he wanted Pete to suffer. He wanted him to break down on national television. For the news, for ratings.

"The producers of Real TV have received an anonymous videotape. It will be airing in a moment. We'd like your live response, sir."

Pete fought a rush of emotions. Fear. Anger. Desperation. He didn't know what the tape was, he didn't know what he was about to see, but he did know these vultures wouldn't be on his property if it was good news.

The reporter, this Hugh King, stepped closer.

Pete slammed the door, heard the satisfying *thunk*, the yelp of pain. He glanced over his shoulder. Hugh King, on the television, covered his nose with bloody hands.

Pete threw the dead bolt, and ran to the couch. He had to turn off the television before Jeremy saw the broadcast.

Too late.

Jeremy stood in front of the television, his mouth open, his eyes not blinking as he took it in. Pete swept in front of him, blocking his view, and turned at the same time. The Real TV crew, now on his porch, filmed Pete and Jeremy through the living room windows.

Jeremy whimpered. He snatched the remote from his hand, going for the off button.

His eyes locked on the shaky video image on the screen.

Pete pressed Jeremy's face into his chest, forcing his eyes away from the screen, but was unable to press the off button. He could not stop the image. He had to see. *Dear God, he had to see this.*

Justine. Naked. Tied with ropes, lying on a rocky floor, bleeding and bruised, her femininity covered with pixilated filters. She was awake, staring at the man with the shaky video camera, shouting at him. "I'll kill you, bastard."

Pete wanted to turn off the television. Wanted to run to the living room windows and close the curtains. Wanted to grab his shotgun and chase off the Real TV cameramen. But his feet were glued to the floor.

Inset in the television picture was his own face. The image pulled back to reveal Jeremy sobbing, clutched in his arms. In the bottom of the inset box was the word *LIVE*. Across the bottom of the larger, shaky image of Justine—naked, tied up and thrown bruised to the rock—the digital words, *Recorded earlier tonight.*

Pete kept Jeremy's eyes covered, in spite of his struggles to see, but he could not take his own eyes off Justine. She wriggled on the ground, covered in her own sweat and blood.

The camera cut to a live image of a man, hanging upside down. Bold type scrolled across the bottom of the screen:

*WARNING to SENSITIVE VIEWERS! THIS IS BREAKING
NEWS NOT SUITABLE FOR SENSITIVE VIEWERS.*

Pete watched horrified, as the small, muscular Asian man screamed.
His face was filled with terror. There could be no doubt that this was
real. His lips pulled back in a snarl.

The camera zoomed in. The man had no fingertips. Blood dripped
from the fresh wounds. Drip, drip, drip into a bucket of blood. The man
wriggled in the ropes that bound his ankles, turning and spinning like
meat on a spit. Pete felt the pain as if it were his own.

Pete leaned forward and knocked the cable box from the top of the
television. It flew across the room and hit the living room window. Hugh
King stepped back. Too late. The glass showered him. King shrieked and
ran.

Reality television had become Death Television. Torture Cam.

And Justine was next.

Chapter 28

....

January 25, 11:13 pm
Undercroft, Mason Place

Bane hit dark water. He went deep. Ice cold enveloped him. He thrashed, fought to the surface, swallowed foul liquid.

He treaded water and looked up the narrow chute. Arm leaned over the opening, a spectral blue shape floating above, lit by the glow-sticks. "Bro, you alright?" Bane winced as Arm shone the flashlight into his eyes. The light seemed to spin as dizziness took Bane. His cheek burned and his finger throbbed where the nail tore off, but none of that mattered. He was trapped. In the dark.

The wells. Bane had fallen through one of the rotted wood covers.

"Freeze! I'll fire!" Arm's roar sounded muffled and distant. He disappeared and with him the flashlight. Only the dim blue of the glow-sticks lit the small square of the well opening.

Arm came back a moment later and peered down the well with a scowl.

"I'm okay," Bane lied. "Get the bastard!"

Arm gave Bane a thumbs up and disappeared. Darkness. Bane plunged into the dark world of his worst nightmare.

He was alone.

The damn wells. He had seen them on several occasions, mentally warned himself to be careful, told his search crews to be aware of them. The man in the shadows had deliberately lured them into this trap.

He clawed at the stone walls, slimy with algae.

Remain calm.

"You screwed up, Bane," he said, to himself.

An inner voice answered him: *Fine. I won't do it again.*

"We're not getting out of here."

Well, aren't you cheerful? I forgot what a wuss you are.

"It's impossible."

Wuss, wuss, candy-ass.

He touched the slick algae.

He took inventory. Just bruises and cuts. As his eyes adjusted he could see the chute above him, glowing in the cold blue glow-sticks. Barely four feet across, maybe thirty feet deep, roughly hewn out of limestone, now slimy with algae.

The water, reeking like a swamp, splashed his lips. A breeding place for bacteria and insects.

Bane no longer heard Arm.

He's alone, Bane. Get climbing.

"Arm!"

At least he won't have to listen to your stupid one-liners anymore.

He tried to climb, clinging to the crevices and clutching at a crack. His hand slipped on slime and he fell back with a splash. He struck something hard and sharp; pain lanced upwards from his hip. Black fetid water, polluted by decades of rat droppings and insect eggs, swept into his mouth as he sputtered and resurfaced.

If only he had his flashlight. He fumbled for his radio. It slipped from his hands, nearly fell into the water. He turned it on, but after a quick crackle, it died. Treading with one hand he fumbled for more glow-sticks, but his pockets were empty.

Why don't you just wait for rescue?

"Arm's in trouble."

Arm's tough.

"Do you think he'd sit here treading water?"

This is why I didn't waste money on swimming lessons.

"Climbing lessons."

You're talking to yourself.

Bane placed his hands on one wall, palms down, and his feet on the opposite wall, balancing himself like a human arch. With palms pressed flat, fingers bent to clutch tiny cracks and chinks, he pressed with all his strength, the tension of his bent body between the walls sufficient to insect-crawl his way up. He moved, inch by inch, until his feet were just above the water's surface.

He lost his footing and splashed down into the water.

He tried again. Failed again and swallowed more water.

Damn you, Bane, they're counting on you.

This time he concentrated on an image of Kip's face. He even talked to her, mumbling in the darkness. "I'm coming, Kip. I'm going to find you. You just hang on."

Another excruciating effort and the water lay just below him.

He fell again. Started over.

His shoulders and thighs ached. Sharp pain shot through his back and his legs were cramping. Another few inches. Just hold on.

He started to slide, dug in, felt searing pain where his nail had torn off in his fall. He froze.

How long had it been? He hadn't heard Arm in a long time. The blue glow was dimmer now. The only hint that he might be near the surface was a sense of fresher air, musty but not as putrid.

As the cramps overcame him, he screamed his frustration and fell once more.

Again. And again. In the dark, pain jolted through his trembling muscles, but he was going up. Slowly. Inch by painful inch. But he was going up. For Kip. For Arm. For himself.

The glow-sticks sputtered, a last burst of light, then Bane was plunged into total darkness.

He closed his eyes.

A hand grabbed him and he yelled out, struggling.

"Easy, bro!"

Bane opened his eyes, blinded even in the dim light of a flashlight. He had made it to the top! Arm helped him to his feet.

He grinned at Bane. "Well, don't you look like a mudbug!" He laughed, wiping Bane's face with his hands as the detective's eyes adjusted to the flashlight. Arm unbuttoned his jacket and slung it around Bane's shoulders.

"Well, guess you let our suspect get away."

"Came back for you, pal."

"I was fine."

"I lost him."

"You—I go swimming, climb out of that hellhole, and when I get out, all you can say is 'I lost him.' That the story?"

"*Jesus*, Bane. Next time I'll leave you to drown."

"Do that."

"Miserable donkey bastard."

"Donkey?"

"Stubborn. Eee-aah, ee-aahh!"

"You're an ass."

"You're a mess."

They laughed. "I don't know why I still call you friend, bro."

"Because I'm so lovable." Bane bent to pick up his fallen gun and shoulder bag.

"Kip's still missing. We keep looking."

"For true, bro. Just you let them troopers have a look."

Bane didn't move.

"Look at you. You're shivering like a wet cat. Get your donkey ass upstairs. I'll stay down here with the search. 'Kay?"

Flashlights shone ahead. Three troopers ran up. Arm shouted "Here! Fordor. You take your boss upstairs and get him some dry clothes."

Bane nodded. "Cover every inch of this level! And those passages. Every inch. No one breaks until you find Detective Kipfer! Understood?"

As he followed Fordor, Bane heard Arm taking charge.

"Are you all right, sir?" Fordor asked.

"Don't call me sir, or I'll call you son."

Near the stairwell, they met Hix with two of his squad.

"What are you doing here?" Bane asked, and he held out his arm to prevent Hix passing.

"I'm senior agent here, Bane."

"My crime scene, Hix. I don't need *your* kind of help."

"Screw you."

"Oh, clever. I'll tell my captain on you."

"I hope you catch your death."

"Thanks." Part of him hoped Hix would fall into the same well.

"You're not to go down there."

"You going to stop me, Bane?"

Bane leaned close to Fordor. "Trooper, you're to stop Hix and his men from entering any active theatre He's here to observe. Put him in the Brain Room. We can rename it the Stupid Room later."

"You can't stop me."

"Fordor."

Fordor didn't move. "But they're FBI, sir."

"Make your choice, son. You know what I'll do."

Fordor slid his service revolver from its holster.

"You have my permission to shoot to kill."

"Sir!" Fordor's gun wavered.

"Son, I'm joking."

"Oh."

"But only a little. He's not allowed down here. Any force necessary."

"Yes, sir."

Hix pushed past him. Bane grabbed his arm and threw him hard against the wall.

"I'll have your badge, Bane."

"*I'll have your badge, Bane,*" he mimicked. "Oh, I'm scared."

"I'll arrest you for obstruction."

"Hey, that was my line."

"Bane, there's something you don't know."

"There are a lot of things I don't know. Like why you thought you even had a shot with my wife?"

"For God's sake, that was twelve years ago!"

"Feels like yesterday." He shoved again. Harder.

"Bane, I'm trying to tell you something! The kidnapers—they delivered a tape. Abbey Chase is broadcasting it. It shows Kip, tied up—"

Bane ran past him up the stairs. He yelled back, "Any force necessary, Fordor. Shoot his feet if you have to!"

He found Abbey Chase in her office. She looked up, startled, then walked quickly to the door, her eyes full of concern.

"You are freezing."

THE GAME ■ 227

"And getting your carpet wet. I know."

"Dry clothes first." She pulled his arm. "Now, Detective. You'll get sick. . . I have some of Colin's clothes. You're about his size."

"Ms. Chase, what kind of a monster are you?"

"By the fire. Now, Detective." Her voice hardened, and she hustled him across her opulent office to the marble mantel. A roaring wood fire cracked and snapped in the hearth, and he leaned close, warming his hands, trying to stop his teeth from chattering.

"Here. These should fit." She held out a pair of wool slacks and a flannel shirt. "Colin's work clothes." She smiled.

Bane shook his head. "The only thing I know about you for sure, Ms. Chase, is that your father molested you and your mother didn't care."

Her face grew still. "Nice. I should be used to your humor."

"No one is."

"I'd say that's a truth."

"That's about the only thing true around this amusement park."

"It's not true," she said, "about my father."

"He beat you, then."

Her shoulders trembled. "How could you know that?"

"I didn't. You over-compensate with men. The way you flinch if I make a fist. I suppose I remind you of him."

"A little."

Bane had no reply for that.

A smile trembled on her lips, and vanished behind a frown. "I'll turn my back. Quickly now."

Bane didn't move.

"I don't peek, Detective."

Trembling, he peeled off soaking wet clothes. He saw her peeking, breaking yet another promise, but he didn't care. He leaned closer to the fire. "Ms. Chase, just so you know, I'll be arresting you."

She turned, and again the ghost of a smile appeared then vanished. "Those clothes look better on you than on my ex."

Bane cleared his throat. "Did you hear me?"

"Yes, yes. Arresting me. Well, you do your job, I'll do mine. But now I assume you want to see the tape they sent, including the parts we didn't air. Stay there by the fire."

She strode to the far wall and pressed a hidden switch. The panels slid back to reveal monitors. She pressed a button on a tape player and all of the tiny screens flickered to life with the same image. He crossed the room and stood beside her.

Kip, tied and bruised. Cut and wounded. Angry and snarling like a captured lioness.

Bane's worst fear. He closed his eyes, mourning silently. Anger spurred him. There would be no mourning. Kip would live. He would ensure it. The tape indicated that she was probably alive.

The tape cut to the unlucky Eddie Kim and the terrible images of his torture. They hadn't filmed the actual acts, but between each cut the video zoomed in on the new wounds. Eddie Kim's screams were terrible to hear.

Bane stared at the monitor, not blinking, not wanting to miss a single detail. All the evidence he needed was there. And his best friend in need. The tape cut without showing the outcome.

"That's all?"

"That's enough," whispered Abbey Chase. "I still want to throw up every time I see it."

"It's a shame the perpetrator has no sense of poetic justice."

Tears actually flowed. "Meaning you'd rather that was me there?"

"Oh, save it. My daughters are better actors."

"Are you going to lock me up?"

"Certainly." But right now he was concentrating on the evidence. He played the tape back, over and over. "Caves. These are caves."

"Yes. Kenji found caves on one of his late night jaunts. There's a network that goes on for miles in these mountains."

"This is why I will have to borrow Mr. Tenichi from your show, Ms. Chase."

"Can't you call me Abbey? I've seen you naked, after all." She shrugged. "I peeked."

"I hope I measured up."

She flushed. "More than."

"Kenji."

Her foot tapped the floor. "I have a condition."

"No conditions."

"My way, or you get a court order." The kind woman, loaning clothes to a shivering detective was gone, and the hard producer stood in her place. "You agree that we can broadcast what our cameras film."

"Oh, that's easy. No." He held up his hand. "But you will anyway, so why waste my time asking?"

She stood up and posed by the mantel, beside a brass clock that ticked too loud. Time. Bane's enemy. She had her act down. "Because my camera crew goes with your search parties. We don't broadcast until after your investigation, of course."

"You broke your promise once already."

"Oh heavens, Detective. You call me a liar to my face."

"You are the goddess of liars."

Her lip twitched. "A goddess at least. Those are my conditions."

Bane leaned close to her, his voice dropping to a low growl. "I'll be shutting you down."

"Only the governor can do that."

"I'll make sure it happens."

"Good luck on that, Bane. This is America."

"How could you send crews to film the reactions of little Jeremy and Pete?"

"How could I not, Detective?"

"You disgust me more than the rat-infested well I just fell into."

She turned, her face a mask. "There are things that move all people, Bane." She sighed. "I have my reasons. Did you know we were nearly bankrupt."

"I knew that. It doesn't justify any of this."

"Would you blame a lioness for killing to feed her cubs?"

"You're more the black widow—"

The lights went off.

He could see out her bay windows as the entire house was plunged into darkness.

He waited for the backup generator to trip. The fire cast a warm glow on the room.

"Damn power failures. Can't rely on New England Power." She marched to her desk and pulled out a large flashlight. The beam lanced around the room and came to a stop on his face. "The generator should have kicked in automatically."

"Unless someone shut it down."

"True," she said, and her eyes blinked rapidly. "We retrofitted the main door locks to the guest wing. They're electromagnetic."

"I know. No locks. No cameras. You stay here."

"It's my show!" She ran for the door, Bane pursuing her. They made their way through bobbing flashlights in the hall, jostled by shouting crew.

As they ran, Bane pulled the two-way off his belt and waited for a clear channel.

Finally, he broke in. "This is Bane. All sections report, over."

One by one, the sections reported in.

"I want the crew and contestants under guard. Lock down until the blackout's finished." Bane released the button.

"This is Barber, over," a voice snapped back.

"Go ahead, Marty."

"I heard screams from the contestant wing. Over."

"Investigate. I'm on my way."

Abbey's face paled in the dim light. "The contestant areas are sound-proof," she said. "If they heard screams—"

"Then the doors are open."

"Oh, Christ!"

The chaos in the hallway was worse now as two Real TV camera crews filmed, their lights throwing beams into the frightened crowd.

Bane broke through the crew and ran up the hall that connected to the guest quarters. His sprint left Abbey Chase behind.

A small hall led off to the right. On both sides of the entrance was a sign: *Contestants Only. Entrance Forbidden.*

Bane heard a long, chilling scream, a woman's. He drew his snub-nosed revolver.

At the end of the hall the security door was ajar, the guard missing.

Excited voices ahead, a woman crying. An unknown man shouted, "Stay together!"

Bane jogged forward and emerged in the vaulted foyer of the house, harshly lit by emergency lighting and the flashlights of the troopers, but so vast the domed ceiling disappeared into blackness. He recognized faces, people he had recently interviewed, as the beam of his flashlight wheeled through the big foyer. His men were already there, and most of the contestants as well.

He ran up to Sergeant Silva. "Report."

Silva stepped into the flashlight beam. "We have another vic, sir," he said. "I've got the contestants here, in the foyer."

As he was speaking, the main power came back on and Abbey Chase ran through the door behind them.

"Who's missing?" Bane asked the producer.

"I don't see Junior," Chase said.

His sergeant pointed. "He's in the library. With a. . . a new vic."

"Sarge, who discovered the body?" Bane asked.

"Margaret. That was who screamed."

"Control first. And call an ambulance and Cross." Bane didn't know which would be needed. He turned and looked at the producer. She seemed to have shrunk in stature. "Look, I want you to stay here. My men will be here with you."

She looked frightened. "The cameras will be on air again, now that the power's restored."

"Oh, hell."

She stepped forward. "We edit for the television show, but subscribers get this live on the internet."

He looked at Silva. "Sarge, keep black widow lady here."

Silva nodded, his face grim.

Bane stepped into the library. He stopped at the door. "Shit."

Junior was on his knees as if worshiping before an altar, looking up with eyes that would not blink. Over and over he mumbled, "Oh God, oh God, oh God."

Junior's eyes remained fixed on the north wall.

Bane stepped closer, preferring not to pollute the scene.

Eddie Kim.

Poor Eddie Kim.

His naked body impaled on the horn of the trophy rhinoceros. The long, curving horn, scarlet with Kim's gore. Kim dangling like a puppet with its strings cut. At least he was not castrated or headless.

"Lord Jesus," Bane said. The perp had been here, moments before. The scene was fresh. They had cut the power—it was clear, now, beyond doubt; the perps were a group, no one person could cut the power, carry a full-grown man so quickly through the tunnels, lift him, and impale him. Bane had missed his chance.

He snatched his radio. "They have to be in the tunnels now. There's more than one. Anyone in the tunnels is suspect. All units, lock the grid down! Don't let anything through!"

Junior didn't seem to notice the detective, his eyes fixed on Eddie Kim. Junior's face was pale, his lip trembling. He held up his hands. Bloody hands.

"Mr. Barns?"

Bane touched Junior's shoulder and the man scrambled sideways like a hermit crab. Bane waved at a trooper by the door.

"Mr. Barns!" Junior's head snapped left and he looked at the detective, his eyes wide and pleading.

"Eddie's dead," Junior mumbled. He looked at his hands, dripping blood. "Oh, God." A shudder took him. Shock.

"What happened, Mr. Barns?"

Junior's head swung round, then back to Eddie. "Oh, God." He wiped blood on his pants.

Bane held his arms. "Don't do that, Mr. Barns." Bane felt him shiver.

With surprising strength, Junior tried to wipe his hands again. Bane swung his arm behind his back. "Cuffs. Give me cuffs." The trooper snatched the cuffs off his belt and Bane snapped them on.

Junior continued to kneel, as if in prayer. "I tried to. . . I tried to lift him off. . . God, he was still alive."

Bane pulled him by the cuffs, helping him stand. He may not be the perpetrator, but he would be an important witness. Of equal importance was the forensic evidence on Junior's hands. The man swayed, as if drunk. "Take him to his bedroom, and keep him there, okay?" The trooper nodded. "And—best read him his rights."

Bane's eyes locked on Eddie's dead eyes, clouded over and lifeless, but still telling the story of his death terror.

Bane shivered. Kim had been with Justine. Kip. What horrible things were they doing to her now? He fought down a sense of panic, the same feeling he'd had when he fell into the well. Helplessness.

But they couldn't get far. With all these men, how did they manage never to leave a trace.

He forced himself to be calm. A trail of blood led across the room to a panel. Another tunnel entrance.

"Silva!" He pointed at the trail. "Forget forensics. Follow that trail while it's fresh." He grabbed Silva's arm. "I want Kip back, Silva."

Silva and three troopers ran to the tunnel and disappeared inside.

He looked up at the body. The horn punched through his ribs, the red tip curving up and out of the chest cavity.

"Dear God."

Eddie Kim's eyes were wide open, looking toward the ceiling as if in prayer, his lips pulled back. Blood dripped from his mouth, a rivulet next to the river that had cascaded out of his chest, splattering the Empire furniture below. Blood still dripped to the floor with audible plops. His fingertips had been severed, like the others, but the blood had congealed into brown nubs. He was alive when impaled.

On the wall, in tall spidery letters—painted in Kim's own blood—was a single word:

FLATLANDER.

Chapter 29

....

January 26, 2:44 am

The Caves, Vermont

She felt hands on her body, vile, callused fingers.

Kip jerked to one side, bucking in her restraints.

Ira Evans laughed at her struggles.

She opened her eyes and stared at him. "Bane will figure it out. He's already coming for you."

She felt triumph and fear at the same time. Triumph, because she saw the face of the monster. Fear, because she would die with that knowledge. Her death would be agonizing. And beyond the terror were thoughts she had long ago locked in a hidden room of her mind; when she had seen Ira Evans with his video camera filming her, it tore her apart to think about Pete and Jeremy watching the tape.

Ira laughed again.

She looked down at her own naked body. His hands had been on that body, polluting the iron flesh she had sculpted with hundreds of hours of hard workouts.

She worried at the ropes, her skin long ago torn away to reveal inflamed muscle tissue. The pain kept her alert. The ache gave her hope. She pulled harder on the ropes.

He left her, alone on the rock, damp and shivering. She knew that, even if she survived this ordeal—and she clung desperately to the hope that Bane would find her—she would never work as a detective again. And that fed her wrath. She was a mother first, detective second, woman third, and Ira had stripped it all away from her in layers. He had told her about the tape and how they had broadcast Pete and Jeremy's reaction to it.

She rolled onto her stomach, ignoring the chill rock against the spidery gashes on her hard abdomen. She tried to bend her arms backwards, and over her head. A stab of pain met her efforts and she grunted, biting back a shout. She hesitated, listening for his return.

Where was Eddie Kim? After the escape attempt their captors had taken him, ignoring his screams: "I am American! You can't do this!" In the end, his pidgin English had fallen away with his pride.

They took him out of sight, and she heard screams. He shouted until his voice was hoarse. She tried not to visualize what they were doing to him. She continued to work on the ropes as he screamed. Then his shouts rose to a new level. "No! No! No! Not that! Kill me! Not that!" Two men laughed, and more screams. She was next.

She worked on the knots, rubbing them on a sharp spur of rock.

There were no more screams, only the rustling of bats driven from their hibernation, dimly visible along the cavern roof in the flickering flame of the lanterns.

Kip cried. If she hadn't handcuffed Kim, he might have escaped. She had killed him.

Slowly she loosened the first loop of rope, but her wrists were so raw that every movement shot pain up her arms. There was no one to help her. She must save herself or die.

She tried not to think of the victims she had seen in the crime scenes she had investigated. Or of Eddie Kim.

As she struggled to control her breathing, her thoughts went where she couldn't afford them to go. To Peter and Jeremy.

The tears threatened, but that only made her angrier. The victims, naked, headless, genitals butchered, fingertips removed—*Please God, don't let Pete see me like that. Please God.*

If only she hadn't been so blind. Bane had suspected Ira from the beginning, had written his name in block letters on the white board in the Brain Room on that first day.

She rolled into a fetal position, trying again to break the ropes.

And that was when he returned.

"Hello Ira," she said, forcing a steely calm into her voice.

The security guard from Winooski smiled at her, licked his chapped lips. His eyes were locked on her breasts. She rolled sideways, half hiding her nipples.

"Bane's on his way."

Ira leered. He rubbed his crotch, absently.

You come near me and I'll castrate you. If she had to bite it off she would. No hick security guard would have her.

But she knew he was not alone. There was another man, big, rustic, a smiling beast of a man, someone she had never seen before. And she had heard other voices in the caves. This went beyond some psychopath on a twisted mission. This was some kind of conspiracy, and though it involved the Green Mountain Freedom movement, she felt instinctively that they were guided by shrewder minds.

He knelt beside her. His big callused hand cupped her breast.

She swiveled, fast as a striking snake, and spat in his face. She watched as the big gob of saliva rolled down his ugly nose, but he just smiled and wiped it with two fingers then thrust it into his mouth.

"I can't wait to have you."

"I'll kill you first," she snarled.

Ira rolled his eyes and laughed.

"You want to know what I did to the China man?"

"He's Korean," she said—hoping to engage him, hoping to delay him.

He lunged in quickly and licked her cheek. Both of her knees came up and drove into his hard-on.

He howled, flying backwards into a rock.

His mouth worked, but no sound came. Then he staggered to his feet and gasped, "I'll kill you, bitch! I'll kill you! You're dead! I'm going to have you both ways. Then I'm going to. . ."

"Shut up, Ira," she snapped.

He shut up.

"Bane is the best there is. I'm his friend. You haven't got long to live." She tried to sound calm, even managed to force the semblance of a smile but she knew it would be unconvincing.

"Bitch. I'm going to cut you bad. Cut you bad. *Cut you bad.* Cut, cut, cut."

"Wimp."

"I'm going to screw you with my knife. Cut you from inside."

"I think you like men better."

He froze, clutching his groin. "I'm no fag."

"Your knife is your penis, right? You cut Eddie up? Right? Didn't you say that?"

"I made him suffer is all. It was fun to see the little China man squirm."

For a long time, Kip didn't answer. She choked on a sudden swell of pity for poor Eddie Kim. She saw his smiling face. Could almost smell his wonderful coffee. "Bane won't follow the rules anymore. Before, he had to. Now, he'll just blow your leering face off!

"I'm goin' to cut you. *Cut you*. Cut YOU!"

She tried not to think of poor Eddie Kim, probably dead now, tortured by this man. Her own ordeal was about to begin.

Chapter 30

....

January 26, 9:31 am

Mason Place, Vermont

Bane ran for Arm's sleek black helicopter, the blades already spinning, churning up clouds of stinging snow. He wore a Kevlar vest over Abbey Chase's loaned camel hair coat and Armani suit.

They didn't wait for warrants. The time for rules had passed.

The helicopter shook as they lifted off. Arm's face was eerie in the green glow of night lighting, and behind him sat six of Bane's men, his best, fully armed and armored with vests. They were all that could fit into the chopper, although Bane dispatched a full troop by all-terrain vehicles and snowmobiles.

Bane pressed the talk switch on his headphones. "Can we find them at night?"

Arm nodded. "This chopper's equipped with night vision, infrared, and a bank of searchlights."

The helicopter veered towards a row of mountains, nothing more than a jagged black line against a clear sky. The stars were sharp and bright, and a full moon was rising, casting a silvery glow on the snow. Good weather. Their first bit of luck.

"This is a big leap of deduction," Arm said, his voice loud in the head-set. "Do you really think a political group would sink this low? Killing people?"

"This is a splinter group of the GMF. Militia and all." He made sure all his men were looking at him, listening. They were hand picked. His best. They knew him. Knew what he expected. But it bore repeating. "No rules. Kip will be rescued at any cost. I'll pay the price, later." They nodded. They knew what he meant. Rule of law no longer applied.

They flew low, too close to the tree tops for night flying, although Arm's pilot seemed to have a deft hand on the stick.

"There. At three o'clock. The camp."

A neat row of tiny cabins, lit by windmill power and diesel generators, stretched over the hillside. A single one-lane road led into the camp.

GMF members ran out of their cabins, and through night-vision binoculars Bane could see rifles and shotguns.

"Shoot to kill if you have to." Bane's men nodded, their faces grim in the green glow. Vermonters against Vermonters. "Treat this as a hostile situation with suspects who are armed and dangerous. No chances! Backup is on the way." Again the silent nods.

Bane drew his .38, a snub-nosed revolver that usually seemed too heavy in its holster at his belt, but now seemed too light next to the shotguns and rifles. Arm drew an automatic nine millimeter.

The pilot's voice cut in. "They're pointing their rifles at us."

Arm handed Bane a microphone. He pressed talk and heard his voice, distant and strange, booming out under the helicopter. "This is the Vermont State Police. Lay down your weapons. You have ten seconds to comply."

"They're still aiming at us," said the pilot, his tone clipped, edged with fear.

Bane pressed talk again. "Final warning. Lay down your weapons!"

The helicopter banked abruptly, throwing its passengers to one side. Two men, not strapped in, flew into the bulkhead.

Into the microphone, Bane said, "This is Lieutenant Alban Bane of the Vermont State Police. If any of you shoot, you will face charges."

The helicopter leveled, and Bane let go of the trooper on the floor.

"They're putting down the rifles!" shouted Arm.

Bane half closed his eyes, allowing his breathing to return to normal. "Land this air beater." He glanced at his troopers. "No chances. Shoot to kill." Nodding heads and angry eyes. They were ready to shoot. "Secure the camp weapons, then get the suspects inside the cabins. No more than six cabins, with an armed trooper on each." More nodding.

The chopper swept in, spotlights lighting the clearing beside the row of huts. The GMF members stepped away from their rifles, covering their faces as snow and the wind of the blades blinded them.

As the blades wound down, Arm slid back the door and the troopers swung out in twos, rifles and shotguns down, covering each other as they landed in the snow. Arm and Bane jumped out last.

As much as his men wanted to shoot, the GMF members remained peaceful.

Bane's troopers herded twenty-two men into three cabins, collecting their rifles. They searched the cabins quickly for more weapons then Fordor gave Bane a thumbs-up.

"Their leader is Seth Allen. I want him first," Bane said to Trooper Fordor. As he turned to go, Bane grabbed his arm. "And see if Ira Evans is here. I want to talk to those two first!"

Fordor nodded and ran across the tramped snow to the first cabin. The operation didn't take long. Within half an hour the ATVs and snowmobiles arrived with twelve more troopers who fanned out into the pine woods.

"You really think this is it?" Arm looked dubious. Bane knew that look. Hated that look. Arm's instincts were good.

"I have to, Arm." *FLATLANDERS. Ira.* But he knew it couldn't be that simple.

The big FBI agent put his hand on Bane's shoulder. "You'll find her."

But on time? The thought hung. "Arm, what I'm going to do here, you might not want to witness."

"I know."

"No, you don't."

"Doesn't matter, bro. She's your partner."

"You may have to arrest me."

"No, I won't."

Fordor ran up, his breath blowing out in icy clouds. "Found the leader sir. No sign of Ira Evans."

He led the way to the first cabin. The wind blew the door out of his hand.

The cabin was a wretched open-frame hovel, warmed only by an old rusting wood stove. Stapled sheets of plastic flapped over a broken window. In every corner of the one-room cabin were piles of litter: crumpled Doritos packages, discarded Stove Pipe Porter bottles, piles of clothing sour with body odor, and opened cans of pork and beans.

Seven men glared at Bane. At their center was a massive lumberjack of a man, his arms folded, sleeves rolled back. Seth Allen. On one forearm The Green Mountain Freedom logo, inset with a crude profile rendering of the man he claimed was his great great great great grandfather. Ethan Allen. Vermont's grand hero. Of course, it was nonsense.

"Seth Allen, I am Detective Alban Bane."

"I remember, Lieutenant." His bearded face revealed nothing. "What is the meaning of this invasion?" His voice was calm, but Bane heard the rumble of danger. "You don't have a warrant."

"We believe there's imminent danger. That's my authority."

"We do not recognize your authority." Seth stepped forward. He was nearly as tall as Arm, though leaner, harder, meaner, with veins that stood out from his knotty arms. His face was molded into a permanent frown. "Any more than we recognize the right of those flatlanders to invade our mountains." He pointed west, towards Mason Place.

Bane stabbed his unholstered .38 at Allen "Maybe you'll recognize this authority."

Seth stepped closer to Arm, looking straight and hard into his eyes. Arm didn't flinch. He was a match for Seth, and he showed it. "I do not recognize your authority when you come with the Feds," Seth said. "A true Vermonter doesn't need *his* kind." A dark flush colored Seth Allen's face.

"Not much truth here, is there Seth? Great, great grandson of our illustrious Ethan Allen, is that it?"

"That's right."

"Funny. When I looked you up I found you were born Jason—"

Seth interrupted, "Let's talk alone."

"Man to man?" He scanned the faces of Seth's men. "Okay, Jason—I mean, Seth—outside."

Bane followed him out. They passed the cabin sentry and Seth led the way to the edge of the wood then turned. His face revealed nothing. "You didn't have to do that."

"Seth Allen, born Jason Seymor Alexander. California, right?"

"That's a fabrication."

"Well, your Vermont is slipping. I can get you an audition with Ms. Abbey Chase. She's the producer over at Real TV."

"What do you want, Bane?" Seth's voice dropped low and menacing.

"Ira Evans is one of yours?"

The sneer was instant. "One of mine?" He leaned closer, towering over Bane, his red mustache twitching. "Ira is one of the nobodies. He goes his own way."

"He's a sympathizer."

Seth laughed, more of a snort. "Of course. They all are. You're not born and bred, are you Bane?"

Bane folded his arms to match Ethan's stance. "I'm asking about Ira."

"Yes. Yes. All good Vermonters are sympathizers."

"I have no time for games, Seth, so I'll apologize in advance. For disclosing your Clark Kent identity to these folk."

Seth shrugged. "They won't care."

Bane pointed his gun at the man's foot. "This is going to hurt."

"That's corny."

"Corny works for me. Saw it in a movie."

"And you expect me to take you seriously?"

Bane steadied his aim. "I would. No witnesses. I shot you in the foot while you tried to escape."

"Fine, Ira was a member. But he's too wild. Doesn't follow orders. See? He's not one of us, really, because we're about a cause, and he's all about hate."

"Oh, yeah, you're just so noble. Breaking chain-store windows and burning down houses."

"Don't you love Vermont, Bane? This is our country. God's country. The Feds strip us of our lifestyle, our wealth. They give us Mickey D's and Wal-Mart and Home Depot, and they cut down trees and build subdivisions."

Bane pulled back his gun. "So you're marching on Micky D's?"

He smiled this time, and his mustache bent up and around big white teeth. "We're preparing for the day when we have our own army. Our own government."

Bane pressed his snub nosed revolver against Seth's ribs. "Even a .38 makes an awful mess at this range. Where's Ira?"

He chewed his lip. "Why?"

Bane pulled back his gun, started to turn it away, fired. "Oops. Sloppy finger."

The bullet grazed Seth's bicep.

Big, burly Seth screamed. "You shot me!"

Two troopers ran in their direction. Bane waved with the gun. "Sorry, boys. Careless." The troopers looked uncertain. One smiled. They turned and left.

"You're crazy!"

"That's me."

"I'm bleeding."

"That can happen when you're shot."

"I'll sue!" He held his arm. It was a very light graze with virtually no blood.

Bane held out one of Lorentz's silk handkerchiefs. "Here. Don't be such a baby."

That seemed to settle Seth. The sneer returned, and he dropped his hand. The scratch no longer bled. "Tough guy, Bane."

"Bet that smarts. You'll get your day in court, now, Seth. Everyone does. Just remember, Vermont judges aren't fond of you guys. And I have four more bullets."

"You're as crazy as Ira."

"Who else is crazy enough to help Ira?"

The placid, expressionless Seth Allen returned. "What do you mean?" His eyes fixed on Bane's gun.

"I mean, if it's not you and your bunch, he must have his own nut cases."

Seth took a deep breath. Released it. "Well, he'd never work with flat-landers. Not 'less he was usin' them. I can tell you that. But none of us. None of my group are involved."

"How do you know that?"

Seth's eyebrows lifted. "We're all here. No one's missing." He held his arm again. "Christ, that hurts."

Bane dug into his pocket. "Painkiller?" When Seth shook his head, he popped two himself. "Known associates? Who are his friends?"

"What friends? He's a loner. Even when he used to come to this camp, he'd sleep out there." He pointed into the dark woods. Somewhere, deep in the forest, a wolf howled, then another.

"Where?"

"In them caves!" He pointed up a mountain to the west, back towards Mason Place. "This valley's riddled with them. Hell's Pit, we call it."

"Show me." Bane kept his voice neutral, although he felt a burst of excitement.

He showed Bane the hand he'd used to cover his wound, smeared with blood. "In my condition?"

"Ach, I had worse wounds as a five-year-old."

"You're something, Bane. You shoot a man, then ask for his help."

"I'm sure you don't want Ira smearing the good name of the Green Mountain Freedom movement."

"If he doesn't want to be found, you won't find him. Those caves are a maze, full of bats. Hundreds of Big Brown bats, hibernatin' out for the winter."

"Show me!" He wagged the gun under Seth's chin.

"You're a right bully, ain't you?"

"Card carrying member of the bully club of America."

He licked his lips. "I don't mess with Ira. He's madder than a rabid fox. He'd kill you as soon as spit at you. No conscience at all."

"And you, of course, have a conscience."

Seth squinted at the detective through half-closed eyes. "Every man has a conscience."

"I'll give you two choices. Help us find Ira. Or face accomplice to murder charges."

"Bullshit. As I see it, you assaulted me."

"Your word to mine. I say you tried to run."

"Screw you, Bane."

"I don't swing that way."

Ethan laughed. "Funny guy."

"Ira was your man. You are a facilitator. Trust me. You'd be facing mandatory prison time. Either way, I'm closing down this camp."

"You can't do that." Seth replied in a hushed voice, barely audible over the wind.

"I just did." For once, Governor Ritchie would be happy.

Seth turned away. The only sound was the winter wind, plaintive and moaning. When he turned again, he was smiling. "Well, your missing detective is one of Vermont's finest. I'll do you one better. I'll give you my men to help search."

Bane shook his head. "Thanks. Very neighborly. We'll manage. Just show me."

Seth laughed. "Afraid we'd ambush you? We could have shot down your helicopter easy as can be. Twenty-two rifles pointed at your little chopper!" He continued to smile. "You'll never find anything in those caves unless you have my men with you. We use those caves sometimes. We know 'em."

"Why are you offering? For real."

"Ira makes our movement look bad. I don't need the bad press."

Bane studied him long and hard, but his built-in human lie detector couldn't tell if Seth lied or not. Trust him? No. But if Seth's men were unarmed, and Bane's armed, it could do no harm. Kip needed them, and deep in the most primitive instinctive pit of himself, Bane knew Kip was up there, in those caves. "Fine. Done. But we go *now*."

"We'll need torches and lights, then," Seth said.

"Let's get on it."

Seth stabbed a finger at Bane's holstered revolver. "And tell your men no guns. You fire in there, you're in for a collapse, and Lord liftin' there's no rescue, you understand me?"

Bane partnered two of his men to every one of Allen's; Seth's men carried the torches while the troopers had the guns. They headed out on a well-worn trail through the forest, heading uphill and west towards haunted Mason Place. The moon was bright, and the torches cast a warm glow around them. If Ira was watching, from high up in his caves, he'd certainly see them coming.

I'm coming, Kip. I pray to God I'm coming soon enough.

Seth held up his gloved hand and moved in beside Bane. He pointed to a cut in the rock.

The crevice in the rock face lay hidden behind a massive shard of fallen marble, long ago eroded from the cliff face by ice and wind.

Seth jumped into the crevice, plunging into the darkness. Bane heard his voice and saw his flashlight turn on. "It's a six-foot drop. Drop a rope if'n you want."

Trooper Fordor dropped through, fitting easily. One by one the troopers dropped through the crack. Then Arm. Bane took a deep breath and jumped in. For a moment he was falling into the well. Then he was the five-year-old tumbling deeper into the culvert.

Bane landed with a grunt, a jolt of pain shooting up his spine. The troopers fanned out into different crevices, marking the walls with chalk for the return trip.

"I'm comin' with you, bro," Arm said.

"There are hundreds of passages," Seth said, mildly.

"You take one of Seth's men. We cover more ground."

"Not a great idea, bro."

"Your boyfriend'll be alright," Seth said.

Arm leaned close, glaring at Seth.

"Arm, Kip hasn't got much time," Bane said. "We split up."

Seth smiled. "Don't worry, Fed."

"I'm not—Jason. Because if anything happens to Bane, even if you didn't do it, it'll just be you and I."

Seth shrugged.

Seth led Bane into a passage down and west.

"You're kind of overdressed for the caves," Seth said.

Bane did feel ridiculous in Lorentz's suit and camel hair coat. The light flickered on pale walls as the passage cut steeply down, icy and treacherous.

"No reason not to look one's best," Bane said. He dug in Lorentz's already torn pocket and handed Seth some glow-sticks.

Seth grinned. "We'll see how you look on the other end."

He turned and made for a tunnel branch that headed down, deep into Hell's Pit. Above them in a different branch, Bane heard Arm's voice, loud and angry, growling like a bear woken from hibernation too early. "You bring him back, Allen, or I'm gunning for you. You bring him back in one piece."

Seth disappeared.

Bane cracked three glow-sticks and waited as the swell of blue light filled the cave. The ceiling was barely five feet. Bane shoved several glows into his belt and snapped on a flashlight. He hesitated just a moment, the claustrophobia returning, the fast beating of his heart, the quick breathing, the prickly sweat, the sense of the ground moving. But he focused on Kip.

Bane caught up to Seth.

"If Ira's here, he already knows we're on to him with all this ruckus." The caves reverberated with the sounds of twenty searching men calling out to each other, footsteps clattering. The sounds were all around them—above, below, in front, beside.

Bane stayed behind Seth to discourage any thoughts of ambush, his hand hovered near his pocket where he had stashed his .38 Smithie.

Voices ahead. Yelling. Had they found someone?

Only one word was clear. "Stop!" It echoed through the tunnels.

Seth ducked around a corner, jogging towards the voices. "They found him!"

Bane and Seth moved in the direction of the voices. The echoes became louder, clearer. Seth sprinted up a steep incline, a sharp crack in the rocks barely wide enough for one man.

Seth disappeared around an outcrop of rock. Bane ran after him, gun in hand.

He reached the outcrop. Hesitated. Listened. He dove forward and crouched, gun down.

A hand grabbed him from behind.

Chapter 31

January 26, 6:12 pm
Sub-basement, Mason Place

Kenji probed the cold limestone sub-basement wall with his fingers, gentle touches, patient.

"Here."

The wall slid back, groaning on decades-old sliders, pulled by rusting wires and counterweights. Colder air swept into the narrow passage, and Kenji's nostrils flared, drawing in scents. A dank aroma that reminded him of mineral hot springs of Kyushu, but without the heat, and a sour smell that reminded him of the caves of Hokkaido. He half closed his eyes, concentrating. Yes, that was it. Bat guano. These were big caves, then.

He tried to ignore the fear. Emotion clouded judgment. All his years of practice, of *zazen*, of meditation on the nothingness of life, on the cycle of suffering—all of it shivered on the brink of extinction as he faced his fears.

Fear is an illusion. Pain is nothing. Death is just the beginning of a new cycle of suffering. Right. Just as before—when he faced Kawasa on the beach.

His breathing returned to normal as the outward calm returned. No amount of *zazen* could soothe his inner turmoil.

Sergeant Silva waved him back with a gesture of his gun and stepped into the dark opening. His flashlight swept the natural corridor of lime-stone. He slid inside.

"Clear," said Silva.

The cameraman from Real TV leaned over, filming the dark passage with ultraviolet film, capturing the exclusive footage that would appear on the show, albeit washed in eerie green. The redheaded cameraman was clearly terrified, his hands shaking on the camera, and Kenji wished Abbey Chase hadn't insisted that man come along.

Kenji stepped in, silent, using all his acute senses trained over the years by mentors in the war arts. He slipped up the sloping corridor, feeling his way, taking his time, the stealthy cat.

We must not be too late. We must not be. He thought of Justine Kipfer, of her smiling face. Bane had shown him a picture of Justine's child. He shivered.

He held up his hand again and Sergeant Silva, his three troopers and the terrified cameraman froze.

"Stay here," he whispered.

"No." Silva shook his head. "You are a civilian."

Kenji ignored him and slipped around the sharp bend, Silva right behind him.

Kenji pressed hard against the rock and halted, holding his breath.

Silva was less alert, and took a step off the edge before he reeled backwards, arms flailing to balance himself, nearly dropping his gun. Kenji seized the trooper's bicep and yanked him back to the ledge.

"*Jeeee—suss!*" Silva prayed and cursed at the same time. He peered over the sharp plunge. The walls had disappeared, widening into open space. "Caverns!"

"Yes." Kenji had found them on earlier explorations. He'd suspected they existed because of the quality of the air in Mason's passageways, the moisture. The cave crickets had led him to the realization that the sub-basement passages likely connected to a cave network. When he found guano of a bat, he felt sure of it—then, at last, he found them. He didn't explore too far, for fear of losing the reality television contest. The prize money was so important to his village, to the temple in Honshu. Twice Abbey had lectured him on breaking the rules, and both times she had let him off with a warning and a butt pinch.

"Thank you," said Silva, and his voice echoed off high walls. "Where the hell is this?" His flashlight punched outwards into the gloom, highlighting dust motes and glittering stalactites.

"Caves in the mountains." Kenji ran his hand over the rock. "Shale, here." He pointed at a stunning formation, a massive pillar of reddish rock. "Limestone there."

Silva shook his head and tried his radio again. He was answered with only static.

"You go back, Kenji. You and the cameraman."

"No."

"It is not safe, martial arts master or not."

Kenji smiled. "Life is never safe. You need me."

Silva leaned close. "Can't argue with that, can I?"

Kenji led the way, pressing his back to the slate wall as they descended into the cavern, alert, but also stunned by the beauty of the place.

"Ssh." Silva stopped them again. "Hear that?"

"Yes." Kenji listened. "Bats. We disturbed their hibernation. We should be quieter—"

Silva interrupted. "Damn bats." He scanned the cavern roof with his light.

"Do not. The light will wake them."

"Don't want that, do we?"

Kenji knew they would die if they woke and found no food. He crept on, quieter, leading the way along the ledge, surprised that the terrified cameraman continued to follow them, the eyepiece pressed to his eye.

Again, Kenji suppressed the fear.

Fear is not real. Not real. But it felt real.

He had chosen the middle way, the way of the Buddha, ever since that day when he was fourteen and nearly killed his best friend in anger. The frenzy had taken him to a level of ecstasy that he had never before experienced. As he pummeled his friend's face, the madness left him—and he realized he needed help. He had apologized to his wheezing friend, packed his few belongings, bid farewell to his parents and hiked into the mountains to the temple.

They had nearly rejected him, recognizing his violent tendencies, but in the end, after Kenji had fasted for days at the gates, they took him in, shaved his head, and trained him in the ways of peace. Often, in those early years, the fury rose up, dark and monstrous, and he fought it, retreating into silent meditation. Fear also troubled him, that primitive emotion that he could never entirely abolish. And lust, yet he remained a virgin. By suppressing sex and anger, by redirecting the energy from carnal to spiritual, he managed a peaceful life, the monk's life. But always, simmering beneath the surface, madness remained. Ready to take him.

Now, deep in the caves of Vermont, the madness threatened him again. Another monster. How was it possible that this could happen? Was it karmic retribution for his own feelings? It horrified him. He had it within him to be a monster.

"This must be where our perp did the crimes." Silva's voice sounded excited.

"Perp?"

"Perpetrator. The man who committed these crimes."

"Men," Kenji said.

"What do you mean?"

"It is obvious one man could not have done all of this alone."

Silva nodded. "You're right." He glanced back at his men. "Be careful. We're dealing with multiple perps, armed and dangerous."

They nodded, and Kenji saw the fear on their faces.

Fear—even harder to subdue than anger.

He led the way down the narrow path, cautious. He rounded another bend, stepped out and put his weight down before he realized the ledge had crumbled away. He started to slip, swung back, bending his knees instinctively into an ancient stance, grabbing for a hand-hold. Silva reached out to grab his hand and lost his own balance.

They slammed against the wall.

"That was too close," Silva said.

And that's when they heard the first screams.

Chapter 32

· ·

January 27, 12:06 am

Hell's Pit, Vermont

Bane struggled for a moment, shrugging off the big hand and swing-ing around for his .38.

"Quiet," Seth said.

"You got a death wish, Seth?" Bane whispered it. He had nearly shot his guide.

Seth's grip on the detective's arm was iron, then he dropped his hand. He held a finger up to his own lips. "Ssh."

Seth and Bane pressed back against the cold stone. By the light of glow-sticks, Bane could see they were in a larger cavern with scattered rock shards.

Bane listened. Yes, he heard it too.

Laughter. It echoed and re-echoed, haunting and surreal.

Seth didn't move.

Bane snatched several more glow-sticks from his bag and tossed them across the cavern in the direction of the voice. They clattered to the hard limestone floor. Fingers of cold blue light reached out and soon the cavern was awash in spectral blue.

Bane drew his .38. Seth's fingers pushed down on the gun barrel and whispered. "Don't do that, Bane. Bring the roof down on us."

Reluctantly, Bane put the safety on.

"That's Ira," Seth whispered. "Mad as can be."

The voice grew fainter, they heard footsteps, a splash, more foot-steps.

Bane and Seth ran, bent low, in pursuit. There was no way to call for backup. Radios were useless in the caves. Yelling out would confuse.

Seth squeezed on hands and knees through an opening barely big enough for a German Shepherd. His flashlight moved around in sweeps, throwing wild shadows. Bane fell to his knees. Hesitated. Small round hole, the size of a culvert.

Suddenly he was the boy in the culvert, crying for momma, terrified to move as the water cascaded over him.

Seth called out. "Stop, Ira. I'm tellin' you!" Then a grunt.

Bane plunged into the hole, flashlight and gun first. Hands grabbed him, twisting the gun from his hand.

Ambushed and a fool! Bane yanked back, but the hands had his wrists and pulled him through.

Seth shone the light in his face. "Yer a damn fool, Bane." He tossed the gun in his pocket. "I told you no guns." He unbuttoned his parka and drew a twelve-inch hunting knife, glittering and deadly in the harsh flashlight. "This here's what you need."

Bane snatched a clutch of floppy glow-sticks in one hand like weapons. One of the sticks in his belt sputtered, flared bright then died. He fired up a replacement. "What happened?"

"He ambushed me. I almost had the weasel, but he got away." And then he grinned. "We'd best hurry."

Bane held out his hand. "My gun."

The only sign of emotion was a quick twitch of his mustache. Seth's hand dove into his pocket, yanked out the gun, and handed it to Bane.

"It's like one of them kid's pop guns."

"Size isn't everything." He saw Seth frown. "Okay, my jokes get thin when I'm tired." Bane checked the load, then caught up to Seth, his head brushing the lower cave roof. Down here, only bats, rats, salamanders and spiders lived. And Ira and Kip.

They emerged into another large cavern and scanned it with flashlights, taking in the vaulted ceilings. Bane snapped more glow-sticks and tossed them in three directions. The light glittered off impressive limestone stalactites and stalagmites.

Seth squatted by a boulder. He pointed to the cavern wall. Bane looked up, following his flashlight beam. At first he thought it was just the lofty cavern roof, and then he saw them—thousands of them—brown bats, obvious only by their folded leathery wings.

"This here's Hell's Pit," Seth whispered.

"What was that back there? Purgatory?"

Bane followed Seth, silent and wary. Hell's Pit rose to cathedral heights, limestone eroded out of a deeper cleft of green marble. Stalactites hung like giant icicles from the vaulted ceiling, some connecting with fatter stalagmites to form nature's pillars. Bane had never been in caves, even the Cliff Caves Park near Burlington. When Jay and Mags begged him to take them, Bane always found a reason to go somewhere else, anywhere but the caves, anywhere but the dark, dark caves.

Now he realized how beautiful they were.

Seth pointed up to a sharp cleft, three feet off the cavern floor. "He went in there." The slice in the rock was barely wide enough for a child.

Bane looked around. He was certain he heard something. Someone. Sharp boulders littered the cavern, signs of earlier collapses, some the size of pickup trucks.

"No, wait," Bane whispered.

Seth half turned, his flashlight swinging around. His arms flailed, and a dark bloom of blood appeared on his forehead and ran down his face. Seth grunted and reached up as another rock flew past, narrowly missing him.

"Down, Seth!"

He fell. Bane crouched over him, felt for a pulse. Relieved, he stood and slipped the safety off his .38.

"Ira, it's Detective Bane. Come out, hands up. I promise not to break too many bones."

Ira's cackling filled the cavern with monstrous echoes.

Overhead, bats stirred.

A stone shot past, inches from his face. He ducked, leaning over Seth and tried to pull the man, all two hundred and fifty pounds of him, behind a boulder.

"Ira, give it up. My captain is afraid I'm going to accidentally smash your face into a boulder. He might be right."

Silence this time.

Seth didn't move. Again, Bane pressed a finger to Seth's neck and felt a pulse. He snapped off his flashlight and slid back against a rock.

The ethereal glow of the sticks reflected off the formations, washing the cavern in comforting neon.

He waited for his eyes to adjust. His chest heaved, sweat broke on his forehead and prickled under his shirt.

Seth's breathing was shallow. His own came in harsh gasps.

A rock skittered across the floor at his feet.

Wait for it! Wait.

He listened. No sound but the drip, drip of condensation, the growing thrum of waking bats, and his own rapid breathing.

A shadow, darker than the deeper gloom, drifted across the floor.

It would be so satisfying to shoot the bastard. But he couldn't. Kip could still be alive. They might not find her without Ira's help.

The shadow loomed large. Blue light glinted on the blade, blinding almost in the gloom.

Bane pushed himself from the wall and threw himself against Ira, seizing his knife hand and bending it back. They hurtled into a boulder and Bane hit hard, the breath whooshing from him. He saw spots as he lost his air and his vision blurred. A few blinks of his eyes and it cleared. He looked down. Blood on his hands.

Ira lay in a heap at Bane's feet, his own knife thrust deep into his chest. Ugly spurts of blood shot from the wound.

Bane pulled the knife and pushed his hand against the wound, the hot blood washing over him.

Ira writhed on the rocks, like a turned-over turtle.

"Lie still. You might live." He thought about it. "I hope not, but it's possible."

"Don't trust—" He grunted once. His eyes glazed, his breathing stopped. He died.

Bane knew artificial respiration was useless.

Bats flew in circles above his head. Hundreds awake now.

Bane had killed Ira. A righteous kill. An accidental kill. And now the only way to find Kip was to search a maze of caves. Inch by inch. The entire cave system.

Bane stood beside Ira, catching his wind, staring at the blood on his hands. It might as well have been Kip's blood.

A bat dove past him.

Seth stood, wobbly. He held his hand against his bloody skull. "Are you all right?"

Bane nodded. "Not my blood. You?"

"Nothin' to worry on. Ira?"

"Unless he's good at holding his breath, his spelunking days are over."

Seth sagged back into a rock, still holding his head, his breathing coming in harsh gasps. "Why, though? Why'd Ira wanna do a thing like that? A *cop?*"

"Some kind of sick game."

"But she was a strong woman. Tough. How could he do that?"

Bane stumbled, found his footing.

What did he say?

Several bats flew by and Bane instinctively ducked.

"My partner could be dying."

"She might already be dead. Or maybe he was using her for pleasuring?"

There it was again. What a fool Bane was. Exhaustion, overload, fear, distraction—whatever it was he had been a fool. Bane's hand tightened around his gun.

"You know where she is."

Seth's eyes flashed. "What—what are you up to, Bane?"

"How did you know she was a strong woman?" Bane shone the light in his face, gun steady on the man's chest. "How did you even know she was a woman?"

"You must've mentioned."

Bane shook his head.

"Saw it on the news!" His voice echoed off the cavern walls. More bats stirred, a cloud of them lifted off the cavern roof, sweeping down over their heads, close enough to hear the beat of their wings.

"You're lying."

"Why you gonna go say that?"

"Because everyone lies to cops. From lead-foots trying to get out of speeding tickets to psychopaths like you."

They stood three feet apart, Bane's gun leveled at his chest.

"You're a cynic. I know nothin'. Nothin' at all. And I ain't afeared of your pop gun neither."

At the sound of gunshots Bane turned away, and Seth struck hard. He had fifty pounds on Bane, and landed on top, his hand twisting the revolver up and around.

Bane's knee slammed into Seth's groin. He didn't hold back, putting all his weight into crushing Seth's hope for future children.

Seth screamed and rolled off him into a fetal position.

"I may stomp your balls like a pansy fighter," Bane wheezed, "but you sound like a girl."

Too late he realized Seth still clenched Bane's gun. Bane dove for it. His fingers closed over Seth's, bending his wrist in.

The soft hum of bats became strident, a thousand angry little voices.

Like an arm wrestler, Seth bent Bane's wrist the other direction. Bane's muscles could only slow the irresistible force, and he felt his leg cramp under him. The muzzle turned, inch by inch, in Bane's direction. Pain shot up his right arm, as if Seth had shoved red-hot slivers of metal under his skin. Bane yanked back, rolled hard to one side.

The muzzle was three inches from Bane's face.

"You're dead, Bane!"

Bane didn't waste wind on words. He dug his fingers into the meat of Seth's hand, squeezing with every ounce of his strength, pinching the nerve Kip had shown him in one of her martial arts demonstrations.

Seth cried out.

Bane rolled on top of him, turned the muzzle and dove in hard with all his strength as Seth pulled the trigger.

"You first." He'd always wanted to deliver that line.

The gun bucked under him and he felt the hot wind.

Chapter 33

·····································

January 27, 12:29 am
Hell's Pit, Vermont

Justine Kipfer heard the shouts, echoing on the vaulted cave roof. She had long since passed through the panic zone, adrenal gland no longer shooting 'fear' hormones. She continued to work the ropes on the sharp spur of limestone.

Almost through.

Come on, come on.

She heard him before she saw him, then one of the Green Mountain freaks returned, not Ira, one of the others, the one who had jerked off and ejaculated on her. He had a gun in his hand, his eyes wild with fear. The same fear she had seen over the last few hours. Not the confused panic she saw when she had fought off their attempts to rape her; the knee to the groin of one, her teeth sinking deep into the thigh of another —and the time Ira had tried to tie her ankles with the knotted rope, to string her up like poor Eddie Kim and the others—only to get a solid shiner from the heel of her foot. They had thrown rocks at her, beat her with two-by-fours, kicked her, but bruises and all she still fought back.

No, something big had happened. They had come to kill her. She knew that. Hours ago, they had come in a group of four, safety in numbers, all with knives, like a pack of leering, starving hyenas surrounding the wounded lioness, but then they huddled, whispered, argued, and retreated.

Good. Be afraid, bastard.

The last thread of twine broke, but she kept her wrists together.

"Just you? Where's your perv buddies? Afraid of little me?"

He stabbed the gun at her. She didn't wince. She had no fear left.

He looked at her, breathing hard, but this time there was no lust there. "Time to die."

"You haven't got the balls. I know. I've seen them." *Shit, I sound like*

Bane, she thought. She laughed. Out loud.

He recoiled as if she had hit him.

"Yeah, I'm laughing at you, peanut-dick."

The man retreated a moment, leaning back and peering around a rock.

Bane had come. She knew it. His fear made it clear.

She leaned forward and fumbled with the ankle ropes.

"Over here!" She recognized the voice.

Kenji!

Through the fog of pain and exhaustion she thought, *Is he one of them?*

She lunged to her feet, growling like the wild animal she had become. She gasped, her legs cramping, her body not cooperating.

It didn't matter. She yelled, "Hey, peanut dick!"

The gun came around as he spun, but her hands bent his wrist back. She heard the bone snap and was startled by her own laugh. She wanted to hurt the bastard.

Yes.

Hurt him.

She spun him around and broke his other wrist. Then, a quick kick snapped his femur.

Another of the Green Mountain freaks sprinted around the rock, his gun leveled at her chest.

"You're dead, bitch."

She didn't care. She wasn't going to be their plaything now that she had the ropes off.

She jabbed at him, ducked low, bent into a wide stance, swinging up with a scissor kick, ignoring the pain of her cramps. The gun discharged with a roar. She felt its wind, heard the bullet strike limestone behind her, felt a tiny shard of rock strike her shoulder.

Kip spun deeper into her stance and swung up again, but this time he had a firm bead on her.

She must die now.

The blur of motion took them both off guard. A shadow, a familiar martial arts shout.

Kenji's foot dislocated the man's jaw, and the gun clattered across the cavern floor.

She snatched up the .45 in trembling hands and brought the muzzle to within inches of her tormentor's head.

Kenji stepped closer. Instinctively, her gun swung around.

"It is all right, Justine. Bane and his men are here, too." His voice was a soft purr. He smiled, reassuring, calm.

"And Real TV, too?" She pointed the gun at the Real TV cameraman. The young man ducked, nearly dropped his camera.

Justine Kipfer let the anger take her. The gun settled by the fallen jerk-off freak on the ground. The beatings. Their vile hands on her. The unspeakable things they did. The non-stop masturbation on her face. The laughing. Always, the laughing.

"Justine," Kenji said, his voice hypnotic. "I have been where you are."

She looked at him and laughed, fighting the hysteria. He hadn't endured torture and sexual abuse and psychological trauma. No.

"I have killed," he said. "To defend my village. To stop a killer. I have killed." His face carried a sadness, a serenity. His eyes drew her. He stepped closer. Her gun moved back and forth like a pendulum between Kenji and the man at her feet. "I can never remove the memory of that. The monster deserved death, had to be stopped, but it ruined my life. Justine. Believe me." His hand reached out. "I would take it back if I could."

"Stay back," she shouted.

But his hand touched hers, and her anger drained, as if he took it into himself. "Release the madness. You are holding your breath, Justine." She sank into his soothing voice, so warm, loving. "You are better than this. You are strong." Her hand quivered. "Do not become them. Find yourself."

She brought the muzzle close to the Green Mountain freak's head. Her finger put pressure on the trigger.

"No, Justine!" Kenji stepped close, behind her. "Do not do it."

She pulled back her hand.

"You are stronger than this."

She waited until her breathing had slowed then reached out to hand Kenji the gun. Instead, she pulled back her hand and swung it down, hard and true. The grip came down on the man's head, and she saw the red welt rise as he fell back.

The Green Mountain freak fell, unconscious or dead. She hoped he was dead.

Bane's voice called. "Justine! Kip!"

She looked down at the gun in her hands.

"Kip!"

Kenji's breath was on her. She pulled back. No one must touch her. But she looked into his face, so kind, smiling. He put his hand on her arm. She flinched and pulled away. "It is over." He slid off his coat and slipped it around her shoulders, covering her nakedness.

"It'll never be over," she said. She pointed at the cameraman who had followed Kenji. "Prime time."

Bane stepped into the ring of lantern light. His shirt was sticky with blood and his hand held his abdomen. He limped and froze, glaring at Kenji. "Kip, are you all right?"

Kip nodded. She didn't know how to feel. About Bane. About anything.

"She is fine." Kenji answered for her. "You?"

Bane lifted his hand. "Not my blood. Seth's." He didn't bother to explain who Seth was, and Kip didn't care. "Kip, I came as fast as. . ."

Kip didn't want to hear it. She wanted to be with Pete. And Jess. Away from Bane and Mason Place and everything else. She turned away.

Kip heard him before she saw him.

The jerk-off freak at her feet groaned. His hand clutched her ankle, grabbing hard, pulling her down.

Weak, she started to fall. But she brought her knee up, falling with all her weight into his chest.

She saw the blade too late. She jerked to one side, but the knife followed her.

The pain went deep, searing hot. She flailed. He grabbed her again, his face grotesque with hate, and the knife plunged in a second time.

Bane's gun discharged. The man jerked, a bloom of red appearing near his heart. The elegant wound of a .38. But the madman still clutched at her. She screamed, furious, swiveling around with a martial block, bending back the attacker's hands, and driving his own knife deep into his chest.

Bane came up behind her, touched her shoulder. She shook him off, the acrid smell of discharge in her nostrils.

"Silva!" Bane roared. "Medivac! Now! Officer down!"

I'm not down, Kip thought wildly. But then she was sliding to her knees, falling in slow motion, dizzy. And Bane had her by one arm and propped her up. Kenji had her other arm.

I'm fine, she wanted to say. But then she realized she wasn't.

Chapter 34

January 27, 5:16 pm
Burlington, Vermont

Jay clung to Bane's arm. Mags held on to Arm's big bicep. They stood outside the glass of the intensive care wing, watching, worried.

"She's critical, but I think she'll be fine," Doctor Robyn Thomas said. She gave Bane a hug, more the comfort of a friend than a doctor. "You're always the lucky one."

"Only in love, never in cards."

Robyn's laughter at his joke lifted Bane's spirits. Her simple features became beautiful when she laughed, and Bane made her laugh every chance he got. Bane and Robyn had tried dating on and off over the years since Susan's death, but their schedules and Bane's sense of humor transformed their relationship into a gentle friendship and occasional fling. She lectured him often on the dangers of too much ASA.

"I'll keep an eye on Kip," Robyn said. "She owes me lunch."

Bane pressed his free hand against the cold glass, triggering an unwelcome memory of San Quentin, of Tyler Hayden dying inside the glass-walled execution chamber.

Kip was alive. Bane was alive.

Hell, I'm better than alive, he thought. Bruised, battered, exhausted, but none of that mattered. Seth and Ira were dead. Seth had not survived the shot to his chest.

Bane had survived. The Green Mountain Freedom splinter group had been brought down, the entire militia group taken into custody.

Only Kip was critically wounded. Three of Bane's men sustained minor injuries.

Kenji arrived with Silva in time to rescue one of Bane's teams from an ambush, and the entire incident had been filmed by Real TV. Kenji also stopped Kip from shooting one of her captors, again broadcast on national television.

Over and over. Kip striking the perp. Bane shooting him. Kenji leading Silva's men to rescue troopers. Real TV's logo on every clip.

Kip's chest was tightly wrapped in bandages. Behind her, evidence she was alive, the EKG bleeped, up and down, weak, but regular. Pete sat beside her, holding her hand, glaring at Bane through the glass. It was clear Pete would never forgive Bane.

"Was she—?"

Robyn shook her head and smiled. "Rape kit negative. But she's been through hell, Al." She leaned forward and kissed Bane's cheek. "And so have you." Her lips brushed his ear. "Come over tomorrow night. Tell me all about it."

Bane laughed. The nightmare had ended. He could be himself again. "I don't know, Robyn. You might take advantage of my weakened state."

"I plan to."

"I plan to let you."

He watched her as she moved up the hall. She was notorious in the hospital because she refused to wear a white coat—for good reason. It covered up her not-to-be-missed rocker butt. As she reached the nurses station, she turned and blew him a kiss.

"You know Doc Thomas likes you?" Jay squeezed her father's arm.

"I've had a hint or two."

"One more night with Aunt Di won't kill us," Mags said.

Bane hugged them both, one arm around each. "I missed you two. The good news is, I'm back. The bad news is, I can't cook."

Bane pulled his daughters, one by each arm, away from the intensive care window. "I don't think Pete wants us here right now. Come on."

Arm walked silently beside them. Bane knew Arm was brooding on the ignominy of missing the action. But Bane was grateful for his loyal friend, and equally grateful for his silence.

They drove back without speaking.

They ate three party-sized pizzas in the Bane bungalow. Bane probed for boy trouble, his girls carefully deflected him, Arm acted as mediator. Bane noticed how Mags sat too close to big, handsome Arm. She was really into boys. Trouble.

Bane unplugged the television. They'd all seen enough.

Earlier Bane had watched some of it. Governor Ritchie had been on, taking most of the credit, condemning the independence movement as a whole, using one fringe group to destroy the reputations of legitimate independence parties.

Every channel had news of the battle in Hell's Pit, Vermont. Bane's men were heroes. Allen's men were monsters. Real TV played the drama with quick cuts of the madness in Hell's Pit. Over and over they replayed the green ultraviolet scene of Bane aiming and shooting Kip's attacker. Close-ups of Kip being carried off the medivac helicopter profoundly disturbed Bane, especially when the cameras zoomed in close on her son's teary face.

The doorbell rang. Expecting more reporters, Bane intercepted Jay and answered the door.

Abbey Chase stood on the porch.

Bane placed his hand on the door frame.

"Aren't you going to ask me in?" Her smile was sad.

"Wasn't planning on it." Bane closed the door a few inches for emphasis. "This is my home, Ms. Chase."

"I know that, Alban." She reached through the door and brushed his forearm with her bare fingers. "It's cold out here." When Bane said nothing, the smile faded. "Please. It's important. Ask me in."

Bane swung open the door.

She stomped snow from her boots and stepped inside. "This is lovely," she said, looking around the tiny living room. She kicked off one boot.

"Don't get too comfortable," Bane said.

She frowned but bent and slipped off her remaining boot.

Arm stood between Abbey and Bane's daughter like a guard dog.

"I don't bite, Special Agent Saulnier," Abbey said.

"That's a matter of opinion," grumbled Arm.

"And these must be your daughters," Abbey said, stepping forward. She held out her hand to Mags. "Since your father doesn't much like me, I'd better introduce myself. Abbey Chase. I'm the producer of *Haunted Survivor*."

"*Coo-oool!*" Jay ran forward and pumped Abbey's hands. "I'm Jay."

Mags pushed her aside. "I'm Mags."

Bane grabbed Abbey Chase by the arm and yanked her towards the kitchen. "My house is not a reality television show, Ms. Chase." When Mags and Jay followed them, Bane snapped, "Back to the living room." Arm guided them out.

The television came on. Fine. He'd unplug it again when Abbey left. He planned on dumping it on the street corner in the morning.

Abbey Chase unbuttoned her designer coat.

"I said don't get too comfortable. I'm not delighted to see you."

"What happened to happy ever-afters?" She held out her coat.

"There's no such thing." Bane snatched her coat and threw it across a chair, ignoring her disapproving glance.

"You sound positively furious. Didn't you win one?"

"I'm tired. Pissed. Saw the reports on television. Did you really have to show close-ups of Kip's kid? And me—shooting John Doe."

"You're a hero. Enjoy it. May I sit?" She pulled back a wooden chair and sat. "I smell pizza."

"None left." Bane remained standing, arms folded. "Ms. Chase. It's a long way from Mason Place. Why are you here?"

"I wanted to spare you some more pain."

"I doubt that." Bane studied her. "Where's the hidden camera? In your button?"

"I deserved that."

"Think I've seen this show. Unhappy ending." Bane watched her drumming fingers. She certainly seemed nervous. Upset. She looked at him, then away, then back again. She had something important to say, but was afraid to say it. Was this the actress Abbey Chase, or the real one? With a sigh, he said, "Would you like a beer?"

"Love one."

He snatched two from the fridge, passed her one, and sat opposite her. He watched her slug back half the bottle. "Okay. Your dark world has taken me away from my kids for too long. I don't need you here. Can we make this happen fast?"

She put down her bottle and leaned closer, her hands inches from his on the table. "I envy you. A bungalow with a view. Two delightful girls."

"Ms. Chase. No one is this stupid. You've got to know I hate you."

She frowned. "Fine. I understand. I'm despicable."

"Did you write your own script?" He finished off his bottle in one long chug. "Because words mean nothing—not coming from you."

"People change. I think I changed the day I found out about. . ." Tears flowed, unrestrained now. "About Colin."

For the first time, Bane felt sorry for her. Who was the real Abbey Chase? The conflicted, hard-as-steel producer, or the teary-eyed ex-wife? How could a woman be so attractive and unattractive at the same time?

In the living room, Bane's daughters whispered, the television muted as they eavesdropped on their conversation. "Mind your business," Bane shouted, and the television volume came up.

"They're sweet. So lucky to have a good father."

Bane rapped the table. "Ms. Chase! Neither of us is the small talk type."

"That's true." Abbey drew a deep breath. "It's just that. . . Oh, never mind. I wanted to say thank you. I wanted to. . . I like you, Alban." She held up her hand. "No, I really do."

"You've shown how much you care." Bane shook his head. Bizarre woman. "You think life is a television show. That's the only explanation. You think it's cool to broadcast everything that happens in real life, no matter how hurtful."

"When I was a suspect, it was all business for you, wasn't it?" She leaned even closer. Her eyes blinked. She sniffed. "Right?"

"Yes. Of course." Bane let his voice soften, remembering Abbey in the conservatory at Mason Place. Her tender side.

"Well, Abbey Chase the producer's no different. Business is business, Alban. You know? I answer to investors."

"Obviously not to your conscience." Bane didn't need to hear more. He didn't want her apology. He didn't want to like Ms. Hollywood. "There's lots of people out there you can turn your cameras on. The governor loves it. I'm not interviewing today."

"You made our show a blockbuster. You stopped the slaughter."

"Get out of my house, Ms. Chase." Bane hesitated.

"My point is. . ."

"Yes? Your point is? Please, by all means make it. Then slither on out of my house."

"You're not making this easy for me."

"That's the point of my insults, Ms. Chase."

Abbey stood up, went to the fridge and helped herself to two more beers. She passed one to Bane. "I didn't want to use you. I felt guilty. Really I did." She held up her hand, sniffing again. "I've never felt this before. This guilt."

"Maybe you should turn that into a show. Guilty Pleasures, how's that for a name?"

"Alban, please! I grew up in a—well, let's just say I had to fight for everything I have. Let's just say I had a bastard father who beat me until I beat him back with my brother's baseball bat. You were right about that."

"I know."

"You looked it up in the file?"

"No. Your actions. It had to be something like that."

She frowned. "Do I detect a little, tiny bit of sympathy in your voice?"

"No, Abbey. I don't give a crap about your shit life."

"You called me Abbey at least." Abbey looked up, her green eyes searching his. "I've given you no reason to care. I know that. But I don't want more suffering. I've had enough of it."

"Yes?" He noticed the added level of stress in her voice.

A single tear rolled down her cheek. "Don't be mad at me. It wasn't my call. I argued against it, but Stephen Chow insisted."

"Ah. More freak show coming." He stood up, snatched her coat off the chair and thrust it at her. "Take your Prada clothes and your phony smile and get out."

She took her coat. "I'm sorry. I suggest you not let your daughters watch the news tonight."

Bane stepped closer, his face inches from hers. "What have you done?" Exhaustion fell away, replaced with tingling anxiety.

"The report is. . . well, I'm like you, Alban. My professional personality and personal life can't mingle. You know? Like when you interrogated me? Remember?" She sounded desperate.

"Why do you care what I think?"

Her voice dropped to a near whisper. "Because. . . I don't know. I've never cared before."

He pointed at her designer shoes. "The only thing you care about is fashion. You wear high fashion, no matter how uncomfortable. Why? Because appearances are all that matter. Don't try to con me, Ms. Chase. You care about yourself. Your show. Nothing else."

"This is hard for me, Alban. This is too damned hard." More tears. "Before I met you, all that mattered was doing my work. Exceptional work. Being the best. It's all I have."

"You're not winning any Emmy's for this schlock."

"That hurts."

"Good."

Jay ran into the kitchen, excited. "They're doing a special on Real TV! All about you, Pops!"

"Don't hate me, Alban?" Bane knew by the look on her face the report would be a killer.

Bane walked past her, pushing her out of the way. Jay and Mags sat on the floor, three feet from the television, watching in fascination. Zoë Okiko's face filled the big screen. In the background was Bane's picture, a still shot of him with his .38 in hand. When did they shoot that?

They cut to a video shot of him shooting Kip's attacker in the cave, then another of Bane bending over one of Seth Allen's dead. And beside him, Kenji. Zoë Okiko excitedly narrated: "Today, in a daring raid, the Vermont State Police captured the conspirators behind the killings on the set of *Haunted Survivor*." The scene cut to a dramatic shoot-out, filmed in the green wash of night-vision film, mostly images of frightened ghostly faces with otherworldly glowing eyes, and flashes of gunshots. The camera shook and spun as the cameraman dove for cover.

Real TV made Kenji out to be the hero, the man who led Silva and his men to save the day. They played and replayed the scene where Kenji found the cavern, then an exciting gunfight, followed by a dramatic shot of Kenji kung fu-ing two of the GMF men to the ground, then the touching scene where Kenji stopped Kip from killing her attacker. They showed Bane shooting the man with the knife. They cut Kip's final defense where she plunged the knife into the same man's chest.

Thank God.

Then back to Bane as he holstered his .38. He sensed where the story was going. His own face appeared gaunt and exhausted, monstrous in the green glow of night vision. The narrator continued: "Vermont State Police Detective Lieutenant Alban Bane, A.K.A. Bloodhound Bane, was the Investigator in Charge—" Bane cringed. *That* name again, for the media to play with.

The camera moved in close on Zoë's sensuous face. "There have been five murders on our set. Detective Justine Kipfer was abducted, three police officers wounded and several suspects were slain in Detective Alban Bane's rescue attempt."

The camera cut to a shot of a bruised and bloody Justine Kipfer and her sobbing son, as the medics crossed the snowy landing field to a waiting ambulance.

The camera pulled back from Zoë's sad face, revealing a too-familiar image projected behind her. "Three nights ago, one of our own beloved crew was murdered. We warn our sensitive viewers that this exclusive footage is very disturbing."

Bane tried to lever between his daughters and the television, but they jumped to their feet and continued to watch. He looked for the remote control but it was clutched in Jay's hands.

The scene cut to poor Eddie Kim, hanging from the rhino horn, uncut gore and all.

"Can they show that?" snapped Arm.

"We can," Abbey said, from the kitchen doorway, her voice barely audible.

They cut to quick scenes of Kim alive: in his kitchen, chopping and smiling, frying and smiling, tossing his cleaver in the air and laughing; then Eddie dangling from the rhino horn, face twisted in agony, the words *FLATLANDER* written in his own blood.

Bane turned off the television at the set. Jay flicked it back on, and started scanning channels.

Every channel had picked up the feed, with a notice in the bottom right corner: "*Courtesy of Real TV,*" and "*Warning to Sensitive Viewers.*"

The next image was of their bungalow on the hill. The Bane homestead. Abbey's warning made it clear what was coming.

Bane yanked the television plug from the wall. "Enough!" There was no way his daughters would see the crime scene photographs of their mother.

"Are you all right, hon?" Bane said, kneeling in front of Jay.

"I'm okay." Jay buried her face in his shirt. "At least it's over. You stopped them."

Mags smiled. "I can't wait to go to school."

"Why?"

"You're a hero." She punched his arm. "I'll be even more popular." But in spite of her upbeat bravado, her eyes were filled with tears that she was stubbornly holding back. He leaned forward and kissed her forehead.

They all fell silent as Abbey Chase stood up and walked to the door, her coat draped on her arm.

"I'm so sorry," she said.

No one replied as she opened the door and left.

An hour later, the girls finally made their way to their beds, and Bane sat with Arm in his study. Arm threw his massive feet up on Bane's desk, leaning back in his groaning antique oak chair. Bane poured his friend a scotch, himself a brandy, and they toasted by the fire.

"To Kip," Bane said.

"To Kip."

They tossed the drinks down and Bane refilled.

"You heading back to New Orleans?"

He winked. "Trying to get rid of me?"

"No. You're always welcome here."

"Maybe just a couple days. Catch up." Arm winked. "You know we haven't had time to just talk over a few brews."

Bane nodded but said nothing. Thinking of the good times always brought stinging memories of more painful events.

Like Suze, lying in the snow.

"You know, for a man who took down a gang of killers, you're pretty glum, bro."

"Nothing to be happy about."

He put his glass down. "Feeling sorry for yourself?"

"Nope. Feeling dissatisfied."

"Why's that?"

"Because. I don't believe that this is over."

Arm laughed. "Well, ain't that something!" He sat on the edge of Bane's desk. "What's gnawing on that big brain of yours?"

Bane shook his head. "I don't know. Not yet. But this isn't adding up."

"But they had Kip."

"Yes, they did." Bane stood up and went to the window and stared out at his favorite view of Lake Champlain.

Bane stared at the ice-fishing huts below them, dimly lit by lantern light on the bay, and wished he was out there, in one of those huts, carefree, warming his hands on a propane heater with his line in a hole in the ice.

"It doesn't make sense to me, Arm." Bane rolled brandy on his tongue. "Green Mountain Freedom—they were not terrorists. They were against tourism and development and outsiders controlling Vermont. They weren't even on the FBI watch list."

"Go on."

"Our Prada queen, there, Abbey, she might have prodded them on, I don't know, but they just didn't seem smart enough to me."

"You think there's a brain behind all this." It wasn't a question.

"I guess I do." Bane refilled his snifter. "I understand why they'd target Real TV. *Haunted Survivor* was symbolic of the invasion of Vermont by flatlanders. But they could have done just as well with vandalism."

"No national news, then."

"Yeah, true. But serial killing?"

"Seth was a psychopath."

"Maybe. Maybe. But. . . it just doesn't sit right." There was no doubt Seth and his boys were insane. Mission psychopaths. "I just don't think a has-been actor from L.A. posing as a descendant of Ethan Allen has the brain cells to make all this come together."

"Someone else planned this?"

Bane sighed. "I don't know. There's the Hayden copycat thing. None of it's tied up the way I need. And you know what a needy guy I am."

Arm laughed. "Obsessed, more like, bro."

Bane winked. "Welcome to Vermont. The happiest place on earth."

"That's Disney World."

"Oh."

"We're missing a piece of this bizarre puzzle." Bane shook his head. "Tomorrow that old fool of a windbag Ritchie's doing a press conference announcing that he single-handedly led the task force that captured this sadistic ring of radicals."

Arm put his hand on Bane's shoulder. "Allow yourself to savor a small triumph at least. Kip's alive."

Later, Arm slept on the couch, snoring loudly, his legs spilling to the floor.

Bane slept fitfully, disturbed by dreams of Hayden.

Long before sunrise Bane bundled up in his warmest parka and headed out for a walk.

He walked up Colchester to the university campus, his mind straining like a computer before a crash. He brushed off the crusty snow from an old bench in the university green, and sat, surrounded by the splendid nineteenth century buildings of UVM, his *Alma mater*. He ignored the cold and watched the sunrise.

He was still there when the first classes began, and he watched the students chatting and laughing as they dashed between classes. It was his favorite place to sit and think. Here, on this very bench, he sat with Margaret and Jennifer Bane, his precious lassies, one on each knee, and

274 ■ DEREK ARMSTRONG

told them of their beloved mother, and their Grandfather Auly and Great-Grandfather Ewen MacBane, who first came to the New World in 1882 to cut the massive granite stones in Barre.

Bane loved it here, above all other places on earth, on the green at UVM, and he hoped his daughters would one day attend this beautiful campus and take the Bane name to lofty heights. He had been the first of the MacBanes to rise above intellectual poverty, with a Master's in psychology and acceptance into that illustrious symbol of American democracy, the FBI. He wanted Jay and Mags to soar even higher.

He couldn't put Seth out of his mind.

He popped three aspirin.

Seth and his boys were puppets, not leaders. Someone had twisted their mission. Someone with influence. Again, Bane felt certain he was facing a conspiracy. But who had that kind of influence? And why? Why play this game of terror?

Terrorism. He took a breath. Held it. Terrorism. What was the mission of terrorists everywhere? Terror was power when used by a shrewd player. Hitler had used it. Osama Bin Laden. Terror had always been the tool of the twisted mastermind.

An idea formed.

Who had that kind of influence? Who could twist the psychosis of people like Seth and Ira? Make them worse.

And suddenly he knew.

His sat phone rang, obliterating his frenetic thought line. "Bane."

"Bro, it's Arm."

"Hey."

"Where are you?"

"Just walking."

"Well, come on back. I'm on to something. I got an urgent page from DC this morning."

Bane didn't answer.

Arm sighed, a big windy sound on the phone. "It was the background checks you asked for. You always taught me background is everything."

Bane smiled. Forensic chronicling, his specialty in criminology, relied on background, background, background.

"You there, bro?"

"Yeah. I'm here." Bane watched two lovers stroll across the campus, the same path Suze and Bane once strolled, in all four seasons, every day of their precious life together.

"What did you find?"

"Look, bro. It's odd, that's all. Someone with Supervisory clearance put a clearance-level lock on one particular file you asked for, one level above mine."

Bane got up and walked across the campus. "Arm, tell me you got around it."

"Sure. Once I knew it was there, it was easy." He paused and Bane waited. "Listen, this is weird. Got to tell you, bro."

"I'm interested in one background in particular," Bane said, feeling more certain now.

Arm laughed. "Okay, you tell me then."

"Doctor Jonathon Wingate. Eminent psychiatrist." Bane remembered the nagging doubts after learning Wingate was Hayden's psychiatrist, clouded somewhat by his admiration for the brilliant man.

"Wow, bro, you nailed it."

Bane's excitement rose.

"Wingate's patients included senators, bureau agents, the assistant director himself. Even the current US Vice President."

"Probably the reason for the supervisor-or-higher lock." Bane walked faster.

"But here's the thing. Before his stellar climb at Harvard, there's no record of him."

Bane nearly dropped the phone. "That's not possible. A psyche can't consult with the Bureau without being cleared."

"The Deputy Director cleared him. Fast tracked the approval, too."

"I'm pissing my pants with excitement, here. Go on!" Bane shouted it so loud that students halfway across the Green looked at him.

"Cool out, bro. It's pretty unusual shit. I had to double check it."

Bane bit his lip in frustration.

"Wingate," Arm said. "He's not from England, first of all."

Bane thought back. His accent had been pretty convincing. But as he replayed the interviews with Wingate in his mind he realized the accent had been thick at times, thinner at others. Suddenly, Bane knew. "He's from Boston."

"Wow, again, bro. His real name is Bartlett. Emerson Bartlett to be exact."

"Boston!" Bane ran. Boston. The city where Hayden was born. "So what about the Bartletts then?"

"He's of the Jeremiah Bartletts. They're—oh hell, bro. He's the grandson of the second cousin of Mordechai Mason, on the mother's side, so they're Masons, and they were shareholders in Mason Industries. He's a distant relative of Mordechai Mason!"

"You're too cool for school, Arm. I knew there was a reason I love you, big guy."

"Hey, don't be spreading that around."

"My secret."

Bane ran through the campus and back to Colchester.

"Okay, give me the punch line."

"You know me."

"You saved the best for last, right?"

"This one's better than sex."

"Nothing's better than sex."

"This one is, bro. Wingate was Hix's psychiatrist."

Jesus Christ.

"Arm, pick up the bastard."

"Which one?"

"Both."

Chapter 35

Saturday, pre game, 9:11 pm
Shelburne Bay, Burlington

Dennis's lips devoured hers. His tongue darted out, found her tongue stud.

Mags stiffened and pulled away.

"What?" He sounded exasperated, then realized his mistake and said in a softer voice, "I'm sorry, babe."

"Lights are on, you know," she said, meaning, *Adults in the house.* Aunt Di, in the next room, watching her television. Mags pushed him off her, vaguely aware of the bulge between his legs.

"You always tease." Dennis's scowl made him ugly. His tone made it clear he was not joking.

"What do you want?"

"You," he whispered, but it was too late for seduction.

"Give me a break." She sat up, straightening her Kenji tee shirt. "Just because we're kickin' it, doesn't mean you're getting any."

"I'm sick of this," he said, and his pouting lips made him even more repulsive, broad shoulders, dimples, blue eyes and hard sculpted legs notwithstanding. She loved good legs, especially hairless legs, but not attached to morons who only wanted a quickie from a virgin.

He tucked his shirt and buttoned his jeans.

"You should leave." Mags sighed.

"I should." He stabbed his finger at the image of a bare-chested man on Mags' tee. "You'd rather be with him anyway!"

The image on her tee was her favorite, a shot of Kenji in his briefs, his white smile glittering in his so-beautiful face, his brown body rippling and perfect, knife scars and all. Against a black cotton background, the blood red of the *Haunted Survivor* logo and the slogan "Kenji-bomb" stood in sharp contrast.

"He's ten times the man you are."

His face twitched, his eyes burned then cooled again. He sighed and mumbled, "I'll call you."

"Don't bother."

"Oh, Miss Mighty Celeb. Just because your Dad's—"

"Get out!" She opened her bedroom door and ushered him out. He slammed the front door as he left.

"Everything all right?" called Aunt Di.

Mags ignored her and pulled on her winter wrap.

"Where are you going?" Aunt Di muted the television.

Mags didn't look at her. She hardly ever looked at Aunt Di. The woman reminded her of an older, fatter, dowdier version of Mom. Mags hated having Aunt Di in their house. "Out. And don't ask where."

"Your father wants you to stay in." Aunt Di moved to block the door with her substantial bulk. She had mom's face, but years of marriage had made her rounder and softer.

"Then why doesn't he stay in."

"He's saving people's lives."

"Yeah? Well, screw him," Mags shouted. "And screw you, too!"

As Di lifted her hand to her mouth, Mags slipped past her and out into the night.

"Get back here, young lady!"

Mags ran up the street, her feet slipping on the icy sidewalk, just as the tears started to flow. She was sure Di was on the phone to Dad now, but he would still be with internal affairs, then on to a meeting with the governor again. He would be gone for many more hours.

The sobbing began.

Mags wound down the hill. She held her hand up to block the wind and made her way to the frozen pier, lonely and bleak, but her favorite place in any season. The ice-fishing huts off the shore were warm and cheery. The pier was lit with colder streetlights.

Mags was alone. Her mother had left her years ago. Her father was never around. Jay was too juvenile to tolerate for long and idolized her bigger sister so intensely it made Mags want to puke.

No one. Thank God the trooper escort was finally gone. With Aunt

Justine's rescue, the trooper was released from his tailing duties. She was truly alone now.

Not even Dennis for company, with his bulging muscles and full crotch; all he wanted was sex, to stick his tongue in places she didn't want it. He was a hottie, and all her friends were jealous, but Mags wasn't ready for that. Not now. Especially, not now.

Tomorrow was Super Bowl Sunday.

The tears chilled her skin, and she sobbed.

Thirteen years ago tomorrow, her mother was raped, butchered and left crumpled in the snow. Right there in their little haunted house on the hill. Years of begging had not convinced her dad to move.

And Dad. He was famous now. Again. All over the news. Reporters pounded on their door at all hours, the phone never stopped ringing, and Mags' only delight was that her favorite stars on *Haunted Survivor* were safe. The whole world wanted Dad. Everyone except her.

I hate him. But instantly she cringed at the idea. *He killed Mom.* It was his fault. And worse, he solved every case, found every killer, stopped every crime—except the *only* one that mattered.

Mom, I miss you.

The tears flowed now, washing her face in a chilly mask. She leaned on an icy pier post, staring out over the frozen water of the bay at the glowing huts of ice fishermen.

"Are you all right?" asked a kind voice.

She half expected it to be Dennis.

She had thought she was alone, heard no one approach. She wheeled, still leaning on the post, and her eyes widened. A man towered over her, well over six feet tall. Instinctively, she reached in her pocket for the can of mace her father made her carry. But this was Vermont and she felt foolish. She released her grip on the can.

"You startled me," she snapped. In daylight, with crowds on the pier, she might have laughed at the cowboy hat and the boots and mocked the cowboy in Vermont.

But his voice was kind. "I'm sorry. But you looked upset." Even through layers of winter clothing the man was clearly muscular. In the diffused light of streetlights, she could see the face under the wide-brimmed hat—a stunning face, brilliant smile, young, soap opera star handsome. At any other time Mags would have responded to the man's beauty.

She felt like shouting *Mind own your damn business*, but Vermont was the land of the friendly stranger, and she wasn't upset enough to hurt the man's feelings. Instead, she said, "I'm fine. Boyfriend trouble."

"Oh, been there." He stepped closer, now only one stride away, and smiled again.

"Why, you gay?"

"Disappointed?"

"No!" She didn't mean to sound so rude. "Sorry, I . . ."

"It's all right. No, I'm not gay. You're Maggie Bane, aren't you?" The voice was soft and neighborly.

Mags felt the first icicle of fear.

A hand clamped over her mouth.

Chapter 36

....

Saturday, pre game, 10:11 pm
State Capitol, Montpelier

Governor Ritchie rapped his glass desk. "You're an ass, Bane."

"I know," Bane said. "It's not over until the fat governor sings."

"Bane!" Colonel Clancy stood up, his face blooming purple.

Bane studied all of their faces in turn, measuring their response to his news on Wingate. Cap looked embarrassed. Hix smirked. Arm scowled at Hix. The governor appeared shocked.

"Well, this fat governor's singing Bane," Ritchie said, trying to sound like he wasn't insulted, not succeeding. "You're finished here."

"I wish we were finished, believe me. I'm missing Super Bowl."

"Just because the FBI deputy director blocked Wingate's file—"

"Hid his identity. Wingate's a Bartlett, related to our very own mass murderer Mordecai Mason, born in Boston—"

"Yeah, we danced this dance, Bane," Ritchie said, his meaty hands on hips. "Boston's a big city. You're implying Wingate is Hayden's father. We got that." Bane nodded. "All I can say is I hope you give the D.A. more evidence for trials after you arrest people."

"I'm just saying, don't announce anything. That's simple enough for you isn't it? I don't want to embarrass this office."

"Bane, you'll stay away from the reporters," Governor Ritchie said.

"I'd stay away from them, but they follow me around like puppy dogs."

"Because you're scandal rag material."

"Oh, yeah, my last affair was with a slutty movie star."

"Bane, that's enough!" Cap sounded pissed.

"Gentlemen, I'll make this easy for you," Bane said, staring right into his captain's furious eyes. "The case is not closed until I say it is. If any of you want to look idiotic, feel free to take the podium. But, I'm not done."

"You're done, Bane, trust me on that," Ritchie said.

"Trust a politician, sir?" Bane smiled. "You know, sir, being governor is no excuse for not having fun. Get with the program. I'm giving you a heads-up as a courtesy."

This isn't going well. Bane walked to the wide windows, and looked down at the pandemonium below the state capitol building. Even past ten at night, more than two hundred journalists and camera crews milled at the foot of the marble steps, illuminated by floodlights as they waited for the governor's press conference. Governor Ritchie was determined to have his press conference before Super Bowl Sunday.

"Those freaks down there can't help themselves. It's their job. Our job is to protect them from themselves."

"Shut up Bane," Colonel Clancy said. "You're the hero of the day, so we'll all cut you some slack for that, but no one's buying your theories. Wingate's a friend of the President. You know, our big, big, big boss."

"I didn't vote for him either," Bane said, staring evenly at Governor Ritchie. "And since when do we put blinders on to the fact that politicians sometimes have dirty friends?"

"I can't believe this," Hix said, leaning forward in his chair. "Wingate's worked with the Bureau on dozens of cases. He is a personal friend of our Director. Hell, I think he even consults for the White House. What evidence? All I've heard is innuendo and suspicions." His sneer was punctuated with a roll of his eyes.

"That's stand-up, coming from you, Hix. You're his patient, aren't you?'"

Arm nearly fell out of his chair. Everyone would know where the confidential information came from.

Hix glared at Bane, his hate open for all to see.

Bane ignored him. "Sir, I'm just saying the investigation is open. Don't announce anything else."

"You're off the case, Bane," Colonel Clancy said.

"Since when do I follow orders, sir?" He stepped closer to Ritchie. "Governor, I understand you're mad. You'll go from mad to a laughing stock if you announce."

"Rubbish. I had dinner with Wingate and his charming wife Lara, just the other night.

"He's had us all fooled, sir."

"You might as well call me your Gamester. Or Director Harris of the FBI!"

"I did consider you, sir," Bane said.

"Number one sign of job burnout, Bane. Suicidal career choices."

"I'm trying to prevent your suicide in the polls, governor." Bane shrugged. "Why bother? You're just a one-term throwaway."

"That's enough, Bane!" Colonel Clancy shouted. Even the governor jumped. "You're off the case. You're on paid leave. And I want you in my office on Monday."

Bane stared at his commanding officer.

"Go home, Bane," Cap said, stepping between them. "Go home. Watch the Super Bowl. Chill."

Yeah. Tomorrow was Super Bowl Sunday. Déjà vu. The day Bane found his wife—

Bane stared past his captain, at his Colonel, unflinching. "Let's review, shall we children?"

"Bane." Cap's eyes narrowed to slits.

Bane ignored him. "We have an unaccounted for cowboy assassin." He lifted his hand and stabbed his index finger up. "One. We have Hugh King chased through Boston by, apparently, this same Hopalong Cowboy." He flipped a second finger up. "Two. We have a terrorist ring broken here in Vermont—broken, incidentally, and with all modesty, by yours truly. I wonder what the news people will think of you sacking the man who took down these terrorists?" He shrugged and flipped a third finger up. "Three. Said terrorists are not known to associate with flatlanders. If there was ever a flatter flatlander than a Butch Cassidy cowboy, well—I guess you catch my meaning? Four. We have a psychiatrist with a concealed identity, apparently related to a mass murderer, and responsible for engineering this frightfest on reality television. Hmm. Five. Does this add up to case closed?"

"Balderdash."

"You're off the case, Bane," Hix said.

Bane stepped close to Hix, felt his heat rise, forgot everyone else in the room. "We have a mob tie-in." He lifted his other hand. "Six."

"Manetti—Reid—is dead," Hix snapped.

"Shut up Hix," Bane said.

No one spoke. In front of the governor and his colonel, this kind of rudeness was a career killer. But he didn't care. He could always write his memoir.

"Seven. We have unidentified victims. Does this even seem close to being ready for the news media?"

"You're missing the point, detective," said the governor, quieter this time. "You're a hero. We're not announcing the case is fully resolved. Only that we—you—captured the killers."

"But not their puppet-master." Bane turned on Hix now. "And Hix, here, has somehow convinced the terrorism task force to take custody of the prisoners from the cave. All of Seth's men were flown to a military base."

"They were terrorists," Hix said, his voice quiet. "They are being questioned."

"They need to be interrogated by Vermont authorities," Bane said. "The D.A. needs access to them. I need access to them!"

"It's a federal case, now," Hix said. "We run the investigation."

"You're tainted. You're linked to Wingate."

Hix's forehead creased. "Wingate is a board-certified, FBI-approved psychiatrist. FBI agents endure stress, particularly agents who work on serial cases."

"Wingate is not who he says he is. And you're—" he bit back the word, *dirty*, and finished, "linked."

Hix snorted. "Oh, and you are not? Hayden this and Hayden that. You're obsessed. It's time you admitted it."

Captain Jefferies stood up and thrust his hands behind his crisply pressed uniform. He walked over to the window, stepped in front of Bane. He gave Bane a look that said, *Are you crazy, my boy, you'll ruin your career*, but he said, "If Detective Bane has suspicions, I think we owe it to him to listen."

"It's nonsense," said the governor. "I personally know Jon Wingate. He's a good friend. I play golf with him."

"Emerson Bartlett," Bane reminded him.

"Baloney, son. Baloney, with a capital B."

Captain Jefferies put a restraining hand on Bane's shoulder.

Bane shrugged him off. "Oh, you're good, governor. I see how you got elected. Smooth, convincing, down-home fatherly. If you can fake this, imagine what else you can fake?"

Ritchie jumped to his feet, his wide face livid. "I'll not hear any more about this! Seth Allen was evil incarnate. His damnable rebels are finished! And just sit down gentlemen, I'm not done talking."

Bane remained standing, but out of respect, faced the governor. Everyone fell silent under the Governor's vehemence.

"I'll not have you damaging the reputation of Doctor Wingate. Don't even think about it." His lowered his voice, but his eyes fixed on Bane's, hard and cold.

Arm's voice boomed out, "Bane was the Bureau's leading forensic chronologist, sir."

The governor wheeled, his gaze boring into Arm. "Who asked you, son? Seth would never deal with a flatlander. Wingate's from out of state. They couldn't be conspirators. Did you think of that?"

Bane smiled. "Oh, that wasn't rhetorical? Well, since you ask, let's not forget the Bartlett's are relatives of Mason, a Vermonter. Seth was a pawn. Wingate played us like a chess master." Bane hesitated, remembering the note, *Welcome to the Game.* Wingate was playing chess from the beginning.

"Bullshit," the governor said. "You're running on intuition, an instinct I'm not even slightly inclined to be influenced by."

Bane ignored him. "Has it occurred to you that something bigger is happening here?"

"Like what?"

"Like, Reality TV as a forum? Live TV? A doddering governor who allows his state to stage an elaborate terrorist message? I only say this, sir, because at earlier press conferences you crowed about how big an achievement it was for Vermont getting Real TV here."

Governor Ritchie looked uncomfortable for the first time.

"Am I the only one who smells smoke?" Bane asked.

"But *why*, Detective? For heaven's sake, *why* would Wingate do this?" Governor Ritchie spoke softly now, and Bane could see that his neutral expression framed worried eyes.

"There's some connection to Hayden. Hayden was Wingate's protégé? I know Hayden was his patient." His suspicion went even deeper. Hayden's father was from Boston. Wingate, born a Bartlett, was from Boston.

"What arrogance," Ritchie said. "You think the whole world revolves around Bane and Hayden?"

"Hey, they made movies," Bane said.

"No one's laughing, son."

"There's no other explanation for the coincidences: Wingate-Bartlett, related to Mason; Wingate, the psychiatrist of Hayden; the Hayden copycat in Vermont, the state where I work as a homicide detective. And don't forget, I arrested Hayden. It all fits."

Ritchie's voice rose. "This is all just a lot of coincidences." He glanced at Captain Jeffries. "This is what passes for detective work in our great state?" Ritchie shook his head and leaned back in his chair. "I don't want any more talk on this."

"Let me ask you something, governor," Bane said.

"Bane," Cap snapped it.

Bane knew something bad was coming but he couldn't stop himself. "Did you run your election campaign from the psychiatric ward of Burlington General? Or are you just stupid?"

Ritchie cleared his throat. "I think I've endured enough."

"Quite," Colonel Clancy said. "Bane, keep this up, I'll call a review board on your conduct."

"What happened to the medal you promised me?" Bane stared at his Colonel.

"You have no more resources, son," Clancy said, but his teeth were clenched. "You're on leave. Let this go before it's permanent."

"No medal then?"

"You'll get your damned medal. Then your pension."

Bane nodded. "Deal."

Before his commander could respond, Bane's phone range. His pager beeped and his belt radio vibrated. "Someone wants me real bad." Bane moved away from his smouldering Colonel to the bay windows and flipped open his phone.

"You've reached soon-to-be private investigator Bane."

"*Shit*, Bane," Cap said, behind him.

"Al, it's Di," said the voice on the phone.

"Girls giving you trouble, Di?"

Di told Bane about Mags' blow up. How she hadn't come home. "I'll be right there, Di." Bane snapped his phone closed and stared at the journalists in the parking lot. He felt queasy.

"Sorry, gentlemen. Teenager problems." Bane ran from the room, pursued by Arm.

Bane ignored the journalists chasing him to his pickup truck. He slammed the door open too hard, knocking over a correspondent from a Canadian network. Arm jumped in the passenger seat.

"What's up, bro?"

"Mags is gone."

Bane carved a three-sixty in the snowy parking lot, nearly side-swiping an NBC news van.

He roared through Burlington at three times the speed limit, police emergency lights flashing. He slammed his breaks and spun the truck onto his front lawn.

Bane and Arm ran for the front door.

His hand froze, hovering over the knob.

The porch mailbox was open.

A letter stuck out of the slot, half in, half out.

He looked at Arm.

Bane felt a cold, desperate certainty. No post mark. No address. Just his name.

He slipped on latex gloves from his shoulder bag and picked up the letter, turning it over in his hands, sniffing it, holding it up to the light.

The same linen stock. Laser label.

He slit the envelope down the short side. A single sheet of twice folded premium paper.

Carefully, he unfolded it. He held his breath, reading quickly:

> My Dearest Friend Alban,
> Well played, I must say. Very well played.
> I suppose, dear friend, that you know the Game is
> not yet finished.

"Lord Almighty," Arm whispered, as he peered over Bane's shoulder.

> I suppose it is only fair that our final moves in the
> Game come down to this.
> The rules, Detective. It is all about the rules.
> Balance. Yin and Yang. Your mind to my mind.
> Your child for my child.

Oh My God. Bane's hand trembled.

> Did you know, Detective, that your delightful Mag-
> gie is the very image of Susan, aside from a few
> piercings and studs?

Bane fumbled with his keys, hands shaking, reading the last lines, unable to breathe:

> Well, I am waiting for you. You have all the infor-
> mation you need to find us, your Maggie and me.
> I am waiting, a long way off. Come before it is too
> late. With my best regards, the Gamester

Chapter 37

···

Game Day: Super Bowl Sunday, 2:21 am
Bane Bungalow, Burlington

Cap burst into their living room, a look of concern on his tired face. His big handlebar mustache twitched. "Bane, I'm sorry."

"Jay," Bane said. "Go with Di to the kitchen."

Jay clung to Bane's arm.

"Please?"

Without a word she transferred her grip to Di's hand. They went to the kitchen and Bane heard Di's crooning voice. For a moment, neither Bane nor his captain spoke, and the only voice was Arm, talking on the phone in the study.

Bane held out the letter to his captain. Cap slid on gloves. His face reddened as he read the letter.

"I'm sorry, Alban." His voice was low. "I'll put Jay in protective."

"No."

"You have to."

"No. She's going to her Uncle Barry. The horses will keep her mind off this."

"In Canada?"

"Yes."

He leaned closer and Bane smelled the brandy on his breath. Brandy with the governor, toasting the end of the case? "I was wrong. I'm sorry."

"Well that's really helpful, Cap." For the second time, Bane's little house on the hill overlooking the bay was a crime scene. "I want a trooper to escort Jay across the border."

"Done."

"I want my team reassembled."

He shook his head. "Isn't going to happen. I've put Martin Barber in charge. And Hix."

Christ. Mags would never be found.

"You're too close. Bane, let us handle it."

"I'm a time bomb, Cap, and I'm just about ready to blow. Just stay out of my way." How did his voice remain so calm?

"I can't let you do that, Bane."

Bane pushed his face within an inch of Cap's. "You think I'm going to let *dufus* Hix and by-the-book Barber find my Mags? You know me better than that."

"You're too emotional."

"Read the damn letter. He's challenging me. It's always been about him and me."

"I don't believe that."

"Then you're as big an ass as our fat-assed governor." Bane couldn't control a tremble that cascaded through his body. "Christ, Cap! I can't even quit the case. He *wants* me in his Game. He'll kill her if I quit."

Cap nodded and put his hand on Bane's. "I want your badge and your gun."

Bane shook his head. "No."

"Let *us* find her. I don't want some vigilante out gunning down a suspect."

Bane stood up, dug in his pocket for the badge and tossed it on the couch. "Take it."

"The gun."

Bane opened his jacket to reveal the Smith and Wesson Air Light. "My gun. A gift from the Director of the FBI." He pulled it out by the grip, turning the jewelry-fine revolver in his hand. Bane heard the near hysteria in his own voice as he blathered. "Weighs just seventeen ounces. Titanium alloy. Point three-fifty-seven target. Engraved. See here? It says: '*To Alban Bane, with best regards, Director Harris.*' Gave it to me in the hospital two days after I caught Hayden—when I didn't know if I'd live or die."

Cap's eyes were fixed on the chrome revolver.

"Funny damn thing to give someone in the hospital, isn't it?" Bane considered handing the gun to his captain. *Let cooler heads work this.* He caressed the double-action trigger. "This is personal, it's licensed, and the only damn way you're taking it is if you draw your own piece."

"Christ, Bane."

Bane shoved his Air Light back in the worn holster and looked at his Captain. "Call that escort, Cap," he said. "And you see to my daughter's safety."

Cap nodded and Bane thought he saw tears glistening in his captain's eyes. "I will. Personally." He glanced one more time at the gun on Bane's belt. "And you be careful, my friend."

Bane shook his hand. "I can only promise no one will harm my Mags."

Bane joined Arm in the study. Arm stared at him with mournful eyes. Bane booted his desktop computer, the hard drive spinning with a tick-ticketytick. Bane's own breathing was loud in his ears.

"Arm, 'your child for my child'. The Gamester's letter."

Arm shook his head, not understanding.

"Your background checks say Wingate had two sons, Austin and Sampson Bartlett." Bane's mind worked quickly now. "Assuming Austin is the cowboy assassin, maybe it was Sampson who attacked Susan in San Francisco. I'm sure he had a third child. A *bastard*. Like his father."

Arm shook his head. "Where's all this coming from?"

"Wingate is—Hayden's father. I'm sure of it."

"But how?"

"Instinct. I don't know. But I think I know how to prove it." Bane's hands flew on his keyboard.

"Wha's up, bro?"

"I need your supervisor's password."

"I'll be damned." He stabbed his finger at the monitor. "You're in the Bureau's violent offenders database. How'd you do that?"

"Databases and books are the chronologist's best friend. Your password."

"Bro. I can't."

Bane swiveled in his chair. "It's Mags' life. Don't argue with me."

Arm reached past Bane, tapped the keyboard and they were in.

Bane dove through the directories, found his way to the root directory, skipped down to the closed files, past another security barrier, bypassed two warnings, and he was in.

Hayden's file.

Bane scanned, scrolled page after page, wincing at the crime scene photos. Children, hung and bled. Bane's nightmare.

"Yes. Here."

Arm slid on a pair of glasses and at any other time Bane would have laughed. Arm wore reading glasses. He never knew that. Mags would have teased him for days.

Mags. Bane's vision blurred. He was crying. He wiped the tears.

"Hayden was brought up in foster homes. So?"

"Killed his foster parents, see? Went to juvie."

"So? We knew that already."

"That file's locked. The juvie file."

"Of course.—no don't, Bane. There'll be a log."

Bane just said one word. "Mags."

He reached past Bane again, entered his highest clearance password. "Shit. I'm dead, if they find out. We'll be private investigators together, I guess."

"If we're not in jail."

"Right."

"Yeah. This is it." Bane read quickly, felt his excitement rise. "I'm in."

"You hacked into Child Services?" Arm scowled. "Hacking's a federal crime."

Bane shrugged. "Hacking is a research tool. I trained at Quantico, learned everything I know from old Tierry."

"You're scaring me, bro."

"Nothing. Sealed records."

Action. That was what Bane needed. He needed somewhere to go with guns drawn.

"I have another way. Your password works in Revenue too?"

Arm shrugged. "At some levels."

Bane was already typing and the screen changed to the IRS home page. He jumped through the directories and a password field popped onto his screen. "Now's the time to find out."

Arm took a deep breath, typed in his highest clearance code, expelled with a windy sigh.

"We're in." Bane dropped to the root directory but was denied. He jumped higher and swung through the tax returns directory.

"What are you doing?"

"Accessing Laura Kincaid's returns."

"You can't do that without a warrant!"

"I'm a hick detective in Vermont. I'll plead ignorance."

"It's my pass code."

"I'll say I threatened you." Bane's finger stabbed at the monitor. "Here it is."

"What?"

"Look at this. The appendix ledger."

"Holy shit."

"Emerson Bartlett paid Hayden's legals. Over eight million dollars."

"Holy shit."

"Hayden was Wingate's son." Bane felt a cold shiver as he said it.

"That's a leap, even for you."

Bane shut down his computer. It was enough for him. He stood up, faced Arm. "I'm right."

Arm nodded. "I'm with you. Right or wrong."

"If I'm wrong—" Bane couldn't finish the statement. If he was wrong, Mags was dead. If he was right, they still had to find Wingate-Bartlett.

Stabbing pain shot through Bane's head and he dry swallowed four aspirin.

"You telling your captain?"

"Too risky. He might lock me up."

"Isn't he a friend?"

"Another reason not to tell him." He put his hand on Arm's shoulder. "I've screwed with one friend's career already."

Chapter 38

Game Day: Super Bowl Sunday, 7:12 am
Burlington, Vermont

I am waiting, a long way off.

Long way. . .

As Bane drove past the city limits, well over the posted speed limit, he said, "Arm, he has a clinic and a house on Long Island."

The speedometer hit eighty-five, his tires slid on the icy corners.

"For true."

That had to be it. Was it too obvious? Bane braked as he approached a blind corner too fast, and they went into a controlled skid.

Mags, where are you?

He had to be sure. Twenty-four hours. *The Game.* A *long* way off. *Long* Island.

It wasn't enough.

There were only two of them, no task force or inter-department cooperation, no network of exploitable resources who could search for Mags in any of Wingate's clinics or homes. No one else believed it was Wingate.

Arm put his hand on Bane's thigh. "Bane, I have influence, but without grounds, forget a warrant."

Bane knew that. "Fine. Forget the warrants."

"You know what you're asking?"

"We're already headed for a jail cell. Might as well make sure we give the governor and my colonel ulcers."

"If you're right, the case may be thrown out on a technicality. Hacking federal computers, entering without warrants. Christ, we may rot in jail right alongside the Green Mountain Freedom boys."

"I have no plans to make arrests, Arm." He kept his eyes on the road as the speedometer hit ninety-eight on ice. "You want out, jump now."

Arm said nothing.

"You understand me? No trial, no warrant, no badge, no prisoners. People like Wingate have lawyers that will get him off on a technicality. Got it?"

"Yeah, bro. But you're not ready for murder."

"I've been ready since the night they killed Susan."

Arm folded his arms. "But Long Island? Would he be that stupid?" He pointed down the highway. "Hey, watch your lane, bro."

Bane swung the wheel, careening back on the slushy pavement. "He wants us to find him. To finish the game. He'll already know I'm off the case."

"You're jazzed, bro, but I'm with you. I trust your instincts." He rapped the dashboard. "But ain't you heading the wrong way?"

"The answers are at Mason Place." Bane skidded to a stop. "You drive, Arm." He needed to think without distraction. "In my condition, I might kill us both."

"Good idea."

As Arm swung back out onto the highway, Bane punched a number in his satellite phone, praying that Hix and his own captain hadn't talked to Abbey Chase.

"Abbey Chase's office."

Bane disguised his voice, dropping down and going husky. "Fishburn and Rubie, for Ms. Chase."

Chase's assistant wasn't fooled. "I doubt she'll talk to you, Alban."

"Just tell her I have her next big story."

"I don't know, Detective." She put him on hold; audio recordings of outtakes from Real TV played, Zoë's voice narrating the incidents of the last few days. *In a dramatic turn of events, Detective Bane, the man who led the daring raid on the Green Mountain Terrorists, as they're now known, was removed from active duty pending a judiciary review. . .*

"Hello?" Abbey Chase sounded tired. "Alban?"

"Thank you for taking my call."

"I will always take your call."

Bane closed his eyes, shutting out Arm's wild driving on slippery roads. "Abbey—I need your help."

"They're wrong, you know."

"Who?"

"All of them. They're fools for removing you from the case."

"Thank you. . . Abbey, why would you say that? I gave you a rough ride?"

"So? You did your job. I did mine. Let's leave it there."

"I need to—I need access to Doctor Wingate's office."

Silence. For a moment Bane thought the line had dropped.

"Of course." Her voice was neutral. "Alban, you should know, I was officially informed that Lieutenant Barber is in charge here. Finishing off the investigation. Nearly all your men have left Mason Place."

"Abbey, just do me a favor." *Please remember, I chased the monsters out of your haunted house.* "I need you to be a friend—not a producer."

"Were we ever friends?"

"No. But maybe that can change?"

"What, no zingers?"

"You mean like, come on, Abbey, just let me search his office and I promise to tie you up and give you a night of rough sex."

"I might take you up on that."

"I know you will."

"Okay, come to the south gate."

"Thanks."

"And make it two nights of rough sex. I tie you up."

"Done."

When they arrived at Mason Place, the changes were obvious. Instead of a parking lot full of trooper SUVs and coroner vans, the lot was jammed with news broadcaster trucks. They were no longer exiled to outside the big iron gates, as they had been under Bane's authority. Now, there was no way to avoid the press line. They drove as close to the entrance as they could to avoid the worst of it.

Hugh King noticed them first. "Bloodhound Bane!" he shouted, and ran through knee-deep snow after them.

Camera lights went on, filling the early evening with glare, and the pack of journalists ran towards Bane and Arm, microphones lifted like weapons.

King arrived first, barring their path to the crew's entrance. "Blood-hound Bane! Is it true your daughter has been kidnapped?"

How did he know that? How could he possibly know already? Bane sprinted forward like a running back and levered King out of the way. King fell back into a drift of snow with a grunt.

Christ. They knew already! It would be on the news—and so would Bane, knocking down Hugh King. The headline in King's *Crime Times* would likely read, *Fugitive Cop Attacks Journalist*, and then the story would go on to delve into Bane's personal life, with a profile of Mags and her C average in school, and her boyfriend the football linebacker. King would probably run archived crime scene photos of Susan Bane lying in the snow.

But Bane had no time to worry about reporters.

Abbey Chase was waiting for them. Her security guards kept the reporters out of the house and she took him by the arm and guided them down the hall towards the executive wing. She squeezed his arm. "I'm so sorry."

"Thank you."

"Your Lieutenant Barber is waiting for you," she whispered. "He didn't find out from me."

"Is there any way around him?"

"This way." She led the way down a flight of stairs to the finished production suites. They wound through the familiar corridors and up a second flight of stairs to the other side of the executive wing.

Bane glanced down the marble hall, dimly lit with bronze sconces. Troopers stood near her office. They ducked around the corner and slipped into Wingate's office, closing the door behind them.

Abbey Chase put her hand on Bane's and he let it rest there, oddly comforted. She leaned close and kissed him on the cheek. "For luck, Alban."

She left them with a final lingering look and a sad smile that spoke volumes—Abbey the woman, not Chase the producer.

Arm, under any other circumstance, would have ribbed Bane about the kiss. His face was unreadable. "What are we looking for?"

"Anything that might tell us where he'd have Mags."

"Thought you said Long Island."

"We have one chance at this."

They searched every inch of the office, not worrying about messes or forensic searches that might follow. Bane jimmied the locks on Wingate's desk and emptied drawers on the desk.

On the bookcase Bane found a gallery of Wingate photographs. Wingate with the President of the United States on the White House lawn. Wingate posing beside a marlin on a boat with Senator Stephens.

Bane picked up the photo.

Arm paused in his search, bent over a drawer in Wingate's credenza. "What's up, bro?"

"Senator Stephens was Wingate's friend."

"So? Wingate knew everyone, didn't he?"

"He was Hix's alibi."

"There you go then."

Bane smashed the glass and snatched out the photo. He crumpled it into his pocket.

"I don't see how this helps us find Mags," Arm said. He resumed his search.

History. It was all about history. Bane scanned the bookshelves, a shrine to Wingate's brilliant work. Book after book by the illustrious psychiatrist who was really a Bartlett, and a relative of a mass murderer. Not quite a fraud. He *had* graduated. He *had* worked his way to the Chairmanship of the Psychiatric Society, to the confidence of the elite. His brilliance *was* genuine. But how far apart were brilliance and madness? Was sociopathy genetic?

Bane yanked a book from the shelf. He held a bound galley—a new book, not yet published, bound for reviewers. *Vampire Killer: A Study in Schadenfreude Disorder*, by Doctor Jonathon Wingate.

Liar, Bane thought. *It should be Doctor Bartlett, distant cousin of a mass murderer.*

The pictures of Hayden in the book were all of his early years, before the madness began. School photos. Hayden was handsome and smiling and movie-star perfect.

Wingate's perfect son.

Bane stopped on the acknowledgments page and read quickly. "I must acknowledge all of my mentors and teachers at Harvard. To my dear friends and colleagues." A black and white photograph under the acknowledgement was a posed shot of Wingate with some associates. His friends and colleagues. Bane couldn't make out the faces, but the caption riveted him.

As Arm hovered over his shoulder, Bane read it out loud: "Posing at the opening of the Wingate Clinic in the Hamptons: Sen. Stephens of Maine, Dr. Jonathon Wingate of Long Island, Congressman Willis of Orange County, CIA Director Lambert, Hunt Pharmaceuticals CEO Dr. Charles Macmillan, Dr. Sherman Skillman of Miami. . ."

Bane stared at the tiny photo, trying to make out the features. Skillman, with his wacky blond Afro. And, of course, Stephens. All directly linked to Wingate. To Hayden. Historical links Bane had missed in their mad rush to investigate a rapid series of killings.

Think, Bane. What does it all mean?

Hayden. Doctor Skillman, Stephens, even the CIA Director Hermann. It was a conspiracy. And conspiracies required a mission.

"We need to talk to Skillman again."

Bane ran for the door, more convinced than ever, and swung it open.

Lieutenant Martin Barber stood outside, with two troopers. "Alban."

Not now, damn it. "Marty."

"You're not supposed to be here."

"Couldn't stay away. Love this place so much. You know, now that I'm a private citizen, maybe I'll volunteer to compete in this show. What do ya think?"

His steel gray eyebrow lifted. His most striking feature was a sweep of silver hair matched by gray eyebrows over hard gray eyes. "This is my investigation now, Alban."

"I know."

He nodded. "Do I have to detain you?"

"You can't. And you know why you can't."

Again, he nodded. "I'm sorry about Mags, Alban." He thrust out his hand. "Officially, I can't help. Unofficially, ask."

Bane pumped his hand. "You're a good man, Marty."

They all followed as Bane led the way back down to the basements towards the offices of Doctor Skillman in his small clinic.

It all fit now. Skillman was linked to Hayden. And to Wingate. The scalpels. Skillman had been one of the doers.

Skillman, Bane knew, suffered from Gulf War Syndrome. Wingate, his teacher and psychiatrist, was—instead of helping him—fanning the embers of insanity. Just as he had with the Green Mountain Terrorists. And perhaps many others. Wingate had been a consulting psychiatrist for the FBI. How many agents had he screwed with?

As they ran through the hall, Lieutenant Martin Barber close behind, they picked up one of Abbey Chase's camera crews.

The clinic door was ajar.

Bane glanced at Marty, who nodded, giving him the go-ahead.

Bane pushed back the door.

Skillman nodded as Bane entered the clinic. "More stitches?" He laughed.

Bane scanned the tiny clinic room, noticing the open cabinets. A tray of surgical instruments lay across the tile floor. He stepped into the room, his hand on the grip of his .38. Arm slid against the door, drawing his automatic.

"Zoom in," Abbey Chase said, stepping aside to allow her camera crew a clearer view.

"We need to talk, Doctor."

"I know." Again the half-mad giggle. "But I won't sing, I won't sing."

In both hands he had fully loaded syringes. "Been waiting for me, have you?" The man was high. And clearly crazy. He stabbed the air with the hypos.

Bane aimed carefully with his .38—at the man's crotch. Even crazy people cared about that.

Skillman froze.

"Cover me, Arm." Bane moved in with handcuffs and his revolver. "Put the hypos down, Doc."

Skillman stabbed the air.

"If he does that again, Arm, you can shoot him. Aim for his jewels."

Skillman put the hypos down on a roll-away table.

"You're not as crazy as I thought. Hands behind your back, Doc."

"Hands behind my back, behind my back!" Skillman saluted, then tucked his hands behind his back.

Bane moved in.

Abbey Chase and her cameraman also moved in.

"Abbey, stay back."

In that moment, Bane's attention diverted, Skillman dove forward and snatched a hypo. Bane jumped aside. Arm shot once. But Skillman was not after either of them. He dove to the left and tackled Abbey Chase.

She screamed.

Chapter 39

Game Day: Super Bowl Sunday
Mason Place

Abbey smelled his breath. Bitter coffee breath, and something else. Something metallic. Her own breathing accelerated.

"Don't struggle," Skillman said, his lip brushing her ear.

Abbey choked back a scream. Her own cameras were turned on her now. She would now be seen by the world as a whimpering victim of a madman. She stiffened, closed her eyes for a moment, controlled her breathing and tried to think. She must not panic. Skillman tightened his grip and his bony frame was unyielding behind her. She struggled again to choke back a scream, aware of the cameras and ashamed of her weakness.

"Keep filming," she said, her voice a croak.

"Yes, by all means, film away!" Skillman laughed.

Bane and Arm moved in opposite directions along the clinic wall with guns drawn. At the doorway, Bobby continued to film, looking pale and scared, but not missing a shot. Other cops moved into the room, until the room felt crowded.

Keep back, she thought, wildly. *Keep back. Why are you crowding us?*

"Doctor. There's no where to go," Bane said. Did he sound afraid? Was he afraid for her? With his own daughter kidnapped by a killer, he could spare her pity?

There was a pressure at her neck, a sharp point.

"This hypo contains pancuronium bromide," Skillman said, his voice shrill.

Abbey felt sharp pain. She choked back the rise of panic, fought it back. The cameras! The cameras were on her. If she was to die it would be with dignity. Only image and dignity mattered. It kept her sane in a world of madness, a place where fathers could be demons who tortured their children. Dignity!

"Recognize that? Pancuronium bromide. Recognize that, Bane?" His voice sounded like a chant.

Bane moved, his foot sliding so slowly she barely registered it. "Yes, Doctor. Your friend Hayden had a nice dose of that, thanks to me."

Skillman's grip tightened. The pain sharpened at the back of her spine. "I can pump her. Pump her. Pump her! Remember that."

"Yes, I remember," Bane said, flinching. His eyes blazed, the knuckles on his clenched fists turning white. He cared about her. He was afraid for her. She felt a sudden rush of emotions that confused her. Her heart pumped faster, adrenalin feeding her, a heat rising. She was about to die. About to die on national television, and all she could think about was Bane.

He cared for her.

Bane shuffled half a step closer, his .38 pulled close to his chest. "You can pump her if you want. Ms. Prada is of no more use to me."

"You're just saying it." Skillman's voice sounded so loud, his mouth next to her ear. "Saying it! I know you want her. You want her bad."

"No, really. She's damaged goods."

Abbey stared at Bane. What was he doing?

"I'll stick her!"

"I said go ahead. Then I shoot you. And enjoy it."

"Enjoy it! Enjoy it!" Skillman shouted in her ear, and she stiffened. His arm tightened again. His breath again. Sickly sweet and bitter at the same time. Something metallic. And body odor. As if he hadn't washed in days.

She knew something important. Something Bane would want to know. Something that might make a difference.

"What are you waiting for, Skillman? Just do it." Bane was a little closer, now. "Life isn't worth living anymore, is it? Why bother?"

Abbey stared at Bane. What was he up to?

"I mean, you're a limp dick, am I right? Tried the blue pill, but it doesn't work. Why bother living?"

Skillman no longer sang. The hypo no longer pressed as hard against her skin.

Abbey was sure of the sweet metallic odor, now. She smelled it in his sweat, too. Felt his trembling. He was strung out on drugs. His breathing was rapid and she felt him dancing from toe to toe.

She controlled her breathing, locking her eyes on Bane's. She blinked her eyes three times. Three more times. He noticed, but didn't understand. "Get close-ups, Bobby," she said.

Bobby slid into the clinic, filming the high drama.

"That's not my good side," Skillman said.

"You don't have a good side," Bane said. "Look, Skillman, this is all very dramatic. But why not just hurry up and die. That's what you want, right?"

"Hurry up and die! Hurry up and die!" Skillman sang the words.

How could she not have seen Skillman's madness? Cole had hired the whacked-out Gulf War veteran. Though she had objected, she never saw anything that hinted at this. She thought of the physicals Skillman gave her, of his fingers on her skin, of his light humming as he had examined her, his sly winks as he had checked her blood pressure and told her she would have to relax more and eat more oatmeal. She shivered.

"Don't let the suuun go down on me. . ." Skillman broke into the Elton John song, his mad voice melodious. He pulled Abbey back a step.

"You want to die, don't you, Skillman? That's why you waited for me, isn't it?"

"No closer!" The mad doctor continued to sing. *"Too late to save myself from falling. . ."*

Arm steadied his automatic pistol. "You give up now, Doc, you live. You do anything else and you ain't got no head."

Abbey watched Bane's calm face, drawing strength there. She saw his eyes moving, calculating. He winked at her and she saw the slightest nod. How could he be so cool? It wasn't him that was about to die.

Skillman's voice rose to a crescendo. *"Although I search myself, it's always someone else I see. . ."*

"I see a pathetic doctor who sold his patients to Tyler Hayden," Bane said mildly.

"Whatchya mean?"

"You know, the best way to break a bad habit, Skillman?" Bane stepped closer. "Just say no. Just say "no" to psycho-killing. Cold turkey."

"Don't discard me just because you think I mean you harm. . ."

"Skillman, just let her go," said Arm. His big gun was pointing right at them. To Abbey it seemed to be pointing at her!

"I'll poke her! I'll poke her!" shouted Skillman.

"Stand down, Arm," said Bane. He lowered his gun. After a moment Arm complied.

Think, Abbey. Think. She knew Skillman better than anyone here. She couldn't die now. Not with her career rising. Not with the number one show in the ratings. No, Bane would save her. Bane would find a way, and then they'd broadcast this tape of her as a hostage and gain another six points in the ratings. Minimum.

She studied Alban Bane. He was calmer. She had to give him the opportunity. He had fans now. If he saved her on broadcast television, it would increase the show's popularity.

Skillman sang on, his wild voice rising to a near scream. *"And these cuts I have. . ."* he burst into hysterical laughter, and she felt tears flowing down his face.

"Doc," she said. "Doc, listen."

Skillman laughed, but she felt him hold his breath. Listening.

"Doc, this isn't going to work." She tried to turn to face him, but Skillman pulled harder.

"Abbey, shut up," Bane said. He shrugged and winked. "Women."

"Can't live with them," Skillman said. The needle pushed deeper.

Arm stepped forward, but Skillman shouted, "I'm on her jugular!" Arm stepped back as the doctor broke into a new song.

"You want to die, right, Skillman?" Bane was half a step closer, now. "Can't live with all this, right? Helping Hayden. Then, Bartlett?"

She felt the needle pull away.

It was no use. Skillman slipped back into song. *"Don't discard me just because you think I mean you harm. . ."*

"You know this is an awesome television moment," Bane said. "That's what you want, right?"

"You know nothing! Nothing!" And he sang again, *"Don't discard me."*

Bane took one more step. "But Bartlett did discard you. He's off in his home on the coast, laughing at you right now! He masterminded this whole thing and left you to take the blame. Isn't that right?"

Skillman didn't sing this time.

Bane shuffled half a step closer.

"Don't move," Skillman screamed. "I'm not telling you again!"

"Doc, we can help you." She half turned in Skillman's loosened arm. She could smell his breath again, on her cheek now.

"No one can help me." Skillman's voice was suddenly the small child. The frightened child.

"Just release me," she said, her voice a low croon. "I'll protect you. I have the best lawyers money can buy."

The hypo pressed against her neck, but the other arm loosened. "It's too late. Too late, too late, too late. . ."

Abbey shouted, "Doc!" Distracted, Skillman loosened his grip on her. "Doc, we can help you. We can make you better."

She felt his moist breath on her neck as he laughed. "No one can help me. No one can."

And suddenly she fell to the floor. She felt cold tile. She rolled over, half expecting Skillman's head to explode in fragments as both Bane and Arm opened fire.

"Don't move," Bane said. He was at her side, pulling her away. She clung to him as he held her. Tears rushed down her cheek. His gun was still leveled at Skillman.

"I'm all right," Abbey said. She stood with Bane's help, straightened the creases in her dress. "I'm fine."

Now she studied Skillman. She should have felt revulsion. Hate. She should have felt rage. She should have grabbed Bane's gun and blown his scrawny head off. But she felt only pity. This was not a monster like her father. Like Wingate. This was a pitiful wretch. The trembling stopped, and she realized that Bane's arm was still holding her shoulder. It felt good there. She slid a little closer.

"He poisoned himself," Abbey whispered in Bane's ear. "I smelled it on him. Like almonds."

"Doctor Skillman. They say dying men don't lie."

Skillman's mouth moved but no words came. Bubbles of saliva percolated from his lips. He laughed. Tears flowed down his cheeks. "Too late," he said.

"Just tell me! Where's my daughter?"

Skillman's hand, still holding the hypo, stabbed the air. "He's waiting for you. You alone. You alone." He fell to the floor so hard his knee caps cracked.

"Long Island? Is Wingate at Long Island?" Bane knelt in front of him.

Skillman's eyes were open, staring. He nodded, wildly. "Go alone. *Aloooonne!*"

Bane pried the hypo from Skillman's hand and felt for his pulse. "His heart's stopped."

Skillman lay beside Bane. A discarded scarecrow. Wingate had no more use for him. He was programmed to expire. Skillman was nothing but a lump of cooling flesh.

She stood in the middle of the room, the tears streaking down her face. "I'm sorry, Alban."

"Why are you sorry, Abbey?"

She didn't look at Skillman. "He would have known—he might have known— "

"It's all right. He told me what I needed to know."

"Okay." She clung to his arm.

"Abbey, I need one other thing from you."

She controlled her breathing, becoming Ms. Chase once more. She released his forearm. "Certainly. Of course."

"Make sure you broadcast this. Phone the governor and tell him to watch."

Chapter 40

February 3, 12:14 am
Wingate Clinic, Long Island

Five hours later Bane parked on a one-lane side road behind a patch of woodland.

If he was wrong, Mags would likely not survive. He would have lost the Game.

If he was right, Mags still might not survive.

He couldn't think about it anymore.

He shivered as a bitter wind swept up the snowy beach. The surf pounded on the iced breakwater. Moonlit clouds scudded from the southwest, the remains of a storm that had battered the south shore.

The estate was huge, probably a hundred acres of prime oceanfront, with a private spit surrounded by surf and beach on three sides. The house perched on the higher land with a view in all directions. Bane remembered from the picture in the acknowledgment page of Wingate's book that it was a grand Cape Cod style clapboard, with gables and a homey wrap-around porch.

Bane had fretted all the way down He ran on pure instinct. Long Island. *A long way off.* The picture of Senator Stephens, Wingate, Skillman and Congressman Willis, posed at the opening of the *Wingate Clinic*—in the Hamptons. On Long Island. Bane had no choice but to go on faith. Mags was here. She had to be. He had mumbled prayers to his angel—Susan Bane—to protect their daughter.

Bane's hiking boots crunched through icy crust. In summer, this would be a stunning beach front, all sand and waves and sunshine, with screaming seagulls soaring above and sailboats dotting the blue water. In the bitter chill of black night, summer splendor was hard to imagine.

On the spit point they could see the clinic, a glowing, jaunty New England mansion. Doubt assailed Bane again. The house looked so charming, so wonderfully Long Island. He was about to barge in, gun drawn on a possibly innocent house, or worse, might traumatize patients as he searched the clinic after midnight and without a warrant.

No second thoughts, Bane. Mags is all that matters.

It was a long trudge through the snow with the wind chilling them to the bone.

"You're sure you want to do this?"

"I'll go alone." Bane brought his flashlight up to illuminate a wide, worried face.

"Not likely, bro."

"Who's going to call for backup if I get in trouble?"

"You left the message for your captain and I left one for my team in New Orleans. If we don't report in—"

"It'll be too late," Bane finished for him, shaking his head.

"For true, I'm going, bro."

"Your wife won't forgive me for this." Bane had to try one more time to dissuade him with reminders of his wife and son.

"She never liked you anyway."

"Well, that sucks. Cause I thought she was yummy myself."

Arm laughed.

"Think again. Think of Warrick." Arm's son, the future football player, already six foot one at twelve years of age, the image of his giant dad.

"Think of Mags. If you're going, I'm going." He nudged Bane forward.

They reached the estate fence, a tall stone wall that crumbled where it met the sea break.

Arm was first up, and his heavy frame pulled down cracked stone. He balanced, awkward, on the top of the sea wall, before dropping to the other side.

Bane pulled himself up, splayed his legs across the top of the wide wall, a bare hand on either side for balance, and scanned the estate from the higher perch. He teetered on the top, buffeted by wind that bit his skin. When he was sure there were no sentries or guard dogs, he slid over and down. There would be patrols and cameras closer to the house. They could only hope the Wingate Clinic had few live-in patients and a minimal night staff.

Bane slid along a cluster of jagged rocks. His Sox baseball cap and butt-freezer jacket gave him little protection from the wind. The moon broke through the clouds, and Bane hesitated. Where were the cameras? When they were close enough to the house, they crouched behind a wind-burned boxwood hedge that defined a formal garden. He peered over it at the grand old mansion. Lights blazed in every room on the ground floor. The upstairs rooms were mostly dark, their windows shuttered. Elegant drapes framed the ground-floor bay windows and crystal chandeliers threw warm light.

"Not much activity," Arm whispered.

"No."

"You sure you want to break and enter?"

"Define sure. If you mean, are we going in, yes. If you mean, do I want to go in, no."

Arm straightened and sprinted across the snow-covered gardens, weaving in and out of the topiary like an assassin. He squatted under the verandah then waved at Bane. Everything seemed loud now—his breath, gusting out in clouds, his feet crunching in the snow. Somewhere in the darkness a dog barked. When no alarm sounded, they hustled to the stairs, pressing their backs to the yellow plank walls. Bane slid towards the country-style screen door. He tugged on the handle, and the hinges screeched as it opened. He tried the knob inside. It was not locked.

"I don't like this, bro."

"Let's not be rude. We're obviously expected." Bane drew his Smith and Wesson. Arm already had his Glock cupped in two hands.

Bane turned the knob again, and the door swung open. The wind caught it and slammed it wide.

"Shit." Bane ducked inside, blinking his eyes to adjust to the light.

"Can I help you?"

Bane whirled around, dropping his .38 to chest level, finger off the trigger.

"If this is a burglary, we have nothing of great value here." The man in the white coat stared at Bane's gun, his lifted eyebrows the only sign of alarm. At six foot two, with shoulders as broad as Arm's, the man seemed out of place in the doctor's smock. Hard black eyes and a cool smirk put Bane on alert.

Would a doctor in a clinic be so calm in the face of a break-in?

"Thinking about checking in my dad," Bane said and he holstered his gun. Arm hesitated, then belted his automatic.

"Is that so?" The man in the white coat stepped forward, crisp and cool. "I suppose you expect a tour?"

Arm dove into his pocket for his ID, probably remembering Bane had no badge, and handed it to the man. Bane watched the man's face, wary. He seemed too calm. "FBI? What is your business here?"

"We're here to see Doctor Wingate."

Bane studied the foyer. Country charm. Wide plank floors, painted wainscoting. Martha Stewart would be right at home.

"Is he expecting you, drawn guns and all?"

"Actually, I think he is. Guns and all," Bane said.

"You're a smart-mouthed Fed, aren't you?" His foot tapped on the hardwood floor. "Well, Doctor Wingate does not see anyone without an appointment, Mr—"

"Bane. Alban Bane."

"Oh, yes. I've seen you on television, haven't I?" Again, the sarcasm. "Do you have a warrant, Detective?"

"We have probable cause, here—besides, we have guns."

"Yes, I see that."

"What are you then? A doctor?"

"If it's any of your business, a therapist."

"Do you have a name? Or should I call you Mr. X?"

"Mr. Smith."

"Of course." Bane peered at the plastic identification dangling from the smock. It said Mr. Smith. "May we look around?"

"No, sir." Mr. Smith's foot continued to tap. "Where's your camera crew? Aren't you some kind of television star now?"

Bane scowled at him. "With probable cause, we don't need your permission."

"I doubt that." He shrugged and pointed to the far corner of the foyer, beside one of the colonial pillars. "We have our own cameras, Detective Bane." He winked. The red light indicated the camera was on.

"We'll just poke around anyway. Make sure the kitchen's clean. Use the bathroom. You know."

"Suit yourself. You don't mind if I call the *local* police?"

Bane smiled. "No. And you don't mind if I shoot out a few locks?"

As expected, Mr. Smith did not go to the phone. Bane crossed the room with Arm at his back. Mr. Smith made no move to follow. They passed through a salon, richly appointed in leather and colonial antiques.

"They just practically invited us in, Arm."

Arm snorted. "*Mr. Smith.*"

A raven-haired woman reading a book in a wingback chair looked up, opened her mouth to speak then said nothing. She closed the book and watched Citizen Alban Bane and Agent Arm Saulnier cross to the next room. They paused in a dining room dominated by a mahogany table with twelve chairs, illuminated by a crystal chandelier.

"This is some clinic," Arm said.

Bane wasn't feeling good about this. It had the look of an upscale clinic or a home, and Bane was breaking and entering.

If he was wrong, the police would come, they would be arrested, and Mags might die.

I can't be wrong.

The front door had been unlocked. Lights on. It wasn't what Bane expected. He was exhausted, he'd made the wrong choice, he'd never find Mags in time. His throw of the dice would kill Mags.

They saw only therapists and the odd patient in the mansion. In the kitchen, a man peeled an apple.

"Who are you?" he asked. He slid a slice into his mouth.

"Exterminators. Looking for rats." Bane scanned the kitchen. There was a narrow stairway.

They moved up the stairs, every step creaking, and emerged on an open landing. A man and a woman chatted on a plush love seat.

"Bane, I don't think—"

"I'm not thinking anymore, Arm. Thinking's over-rated." It was too late to worry about being wrong. Bane would already be up on charges. Every room of this clinic had to be searched now. There was nothing to lose. He opened the first door on the second floor. Unlike the ground floor rooms, it was dark. Bane flipped the light switch.

"Hey!" a voice shouted. A man rolled over, the blankets falling away from his body.

"Sorry," Bane said, turning off the light.

Wingate had played them. The doctor was probably watching right now on their security closed-circuit cameras. Laughing at them. Bane was conscious of the cameras in every hall and knew that when the case came to trial—the case of the rogue detective breaking and entering the famous Wingate Clinic—there would be no defense, beyond, "Ladies and gentlemen of the jury, Alban Bane acted with the emotions of a father."

Arm watched from the hall as Bane burst into the second bedroom. For the first time since Bane had known him, Arm seemed embarrassed. Perhaps he too was thinking of his career, of how Bane had destroyed his chances at promotion. As Bane emerged from the empty bedroom, Arm said, "Let's get out of here."

"Not until I embarrass every patient."

"You're embarrassing me."

"Arm, chill."

There was a patient in nearly every room, and Bane woke all of them. There would be hell to pay.

They headed back down the main staircase to the foyer. Mr. Smith in his white coat smirked at them. "Satisfied?"

"No."

"I've called the police."

"Good." Bane pointed to another door under the main stairs. "Are the treatment rooms through there?"

Mr. Smith hesitated, stepped closer, then nodded.

Bane turned the knob. Locked. "Open it."

He folded his arms, and Bane noticed the naked forearms were as gnarly and hard as an old Scotch pine tree.

Bane pulled his gun. "Open it."

"You going to shoot me?" Mr. Smith winked.

"Maybe. Or I'm going to shoot the lock."

The smile never failed. "They must do things differently in Vermont." When Bane didn't holster his gun, Mr. Smith walked forward and pulled a key ring off his belt, extending it on a retractable line, and unlocked the door. He stepped back and gestured with his hand.

"There you go, Detective."

Bane studied the man's body language. His foot tapped, his arms were folded, he smirked.

The man's attitude gave Bane reason to hope he was not wrong.

With his .38 in hand he pushed back the door. The room was pitch black. He looked back at Smirky. "Light switch?"

"Inside the door, to the right."

Bane held the gun close to his chest, finger resting on the trigger guard, and reached around the door jam with his other hand. He felt the switch.

Started to lift it.

Something stung his hand. He yanked it back. There was blood in the meat of his thumb. He looked over his shoulder.

Smirky was gone.

"It's a trap, Arm."

"Christ." Arm pressed his back to the wall, Glock in hand.

Bane pulled his flashlight from his belt, flipped it on and swept the room with it. He stumbled forward.

"What's wrong, Bane?"

"Woozy. I feel dizzy." Bane looked at his hand.

A hypo. He'd been drugged or poisoned. Either way there wasn't much time. It meant Mags was here. Had to be here. Bane focused on Mags. They wouldn't assault an officer, even breaking and entering, if she wasn't here. Bane clung to the thought, used it to focus his cloudy mind. The hypo proved she was here.

The floor seemed to buck under him.

He stepped forward, swung sideways and knelt with his back to the wall, gun held low. He scanned the area with light. Bane tried to stand without leaning against the wall, but dizziness took him and he swayed back. Arm reached over with his gun grip and snapped on the light with the handle. He helped Bane stand. The room was empty. Bane leaned closer to the light switch. A tiny hypo needle, still pink with his blood, was taped beside the light switch, a crude but effective trap. *I'm a damn fool.*

"Careful Arm," Bane slurred.

Nausea took him now, he wanted to puke.

Bane concentrated on the room. Empty. It appeared to be a waiting room for patients. On the far side was a paneled mahogany door with a bronze handle.

"Arm, call backup."

Arm reached for his satellite phone, unsnapping the strap on his belt.

The door across from them burst open.

Two men dressed as security guards, both with guns, stood in the doorway. Behind Bane and Arm, a voice called out. "Drop your weapons and stand against the wall."

Bane glanced over his shoulder. Smirky Smith stood there, a big kitchen knife in his hand. "Lower your weapons." Bane moved his gun hand, and Mr. Smith snapped, "Slowly, Detective!"

Bane let the .38 spin upside down on his index finger and held it out. Arm copied the move. Mr. Smith stepped forward and slid the guns from their fingers.

"We're arresting you for trespassing. Understand? I'd read you your rights, but this is a—how do you say it? A citizen's arrest." He laughed, a short staccato burst.

He started to turn away. Bane lunged, grabbed Smith's forearm and spun him. Bane's limbs were heavy but he bent the so-called therapist's arm behind his back in a lock.

Arm crouched and let fly with a roundhouse kick that caught one of the guards. The guard flailed backwards, his gun discharged. Arm knocked the second guard back into the wall.

Bane's knees wobbled. Dizziness took him. He leaned against the wall, clinging to Smith. Arm bent and snatched up their guns, one in each hand. He aimed one at a guard's chest.

"No one move!" Arm stepped closer to Smirky, but the guards didn't seem to care. Both guards fired.

Bane tried to fling himself to one side, but his muscles wouldn't move.

He felt the pressure before the pain. The bullet tore through his shoulder. He slammed against the wall, and slid to the floor. He lay on the floor and pressed one hand over the wound to stop the blood.

"Bane!" Arm dropped to one knee and fired.

A burly guard fell with a grunt. The second guard fired back, but Arm twisted to the side and fired back with both guns. Smith circled around behind Arm.

"Arm, behind—" His voice slurred as the drug took him into a fog, in spite of the pain in his shoulder. His vision blurred. "Watch—out—"

Arm spun to face Smith and his knife.

Another gun fired. Smith dropped.

As if in a dream, Bane looked up and around.

"Hix," Bane said.

Hix smiled down at him. "Are you all right?" He held his gun in both hands.

"I'm fine—how did—how—" He couldn't hang on. He surrendered to blackness, and his last thought was of how he had apparently misjudged Noland Hix.

Chapter 41

February 3, 12:41 pm
Montpelier, Vermont

Abbey Chase put her hands on her hips and stepped in front of the fire. "Gentlemen, I suggest you listen." But were they listening? Chris Harris on the speaker phone sounded condescending. Governor Ritchie by the fire chewed on his index finger nail, clearly uninterested. Only Bane's commander, Colonel Clancy, seemed attentive.

"Ms. Chase. We appreciate your concern," said Governor Ritchie. He sipped his Bailey's Irish Cream. "But Alban Bane is working outside of our jurisdiction."

Abbey ignored him. She couldn't abide fools. She stepped closer to the desk, sat on the glass top, and spoke into the speaker phone. "Mr. Director. Chris. This is not outside of your jurisdiction."

"Now, look here—" Ritchie rose from his overstuffed arm chair.

Abbey held up her hand. "No, Governor. Let me be clear. This goes beyond politics, but if you want to talk that language, let me assure you that I am willing and able to pull my productions from Vermont." She smiled. "Unless, of course, Vermont creates a more cooperative business environment for Real TV." Governor Ritchie fell back in his chair with a grunt. She leaned closer to the telephone. "Chris, this is serious."

"I appreciate your interest, Abbey," said FBI Director Chris Harris on the phone. "But we don't have probable cause."

Abbey sighed. Were all men fools? "Probable cause. Skillman held a hypodermic to my neck," she said, trying to control the emotion in her voice, trying to suppress the memory of Skillman, his chattering song loud in her ear, pressing against her, drawing her blood. She closed her eyes. Now was not the time for hysterics. "I clearly heard Doctor Skillman implicate Wingate only hours ago. His foul mouth was inches from my ear. I will testify to that."

"Yes," Chris said tersely. "I'm sorry for that. Terrible thing."

Eyes pressed firmly closed, Abbey spoke through clenched teeth. "Terrible thing? Terrible thing! It was a nightmare. I'll never forget his breath on me. The feeling of..." The only sound in the room was the snap of the fire. "Chris," she said, forcing all her will into calming her voice. "Do this one thing for me."

"Abbey, I'm sorry." She heard no real sympathy in his voice. "I'm sorry you went through that. It should never have happened. But—"

"Don't you damn well 'but' me, Chris." Her voice rose. "I'll testify to Wingate's complicity. Bane saved my life. I don't want to hear any damn 'buts' from you. You get this warrant." Eyes still closed, she focused on Bane's face. Bane, the father looking for his kidnapped daughter. Bane, the man who saved her life. Bane, the man whose face haunted her.

"A warrant is under the jurisdiction of the judiciary, Ms. Chase." Harris sounded angry now.

"And don't 'Ms. Chase' me, either." She calmed her voice, and opened her eyes. She knew how to play the game too. Abbey Chase understood that the fastest way to coerce men of power was to play them against each other. "Let me be clear. Real TV plans a major exposé on this entire case. I already have planned specials which will highlight the involvement of both Governor Ritchie and the Federal Bureau of Investigation."

"Abbey—"

"Chris," Abbey interrupted. "Your own agent is in danger. I can attest to Wingate's involvement. Lieutenant Martin Barber of the Vermont Police can verify the information. What the hell more do you want?"

"Abbey, it's not that simple."

She rapped the desk. "Are you telling me that Wingate's influence runs so deep that judicial rules no longer apply? Is that what you're telling me?"

Director Harris didn't reply. Abbey glanced at the Governor and Colonel Clancy. They squirmed in their chairs. This wasn't just a matter of throwing her weight around, of having her way. Bane was in danger. Mags was in danger. She owed them. And she would do something about it.

"Get the warrants, Chris. I demand it, as a helpful citizen, if you take my meaning. Do you, Chris? Do you take my meaning?" She knew he understood her to mean: *I can make your life very miserable.* She had done it before. On her show, *Real Law*, she had shown that the entire Bureau was filled with nincompoops. And she could also make life easier for her friends. Her influence had, in part, secured Chris Harris his current lofty position. A word in the right ear.

"I'll try, Abbey." Chris sounded defeated.

"Do it now. Not tomorrow. Wake up a Federal judge."

"Do you know what you're asking? What if Wingate's not involved? Do you understand the repercussions?"

Abbey snatched up the handset and pressed it to her ear. "Damn it, Chris. I only know the impact if you refuse. You'll be tomorrow's news. If Bane and Arm show up dead, you'll be headlines all over the nation! That I promise."

Chris sighed. "I'll do it, Abbey. But you'd better be right. Wingate knows the fucking President."

"That makes this rather urgent, wouldn't you say? Imagine the news headlines if the Feds didn't break Wingate. What if Real TV's lead news story is 'Detective Alban Bane dies at hands of madman in spite of warning to Feds?' What if the media breaks the story before you act? Imagine that."

"I'm imagining, Abbey. I'm seeing it quite clearly." Again, the sigh. "But Abbey, we don't even know they're in trouble."

"Isn't it the Bureau that states in your guidelines that kidnap victims have only twenty-four hours to live, on average? Bane told me that."

"Something like that."

"This is a kidnapping. Don't forget. Maggie Bane is a victim here. In a Federal Crime."

"Yes. Well. You are right, of course."

"Thank you, Chris."

"Don't thank me. Because I don't ever want to hear from you again." He hung up, and she knew he meant it. But she also knew he'd get the search warrants on Wingate's clinics and homes.

She hung up the phone and turned to face a pale-faced Governor and a fidgeting Colonel Clancy. "Well, gentlemen. The warrants are on the way. Colonel, I suggest you contact the New York State Police."

"I will, Ms. Chase. He's my man, too." Clancy stood and held out his hand.

Too? What the hell did that mean? She shook his hand, nodded at the Governor, and left the office, slamming the door.

She stormed through the silent halls of the capitol building, heels clicking loudly on the marble floors.

What had she done? She had thrown her weight around, threatened an FBI Director, Governor and State Police commander just for the sake of a down-home country bumpkin police detective and his daughter. Had her feelings gone that far? Yes, they had. Something had happened in that room when Skillman pressed the hypo to her neck. She tried to rationalize that it was because of the violence she had witnessed. But her career had brought her close to terror many times. No. It was more than that. There was rage. And something else. The rise of an emotion she didn't know she still possessed.

Bane must not die. Mags must live.

She hoped she wasn't too late.

Chapter 42

....

February 3, 2:41 pm
Long Island

He felt cold, nauseous, weak. He shivered. Pain lanced his shoulder, down his right side and into his leg. A blur of color punctuated with small suns of brilliance passed before his eyes.

Pain.

His eyes focused slowly but he couldn't turn his head.

He remembered now. Hix had come, just in time. He grappled with the idea of Hix as his savior. It made no sense.

He felt weak—how much blood had he lost? He tried to lift his arm and couldn't. Or his legs. He was restrained, on a gurney. He bucked in the straps, claustrophobia pressing in on him as if a pillow were pressed to his face. He closed his eyes and everything began to spin.

Why was he strapped to a gurney? He took a deep breath. *Breathe, Bane. Breathe.*

Something was very wrong here.

"Hello?" His voice echoed. "Is anyone there?"

A man in white lab coat, surgical cap and mask leaned over him.

"Just be calm, Detective," said a reassuring voice. A familiar voice. Bane tried to clear the fogginess from his head.

"Why am I restrained?"

The man laughed. "For your well-being," he said. So familiar. He knew that laugh. Where were the other hospital personnel? Nothing made sense here.

"Is Arm... my friend... all right?"

The Doctor nodded.

"Don't worry, Detective. We have treated your wound." Who was that? Bane pulled on the straps, tried to lift his leg.

"Detective, please don't move or you'll open your wound. You really must lie still."

"What's going on? Where are we?" But he knew. As the fog of sedatives dissipated, he understood.

"In my clinic."

Bane thrashed in his bonds until his shoulder wound burned.

"Bartlett!" The name was a curse on Bane's lips.

"*Doctor,*" Wingate said, his phony English accent returning.

The drug-haze confusion was gone and he was left in stark, cold reality—Wingate's version of reality.

"You have lost a lot of blood, my dear Detective." Wingate laughed. "Oh, if you could see your face. Priceless."

"Where's my daughter, asshole—?" Bane gasped as Wingate placed a hand on his shoulder wound.

"Really, dear boy, I must insist on respect." He dug his fingers into the bandages over the bullet wound, and Bane grunted.

"Big jump from 'kindly doctor' to 'mad scientist.'"

"Funny."

"No, really, I don't mind. My captain says I'm a masochist. Do your worst. Just tell me where my daughter is."

Oh God, it hurt.

"Oh come. Let us be mature about this, hmm?"

"Where is she?"

"Do not shout, Alban." He still wore the surgical mask. "Forgive the little deception. I was playing. I wanted to see your reaction, my boy."

"My reaction is, 'Oh boy, where's the straightjacket?' but I'll keep an open mind."

Bane closed his eyes as Wingate dug into the shoulder wound again.

"I know, I know, respect," Bane said, through clenched teeth. "Where'd you go to medical school? The Josef Mengele school of—" A stab of pain cut him off. After his breathing returned to normal he asked, "Where's Mags?"

"Always your daughter. What a good father you are."

"Where is *SHE?*" The words burst out of him.

Wingate wagged his finger in his face. "Now, now. Impatience does not win the game." His smile was warm. "She is here, Alban."

The gurney back started to lift. "Here, let me make you comfortable."
Wingate reached over Bane's head and unbuckled the restraint.
"There. Look left."

Bane turned his head left. His daughter, Mags, sat up in an inclined
gurney. She was strapped in, IV's into both arms. "See, there she is."

"You bastard."

Wingate's hand snapped out and rapped Bane's wound. "Manners,
manners, dear boy."

"Mags, it'll be all right. Mags!" Her head was restrained as his had
been. Her eyes were wide open, pupils dilated, druggy yet panicky. A
leather strap in her mouth prevented her from talking. She moaned.

Over Mag's head, Bane saw a suspended LCD monitor, with a
close-up image of her face. Above her image, the words *MAGGIE
BANE*. Under her image, a big **0**.

"What have you done to her?" Bane snarled it. He lurched up, pulling
hard on the arm straps.

"Just a light sedative, dear boy. She was having a panic attack."

"What are those IVs?"

"Oh, you must wait for that, my friend."

"Screw you, Wingate."

"I thought you liked games?"

"I like jokes. Games are for assholes."

Bane scanned right. Arm lay on a similar gurney, also restrained.

Arm's big arms were double strapped, an IV in each. His eyes were
open. His teeth clamped down on a leather strap through his mouth.

Over his head was a large LCD screen with his face and the words
ARMITAGE SAULNIER and **0**.

"Get the idea, Alban?"

*Hayden. Hayden, had been executed this way. Two IVs, one in each
arm.* "Yes."

"Good. Then, let the Game begin."

Bright lights blazed, blinding Bane. Applause broke out.

"What is this, Wingate?"

"Is this not fun? An American tradition, no?"

The sick bastard was playing a game. *The* Game.

"Retro of me, I know. Reality TV with a Game Show spin."

An audience laughed.

"Laugh tracks and clap tracks," Wingate said, smiling. "And lots of cameras, see?"

And Bane did see. The room was an operating theatre, filled with surgical instruments. It was also a television studio, filled with lights and cameras. One of the cameras, the one closest to him, moved on a motorized track, sliding closer, the red light over the lens coming on. Someone was controllling from an editing suite somewhere.

"Yes, I see. A juvenile game show combined with imbecilic reality television. Wingate, get a life."

"Get a life. Ha. Very good. I like my life. What about you, my friend? What do you want out of life?"

"Oh, you know. Love, family, the American dream."

"Well, here we are then. Wingate provides all. Your loving family is here. And is not reality television the American dream?" Wingate smiled. "The video will be delivered to Abbey Chase and Real TV."

"America will love it," Bane said.

"I think so, too. You know, Abbey may have feelings for you, but in the end she will broadcast your ignominy."

"I have no doubt."

"Bane, humiliated. Wetting himself. Throwing up. Screaming like a baby."

"I hope you are patient. I may wet myself if you don't take me to the toilet, but I don't scream."

"We shall see."

"So this will be the new hit TV show," Bane said, "Torture TV."

"Always the joker. Let me explain the rules, my friend. Round one, we find out just how good a detective you are. I ask questions. If you guess incorrectly, one of our two contestants loses points."

"One of. . .?"

"Yes. You see, you choose. Your friend Armitage, or your daughter Maggie. If you are wrong, the IVs drip. See? What fun." His smile was mirthless. "Tiny doses of pancuronium bromide."

Bane said nothing.

"You recognize it, do you not?"

"Yes. San Quentin."

"For executions. Very good." He caressed a small panel of buttons and digital gauges. "You answer wrong, I press this button." He pressed it. "Look right, Bane." Bane stared at the monitor over Arm's head. The **0** changed to **1**.

"Bastard."

"Just 1 cc of pancuronium bromide. Uncomfortable to be sure. Now, you might want to spread the pain, because five cc's will begin to collapse the lungs and diaghram. Hideously painful without an anesthetic. In Arm's case, big man that he is, he might endure ten ccs. before the lungs basically implode."

Arm strained against the restraints. His eyes widened. His teeth clenched on the leather strap in his mouth. His voice was angry but Bane couldn't make out any words.

"Now, there is also a wild card." Wingate pointed to another screen. It had Bane's name. And a picture of three scalpels. "Three times only, and only if I say so, if you are wrong, you can choose to use a wildcard."

Wingate leaned over his tray of surgical knives and clamps.

"A wildcard means you substitute for Armitage or Maggie. Just a little snip or cut. Perhaps I'll cut off your finger. Operate on your intestines? We shall see how noble you really are."

The artificial audience booed.

Delay him. Screw with his head. Don't play the game.

"Very Boris Karloff," Bane said.

Wingate picked up a stainless steel tool, turning it over in his hands. "Bone clamp." He levered the clamp open and pressed the serrated teeth over the meat of Bane's right hand. "Now, here is how The Game works. You start by telling me what you *think* you know. Each time you're wrong—" He snapped the bone clamp closed. "It hurts, for someone dear to you."

"Like a game show. I get it. Cool." Wingate was going to torture his loved ones and him; not original, but with a twist.

He stared into Wingate's cold eyes. Hayden's eyes.

"Question one: what motivates me to play this game with you? With you, personally."

Delay. Stay calm and delay the sick bastard.

"That's an easy one. You blame me for your freakish son's death. Although, personally, I think I did you a favor."

A sound effect—*beoong.*

The doctor screwed the bone clamp. Bane felt the pressure and spoke quickly. "Aren't you breaking your own rules? I was right, wasn't I?"

The pressure released. "Fine. But what, Detective, was my motivation?"

"You get off on sadism?"

"Wrong." The clamp closed hard. Bane closed his eyes. He heard the crack of his finger bone before he felt it. "Correct answer: a child for a child, Bane. I gave you this as a free wild card. Say thank you."

He managed to croak, "Thank you—mother fucker."

The clamp closed. He clenched his teeth. He would not scream. No way he would scream. He would continue to provoke Wingate, and the madman would torture him, not his family.

The artificial audience cheered as the clamp cracked another finger.

"Sounds like a nutcracker," Wingate said. "No scream for me?"

Bane shuddered. Through clenched teeth, he quipped, "I'm into S&M."

"Oh, then you will love what I have planned."

"I can't wait. You know, your son was an idiot. Are you sure he was really yours? He wasn't quite retarded, was he, but—did he suffer from lack of oxygen at birth? Breach?"

The pain came hard. He choked back a scream.

"Very good, Bane. Perhaps you were serious? You want more of this?"

"Please. Oh, please."

The audience booed.

Wingate sighed. "Not a very convincing act, my dear."

Wingate squeezed the clamp again, tore away flesh. Bane clenched his teeth and his body convulsed, then stiffened into an arch. No scream for him. Bane wouldn't give Wingate that pleasure.

He spat blood. But he managed, "Oh, that felt so—good!"

"Always the clown, Bane. Very brave. But I wonder how long you can keep up your act with my finger on the bromide dispensers?"

"More torture please. I love it." *Boos.*

"You are something special, Bane."

"Oh, yes. Do you want to know about your son?"

"There we go. The expected diversion technique."

"Sorry to be so predictable."

"I know everything about *your* life. Everything."

"So you know how much I enjoyed watching your son die."

Wingate leaned close. "I was there, remember? Quite the show."

"That's cold."

"He was my black sheep. His time had come."

Bane focused past the pain. "For me, I enjoyed watching him die."

"Just as I will enjoy your daughter's death. And Arm's. And yours." He smiled. "Ah, see, not so cock-sure now, are you?"

"Why bother? Isn't revenge for the simple mind?"

"No. Killing for pleasure is for the simple. Killing for food is for survival. Killing for power is facile. Killing for revenge is poetry."

"You are a family of poets."

"Precisely."

"And this whole Reality TV and Gameshow schtick is poetry?"

"Reality TV as metaphor, dear boy."

"And I thought Hayden was sick."

"My son was perfectly normal."

"So, sociopathic behavior is normal. Perfectly normal."

"Exactly. Social order is an artificial, learned condition. We are born sociopaths. We learn the social graces."

"From our families." Bane's head pounded. He needed his aspirin. He couldn't fence with Wingate, not in his condition. But he had to. For Mags.

Wingate picked up a bottle of antiseptic. "Let me clean that mess for you." He dabbed the wound.

Bane jerked in the restraints as antiseptic burned his flesh, clenching his teeth, refusing to scream.

Wingate smiled. "I feel we are so close. You are like a son to me."

Bane closed his eyes. Wingate really did think he was God. God Complex. And Hayden had been his sick messiah.

"Now, question two. Be careful now, Bane. If you are wrong, you must choose this time between your buddy Armitage and your beloved daughter Mags. Five doses for Mags should be plenty. Eight or ten for big Arm.

"Question two: Who is six foot six and wears a cowboy hat?"

Bane focused. *Delay.* "Another Bartlett-Wingate spawn. Your son."

Beoong!

Wingate smiled. "Yes. My oldest boy. Austin. Fancies himself a Clint Eastwood." Wingate shook Bane's aspirin bottle. "You want these, no?" He wagged his long finger. "One aspirin a day, good for you. Fifteen a day, very bad." He snatched a hypo from the tray. "Here, try this. Much more enlightening."

Bane tried to roll away from the hypo. He tensed as it went in.

Bane felt instant relief. The pain numbed. His head cleared.

"See? Wonderful is it not? Question three: What is The Game?"

"Your juvenile, pathetic attempt at revenge."

Beoong!

Wingate rolled in a chair and sat beside Bane. "I really shouldn't give you that one." He cupped his chin in his hands, face close to Bane's. "What about you, dear boy. You want revenge, no? If only you could loosen a restraint."

Bane controlled his breathing. The drug had really helped. The pain was gone. "I'm missing the Super Bowl for this."

"Oh dear. There is that sarcasm again, a defensive instinct. It shows weakness, you know."

"You're the expert. I'm just not a people person, right?"

"Oh, you are. You are pathetically a people person. Your actions show this. Just insecure in the niceties is all."

Wingate twirled a scalpel between two fingers, a deft and scary motion. "Question four: Is Stephen Chow an accomplice or a dupe?"

Oh Christ. Bane's investigation hadn't stretched that far, yet. He stared at Mags. Turned his head to Arm.

A buzzer sounded: *zonk!*

"Oh, did I forget to mention the time limit?"

"Dupe. He was a dupe!"

"Correct, but too late. Sorry, dear boy."

"You didn't mention the time!"

"Armitage or Mags. You have seven seconds, after which I choose."

"If you're going to play a game, explain the rules—"

"Four-three-two..."

"Arm. I choose Arm!" He rolled his head to the right. "I'm sorry, bud. You're stronger."

He saw Arm's quick blink. *Yes*, he understood.

Bane heard a jingle sound effect. The scoreboard over Arm's head flipped to **2**.

Arm bucked in the restraints again, his back arching up in a long curve, his eyes wild.

The artificial audience clapped.

"I'd say five more doses at most," Wingate said. "What do you say, Bane? Go for question five?"

Bane regulated his breathing, fighting to stay lucid. He couldn't let the anger take him.

"Question five: Seth Allen. Willing accomplice or dupe?"

Bane closed his eyes.

"Tick tock, Alban, tick tock."

"Willing!" Bane opened his eyes.

Zonk!

"Seth?" Wingate sneered. "Wrong, dear boy. His ire was so easy to manipulate. Do you not understand? Our first move in the game—I suppose you would call him a 'victim'—that was Seth's right-hand man, a horse farmer from Hancock."

With sudden clarity, Bane remembered the alfalfa and his suspicion that the first victim was a farmer. "You killed one of Seth's men, then you blamed the outsiders." Manipulation. Control. Cold-blooded chess.

"Of course. But you can't change your answer. The flatlanders were symbolically represented by Colin Lorentz and Real TV. So simple. It's so easy to manipulate fanatics." He smiled. "Hanging the old farmer—Thom Hanson was his name—to drain over a bucket was dear Austin's work. He thought it would resonate with you."

"Technically, he was willing then. Play by your own rules—"

"Sorry. Seven seconds. Armitage or Mags. Six, five, four, three, two, one—"

"Arm!" He felt his eyes watery with unshed tears. "Arm, I'm sorry!"

Bane heard the dreaded jingle. The scoreboard flipped to **3**.

"There you go. Such an easy choice. But you have ten more questions to answer. You may have to use some of Maggie's points."

Delay. Delay. Say something!

"There's something I don't understand, Doctor. How is it that your children are so—mentally inferior—to their father."

Bane expected scalpels, a momentary pause in the game, but Wingate answered, mildly, "Austin is not the brightest progeny, it's true."

Concentrate. Keep him engaged.

"Question five: Jackson Reid, a.k.a. Manetti, planned execution or improv? Seven, six, five, four—"

"I can't think with you counting!"

"All part of the game, two, one—"

"Plan—no, improvised!"

Wingate bent close, grinning. "Oh, *almost*. You had it right the first time. Oh well. Armitage or—"

"But Ira killed him because he was a flatlander! It wasn't planned."

"By Ira, no. By me?" He smiled. "Time's up."

"Arm!" Again he watched helplessly as the score board flipped to **4**. Arm didn't thrash this time. Bane saw his pupils dilate.

"You will have to choose Maggie soon, or Arm will simply be gone."

"You realize Mancuso will be coming for you?"

"How would he know to try?"

Bane smiled. "I told him. Yesterday."

"You are bluffing. A nice play, though."

"No bluff. I was cut from the force, I needed support. I called Daddy-in-law." Bane wished it was true.

"Nicely played. Your eye movements tell me you invented this. You glanced right. Blinked three times."

Bane focused on Wingate's face. "No. I never lie."

"Is it not you who says 'everyone lies?' Cynical, but not far from the truth."

"Nice play on words."

"Thank you."

"Question Six: Who were the victims in the attic?"

Bane closed his eyes, visualizing it. He saw them, hanging from the rafters. "Lorentz and—"

"And? Quickly!"

"And Maya Rubie."

"A neat guess, considering she was the only one unaccounted for on the set."

Zonk!

"Sadly, only half right. Lorentz, yes. Rubie, no. The female was a producer from Real TV. Martha Steinberg. She was threatening to shut down the show."

"And you couldn't have that?"

"Of course *not*. Sorry, Armitage or Maggie?"

"I got half right!"

Wingate laughed. "Half right? He looked at the nearest camera. "Judges?"

Artificial boos.

"Oh, sorry, Bane. How about this? You can use a wild card."

"Fine. Cut me. I love it. Cut me. Make me bleed."

"Brave."

"I love sick games."

"Life is a game, dear boy. Nothing else. The more we learn about our

universe, the more we realize there is no purpose. So we distract ourselves with video games, reality television games and game shows."

Wingate balanced the scalpel between two fingers, just above Bane's
eye. A drop of Bane's own blood rolled off the pink edge.

Bane focused. *Delay. Don't let the game continue.* "So Abbey Chase
has it right. Reality TV is the best reflection of America's zeitgeist?"

"Abbey Chase. Ah, yes, well I think she might just have it right. My
theory is that the only thing that matters is *The* Game."

Bane shuddered. "There isn't much sport in torturing a tied man."

"You still have your most important weapon."

"The mind."

"There you go, Alban. Question seven: Who killed your wife?"

Bane lunged, but the chest strap restrained him.

"Noland Hix."

"So sure?"

Bane nodded. "I'm sure."

Beoong!

"Bravo, my boy. Bravo!"

Bane felt an odd thrill. Not for answering the question correctly, but
for confirming what he'd suspected for years.

"Hix was your patient."

"Yes."

"You arranged for his alibi?"

"Yes. And here is your bonus prize."

Hix stepped into the operating theatre. Bane saw his own face on the
monitors over Hix's head. His face matched the red of his hair, his lips
were pulled back in a snarl.

Hix.

The wife killer.

"This is part of Hix's therapy," Wingate said.

"Glad, I could be of help." Bane whispered.

"Funny, to the end."

Hix leaned close to Wingate and spoke. Bane didn't have Arm's abil-
ity to read lips, but he could see Hix was upset.

Wingate's eyes looked thoughtful and he said a few words in return, quietly enough that Bane heard nothing other than brief snatches— "Mancuso" and "thirty minutes."

Wingate turned. The smile was gone. "Oh, dear me," he said, the mask moving, his face still mostly hidden. "It seems you have cheated. Is that the American term? You squealed—ratted out is the vernacular, no?—to the Mafia. Naughty of you. Hix's informants tell me they'll be here shortly."

"I told you I left Daddy-in-law a message. And Mancuso doesn't play games, Wingate." Bane tried not to sound triumphant. Tried not to gloat. Because if he did, it would take only seven quick stabs of Wingate's fingers to end it for Arm or Mags.

"Yes. Now, Hix, here, can certainly handle all of this. It appears one of my patients has gone mad. Poor fellow is in the next room, ready to—how do you Americans so colorfully put it—ready to be the 'fall person?'"

"Fall guy."

"Turns out our 'fall guy' has been doing this for years," Wingate said. "And I will be on the telly saying, 'Oh, this is just horrible. How could such a thing happen in one of my clinics?' Well, I will write out a script."

"Of course you will," Bane said. "You'll still sound smug and guilty. But trust me, Wingate. Mancuso won't care. You're dead. If you're lucky, he'll strap you to one of these gurneys."

"Do not worry about me, dear boy. I have friends everywhere. Did you know, dear boy, the President himself was a patient. I can not reveal anything from his sessions—confidentiality, you understand—but my goodness, this man owes me a lot. Oh yes."

Hix smiled. "Mancuso's coming. We must be fast."

"Screw you, Hix."

Wingate wagged his finger. "Now, now. Boys. Hix, no need to send me the tapes, dear boy. This has been wirelessly transmitted. And do not worry. We are no longer filming." He pointed at the cameras. The record lights on the television cameras were all off. "So have all the fun you boys can stand."

"Cheerio, Bane. I promised you to Hix. I am a man of my word. But I shall miss you, dear boy." Wingate left the room.

Hix smiled. He stepped close to the prize panel. His finger hovered over the dispenser control for Mags.

Chapter 43

· ·

February 3, 4:01 pm

Wingate Clinic, Long Island

Bane fixed his eyes on Hix's face, the man who had taken Suze.

Hix finger touched the dispenser button for Mags.

"Should I? Just a little?" Hix smiled.

"I so love being right," Bane said. *Distract the bastard. Away from Mags.* "I always knew it was *you*."

"Too bad you're all tied up."

"Too bad you're such an ass-kisser. I can see the brown stains on your nose."

"Shut up, or I'll do her."

"*Shut up, or I'll do her*," Bane mimicked. "How infantile. I should spank you. No, you'd like that, wouldn't you?"

"Shut up!"

"God, you are so not on my Christmas list anymore."

"Funny, Bane."

"And no invite to my Super Bowl party."

"Ha. Ha."

"I always knew you were a coward."

"You can't bait me."

"I think I can. How about we bet? I bet if I can bait you successfully, you have to take ten full doses of that pancuronium bromide."

Hix stared at Bane, his hatred obvious.

"You're no fun, Hix. My wife told me you were impotent."

Hix picked up an electric bone saw from the tray of instruments. "Shut up, or I'll cut off your dick."

"At least I have a dick."

Hix buzzed the rotating saw blade. He leaned closer, and spat in Bane's face.

"Oh, you're such a man, Hix. Do it again. Show you've got spit."

The saw buzzed.

The face of his betrayer leaned over him. Too close. Bane's only chance. He readied himself for one burst of madness.

In a frenzy, he thrust his head forward, pressing from the shoulders, lifting his upper body as far as the restraints allowed, using all his abdominal muscles.

With a shout he clamped his teeth onto the tip of Hix's long nose.

Hix screamed, punching at Bane's wounded shoulder. Bane focused, ignored the pain, concentrated on Mags, clenched harder. Held on.

He felt the wind of the saw. Heard the howl of the blade spinning, coming down, down, lower and lower.

Hix pushed with his other hand, trying to tear his face away from Bane's canine grip. But Bane turned his neck and body, shaking like a coyote on the jugular of its prey.

The saw blade buzzed again. He felt the pressure first, then a numb heat. Finally, pain. The blade slided through Bane's chest skin, leaving a long trail of red. Pain bloomed. He felt the warm splash of his own blood.

Still, Bane held on, clamping harder, concentrating on biting off the man's nose tip.

Hix tore himself away, squealing like a stuck pig. As he tumbled back, the saw blade came up, cutting into Bane's abdomen, just lightly tearing skin as Hix fell back. The blade also caught the chest strap. As Bane had hoped.

The blade cut through Bane's skin—and the strap. The smell of hot oil made Bane gag as more of his own blood splattered his chin.

Hix stumbled back against the wall, arms flailing, rivulets of blood flowing over his lips and chin. He clutched upwards, pressing his hand over his wounded nose.

Bane fell back, a chunk of Hix's nose in his mouth. He spat out the vile meat.

And sat up. His hands were still bound to the chest strap, but he was able to bring his two hands together. It brought steadying pain, and a spurt of blood on his chest as he bent forward and fumbled with the straps. Pain was good. It took him to a new place. A place where he was strong.

He saw through the cloud of dizziness.

"You'll pay for that!" Hix shouted, holding his nose. "I will castrate you. I will cut off each of your fingers, one by one."

But Bane was already busy, bending over, snatching with his freed hands at the thigh straps. Then a further reach to the ankles.

Hix, still holding his torn nose, saw what he was doing.

Bane laughed, swung his numb legs over the gurney, and sat facing Hix. "Let's play a trivia game. What happens when an idiot brings a saw too close to a cloth strap?" He ignored the ugly trail of red that arced across his chest. Nothing mortal. Just a very painful foot-long welt. A new scar to add to his collection.

Hix snatched his holstered gun and pointed it at Bane. "You've got about one minute to live."

"Oooh. Hix has a big gun. Very dramatic. Maybe Hix has grown some balls."

Hix shook his head, his nose still bleeding. The gun wavered.

Bane chuckled. It sounded forced, but it also infuriated Hix. "You know, Wingate has no more use for you."

"Your amateur psychology isn't going to work." Hix thrust the gun at Bane. "Back on the gurney. Now."

"Normally, I'd just smile and climb right up there. But right now, I feel so free. And darnit, it feels pretty good." He wiped his own chest, held up a bloodied hand. "I don't like the patient care in this hospital."

"I'm going to enjoy this," Hix said. He took a step towards Bane.

Good. Hix was focused on Bane, ignoring Arm and Mags.

"Even tied up, I destroyed your nose." Bane laughed again. "You'll need cosmetic surgery there, Hix. Maybe Wingate knows plastic surgery too? Or would you trust him to wield a scalpel near your face? He's done with you, isn't he? Why does he need you anymore? My Daddy-in-law'll be here any minute, so he's gone."

Hix's lips trembled. Was it anger? Fear? But his voice was calm. "Wingate isn't done with me. He's done with *you*."

Hix changed the subject. *Good.* "He's done with you—trust me. Maybe if you weren't damaged goods, he could still work with you. Groom you to be director of the FBI, some day. Is that what he promised you?" Hix's startled expression told Bane he was right. "Of course, if you believed that, I have a nice piece of swamp property..." He groaned, sagging hard against the gurney. He fought to stay conscious as a massive tsunami of vertigo took him.

"I'm twice the man—and twice the agent—you are!" Hix stepped closer, gun wavering.

"What are you—six years old?" He shook his head. "Well, you've really given me a lot to think about. You're twice the man I am. I never knew that." Now what? He was running out of insults. He barely clung to consciousness, still leaning hard on the gurney just to stand. His only hope was that he could exploit Hix's inferiority complex and phobias.

Through a veil of pain, Bane managed one more effort. "If you were *any* kind of a man, you'd face me without your gun. I can barely stand. And you still hide behind the gun. It'd be like taking on a child on crutches. But you still need your gun." He laughed at Hix. "That gun's bigger than your dick, isn't it?" He swayed. He had moments left before he passed out. He lost it for a moment. When his vision cleared, he found he had sagged to the tiled floor and Hix was close. Too close.

Hix stood only a roundhouse kick away. Unfortunately, Bane couldn't manage a roundhouse kick. A kick required he stand on his own two legs. He could barely get up off the cold floor.

Hix was close enough now that Bane smelled his sour breath. He was breathing through his mouth, his nostrils too full of blood.

Still on the floor, Bane gripped the gurney that had been his prison, and rolled it over his head. He grabbed hold of the opposite side and pulled himself to his feet, the gurney both crutch and protection.

Hix now had a battery-powered surgical saw in one hand, the gun in the other.

Hix lunged across the bed, the saw buzzing to life. Bane reached out and seized his wrist. He pulled, yanking Hix forward and down across the gurney, then drove an elbow into his back. But he was weak. Queasiness swept through him. He fell back as Hix lunged in again.

Hix smiled. "Very good, Bane. Not bad for an old man."

Bane blinked several times, clearing his head, leaning on the gurney. "I jog six miles a day. Keeps me young."

"Even dying, you try to joke. You're still bleeding, Bane."

Bane stumbled towards the tray of surgical instruments. Hix darted around the gurney and rolled the tray aside. He stepped in front of Bane.

Behind him, Bane heard Mags crying. He curled his hands into fists. "But I have plenty of adrenalin."

Hix shook his head. "Always so stubborn." He smiled. "Is it true that you haven't been able to watch the Super Bowl for twelve years?"

"That's right," Bane said, keeping his voice even. The night Hix killed his wife. The verbal needle was enough to give Bane strength. "But after tonight, I think I'll plan a big Super Bowl party." The last part came out in gasps and heaves.

Hix's smile faded. He moved in. Bane stepped back, felt the gurney behind him. He ducked under it and stood up on the other side.

Hix closed in again, saw buzzing, gun still ready in the opposite hand. Bane moved the gurney between them. Hix revved the saw to a high scream. He lunged. Bane pulled back and the blade sliced into the mattress. Foam erupted from the cut.

Bane smiled.

The blade whirred. Hix shoved the gurney hard into the wall. It clattered and bounced across the floor, taking Bane along with it. Hix took one long stride forward, swinging the saw. The saw flashed silver. The saw blade screamed so close he felt its wind. Bane pressed back against the wall. He looked around for weapons. The tray was across the room now. Bane had only his fists against a saw and a gun. Hix was playing with him, ready to shoot him if need be, but prefering the blade.

"Goodbye, Bane. I'll be sure to attend your state funeral."

Hix lunged. Bane stumbled to the side, dizzy, grabbing hold of an IV dolly. A bag of blood swayed to one side. Bane swung around it, using it as a support.

When Hix dove in again, Bane pushed the dolly. Hix's legs caught in the casters and he fell forward into Bane.

As Hix bulleted past him, Bane flung out the IV line and wrapped it around Hix's neck. Hix's momentum tightened the loop. Bane was pulled along like a waterskier, his legs moving in a tangle. Bane's body became an anchor. The line snapped taught, whipping hard around Hix's neck.

The saw swung round, hungry, cutting through the line, slicing into the bag of blood. Warm blood spewed, splattering the room, Mags and Arm. Bane yelled out, grabbing for Hix's extended arm.

They both slipped on the blood.

The blade gashed Bane's left tricep. He spun with woozy momentum, holding Hix and pulling him down. Hix shrieked as they fell and landed on top of Bane. His body convulsed, he scrambled backwards, dragging himself away. Red muscle fiber hung out of a gaping wound in his thigh.

Blood fountained out of Hix's wound.

"Artery, Hix," Bane said, pulling himself up to his knees.

Hix pressed his left hand over his thigh. Bane crawled forward, ready to grapple again, but Hix still had his Browning automatic in one hand.

"Back up, Bane."

Still on his knees, Bane shuffled back. He shoved away the saw and crawled across the floor toward Arm's gurney. He used the bed to pull himself up.

Hix lay with his back against the wall, pressing one hand to his wound, his gun in the other.

Bane gasped, leaning over Arm.

Bane looked into Arm's face. His friend grinned. Hands trembling, Bane unbuckled one of his restrained hands. He reached over to release his other hand.

"Leave him!" Hix leveled the gun at Bane's chest, his hand waving unsteadily. Bane took a deep breath and held it. He clung to cloudy consciousness.

"Arm. Hear me," Bane whispered, still holding the gurney.

"I hear." Bane felt Arm's freed hand on his back.

"Protect my daughter. No matter what."

"With my life."

Bane dove towards the surgical tray, caught the edge of the gurney, and pushed hard to the right. He clawed at the tray. Hix's gun discharged. The bullet tore open a welt in the drywall, inches from Bane's head. Bane yanked the IVs out of Mag's arm as he flew by. She screeched.

Two more shots as Bane skipped across the room.

"No closer, Bane, or I'll do her!" The gun was pointed at Mags.

Bane roared and launched himself between the muzzle and Mags. Hix's gun discharged, the bullet tore into him, he smelled the acrid discharge. He fell hard on top of Hix.

Bane plunged both IV's into Hix's neck. He fell backwards, clawing for Wingate's score board. Both hands came down on the Maggie buttons. Over and over. Dose after dose.

Hix screamed, clawing at the needle, his eyes bulging first then seeming to sink. His eyeballs seemed to implode into his head. Bane knew his lungs were collapsing, too.

Hix's face crumpled, the muscles relaxed, uncoiled, sagged. His eyelids dropped. Bane sagged to one knee and pressed his hand over Hix's heart. Its thready beat grew slower. And slower. Winding down. Relaxing.

Bane had to hang on to consciousness long enough to see the bastard die. Blackness was coming. Comforting blackness.

He collapsed on top of Hix, then rolled to one side. He stared up into the lights.

Hix, the wife killer, died.

C h a p t e r 4 4

....

May 18, 3:37 pm
Pantages Theater, Hollywood

The audience applauded. Bane sat straighter as Kenji Tenichi stepped on stage and bowed. From the front row seats, Bane noticed Kenji's darting eyes and clenched fists, although he walked with quiet elegance across the set and joined the other contestants of *Haunted Survivor*.

Mags and Jay screamed with the rest of the crowd. "Kenji! Kenji!"

Kenji's face was mostly hidden behind his long bangs. He smiled. He wore faded jeans and an open shirt, spurning the rented tuxedos of the other contestants and most of the audience. Behind him stood the other contestants, framed in a perfect reproduction of the cobwebbed library of Mason Place, complete with rhino head. It seemed an odd contrast to the soaring gilt décor of the Pantages. The audience shouted.

Kenji turned and hugged each of the losing contestants. Ahmed was conspicuously absent.

Bane remained rigid in the velvet seat, awkward in his rented tuxedo. He had come for his girls and because Abbey insisted: "It'll do you both good. Mags needs it, Alban. You need a change, too."

The applause thundered when Kenji smiled and gave a big thumbs-up to the cameras. Even big Arm was on his feet, grinning. Kip, Pete and Jeremy shouted along. But Bane remained sitting with arms folded. Bane couldn't be happier for Kenji. Looks and heroism might have bought him the viewer votes, but Kenji deserved to win.

Bane lost interest in the stage show and glanced up and down the front row at his loved ones. Mags and Jay on either side of him leaned forward, cheering. Arm laughed and clapped. Kip shrugged at Bane, then gave him one of her long rolling winks. Her ordeal had shattered her nerve but not her will, and she recovered faster than Bane.

Nearly fourteen weeks of hospitals and internal affairs investigations left Bane mentally scarred, but physically sound. His Colonel and the

District Attorney overlooked his vigilante vendetta as Wingate's terror network unraveled.

It was the time for healing, a change of pace. Abbey Chase preempted his plans to slip away with the girls to the mellow street bands and relative peace of Arm's New Orleans. Abbey insisted they attend the final live special for *Haunted Survivor* and sent first class tickets to Bane, Kip, Arm and families. Bane's girls went ballistic when Abbey invited them to the wrap party, with a guest list of their favorite movie stars. Bane could hardly say no, although he would have chosen anywhere except Hollywood for a holiday. Seeing his girls happy and laughing was important therapy.

The lights dimmed and three giant screens lit up with the *Haunted Survivor* logo. One screen dissolved to a close-up of Kenji, smiling but blinking into the stage lights. A second screen had a long shot of all the contestants on stage. On the larger center screen the opening credits for the show rolled.

A familiar scream echoed through the theatre as a giant projected image showed Kelly, covered in fake blood, running up a hall of Mason Place. The audience laughed. To the unforgettable music of *Haunted Survivor*, familiar clips rolled in quick cuts, the audience laughing and cheering at each scene: big laughs when Junior jumped into Kenji's arms while snakes writhed like a living carpet at their feet; a big gasp during a quick scene of Carlos bonking Kelly in a steamy shower scene that was too revealing in spite of pixilated filters; cheers for an angry Mya batting away rats and kicking them across the room; a chant of "Ray! Ray!" when Ray the stockbroker look-alike squashed big hairy spiders.

Bane's daughters shrieked, pointing at the giant image of their father. The projected Bane, gun drawn, rushed into the foyer of Mason Place after the power failure. An abrupt close up of poor Eddie Kim hanging from the rhino horn shocked Bane, and the hidden camera pulled back to reveal Bane in the foreground, controlling the scene. Seconds later the scene dissolved into a shaky camera shot of Abbey with mad Doctor Skillman's poison-filled hypo at her throat and Bane diving forward to catch her as she fell.

The Pantages theatre stilled. Then a single woman at the back of the room shouted, "Go Bane! Go Bane!" and the entire audience took up the chanting.

Bane slid even lower in his chair. Laughing, Arm reached past Mags and grabbed Bane, yanking him to his feet. A spotlight came down, blinding him, and the audience clapped.

He pulled away, elbowing Arm and slipping back into his chair. Mags slid closer and nestled her head against Bane's shoulder.

The spotlights lanced through the darkness to illuminate Kenji, live on stage. Abbey Chase stepped out of the darkness, beautiful in a designer original, her hair and makeup perfect. She smiled at Kenji, hugged him, kissed his cheek, and the audience fell silent.

"Kenji Tenichi, Real TV is proud to present a check for one million dollars made out, at your request, to the charitable works foundation of the temple at Eiheiji." She handed a check to Kenji, who casually folded it into his jeans pocket.

Abbey slid close to Kenji's side, facing the audience. "Tonight we are proud to announce that Kenji Tenichi will return as host of our new blockbuster reality show." Kenji's face appeared in close-up on one screen as the audience screeched approval. A long shot of Kenji, nude in the shower, brought screams from the women in the audience. "America's new superstar will head the search for the world's next superstar!" Clips of Kenji rolled in collages on the screens, revealing his winning smiles and hard muscles. "Real TV will tour the world, starting this summer in romantic Venice, in our hunt for the next beautiful talent to earn the title in our live show *Superstar!* The finalist will win a ten million dollar contract with our movie studio." The crowd went crazy.

It was all too much.

The wrap party was the worst for Bane, though his daughters were in heaven. The ballroom filled with the Who's Who of Hollywood and he found no place in the crowded room to escape. Arm followed him, amused. Bane hovered within sight of Mags and Jay, watchful.

"Lighten up, bro," Arm shouted at Bane over the crowd's rumble.

Bane watched as the girls pursued Kenji. "Wingate's still out there, Arm."

Arm laughed. "I know it, bro. But he'd never show here." Arm nodded at the armed security guards.

"I've learned never to underestimate him."

Arm pulled Bane towards the bar. "Where's that new squeeze of yours?"

"I'm right here, big guy," said Abbey Chase. She sandwiched between them, clutching three beers.

Bane put his arm around Abbey Chase, surprised how comfortable she felt after only three months. It felt like a lifetime.

How had it happened, this closeness to Abbey? She'd visited him every other day in the hospital, in spite of duties on the set, surprising him with her tenderness. At first he thought it was nothing more than gratitude, for saving her from Skillman's poison. But she went beyond that, returning to the hospital day after day, the hard, all-business producer persona dissolving to reveal the vulnerable Abbey who had—surprise surprise—been frightened all along. Once Bane awoke to find her holding his hand. She had bent and kissed him on the forehead but said nothing. Having her there, nurturing him, had helped him recover.

Abbey snuggled closer, watching the milling crowd. "Cheers." They pushed their bottles together and chugged back beer.

"You've got a huge hit," Bane said.

"The hugest." Abbey blew a kiss to Jodie Foster, who waved back. "We blew away every other show in the ratings. Set a record."

Bane kissed the top of her head. "Are you really planning a sequel?"

"It's television. Of course. We have a monster franchise here." She pulled him by his elbow and Arm followed along. They intercepted a strikingly handsome Asian man, with Kenji-like sheepdog bangs. "Alban Bane. Allow me to introduce Takeshi Kaneshiro." The young man shook quickly, then was swept away by a crowd of women. "Takeshi has agreed to play Kenji in the movie."

Bane fought to control the anger. They had battled the movie issue several times and Abbey ignored his protests. Real TV had sold rights to the *Haunted Survivor* story to a big-time studio, and both Hollywood franchises were fast-tracking the story to the theatres. "Who plays Abbey Chase?"

"Alyssa Milano," Abbey said, ignoring his sarcasm. "And we're going for Ewen McGregor for you again. Gary Dourdan is considering playing Arm."

Arm rumbled with laughter. "I'll sue."

Tired, Bane escaped the party to a private salon off the main ballroom. He needed to be away from the crowds. And Abbey. Tomorrow, when the Bane clan returned to Vermont, he would leave Abbey Chase behind. Fling over. No more games. No more craziness.

He found a private lounge and sat in a plush armchair by a marble hearth with a roaring fire, alone for the first time in weeks. He had too much to think about. He enjoyed a small buzz as he chugged back his seventh beer. He stared at the fire, enjoying the warmth, wishing he was in Vermont. Thank goodness he was alone.

Not for long. A man entered the salon, two beers in hand.

"G'day," said the man, his voice cheerful, a big smile on his handsome face.

"No autographs," said Bane with a yawn.

The smile seemed to widen as he crossed the room. "I don't want an autograph, Alban."

"I'm not selling my story." All week he had dodged agents and writers wanting the rights to his story. He studied the man as he came closer. He didn't seem Hollywood. More Midwest. No tuxedo, just tight jeans and a neat shirt tightly drawn over a muscular chest. He was at least as tall as Arm.

Bane tensed. His hand hovered near his waist, where his .38 normally nestled. The light-haired man was strangely familiar. "Do I know you?"

"No, sir. But I know you. Yes, I do." He handed Bane a beer.

Bane put down the bottle on a marble side table and folded his arms. "Well, how about that." He forced a scowl. "How is it you know me?"

The man slid into the other arm chair and crossed his long legs. He wore battered cowboy boots. "Everyone knows the great Alban Bane, right? Didn't I just see you up there on the big screen?"

Bane felt his muscles tighten, eyes fixed on the cowboy boots, ready to spring from his chair. Outside the door he knew there were crowds and armed guards with guns. His own gun was back in Vermont.

"I hear congratulations are in order," the man said, his voice full of warmth.

"Oh?" Bane took a breath. Held it. He knew who this was.

"Head of an elite terrorism task force."

Bane slid to the edge of the seat, ready to lunge. "How would you know that?" Only Arm knew about the offer.

"Then it's true?" The man laughed, a good-natured sound, and held out a hand as if to shake.

"Can't say it is."

"Well, I'm sure we'll cross paths many times either way." The giant man, so familiar but unfamiliar, stood up.

Bane jumped from his chair, blocking him. "May I see some identification?"

"No."

Bane stepped closer. "In that case, our conversation is not finished, Austin."

"Who?" Piercing eyes focused on him.

"Austin Bartlett."

"My name is Michael Hensely."

Bane gestured with his index finger. "Identification."

The man reached into his pocket. Bane stiffened, his hands curling into fists. Laughing, the man pulled out a badge. FBI Special Agent Michael Hensely.

"I can buy one of those online too," Bane said.

The smile faded for the first time.

Bane barely registered the motion. The giant spun on his boot toe and slid low, taking Bane down in a leg sweep. Lightning fast, the hands came down and seized Bane's tux lapels. Bane half turned, bringing up both his arms and pushing out. Bane's knuckles snapped up and inside. Surprised, Austin stumbled back, releasing his grip and Bane rolled to his feet.

"Not bad for an old guy." The smile returned.

Bane sank into a ready stance.

"Kung Fu? Your little partner teach you that one?" The giant lunged forward. Bane parried with a snapping kick. He didn't connect, but Austin stepped back. Austin dove in, then left, and Bane stepped back and blocked with both arms. His forearms snapped back and stinging pain shot up his arm. Each blow brought numbing pain. Austin's motions were long and carried bone-snapping power. Again he pushed in a flurry of fists, and this time Bane crashed back, tumbling to the floor. Bane landed on the Persian carpet, winded. The man had appalling strength.

The door slammed shut.

Taunting words echoed on the ceramic tiles. "Father says hello."

Bane scrambled to his feet and stumbled to the door. He burst into the carpeted hall. The door thudded against the wall.

The crowd from the ballroom spilled into the hall. He focused past the unfamiliar faces, looking for someone tall. Someone in jeans in the tuxedoed and gowned crowd.

On the floor to his right he saw an envelope. A woman in a shimmering white gown bent to pick it up.

Bane ran, pushed her aside. He ignored her cry of alarm and snatched the letter. He ran through the crowd, pushing up the hall to the main doors, down the stairs, into the foyer. Austin was gone. A ghost, like his father.

Not caring for rules of evidence, Bane ripped open the envelope and read the eleven words, in elegant script:

"Congratulations on round one. I look forward to our next Game."

About the Author

If you enjoyed Derek Armstrong's Alban Bane mystery-
thriller, don't miss the sequel MADicine, due late 2007
from Kunati.

Derek Armstrong is the author of
The Persona Principle
with co-author Kam Wai Yu.
Derek Armstrong also authored the historical trilogy
Song of Montségur. The Last Trouabdour, first in the trilogy,
releases from Kunati in late 2007.
Learn more about Derek Armstrong
at his authorized web site,
http://www.derekarmstrong.com

KÜNATI

Provocative. Bold. Controversial.

Rabid | A novel by T K Kenyon

A sexy, savvy, darkly funny tale of ambition, scandal, forbidden love and murder. Nothing is sacred. The graduate student, her professor, his wife, her priest: four brilliantly realized characters spin out of control in a world where science and religion are in constant conflict.

■ "Kenyon is definitely a keeper." STARRED REVIEW, *Booklist*

US$ 26.95 | Pages 480, cloth hardcover
ISBN 978-1-60164-002-4 | EAN: 9781601640024
LCCN 2006930189

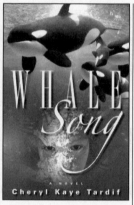

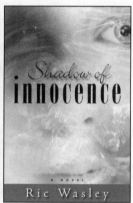

bang BANG
A novel by Lynn Hoffman

In Lynn Hoffman's wickedly funny *bang-BANG*, a waitress crime victim takes on America's obsession with guns and transforms herself in the process. Read along as Paula becomes national hero and villain, enforcer and outlaw, lover and leader. Don't miss Paula Sherman's one-woman quest to change America.

■ "Brilliant"
STARRED REVIEW, *Booklist*
US$ 19.95
Pages 176, cloth hardcover
ISBN 978-1-60164-000-0
EAN 9781601640000
LCCN 2006930182

Whale Song
A novel by Cheryl Kaye Tardif

Whale Song is a haunting tale of change and choice. Cheryl Kaye Tardif's beloved novel—a "wonderful novel that will make a wonderful movie" according to *Writer's Digest*—asks the difficult question, which is the higher morality, love or law?

■ "Crowd-pleasing ... a big hit."
Booklist
US$ 12.95
Pages 208, UNA trade paper
ISBN 978-1-60164-007-9
EAN 9781601640079
LCCN 2006930188

Shadow of Innocence
A mystery by Ric Wasley

The Thin Man meets *Pulp Fiction* in a unique mystery set amid the drugs-and-music scene of the sixties that touches on all our societal taboos. *Shadow of Innocence* has it all: adventure, sleuthing, drugs, sex, music and a perverse shadowy secret that threatens to tear apart a posh New England town.

US$ 24.95
Pages 304, cloth hardcover
ISBN 978-1-60164-006-2
EAN 9781601640062
LCCN 2006930187